Shagging, Shooting & Death

ଓ A Novel ଃ

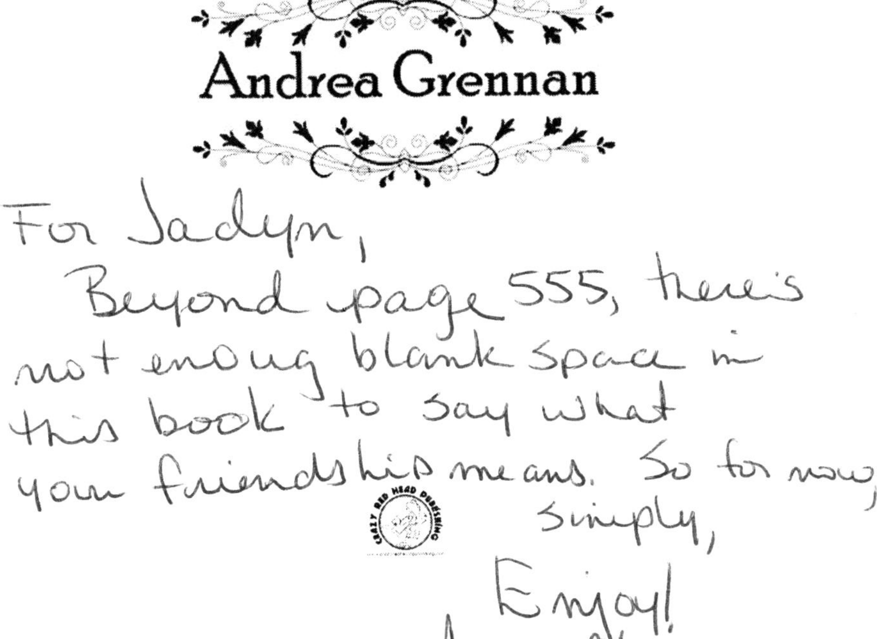

Andrea Grennan

Crazy Red Head Publishing
West Bloomfield, MI 48323

 First e-book and paperback printing, 2017.

Publisher's Cataloging-In-Publication Data
(Prepared by The Donohue Group, Inc.)
Names: Grennan, Andrea.
Title: Shagging, shooting & death / by Andrea Grennan.
Other Titles: Shagging, shooting and death
Description: [West Bloomfield, Michigan] : Crazy Red Head Publishing, [2017]
Identifiers: ISBN 978-0-9992968-0-6 | ISBN 978-0-9992968-1-3 (ebook)
Subjects: LCSH: Upper class women--England--History--19th century--Fiction. | Female friendship--Fiction. | Murder--England--History--19th century--Fiction. | Country life--England--History--19th century--Fiction. | LCGFT: Humorous fiction. | Epistolary fiction.
Classification: LCC PS3607.R46 S53 2017 (print) | LCC PS3607.R46 (ebook) | DDC 813/.6—d

For My Mom,
Who gave me the love of literature and words

and

My Dad
For the *craic*

☙ Prologue ❧

My Darling Annabella,

If you are reading this then I am dead, I suppose. I am very sorry to have died, and hope you are as well. I presume I am dead because the library is the one room in our house that has never interested you in the slightest. If I am not dead, please put this away right now and read no more.

Oh, dear, I suppose I am dead if you are still reading. Well, that is a shame, for I really did intend to live forever, but so few things go as expected.

You are likely in a state right now, for although I love you very much, you have never been a very serious person, nor a person interested in much outside of fashion and scandal. I found that to be a delight, for it distracted me from the business of the world, and because you are so very charming.

You were a good wife to me, Annabella, and I thank you for that, but you are my wife no more. I have tried to arrange things so you might be safe without me, but that shall not happen unless you undertake to be responsible. I know that shall be difficult for you and apologize for placing you in such a position, but it cannot be helped.

As you surely know by now, you inherit everything, and the "everything" you have inherited is likely more than you ever imagined. That is why I ignored your gentle teasing about my "tinkering," dear, for it was the tinkering that made us so very wealthy.

But now it is time for you to grow up, those are the only words I can think of for it. And you must do something that is anathema (look it up, dear) to Ladies of your station. You must educate yourself, Annabella, and you must do it soon. You know nothing of how the world works and there are many who would cheerfully defraud you and leave you with nothing.

As I do not wish for that to happen, you must begin a program of study. Begin here in the library. Read the books, Annabella, even if it is difficult, vexing, and gives you a headache. Use the dictionaries whenever you need (we have several), ask Mr. Weerly for help (he is discreet), whatever is required. You must also begin to read the newspapers every day, but not for gossip and society information. You must read it to understand the world that you now live in without protection. I promise, it will become easier as time goes by and you have a broader body of knowledge from which to draw.

You must promise to do this for me, Annabella.

When you have read the books you will understand why I am so very adamant on these issues, and you will know what you need to continue to investigate on your own. If you do not wish to be penniless, or perhaps forced to marry someone who will not treasure you as I did, you will do this last thing I ask of you.

Annabella, I am very sorry that I have died. Please let this thought comfort you: I am with Sarah again, and I will give her your love.

Your Husband,

Quince

Wetmoor Hall

Essex

☙ *Lady Annabella* ❧

24 September, 1820

Dearest Susannah,

I am thrilled beyond belief to write you my first letter from Wetmoor Hall and, although my tenancy is thus far in its earliest infancy, there are already new and exciting things happening: namely, I was near murdered yesterday.

Is that not the most exciting thing you have ever read? I, Annabella Upton-Church, formerly of London, now a country lady, came quite close to being cannon fodder. Of course it was an accident. I fervently hope so.

The principal reason I wonder such a thing is because of the two promises you made me, only one has been found to be true: the promise that time would remedy much. The second, that people would forget and the scandal fade to nothing, appears to be more hope than reality.

Perhaps once I have restored Wetmoor to its former glory my reputation will be less wicked. I confess I do not see how having a lovely house will accomplish such a feat, especially in the country, of all places. Well, there is nothing to be done about it now, for I am here, the London house completely closed, and I have embarked on my "new life." Thus far it certainly has proved to be more interesting than the old.

The move to Wetmoor was uneventful, but once we arrived everything deteriorated into tumult. I had given up trying to oversee the unloading of the carriages and wagons, leaving it to my last footman, Taylor, the newest and most inexperienced of my former set of six. I had removed myself to my rooms for a spot of claret to calm my nerves, for my physician advised me to avoid any further anxiety. Suddenly Prudence added to it by announcing a caller.

I was appalled – I had not even sent out cards to my new neighbours and I was being importuned by a caller! I was going to have them (whoever they were) sent away when I realized whoever it was might be Important and I could set a foot wrong without ever setting a foot out my own front door. With a sigh I set down my claret, knowing it could give an unfortunate impression if I took it with me, and left my lovely suite, walking down the wide halls to the grand staircase.

Well, it will be grand again someday. From the top of the stairway I swept as much as possible in a gown without a train to the foyer, which was annoyingly empty given how well I thought I swept. It was not empty, but rather full to bursting with everything that had come with us from the London house. I found myself having to climb over crates and trunks to make my way to the drawing room. When Taylor and the moving men came through the front door, laden with ever more of my possessions, I was inelegantly balanced atop one of the sideboards. Taylor near dropped the box he was carrying when he saw me. As he ran to help me down I told him to at least clear a path, as I have suffered through enough foyer incidents to last the rest of my life. I was quite imperious until he lost his grip and I tumbled to the floor. I ought to have known better than to lean on him, he is a wonderful footman but has the strength of a rabbit. As he helped me to my feet I saw he had blanched at the memory of the last foyer incident, even if it was over one year ago, and he quickly instructed the moving men to do as I asked.

Limping only a bit, I entered the drawing room expecting to see a female caller, it would be unseemly for a gentleman to hurtle through my doorway so soon after coming out of full mourning, and was brought up short by the sight of a servant. Someone else's servant; I was quite sure he was not mine. I know exactly who my servants are, as there were so few who survived everything. The one standing in front of me promptly bowed low.

"I am sent from Sumwattle Estate, Lady Upton-Church, by Lord and Lady Shardley" he said, voice breaking a little on my name. I scrabbled through my memory, I knew that name but could not place it, and found not a single reference to a place called Sumwattle Estate, although I have always been hopeless at remembering place names. Wetmoor Hall is not very elegant but "Sumwattle" sounded awful.

"What is the purpose of your visit, young man?"

He thrust an envelope toward me, and began speaking even as I opened it. "It's an invitation, milady, to the hunt." I perused the invitation and noted with alarm the date set.

"The hunt is <u>tomorrow</u>."

"Yes, milady, which is why I was told to wait for your reply. Lady Shardley wants to know right away if you accept her very kind invitation." I narrowed my eyes at the little snot, for implicit in his statement was arrogance. I wondered if it was his own or merely borrowed from his mistress. Considering his callow and unfinished face I realized it was likely the latter, the former being too young and hopelessly outclassed for such a jab.

I then considered the request itself. That Lady Shardley knew I was just arrived from London and still extended an invitation so quickly was either evidence of either utter foolishness on her part – the furniture was not yet uncrated! – or she was looking for an opportunity to be slighted, the slight then used against me with others in our set. That may sound preposterous but given my reputation in London, I had the distinct feeling the latter purpose was also the true one. I did not want to make the wrong decision, Susannah, for I mean to make Wetmoor my home, and could not afford to put a foot wrong on my very first day. I sighed, as there was nothing to be done about it: I would have to attend. Worse, a lawn meet was to be had as well, which meant my morning would begin all the earlier. I asked Taylor, standing in place at the door, where my writing desk was located. He gulped and looked over his shoulder where I could see the crates piled high, which produced from me another sigh. I turned back to the servant.

"Please tell Lady Shardley for me that I thank her for her very quick kindness and sudden hospitality and greatly look forward to meeting my neighbours." He nodded through my statement but looked a little confused at the end. "Have I missed something?"

"Umm, does that mean you'll be at the hunt?"

There went any hope of my original response getting to the recipient as originally stated. "Yes, it does. I accept with many thanks."

"Thank you, Lady." He bowed low again and I gave him his leave. As we watched him climb onto his horse I handed the invitation to Taylor.

"Taylor, have my gowns found and sent to my rooms. Send Prudence as well. And make sure – " I cast about for which servant would handle my next request, and realized I had no idea " – someone finds Driver's best uniform. I am going to a hunt on the morrow. Have Driver make the carriage presentable for such an outing – the closed carriage, not the cabriolet."

"Yes, Lady," and Taylor was off at a run. I walked through the foyer at a statelier pace, courtesy of a miraculous little path cleared for me during my time in the drawing room. Wetmoor Hall is still very new to me, Susannah, and I found myself gaping at the high ceiling above me, hearing footsteps echoing up and down the hallways. I went directly to my rooms to see if there was already a suitable gown unpacked. My full mourning period is over so I am not constrained to black, but I was not merely going to a hunt. I was going to be introduced to my neighbours, and wanted to make sure I looked my best within the limits of grey, black and general sadness, as that is no excuse for not looking fabulous.

The rest of the day was spent seeing the crates pried open, spilling the contents of my life into the foyer, the items then carted off to the correct rooms. Occasionally I needed a bit of claret, for the last mess in my foyer was . . . well, there really is not a word to describe such a thing, is there?

Dinner was a meagre affair, which I took in the morning room sitting on the floor, for the dining room table had a leg gone missing and could not be used. I wondered if Driver had made off with it, to show that being without a leg is more vexing than one would imagine, although he gets around very well on the new one. I mean that of course it is not the original leg, but not even the original wooden leg. He keeps doing things to them, no matter how I importune him to take care. As it was Quince's fault Driver is lacking in a limb I order the wooden ones from the finest body carpenter in London, who charges dear for his services. Whenever one goes awry I order Driver yet another, although I think if he had to purchase them himself he would take more care. Servants.

But eating this way reminded me of the first days with my Quince, after we married. He had cleared the London house so I might remake it in whatever fashion I chose, forgetting that until I had done exactly that we would be reduced to sitting on the floor and eating from plates balanced on window-sills. It was by eating from window-sills, sitting on the floor, that we began to know each other. He was a dear man, although terrible at everyday things. I do wish he were still alive.

By the end of a long day things were looking much improved. Many things were still piled chock-a-block throughout the foyer and the Hall, but I was very pleased to see that my rooms had been mostly put to rights. My rooms comprise a bedroom, sitting room, dressing room and positively decadent and modern bath. The full suite spans the back end of the Hall, directly over the ballroom. I could easily live in those four rooms if I chose. I think Sir Manfredson, the previous owner, did by the time he went mad.

By the time I wanted my nightdress Prudence had built a merry little fire in the fireplace and properly turned down my bed. It was near midnight when I climbed into it and blew out the candle, and I was very tired. It was more difficult than I imagined to move, even if servants moved everything.

Once I was finally alone I let out a sigh that, once released, I realized must have been pent-up for well over a year. I snuggled into the down mattress and looked up at the pretty canopy and drapes, remembering my bed in London, which had become so austere by the end. I like my new bed far better, with its silks and down, pillows piled high, drapes and cording swathing the four posts. My life has changed so much from what I thought it would be in my youth! Who would have thought I would be 27 and a widow without a single child to show for it? As going down that avenue of thought was dispiriting I turned my mind to what I was doing one year ago, locked away in mourning in London. If I remembered rightly I was just embarking on my studies. What a difference a year makes! I was wondering what Quince would have thought of my decision to move – bless him for leaving me Wetmoor in the will! – when I drifted to sleep.

At six o'clock in the morning I woke to Prudence bustling in with my breakfast tray. I looked around blearily; it took me a moment to remember how I wound up in a bed not my own. That is not a situation I ever before encountered and it was quite discomfiting. Then I remembered it is my own, as well as everything surrounding it, and smiled at my dear personal maid to show I was well. As I tucked into a proper breakfast I told her the carriage should leave within the hour and to make sure Driver would be ready.

As you can see, I had no intention of missing the lawn meet. I surely would have arrived there on time had I not forgotten one simple thing: the actual location of Sumwattle Estate.

Once in my carriage I was thoroughly enjoying having a few moments to myself, no one importuning me for decisions, and watched my new surroundings go by through the windows, the panes sparkling in the early morning sun. That did become rather dull after a few moments, however, there is much Nature everywhere, so I was pleased to find a bottle of brandy and a glass tucked under my seat. As it was my first outing in my new neighbourhood I was excited and anxious about what I might encounter, and the brandy helped settle my nerves. I am remarkably clever, Susannah, for I even thought to put mint leaves in my bag so no one would notice if I fortified my spirits with . . . spirits.

Birds were flitting about, I was feeling quite gay with the help of the brandy, when I realized other horses and carriages were passing us in the other direction. I rapped on the carriage ceiling and felt it slow before coming to a stop just off the road. I heard Driver clamber down, wooden leg banging on the carriage side, before he poked his head in the carriage.

We then had a near set-to, for it appeared he had no idea how to get to Sumwattle, and was planning on going to town for directions, which would have made me look terribly stupid. When I informed him of the error in his thinking he managed to find someone living nearby who could tell us, and paid a farthing for silence. I was nearly mollified until he said, "So no need to fret, Lady, your reputation'll be . . . the same."

Of course Sumwattle was in the opposite direction, but it did afford me the opportunity to see Wetmoor as we passed by it again. Goodness, the renovations of the grounds alone shall take forever. It appears quite forbidding and wild from the road, and I made a note to see if something could be done to make it look less disgusting as soon as possible.

Because of the delay I did not arrive at Sumwattle Estate, the most rigidly perfect example of a country estate I have ever seen, until near half-past ten. Carriages were all along the drive, with their owners and servants nowhere in sight. I hoped I should not have to bring Driver in with me – with that wooden leg he has a terribly lurching gait.

I learned from Driver later that the absence of servants in the front of the house was due to an odd preference of Lady Shardley's: servants have to stay under stairs and are not to be seen outside unless they are working on the grounds.

Once the horses are hobbled and left to graze she does not wish for inferiors to "loll about, mucking up the façade."

I am very pleased for her snobbishness, Susannah, for I was the only witness to the scandal.

As we pulled up in front of the doors of Sumwattle, they flew open with a bang! I thought the butler had seen our arrival and was running to help me from my carriage. I was utterly incorrect.

It was one of the maids coming out the front door and she was shrieking and screaming as if possessed! I was absolutely terrified, for she was disheveled and apparently quite mad – she did not even use the servants' entrance! Driver had clambered down the side of the carriage during this scene and opened the door for me. I (quite properly, I feel) pulled it closed again. I held tightly to the handle, for I knew Driver would try again, he has no understanding of etiquette. One does not knowingly step into a scandal in the making. One stays quiet and pays careful attention so as not to miss a single, sordid detail. After a few more tugs he gave up and I heard him clomping off to the other side of the carriage. I scarce noticed; I was too transfixed by what I was seeing in front of mine own eyes.

The wretch then collapsed on the ground and began beating her fists against the earth! The front door opened again and out bustled the housekeeper, who gasped at the sight of my carriage. I looked down from the window, where my nose had been veritably pressed, and pretended to be occupied with an item in my little velvet reticule, so as not to add to the embarrassment caused by the maid's behaviour. Satisfied I was otherwise engaged, the housekeeper strode over to the maid – her name is Gwynneth apparently, what a ridiculously high-tone name for a mere maid – and yanked her to her feet.

There followed the most tumultuous row between the two – I was astonished at the cheek of the girl at first, until I realized that she did not simply seem mad – she was, in fact, quite off her head.

Gwynneth is of the unshakable belief that the master of Sumwattle, Lord Shardley, is in love with her, and is the father of her coming child! She is convinced of this, unlike the other maids who so often make the same accusation, hoping for some financial windfall, when they lose their positions for moral turpitude.

Gwynneth sincerely believes Lord Shardley loves her. She screamed up at the windows for him, quoting the promises she believed he made to her. I was beginning to actually pity her when I realized what a crafty little thing she is! To cause such a scene in front of a guest – obviously she has no loyalty to her house, and not a whit of decorum! This fit was being tossed on the day of a hunt and anyone could have heard! I thanked the Lord it was myself. Such a one as her deserves to be turned out, and the sooner the better. One rotten apple will spoil the entire staff, I believe.

Apparently the housekeeper felt the same as I. With a nod to the stable hands, who were drawn by the noise and creeping near, the girl was scooped up and carried down the drive. She never stopped wailing that she loved his Lordship, they were soulmates, and all manner of hopelessly romantic drivel.

After that came quite a silence, as from below the brim of my hat I could feel the eyes of the servants staring at the carriage. What had I seen or heard? I knew they wondered. I continued to pretend to find something fascinating in my bag. Finally, the carriage door was re-opened by one of the Shardley footmen and I exited the carriage, trying with all my might to appear completely unaware of the events just past.

Everyone's breath was held as I reached the porch. A footman leapt to my side (a fetching young man, actually), opened the door and ushered me into the house proper, even as I tried to remember every word I had heard. The staff was mute, but more from horror of what I had overheard than training.

It is clear the Shardleys are very, very, <u>very</u> fond of the Greek style that has been so popular in recent years. I find it a bit of a bore myself; it is strange to see busts of Zeus sitting on pianos and the like. Before I could see anything else I was ushered through the house to the back veranda, which swept the length of the house itself. I was announced and Lady Shardley stepped forward from the crowd of titles clustered about, all of whom were staring at me. Lord Shardley did not appear to be in evidence.

Lady Shardley is the most intimidating woman I have ever seen. I knew that I might have heard the name but we had never met, she is unforgettable. It is easy to see that in her youth Lady Shardley was a handsome woman, but now appears more forbidding than forgiving. Her bust, like the prow of a great ship, disproportionately preceded her and she was covered in tweed, tartan and other wool patterns. Her hat appeared to be made of a clutch of pheasants, all of whom appeared as if they would swoop down upon me, talons extended, if I were found wanting in any way. Lady Shardley did not speak at first, merely looked me up and down. I felt as if I were a horse on market and considered whinnying. I was beginning to wonder if she was going to check my teeth when she spoke in an unforgettable voice: fruity and gravel-strewn simultaneously.

"You are Lady Upton-Church?"

"Yes, I am."

"I am Lady Shardley. You have not yet invited me to your Hall, Lady Upton-Church. Have I offended you in some way?" What a beginning to our acquaintance! Accusations of either etiquette breach or snobbishness. Thank God I lived in London, where such things are easily handled.

"Of course not, Lady Shardley. Why ever should I wish to offend one whose existence is not known to me?" That was good; it let her know her fame was indeed small, and did not extend to London. Or if it did, it did not extend to me. The fact that I could never keep straight who was important in the Ton was irrelevant, I feel. I know not how anyone manages to remember who in the peerage is what, not only of themselves, but of every family and title relationship between all of them. I used to despair every time an engagement was announced. As I need not worry about <u>that</u> anymore, I maintained eye contact throughout my statement, head held high. For goodness' sake, I had not even been in the country a full day! She must have an astonishing sense of her own importance.

Her eyes narrowed. "I am mistress of Sumwattle Estate."

"So I am given to understand by your invitation."

She made a snorting sound. "You are late. Do you not care for lawn meets?"

Goodness, she was awful! I maintained a civil tone. "I adore them, Lady Shardley. I wish you had enclosed directions with your generous invitation, else I may have arrived at a more sociable time."

She faltered, as intended. Not everyone in the universe, of which she clearly feels Sumwattle is the center, is acquainted with her estate. She tried to recover. "How do you find Wetmoor Hall?"

"Lovely." I looked about, she was rather boring, actually.

"I read of you last year in the newspapers. You are quite famous." She sniffed, actually <u>sniffed</u>! Rudely!

"Really?" I tilted my head at her, silently daring her to say anything.

She did not have the courage. "Pity about your husband."

"Thank you. Is Lord Shardley here?" I knew my voice was icy, but I did not like this woman, even on short acquaintance.

My question struck home somehow, I was pleased to see, for she faltered somewhat in her disdain. "He is in London at present. For the Crown."

"Of course." I did not give her any leeway, as unChristian as it may have been. I disliked Lady Shardley on sight.

She seemed to feel the same. "If you wish to live in a haunted Hall in the country instead of London, it is none of my affair." She turned away, but I was irritated. And what was that bit about Wetmoor being haunted? No one ever mentioned that to <u>me</u> when I contemplated the move. However, it was not the time to dither over that, it was time to engage in a verbal skirmish with a horrid woman.

I followed her. "Lady Shardley, a moment, if you please."

She turned back to me. "You are going to tell me your Hall is not haunted, I suppose."

I smiled prettily and readied myself to wipe the smug look from her face. "Actually, no one has informed me of a haunting." She opened her mouth to interrupt but I continued quite smoothly in a whisper. "I was going to request, Lady Shardley, that you discuss with your housekeeper what I witnessed on my arrival before impugning my house in public – or private, I should like to add – ever again."

She gaped. "I beg your pardon?"

"Once you have spoken to your housekeeper I believe you shall." I stood waiting and smiled. She looked somewhat flustered and at a loss for words – in less than two minutes – quite a poor showing for a verbal spar.

Thankfully another guest was announced and Lady Shardley turned from me, saying over her shoulder, "You have not brought your own firearm. One of the servants will equip you."

"Thank you, Lady Shardley." There was no reply, presumably the newest arrival was more pliable. However, that awful woman left me without making any introductions or offering sustenance. I looked around, for this was my first social event since . . . everything . . . and being unescorted, I was hoping to see a familiar face, so as to have someone with whom I could chat. It has been so long since I have had a nice chat!

Not a single face seemed familiar, which surprised me, for Lady Shardley did not seem the type of woman to accept demurral without consequence. In fact, there were fewer people than I expected, given the popularity of hunts. I did note that the men on her staff are incredibly handsome, every last one. Especially the one who was looking at the rifles to be used. He did not have a regular uniform, but was talking and laughing with some of the other servants, so I assumed he held a high position in the household. He was absolutely staggering. He did not behave properly, for instead of looking away he openly stared at me. I wondered for a moment if he had overheard Lady Shardley before dismissing the thought; he was near thirty feet from us. I suddenly thought that a rifle might be acceptable if he were to choose one for me, and I might even endeavor to use it.

Then he ruined it by smiling and inclining his head at me in acknowledgment. I quickly looked away, it would not do for him to think himself the subject of particular attention, he might try to take liberties, and then I would have to remonstrate and perhaps smack him, which would lead to him losing his post and starving to death, being unable to find a new position without proper references. It did not seem his clear adoration of me was enough of an insult that he needed to die for it, so I decided to hold my tongue regarding his impertinence.

As I looked about for any familiar faces I realized that people were coming close to staring at me themselves. I suddenly began to feel anxious, for I have been removed from the center of attention for more than a year, and the last time it was infamy, not fame, causing such curiosity. I managed to refrain from actual fidgeting, looking back just as openly, as if I had not a care in the world, nor a thought, and smiled gently, just as Miss Penelope taught us at her School of Charms and Whimsies. Miss Penelope was so odd, and our education odder still, but there were nuggets of wisdom to be gleaned from the dross she called "lessons."

I had fallen into a reverie of my school days when a stunningly beautiful woman, even if near forty, with dark hair and porcelain skin, approached holding her hands out to me. She wore a gown that made me long for my half-mourning to be complete, truly staggering jewels – I am still perforce in jet and onyx, although I was spared the hideousness of having something made from Quince's hair due to what happened to his head. I admit I felt a twinge of jealousy at her fashionable attire.

"Annabella!" She was beaming at me, but I had no idea who she was. She at least seemed pleased to see me, so I took her hands and as we bussed each other on each cheek she murmured, "Well done with Lady Shardley. I am Baroness Gurthwant." A baroness! I was quite surprised. The baroness, as you recall, is not the first baroness for the baron. His first wife, Hilda, was from Germany of all places, and passed away in that horrible ice-skating accident. The new baroness seemed the antithesis of what the name of Hilda might conjure: beautiful, petite, sophisticated and apparently very, very bored. Exactly the sort of person I love to befriend.

She stepped back from me, still smiling. "It is wonderful to see you."

"And I you." She tucked my arm in hers and walked me away from the crowd, behaving for all the world as if we were the best of friends. I was bewildered and trying mightily to think where we may have met in London, utterly without success. She must have heard of me, but did not seem mortified that I was sullying the hunt with my presence.

The very moment we had moved a decent distance away I whispered, "I am Lady Upton-Church," for we had not been fully introduced.

She turned to me with a smile and said, "We have not met, Lady Upton-Church, but I thought it awful that Lady Shardley invited you here and then treated you poorly. It was most unkind and not a little vulgar, in my mind."

I was surprised at her candor. "She is no worse than most in London, Baroness."

She smiled. "Quite true. What did you say to her to make her falter?"

Something stayed my tongue, and I told a tiny untruth. "I told her that her hat was a lovely antique."

Baroness Gurthwant laughed. "Wonderful! She has worn that awful thing at the last six hunts . . . However, I had my own reasons for wanting to secure your attention. You are the owner of Wetmoor Hall, are you not?"

"Yes, I am."

She clapped her hands. "How thrilling! I want to hear all about it. Of course, I am terribly remiss, for although I have heard of you, we were not properly introduced. I hope you will forgive me for having approached you in such a fashion."

"I am quite glad of it. I do not know anyone here." I smiled at her; her gaiety was infectious.

Baroness Gurthwant cocked her head. "Lady Shardley is aware of that, I am sure. This is not my first event at Sumwattle."

"My apologies," I giggled.

"Wetmoor interests me far more than Sumwattle. Is it haunted? I must admit, I eavesdrop without shame." She tried to look abashed but utterly failed.

"As do I. I hate to disappoint you so early in our acquaintance, but there seem to be no spirits in Wetmoor except those in bottles."

She waved away my demurral. "It is quite the talk of the county all the same, and mine as well. I live the next county west of this," and gestured vaguely to her left. "I first came to this part of the country two years ago, and your Hall stood empty the entire time. When I heard it was to be occupied I was so excited, for I have always wanted to see the interior. I understand it is lovely. Oh, goodness, I have been remiss once again. Please accept my apologies on your husband's passing." Of course she would have heard, the same as everyone else.

"Thank you."

"You are the sole inheritor?"

Baroness Gurthwant clearly had access to better gossip and information than I ever did and I, in my former life, had a considerable amount of both, so it seemed pointless to deflect. "Yes, I was as surprised as anyone."

"Of course you were. I cannot credit you had anything to do with your husband's death."

There it was, as I found when going out again in London after my full mourning finally ended. With no one to defend me during that time and required to stay indoors save going to Church, the rumors swirling had coalesced into what was now accepted as fact. The questions were begun by the newspapers, but the Ton swooped upon them and gobbled them whole: Had I killed Quince or not? I am grateful the authorities finally decided I had not done anything to hasten Quince to his Reward but was surprised there were so few others with the same opinion. In fact, you were near the only one who thought me innocent. I had known Quince and I were not the *crème de la crème* of society, but we were – I thought at the time – accepted. We were invited to near every gathering that mattered in London. It was quite distressing to find that without Quince I was as welcome amongst the Ton as a member of the *demimonde,* poor little aspirants. My reputation was as tattered as a peasant's clothing. Perhaps more so.

Given that, I was dispirited that a new acquaintance would bring up the subject directly, but did not want to annoy her. She is a baroness, after all. "You are in the minority opinion, I am afraid," I finally said.

She realized what she had implied. "Oh, do not fret about that. Most of the Ton thinks I murdered my first husband so I could marry the baron. I had nothing to do with it, so I understand what it is like. My new title is the only thing keeping me afloat." She waved at some people walking by before looking back at me.

I quickly revised my earlier thoughts, for it appeared I had an ally. "That is very kind."

"The Ton dropped you, of course."

There was no point disputing it; she was perfectly aware it was true. "Yes."

Her response surprised me. "A crashing bore, the lot of them. You are better off here."

A baroness declaring the Ton a bore? I had thought so myself, you and I have often discussed it. Of course I followed Debrett's for the changes in the upper crust, but I am only a recent lady and always had difficulty keeping all of the alliances and titles in order at parties and balls, which often became more trouble than the pleasure a new ball gown or daring dessert provided. Baroness Gurthwant was nothing but surprises.

I smiled at her, for it was clear she was trying to soothe me. "I believe I am. It is tiring to be peered at as if I might go mad and start shooting everyone in sight."

She nodded. "I know. In my case it was exhausting, as my first husband was shot to death."

I would have cut my own tongue out right then and there had I a knife; how could I have put my foot wrong so quickly! "I am so sorry, I did not know." Luckily she did not seem to mind in the least, waving her hand about vaguely.

"Oh, it was his own fault. He should have gone to the more established brothels, not the ones near the docks." This was such a personal conversation, but Baroness Gurthwant was so charming and seeming honest it did not seem strange. She patted my arm again. "I think what you are doing with Wetmoor is lovely, and hope my kindness today will be repaid with an invitation when you are ready to receive callers." A baroness brazenly angling for an invitation! The Hall must have a much more storied reputation than I was told. It could redeem me socially, if properly handled.

"I would be delighted to receive you, Baroness."

She smiled. "Then it is settled. Do you know anyone here?"

"I confess I do not."

"Well, let me point out the most esteemed of our set. Although esteemed may pay too high a compliment. I shall properly introduce you as opportunities present themselves." She pointed out Baron Theosophus and Duke Twitwhistle, best friends since their school days, and Mr. Gibberwilly, the surgeon. ("In case something awful happens, and it usually does," she murmured. Before I could ask what that meant she moved on to others.) Lords and ladies, a duchess, Knights of the Realm, etc., etc. etc., joined the list, although I was somewhat distracted by Baron Theosophus, who was wheeling about a small cannon with a cavalier air that boded ill for all. I was trying to engrave names in my head when the baroness turned and asked, "I never thought to inquire: Do you shoot?"

Although concerned that I was about to lose all of the social ground just gained, I realized that if I lied, hunted and then vomited while viewing bits of a dead and bloody fox I would lose far more, so decided honesty was the best course. "Truth to tell, I hate shooting, Baroness. Blood makes me feel faint. I came because it seemed an invitation from Lady Shardley was not something lightly refused. I plan on being far away from wherever the foxes lurk and then perhaps getting lost."

Instead of ruining everything my honesty was rewarded, for not only did Baroness Gurthwant smile, she clapped her hands together. "Finally! Someone as civilized as I! I hate hunts, I would much rather spend the afternoon drinking, but my husband could not attend and he and Lady Shardley's husband have business together, so I had to attend on his behalf."

I was so happy to find someone of a like mind. "It is perfectly all right for men to go around shooting at things, it makes them so happy, but I have never understood why I should tromp around in the mud and the rain with a rifle or musket or whatever it is they use."

"I could not agree with you more." We had strayed rather far from the veranda, off to the side, when there was a loud banging sound. My original plan, to turn and see what had happened, was immediately dashed. Instead an old tree branch hanging overhead cracked in half and landed atop me, so surprising me that I stumbled, which proved unfortunate, as I was standing at the edge of a small ravine, and of course some of the ground gave way so that I found myself tumbling down the incline all the way to the bottom. It was a small ravine, but not the sort of thing I ever want to do again. The baroness screamed and I did as well, it was all very startling.

Baron Theosophus had been showing how his cannon was aimed and had not checked to see if there was a cannonball it. That is what I was told later, but at the time all I knew was that I had been clubbed and thrown into a ravine. As I rolled and thumped to the bottom I wondered if Lady Shardley had found out what I had seen on my arrival and arranged to murder me before I could spread tales of her wanton servants.

"Do not move!" Baroness Gurthwant called from the top. Of course I was going to move, my gown was nearly over my head! I yanked it down and rolled over. The baroness saw what I was doing. "Well, except for that." She turned away whilst I attempted to determine if I was in complete disarray. As I was horrified to discover, I had gone past disarray to utter *dishabille*. My hat had disappeared, I was covered with an unfortunate amount of dirt and leaves, my dress was rather twisted about and (I am loathe to admit) somewhat rucked up. As I yanked it down to cover my bared ankles I heard a rustle above me and looked up.

The surgeon, Mr. Gibberwilly, was beginning to scramble down the incline, apparently ready to hack off any limbs that appeared damaged, so I called to him, "I am quite uninjured, sir! Your services are not needed!" He instantly scrambled back up again, which was most rude. I may not have required medical care, but an arm to steady me on uneven ground would have been welcome. I began brushing dirt clods and sodden leaves from my ruined gown and suddenly another man was scrambling down the incline. It was the servant who had been staring at me. He reached the bottom far more gracefully than I had and ran to me.

"Lady Upton-Church, are you all right?" He asked, breathing a little heavily from what must have been a mad run to so quickly reach me. He scooped up my Spanish hat from where it had landed and handed it to me when he reached my side.

"Someone clubbed me. I think." I was utterly nonplussed as I put my hat back on.

I heard Baroness Gurthwant berating Lady Shardley at the top of the ravine. Something about hosts not having guests shot at and being rude to boot.

My introduction to country society had gone terribly awry – ladies casting aspersions upon my character to all and sundry, falling into a ravine, my gown ruined, Prudence would not be able to save it . . .

The man moved to my side and gently took my arm. "No, you were nearly shot. Baron Theosophus. He loves his cannon." My confusion continued and I stared at him. His voice clearly marked him as a Scot, although he appeared civilized.

"Why did he try to kill me? We have not even been introduced."

The Scot smiled. "I don't think he was aiming at you, Lady."

"Who are you?"

He looked embarrassed. "My apologies. I am Mr. Ploughgoode."

He was incredibly handsome, with dark hair and grey eyes – a very unusual colour – which were flecked with bits of green and blue.

I was able to see his eyes clearly because he was looking me up and down quite thoroughly. I thought I perhaps should smack him for such an affront, but realized he was ensuring I was not bleeding from a cut or had a bone sticking out of my head or something similarly awful. However, even if there were, that was something for the surgeon to remedy, so I drew myself up to my full height, which is still altogether too short, and tugged the veil on my hat back over my face.

"Mr. Ploughgoode. Thank you for coming to my rescue. I am Lady Upton-Church."

"I should have kept a better eye on the baron." He looked somber. "He might have killed you."

"However, he did not, so I would not fuss if I were you. It certainly has been an unusual morning." Given everything else I have survived falling into a ravine and near being killed seemed a matter of small consequence. A year ago it would have sent me to bed for a week. How much I have changed! "Is it always like this?"

Mr. Ploughgoode chuckled. "Not always. Sometimes, though . . . Can you walk?"

I took a little step, realized I had turned my ankle and grabbed at his arm as I gave a little squeak. "At least I am not shot." I am very brave, Susannah.

"I shall carry you." He made as if to sweep me right off my feet, which was altogether unwarranted.

I let go of his arm and turned a bit to keep him from throwing me over his shoulder or dragging me up the incline by my hair, for he was a Scot. "That shall not be necessary. Should you carry me Mr. Gibberwilly will realize I am injured and want to cut off my leg."

He smiled. "You're a fair judge of character; he likely would. May I offer you my arm instead?" I took it to steady me and we slowly ascended the incline, he carefully leading. I was glad of it, my ankle really was quite sore.

Baroness Gurthwant was still having a grand time dressing Lady Shardley down in front of the party at the top of her lungs. She had a few interesting observations regarding the Baron Theosophus' cannon aiming skills as well. It seemed everyone was rapt watching Lady Shardley's humiliation. I would have done the same had not been myself who had nearly been killed.

When we arrived at the top of the ravine Baroness Gurthwant was still holding forth. "It is unacceptable, people wandering with cannons and possibly killing or maiming peers, I have never heard of such a thing, what kind of house do you run?" She saw me. "There you are. Are you all right?"

"I am fine," I managed to say. Lady Shardley looked markedly less intimidating.

Baron Theosophus stepped forward. "Lady Upton-Church, please accept my most profound, heartfelt, sincere and abject apology. The cannon was a gift from the King himself, I was just demonstrating – "

Baroness Gurthwant took my arm. "Yes, of course. You are always shooting at things, Baron. Perhaps you might consider aiming beforehand." She turned to me. "Of course you have had enough excitement, dear. Being shot at and nearly killed. It is a scandal!" She glared at our hostess.

Lady Shardley winced at the word scandal and stepped forward. It seemed she had met with her housekeeper, for her manner was markedly different. "Lady Upton-Church, please accept my apologies for such a horrible accident. Are you injured?"

I waved my hand as if it were no matter. "I have twisted my ankle somewhat. I should like to sit down, if that is not disagreeable."

"Of course, of course," she waved at a servant, who came running with a chair.

"Oh." I managed to make my voice quite small. "You wish me to sit out here? How lovely. It is such a pretty day." A ridiculous faux pas on Lady Shardley's part, and it was difficult for me to not laugh. I tried to look pained and frightened instead.

Lady Shardley was furious her hunt had gone so awry before it even began and whirled upon Mr. Ploughgoode. "And you! It is entirely your fault!"

"Excuse me?" He seemed astonished. I was as well.

"Mr. Ploughgoode, your sole responsibility today was safety, and you were sorely deficient in your post, do you not agree?"

I thought that very nasty. If he agreed he would be stating he had done a poor job and being discharged was warranted, if he protested he would be publicly disagreeing with the lady who employed him, as well as casting aspersions on a baron. It was impossible. Regardless, it was the baron's fault, and I was disappointed yet unsurprised that the baron did not come forward and take responsibility.

"This has been an unfortunate beginning," Mr. Ploughgoode murmured.

Lady Shardley remained imperious. "Due to your negligence Lady Upton-Church has been injured. You are dismissed. Take your leave."

I was suddenly sorry I had said anything about my ankle. I was trying to think of a way to protest, regardless of the fact that he was her servant, for it was the baron's fault, not Mr. Ploughgoode's, and got as far as saying "But – " when Mr. Ploughgoode nodded at Lady Shardley and turned to me.

"My apologies, Lady Upton-Church," he said, bowing quite low. He did not seem to mind losing his post.

"Mine as well," I said without thinking. "You were very kind to have helped me." He looked startled as I glanced at Lady Shardley. I decided since my reputation is already in ruins and she did not like me I may as well say what I wished. "The only one to have helped me."

Lady Shardley looked as if she might shoot me herself but as I was injured and a peer she vented herself on poor Mr. Ploughgoode. "Which was only proper, as it was your fault."

He coloured slightly but bowed to her as well. "With your permission, Lady Shardley." She flicked a hand at him in dismissal. He bowed to me once more and departed the little group, which left me sitting on a chair, surrounded by titles and servants, all straining to get a better look. Goodness, would being stared at never end?

Lady Shardley leaned over me, trying to salvage what was left of the hunt, but with the huge birds on her head it looked more as if she were attacking me. "I am having the drawing room fire drawn and lit for you." Lady Shardley was gesticulating to the servants, who seemed quite confused. She finally grabbed one, whispered in his ear, and he took off at a run for the house. "How are you now?"

I was quite put out. "Lady Shardley, you are fussing for nothing. The hunt must go one, does it not? I shall simply stay here."

"I shall stay with you." Lady Shardley finally felt she had put a foot right, and perhaps have the opportunity to stifle me from spreading the tale of what had happened at the front of her house. She was wrong, of course. Baroness Gurthwant put a proprietary hand on my shoulder.

"Oh, dear, you cannot do such a thing. Why, you are the hostess! You need to see to the rest of your guests. I will stay with Annabella, if that is all right." The baroness smiled at me as murmurs rippled through the crowd. The baroness used my Christian name! She smiled at me. "It has been so long since we have seen each other, has it not?"

"Ages," I smiled and looked innocently at Lady Shardley, who realized that by slighting me, she had likely slighted a baroness.

The baroness could not resist. "Annabella and I go back years."

"I did not know that," Lady Shardley finally said.

Baroness Gurthwant smiled sweetly. "So it is decided. Annabella and I shall catch each other up, you can host your hunt, and we shall all see each other at dinner." We both smiled, and Lady Shardley knew she had been bested. By a baroness. Lady Shardley was trying to determine how to gracefully extricate herself when the baroness took my arm and I stood.

"We shall be inside." We walked to the house together, footmen scrambling to reach doors before us. The very moment we were in the drawing room and the door was safely closed behind us we burst into laughter.

Baroness Gurthwant was almost doubled over. "Oh, Annabella, thank you. I have been wanting to do something like that to Lady Shardley since the day I met her."

"You were brilliant." I picked up a bottle of claret from a table. "I do feel badly for Mr. Ploughgoode."

"Why ever should you do that?" Baroness Gurthwant was pulling bottles and glasses from a cupboard.

"He lost his post because of me."

She laughed. "Mr. Ploughgoode does not work for the Shardleys."

"He does not any longer."

She gestured to the window. "Take a look." I hobbled to the window to see Mr. Ploughgoode riding away on lovely horse. She turned to me. "He does not work here, he came to help with the hunt. He provides instruction to members of the peerage in whatever sport they require: shooting, riding, golf, duelling – so they might not publicly embarrass themselves. His instruction has prevented a number of terribly embarrassing moments for many peers."

I watched him ride away. "I am surprised, I would think such an instructor would be quite young, and Mr. Ploughgoode appears to be in his thirties. He is no boy."

"No, he is not." Baroness Gurthwant smiled at me, misinterpreting my observation for a more personal interest, which I quickly quashed.

"I feel badly he will lose clients because of this – " I began to say.

The baroness waved her hand. "Hardly. He is very popular, and being dismissed by the Shardleys happens so frequently that it is generally recognized it has little to no bearing on the person involved."

I was surprised. They must get rid of servants right and left to have such a reputation.

She saw I was not convinced. "I am sure he shall not suffer for what happened today, Annabella. He is teaching my children to ride, and shall remain in my employ. There is a fortunate by-product to his work." She gave a coy little smile.

I was astonished, for it appeared Mr. Ploughgoode provided other services as well. Gossip, I was privy to new gossip!

The baroness still had a smile on her face. "When he is working with the children the baron is most . . . attentive. I have the impression that he fears if he is not, I may go riding with Mr. Ploughgoode."

"Would you?" I blurted it out without thinking.

She looked at me with an arched brow. "Of course not. I love my husband, Annabella. But Mr. Ploughgoode is lovely," she said, taking one more look through the window before turning back to me. "Now that we do not have to ride to hounds and shoot anything, would you like some claret?"

Clearly our discussion of Mr. Ploughgoode's qualities was over, which I found a relief. "I certainly would."

I found myself spending the entire afternoon with a baroness, becoming steadily more unsteady, and being caught up on what is happening in the rarified circles she travels in, which are far higher in society than mine.

I have no idea why she chose to show me such kindness and courtesy, and suppose it does not really matter, for at the end of the afternoon I felt I had a new friend. It was very nice, for she is fun and I do not really have any friends in the country. Any friends at all, save yourself. Of course she travels a great deal and spends most of her time in London, but I do know that as soon as it is possible I shall be issuing an invitation to her to come to Wetmoor for tea. Before Lady Shardley, even though etiquette dictates that I return the "favour" of her invitation.

Rank hath its privilege.

All too soon everyone returned, dead fox heads blessedly stowed away where they would not drip on the carpets.

Dinner was a less pleasant affair, for the baroness was at the other end of the table. I was seated exactly even with the salt, and my dinner companions avoided me for those sitting on the other side of them. I consoled myself that no one mentioned explosions, inquests, or anything connected with Quince's death. That was better than my first forays into London after my full mourning ended.

Even with the coolness shown me at dinner I found myself leaving for Wetmoor with a lighter heart. It was good to be out amongst others, Susannah. I had not realized how very little social intercourse I have had in the last fourteen months. Police interviews do not count, I am very sure.

You see, I have to make a life for myself now, Susannah. The fact that I have no idea whatsoever how to accomplish such a feat seems not to matter now that I am alone. I thought moving far away from my old life would be a good start. I went from my father's house to my husband's, and thought I would have several children and die one day surrounded by they and lots of lovely grandchildren. I never dreamt it would all go so wrong. But it did, and when I came out of full mourning I realized there was nothing left of my old life. Everyone is gone.

I hope my new life is more successful.

I must away now, for there is to be another meeting with Mr. Wicklestaff – he is the man overseeing the renovations – regarding something about the plasterers. I am sure I am about to learn more about plaster and why it is expensive than I would have ever thought possible.

I have gone on far too long as well. Taylor may not have the strength to carry such a massive missive to the post without breaking his arm. I am grateful for the chance to tell someone of my new life, Susannah. Otherwise I should be quite lonely.

Oh, my. I must run, I just heard a crash and a scream, which means one of the workmen has done something clumsy and, quite likely, messy, and will require medical attention. This will be the third one. I must go see what has happened.

I shall write again soon and remain

Your Fond Friend,

Annabella

Lady Upton-Church and Mistress of Wetmoor Hall

☙ Questionable Advice ❧

27 September, 1820

Dear Susannah,

I write to you from my lovely sitting room in my suite overlooking the back of the grounds, wearing my favourite pellise robe and sipping a cup of tea. It is very civilized, although I am still getting used to thinking of Wetmoor as "mine" and that I live here instead of London. I so look forward to you visiting! I know your husband's obligations in Paris precludes such a visit in the near future and I suppose that is all right, for the Hall is still in complete disarray. We shall likely not see each other before Christmas, which fortunately is coming on fast. In the meantime, I will console myself of your absence with voluminous correspondence. I am pleased it only takes two days for a letter to arrive to or from Paris, so it will not seem as if you are reading ancient history when a missive arrives. In my mind's eye, I imagine you read these from your own rooms overlooking the Seine, as your maid prepares your gowns for another exciting and glamorous day.

I had no idea yours and the Shardleys' relationship went back so many years! Actually, I had no idea you knew the Shardleys at all, but your husband's work brings him in contact with so many people. Thank you for allowing me to use your name should I meet with Lady Shardley again. (I am sure we will, the country world is small.) Our friendship, acting in concert with her belief that I am close friends with

Baroness Gurthwant, may improve her initial impression of me, for it certainly did not go well at first. If your Lordship actually lived with the Shardleys for a short time, after his divorce and before he met you, they must be great good friends indeed!

I never did denounce Lady Shardley and the claims made by that wild maid, save to you, whom I tell everything. I think it a secret best kept in abeyance. For now. It is more delicious for her to be nervous about what I may or may not have overheard or repeated.

The maid was clearly lying, for she was not pretty enough to catch the eye of a Lord. She has a plain face, lank hair and a rather unfortunate nose. It is long, like your husband's, with a similar blob at the end which, on your husband, is quite attractive, but on a girl scarce seventeen is quite <u>un</u>attractive. Clearly her mother never cared enough to show Gwynneth the miracles that can be wrought with a bit of rouge and face paint, or worried that her daughter was as wanton as she appears to be and hoped that by leaving her plain she would remain untainted. Clearly her mother has some hope for her, else she would not have given her such a pretentious name. Gwynneth? It is ridiculous on such a creature!

In regard to Lady Shardley's wild claims about my house, you need not fret that Wetmoor is haunted. There have been no indications of supernatural activity thus far, which has been a great relief. I have enough to occupy my mind without worrying that ghosts shall pop out of nowhere to scare me out of my wits.

Your letter was filled with so much love and support and I thank you for it. Your belief in my ability to craft some sort of life from the wreckage of my old one cheered me no end. Perhaps I will be able to actually fashion something for myself that is acceptable.

In that vein, my primary reason for this letter is to address the Woman's Advice you gave when you saw me off from London. I have dithered in even visiting the issue, going so far as to start several letters, but each time ended by tossing the pages into the fire.

Your advice to me, although intended to educate, left me instead highly confused. I wanted to write you before now, but each time became terribly embarrassed. My mother is long dead and I have no sisters, so that sort of advice is something I have never received. I do not think I have ever discussed such things with anyone in my entire life.

You must think me frightfully provincial, but you have travelled and experienced far more of life than I. Our conversation in London did put some of the books I found in Quince's library in London into perspective, for when I found them they were so strange I put them away. They appear to be instruction books on various methods of enjoying oneself with someone else. There are some sketches (appalling) and written tales to provide insight (disgusting). I had never seen them before Quince died, nor had he ever suggested such things. They must be for mistresses, no decent wife would ever entertain such notions, although I do not believe Quince kept a mistress. No such woman showed up after he died.

Regardless, I did not like to think Quince was so degenerate in his romantic feelings. After my afternoon with you I realized romance had nothing to do with what he had been reading on his own. Relations between us were more along the lines of doing one's duty for God and country, although I did become adept at list-making in my head, a useful skill.

I had no idea it was supposed to be so enjoyable, Susannah! After Sarah Quince rarely came near me anymore, for nothing would have come of it anyway, and I did not mind.

However, no matter how I have tried, including pages of notes that I attempted to put into some semblance of order, I find myself reeling from the information you gave me, and have had difficulty getting it to fit into my head, for it was all quite cosmopolitan and sophisticated. France must be terribly complicated. I had not thought of my somewhat unique position as being conducive to finding myself in other unique positions at all. Or that unique positions are not actually unique, but rather intended to improve upon the sensations being sensed. I was married, now I am widowed. I thought I would be rather remote and then die one day.

I am only 27 but remarriage is impossible, for I find that with both the constraints of the will and my education at Quince's behest, I am not feeling inclined to give up everything I have inherited in order to be the adornment on someone's arm, unless there is a remarkable man attached to it. Also, I cannot think that a man would wish to marry a woman who had nothing to offer in a materiel sense nor give him children, so marriage would have to be due to wild passion, something with which I clearly am not acquainted. The only candidates I can imagine finding the above conditions acceptable are the heads of Cambridge or Oxford, and I shudder to be a teacher's wife. Were I to marry one of them I should then have to worry about being murdered all of the time in order to free up the estate, which seems a poor way to spend my life.

In terms of other opportunities for . . . companionship, why should I ever become a mistress? I have no need of funds, and I presumed my belief regarding relations was correct, as mistresses are paid ridiculous amounts to receive men. After seeing some of the drawings in Quince's private collection of books it seemed perfectly understandable why. They surely would not do that for free if it were wonderful. Some of them looked quite uncomfortable, although if you hold the book upside-down they appear more manageable.

As you seem to have thought everything out far more completely than I, please indulge me while I take a moment to understand you properly (and hide this letter the moment you have read it!):

Relations are very fun, if properly conducted. I may find myself feeling out of sorts at times, and relations are very helpful (if properly conducted) in improving my mood. As long as I undertake trysts (it is the only word I can think of) in the knowledge that romance, etc., are not part of it, I should indulge my (goodness, it is difficult to think of the best words for this sort of thing!) inclinations as I please. I cannot ever have a child, so shall not have to endure the tedium of what seem to be awful precautions to prevent scandal.

I believe I understand that part.

It also makes some sense that the Church will not mind any such dalliances as long as I do not have a strong attachment and make up for any lapses by increasing my tithe, although I do not recall any specific sermon stating such things. Perhaps in France the clergy provides more clarity.

The part about not becoming besotted is where my recollection becomes a bit vague.

Please advise me, Susannah, for it was late in the afternoon when the subject arose, and I had drunk a great deal of sherry at that point. If you insist that I would benefit and also not go to Hell, nor find myself an object of contempt and ridicule I might take your advice, but it all seems odd. Quince was not the sort that could make one feel drunk with abandon and he set his hat for me the first time we met, so there were not many of those lingering glances and no stolen kisses you kept referring to, even in my blushing youth.

I feel terribly childish in asking these questions, Susannah, but you were not the least bit embarrassed, and I hope you will not mind explaining again, for it has certainly seemed to benefit you beautifully. You have always been a most happy, kind and generous woman, so I must have missed something in the middle. Perhaps it was the Latin words you kept using. I must have misheard them, for I did find definitions in one of the dictionaries Quince had in the library, and I believe most of the behavior described is not legal in England. My opinion of France is changing.

I will wait in a haze of philosophical confusion, Susannah, for your answer. Did I have it all wrong? We did have a great deal of sherry, you know. If so, please accept my apology for thinking you could have counseled such things. If not, please re-explain them to me.

In the meantime, I shall turn my attention to the Hall, for there are many decisions to be made and many things to be done, which will keep me very busy, liaisons or no.

Your Provincial Friend,
Annabella

☙ Eavesdropping ❧

29 September, 1820

Dearest Susannah,

I write to you today in a fair state, and am so glad that you do not mind lengthy letters, for I do not think I can avoid the length of this, evidenced by the pages you are holding in your hand. It is all so upsetting. I know not what to do save to spill forth the tale. Before I do, please know that I do not credit a WORD of what I heard.

Terrible, slanderous, scurrilous rumours are flying about your darling husband, for if my servants are aware then others must be as well. I am in no way making an accusation nor implying there is any truth to what I have heard, but felt you should know as soon as humanly possible What Is Being Said.

It happened yesterday. The weather has been dreadful, and made me so glad Mr. Wicklestaff insisted on putting the roof, chimneys and windows to rights before any other work was done on the Hall, although the rains loosed some of the repairs done and everyone had to stay indoors to keep from having roof tiles smash into their heads as they flew down.

Mr. Sinclair arrived early (he came from London yesterday and stayed at the inn in Wimbish), and was gone before noon, for the weather was so awful that the roads were in danger of becoming impassable. Again. I was surprised he did not put off his visit, but he would not be deterred. That same weather meant the workmen did not come at all, for the roads would surely be useless by dark, and then I would have to deal with where to put them, which was unthinkable. I suppose I ought to be grateful, they likely would have had been struck by tiles and then I should have had to pay for more apothecary visits. I do hate this foul weather!

I thought the entire day would be taken up with Mr. Sinclair, who also tries to keep me apprised of the social goings-on in London, even though it is something at which he is utterly hopeless. I found I was left with precious little to occupy my time. I went through the papers Mr. Sinclair had left behind, considered sacking someone, tried to read but could not concentrate.

I decided to look at the wrapping room and see if it ought to be swapped with the cutting room – Sir Manfredson had no idea how a woman would run a proper house. The floors have been polished to a high gleam and are slippery in my pretty little shoes, so I took them off and sailed down to the wrapping room.

And I do mean sailed. I ran and then stopped to see how far I could slide in my stocking'd feet. This Hall is huge. My best slide was at least twelve feet.

It also meant I could glide past doorways to rooms that had servants cleaning or polishing something in them and check their work. Thus far I have been unsuccessful in denouncing anyone for sloth, but hope lives on.

Soon enough I was in the wrapping room, only slightly out of breath. I was looking about at the shelves and cupboards when I realized I could hear something.

A voice. I looked around and could not for the life of me determine the source. Perhaps it was the ghosts! I became a little frightened, for I do not want to live in a haunted Hall, it is bad enough being a childless widow. However, the voice continued in a low murmur and I saw a little grate up on one wall. When I stood on tiptoe I realized it was Cook's voice. The grate was to the kitchens.

How often does one have the chance to eavesdrop on servants without their being the wiser? Perhaps I could find out for certain if Cook was stealing from me – I really do not think it costs as much as she says for foodstuffs. I was torn between leaving, thereby retaining some kind of integrity, and staying to sate my curiosity.

It ought to come as no surprise which characteristic thoroughly trounced the other in that particular battle. I stayed, and am so very glad I did.

Cook was talking away to herself, muttering ingredients and chopping things for dinner. This went on for a moment and I was becoming bored, near ready to leave, when a singular step came through the mud room into the kitchen.

Driver. No one else makes that step-clunk sound. I decided to stay for just one more moment, for Driver was supposed to being doing something in the stables, not idling about the kitchens. Perhaps I could berate him! I tiptoed to the door, closed it quietly, and returned to stand under the grate so I could hear every word.

Driver asked where the kitchen girls were, and Cook told him they had been dispatched to the wine and cold cellars to inventory everything, to determine if we had enough preserved food to see us through until spring. He made sure they would be gone for some time and told her he had to speak to her on a matter of urgency and not a little importance. Cook's voice sounded oddly flustered as she told him they had some time and bade him sit while she got him a cup of tea. That annoyed me. Tea is not cheap! And why was she being so solicitous of him? Did she . . . <u>does</u> she . . . fancy him? That thought immediately fled, for Driver told her, once they were settled and comfortable, lolling about and ignoring their duties, that he had been to Sumwattle Estate a few days before and had been trying to see Cook privately ever since without success. Cook explained that I – I – keep her busy from morning until night, that ungrateful creature!

But that is not the point of this letter.

Cook sounded oddly alert at the mention of the Shardleys' house and asked the reason. He asked her if she had been in service to them; he seemed to remember her mentioning it once or twice. She said she had, for five years, before coming into Quince's employ fourteen years before. That is why the name was familiar, Susannah, it was one of Cook's references. One could easily believe she had been with Quince since birth, for all of her high-handedness about her kitchens. But I digress.

Driver then asked about a friend she had there, one she had mentioned from time to time. Cook replied she had a wonderful friend there, a girl who worked in the kitchens named Felicity Canlow, who was long gone from the house due to What Happened to Her. Driver sighed. Cook asked him why, for she had told him of what happened in a weak moment, when she received the news that Felicity was dead, and he had promised to never breathe a word to anyone. He apologized and said it was important that she re-tell it to him, for Something Had Happened. Again.

Cook thought for a moment, clearly slurping some of my tea while considering the request, and finally told him the tale, which is what I have to relate to you now.

When your Lordship, darling Lord Carollton, had divested himself of his first wife (and I agree, she was a horrible creature) he found himself between homes for a short time. The Shardleys, Lord Shardley specifically, offered him lodging at Sumwattle.

He gratefully accepted their offer, but found that their generosity of spirit was not matched by generosity in actuality. Apparently it never occurred to Lady Shardley that he might appear with more than a valise and kerchief, and had not assigned a servant to him. He, of course, assumed he would be assigned at least a footman for the duration of his stay.

It was bad enough that his single malts had to be stored in the stables, but the lack of courtesy on the Shardleys' part in such basic requirements threatened to ruin what had been, up until that time, a profitable relationship between the two men.

Finally Lady Shardley assigned a young maid in the house, Felicity Canlow, to take care of your Lordship's needs: changing the linens, making sure his wardrobe was in order and the like. Your Lordship accepted the arrangement without argument, realizing that although normally not done, he would at least be assured of decent mending of his stockings and such.

What began as a strictly professional and upright relationship became a mild friendship – your Lordship was justifiably unsettled in his new surroundings – and Felicity was, by all accounts, a sweet young girl.

One night your Lordship found a bottle of brandy that was to be saved for his 25th wedding anniversary. He realized there was no point in saving it, and began to drink. At some point Felicity brought in his freshly pressed shirts and he offered her a glass, not wanting to drink alone.

Cook then said that your Lordship, in a moment of drunken weakness, deeply grieving the failure of his marriage, confused Felicity's attempts to console him with amorous advances. And she, naïve and kind, thought that such a one as him could truly care for her. Their liaison continued for some weeks, Cook said, until Felicity realized she was with child. She left Sumwattle posthaste, telling everyone she had been called away to care for a sick and dying aunt.

According to Cook, your Lordship actually seemed to regret her leaving. Felicity moved to London, writing some months later to Cook of What Had Happened, for they were dearest friends. Soon after Felicity's departure your Lordship found his own lodgings and moved to London.

I near fainted by this point in the tale. I could not believe Cook was sitting there, calm as anything, slandering your dear husband in this way! I was stayed from bursting in and denouncing them when Cook began to cry. She said that she had kept up with Felicity over the years, even spending some free Sundays with her and her little girl, until Felicity died three years ago. She read a notice in the newspaper and immediately contacted the little girl. She was about to be turned out of her home, and Cook did the only thing she knew: she wrote to the new Cook at Sumwattle and recommended her, for she knew that at Sumwattle there were always vacancies, as they have such a difficult time keeping help, and knew our own household was staffed perfectly, which pleased me. With Cook's assistance, the girl had been able to secure herself a position in the kitchens at Sumwattle.

Then Driver asked if Cook knew the name of the child. Cook said, "Of course, she was like a niece to me. Her name is Gwynneth."

Susannah, I did not know what to do: faint or sack them both. Instead I withdrew, for I knew the rest of the tale, having seen it all the same as Driver. So I tiptoed out of the wrapping room and, carrying my shoes in my hand, slipped back to the library to write you, although this time I did not run and slide, in deference to the seriousness of what I had heard.

Susannah, these are terrible things they are saying! Shall I sack them both? I am more than happy to do so if that is your wish. Should I lecture them? I am in such shock that I am at a loss as to how to proceed.

I am posting this immediately, for you need to know what is being said right away, so we might minimize the damage. Please let me know what I ought to do as soon as you can.

In the meantime, I remain

Your Curious Friend,
Annabella

☙ The Constable Calls ❧

2 October, 1820

Dear Susannah,

I know I only wrote you a few days ago and am still breathlessly awaiting your reply, but I had a caller yesterday and had to tell someone, and realized you are the only person with whom I can share these things. So as I await instructions on whether or not I should both denounce and sack Driver and Cook, I decided to write.

Mr. Sinclair had just come and gone from London with papers for me to review and sign. I was reading them in the library when Taylor announced a caller. I was exasperated, for he knew how difficult it is at present to find somewhere to put them. The drawing room is not presentable. Before I could state this and reprimand him for the intrusion, Taylor explained that my caller was Constable Pukeston.

Well, that was very different, although I was somewhat annoyed that I could not reprimand Taylor. Also, whatever could a constable want with me? I have been cleared of any wrongdoing for more than a year. Perhaps there was an old murder that had never been solved, and it had happened here at Wetmoor, which would account for the ghost rumours, which remain mere rumours, I am afraid. That might be terrifically exciting!

I asked Taylor to send him into the library, which at least has furniture and drapes, and to have Prudence bring us some tea and cakes. That is what I miss about callers most of all:

the opportunity to eat cakes as a social grace. For some reason that makes them taste better. Eating induces far less guilt when it is for social nicety as opposed to pure indulgence. Callers have been in short supply due to my apparently fearsome reputation. The only callers thus far have been women from Church, come to discuss the sermons. They perch on the edge of their chairs, waiting for me to do something awful. Of course I do not, and they depart seeming disappointed: I am not nearly as exciting as they hoped. Or fear, perhaps.

A few moments later Constable Pukeston was ushered into the library. Taylor presented him and left when I nodded his dismissal. Constable Pukeston bowed and gave me his card: Constable Daniella Pukeston. His first name is so very odd, and he quickly stated, "My parents wanted a girl, Lady Upton-Church." He is not a large man, having the slender frame normally associated with consumption and frailty, but his suit was flawless, not a wrinkle or smirch, and his carriage that of a king. I asked him to sit and inquired after the purpose of his visit.

"Lady Upton-Church, I am here today – "

I could not help myself; I interrupted him. "Is it a murder? Someone was murdered here long ago and you need to search for their mouldering body?"

His silence informed me that to be excited about such a heinous crime was rather distasteful. Clearly he has never spent days on end locked up in his own home. "No, milady."

"Oh."

"I am here to officially welcome you to our fair county, Lady Upton-Church, both on behalf of the town itself and of my offices."

"That is very kind of you." Oh, one of these visits. Boring. . .

"It is my pleasure to extend to you heartfelt congratulations on undertaking this enterprise," he waved his hand around to indicate the Hall.

"It is something I am pleased to undertake, Constable."

"I also wanted to inquire if you have been bothered by anything since taking residence."

That was different, not quite the normal, "Wonderfully pleased to meet you" path of conversation. I needed more information to determine if I need be alarmed. "What do you mean?"

"Problems with vandals, pranksters, that sort of thing."

"No, I have not. Wetmoor Hall is blessedly peaceful." At that moment there was a crash and a terrible scream from the roof area. Constable Pukeston started. "Well, mostly peaceful." I was determined to not react to the scream, even if it did sound worse than normal. "You were saying?" At that moment Prudence arrived with the tea and cakes. Constable Pukeston did not answer until she had served and left, which piqued my curiosity quite a bit. After he had swallowed and daintily patted his mouth with a napkin he smiled.

"If you find any tricksters about, please send for me and I will do whatever I can to assure you are not bothered."

This was odd, but I remained gracious. "That is very kind of you. Have there been difficulties?"

"No, of course not. Well, not many, really, and only a few were egregious – "

"The social unrest continues even in this county?" I blurted without thinking. Those awful Luddites! They were hounding me out in the country!

I do not understand Luddites in the least. And what an awful name! If the founder of one's group is named "Ludd", the first order of business should have been to either find another leader or think of a better name. And why ever should they wish to end mechanization? Mechanization is a good thing, Susannah, everyone with a thought in their head knows that.

I realized Constable Pukeston was staring at me, shocked at my outburst, and I amended my tone and meaning. "It is one of the reasons I moved here from London, to escape that problem. When my husband Quince – Lord Upton-Church – was alive he was the focus of some of the upset. He designed mechanical things, things that made some very angry. It was a terrible time during the worst of it. My physician tells me I should not agitate myself, but if I see a reference to it in the London newspapers I cannot help but read it, and it seems the unrest is spreading, which is very frightening." It is frightening. Do you remember all those terrible misspelt letters Quince and I used to receive? The protests in front of our own house? The smashed windows? For a supposedly civilized group Luddites are quite violent.

"You need not concern yourself," the constable said soothingly, which was not the blanket denial for which I had hoped.

"So my physician has assured me, but I am sure you understand how very alarming it is for a mere woman, one once married to the man who was thought to have caused so much unemployment."

"Lady Upton-Church, there are advantages and disadvantages to living at Wetmoor Hall. One of the advantages is that it is rumoured to be haunted."

"Oh, for goodness' sake, those ghosts again. Wetmoor is not haunted, Constable."

He smiled. "You know that. I know that. The superstitious rabble do not. I do not think they would dare even approach your doors . . . Do you keep pistols?" He asked the question far too casually.

"Pistols that shoot?"

"Yes, that is the best kind for this sort of thing."

"We have, I am sorry, I have ceremonial pistols, and there might be some rifles somewhere. I know not, Constable. Are you suggesting I maintain an arsenal?"

He held up his hands. "No, you misunderstand."

"This is becoming quite upsetting."

"Lady Upton-Church, if ever you are frightened have one of the servants ride for me. That is all. I, or one of my men, will come immediately."

I was not mollified. "Because thieves and brigands wait for arrest, I suppose."

"You are becoming needlessly alarmed, Lady."

"Of course I am alarmed! And if I am it is your fault, sir, for I was perfectly happy before you came here and welcomed me to a county where at any moment I may well be overrun by a riotous and violent underclass!" I pulled a bottle of brandy out of the desk and poured a medicinal dose for myself. "I came here for the quiet." I tossed back some brandy. It was unfortunate that at that moment two workmen walked past the windows, carrying a third that was likely the source of the earlier scream. He was on a makeshift carrier, his groaning clearly audible even through the thick panes, and it appeared that I would be receiving yet another surgeon's bill. I wondered if I should keep that surgeon, Gibberwilly, on staff. Gibberwilly is terribly rude for, although I pay him promptly, he has never sent so much as a thank-you note for all of the business the renovation has brought to his office.

Constable Pukeston looked scandalized at the brandy, curiously at the injured workman being carried by and mortified at my outburst, but seemed to calm when I handed him a brandy of his own.

"Lady, I fear I may have inflamed your concerns, which was not my intent," he soothed.

"It was not your intent, but I am afraid it was the result nonetheless."

"You are safe here, and need not worry. It is my duty to worry for you, and many of the citizenry feel I approach it with too much zeal. In this instance they may be correct." I was not completely calmed and sniffed a little as I sipped my brandy. He sipped as well, nodded his appreciation of its quality, and continued. "I take my station seriously, and this county has been remarkably free of the woes other parts of England have suffered. The reason I came here today was to make sure that nothing untoward has happened, given your late husband's work, so if it had I could strenuously seek to correct any upset you may have endured. After all, we have all been very excited and not a little curious to know of you; you are rather famous here."

"How can that be? I have scarce left the Hall grounds."

He nodded. "Exactly, Lady. A mysterious and, forgive me, somewhat notorious, woman moves into the famous haunted Wetmoor Hall. She is rarely seen but spoken very highly of in town. The injuries workmen have suffered have been attributed to ghosts and curses, and yet you stay. You are the subject of not a little conversation in our corner of the world."

If the Constable's intent was to distract me from being murdered in my own bed by the unwashed and uncivilized masses he was successful. I had not thought of myself that way. I had not thought myself any particular way at all. I was simply trying to restore my Hall so it was livable and throw a marvelous ball in it when completed so everyone could think me tremendously fabulous.

"What sort of conversations?" If my name were being bandied about in the same sentence as "murderess," it would be best to know.

"That you are new here, recently come from London, just out of full mourning. The normal conversations held for any newcomer, Lady Upton-Church." He smiled at me.

"Oh." I wondered if he were being honest or kind. He looked about the room.

"You have a great many books here."

"They were my husband's." I sipped my brandy. Would he?

He would. "Lady Upton-Church, I was wondering . . ." His voice trailed off. I am certain he knew not how to proceed.

"Yes, Constable?" I was not going to assist him in broaching the subject that floated in the room like a giant bat.

Constable Pukeston cleared his throat. "Lord Upton-Church. He designed things?"

"Yes, as I have said."

"Was he really . . . was that really the cause of . . . what happened to him?"

"Are you asking if my husband was killed by one of his own inventions, sir?"

He had the grace to blanch. "Yes, I suppose it is. I am sorry to inquire, Ladyship, but the newspapers, they were a bit . . . vague."

"I am sure you are only asking in your official capacity, I suppose."

He went from blanch to blush in the span of two seconds. "No, Lady. It is morbid curiosity, nothing more."

Honesty was not what I expected. So unexpected was it that I scarce recognized it. "You wish to know the details simply to know them?"

"Yes. I am dreadfully curious and there has been outlandish talk, none of which I credit, but no one seems to know anything." He gulped a fair portion of his brandy.

So I told him, Susannah. He asked in a straightforward manner. Of course, by the end of my tale he was horrified, as you can imagine. Then he sat for a moment in silence.

Finally he spoke, and thankfully it was not to arrest nor denounce me. "I never met Lord Upton-Church, but heard he was a fine man. My condolences on your loss." It seemed more than a rote statement of sympathy, I was surprised to note.

"Thank you, constable. It was very difficult."

"I cannot imagine."

"I advise you never to try, sir." I smiled, for he seemed very sad. I leaned over and patted him on the arm. "Do not fret. It was very quick, and Quince did not feel any pain."

He looked startled. "You're a very brave woman, I think."

I laughed, the mood was entirely too somber. "I am an utter coward, constable! I did not brazen it out with the Ton, I did not denounce all and sundry who called me a murderess. I fled to the country to decorate a Hall!"

I did not brazen it out with the Ton, after all. I did not defend myself, save at the inquest. I was too embarrassed that anyone thought me capable of such a horrible act. Restoring

Wetmoor is easier than restoring my reputation, so that is what I shall do.

I realized that I rather liked the constable. He believed in my innocence, a rare enough trait that it is one I value. "Constable, I am very glad you came to Wetmoor today. I am sorry for my earlier outburst. It has been difficult at times for me." I looked down and tried to look slightly lost. "I am afraid that I become overwhelmed." It is always best for the police to be fond of you, Susannah. Just in case.

Constable Pukeston said he perfectly understood, and was glad I felt better. I asked him if he would like a tour, an offer at which he leapt.

So my first showing of Wetmoor was for the Constable. No bodies fell out of closets, no surprises were found at all, but it was rather pleasant. Taylor walked just behind us as I pointed out things of interest. Both men thought I was being gracious, but I offered the constable a tour so if ever he were needed he would have a good idea of where everything was beforehand and could thus more quickly save me.

The constable was breathless at the scope of the Hall and had trouble maintaining a blasé façade, although he did try. It was when we arrived at the music room that he stopped pretending to find Wetmoor as anything less than wondrous, although I was surprised that did not happen in the ballroom. That is my favourite room. But it was the music room that captured his attention, even in its dilapidated and water-damaged state, and he could not have been more effusive in his praise for Wetmoor as a whole after that point. It was rather sweet, Susannah.

When we finally arrived back in the foyer he thanked me again and I bade him promise to not divulge any details of what he had seen, for I rather like being seen as mysterious. He swore on his office to remain mute, and repeated that if ever anything was needed he was in town and could be found at any time. He thanked me for taking the time to meet with him and left with a rather jaunty step. Taylor closed the door and looked at me. I was feeling quite sprightly after walking through the first floor so thoroughly, as there was clear progress being made everywhere.

I hope I have made a helpful an acquaintance, Susannah, for if one has to interact with Justice, one should have the representative of Justice on your side.

Oh, dear, I have gone on again for far too long. Accept my apologies for such ramblings, there is no one to talk to here, but I must away and see to the menus for the rest of the week.

I hope you are well, and I will write again soon. Until then I remain

Your Mysterious Friend,
Annabella

Scurrilous Rumours

5 October, 1820

My Dear Susannah,

I near fainted when I read your letter, I truly did, for I did not realize when I was telling you what I thought to be slanderous gossip I was instead confirming what you had long known and kept to yourself. Of course I do not blame you for that, I should have done the same, but still it leaves me shocked.

Your husband is Gwynneth's father.

I am not shocked at your Lordship, these things happen from time to time, and he remedied his error as much as possible under the circumstances. Now I understand why you asked about Gwynneth's appearance. Do not fret, the resemblance is very mild, nay, nearly non-existent, save her nose, and England is covered with noses that are singular.

To think that your Lordship found Felicity Canlow in London, so he could offer condolences on her aunt's condition and offer assistance were it needed. She, who moved to London specifically to hide the evidence of her liaison with your Lordship! (I must give her credit for behaving properly, however.)

Of course he was horrified, he is not the sort of man to whom those things happen. I think it lovely that he set up a small trust for Miss Canlow to take care of the child and perhaps help her gain a foothold in the future. He did "as right by her" as he could, far more than most men would have provided. What shocked me was that you knew of it, but I am grateful that strong drink will sometimes loosen a man's tongue when nothing else ever could, and if he believed he was dying when he told you as opposed to being afflicted with a simple fever, you would never have been able to confirm to me the truth. I would have thought Gwynneth to be another silly girl who had gotten herself in trouble.

As to your request: I will be happy to investigate further and determine what has happened to Gwynneth, for it must be the same girl. How many maids are named Gwynneth? It is too fine a name to be casually doled out to every uneducated girl in the world. I will investigate most discreetly, with no one the wiser, and update you of any discovery as quickly as possible. What if it is true? What will happen then? Of course that will unfold in time, but I cannot help wanting to know right this moment. I am so glad that I was late to the hunt at Lady Shardley's that fateful day, and not some other woman of our acquaintance.

In an odd way I am grateful for the opportunity to help you, for you have provided me so much assistance by the simple fact of your friendship these many years, and to be able to return the favour is quite warming to me.

But alas, I must away – I have just heard yet another crashing sound and the now-familiar accompanying scream of agony. These workmen! It is a wonder anything ever gets done with all of their accidents and clumsiness. Every time I turn around someone else is getting carried off, and it is never due to carelessness or malingering, it is the "ghosts." The ghosts push people off things, over them, cause things to fall. For every incident the explanation is "ghosts." It is quite vexing. The last workman broke an arm, a leg and three ribs when he fell out of a window. My own carriage had to be pressed into service to take him to the surgeon and it will be months before he returns, if ever. How he managed to fall I shall never know, but I am grateful he fell into bushes instead of the drive. I have had enough dead bodies strewn about homes to last me the rest of my life and do not want to continue that same awful pattern here at Wetmoor.

So I will find out what happened this time and pay for more medical services – do you know that none of the workmen would consent to working at Wetmoor without assurances that any medical attention required would be paid for by me? You see, I showed weakness with Driver about his leg, and now everyone in the world wants me to be their caretaker. An unfortunate by-product of being wealthy, I suppose.

I shall write again soon and in the meantime, I remain

Your Beleaguered Friend,
Annabella

☙ Quince Jelly ❧

14 October, 1820

Dearest Susannah,

I write to you today not with exciting news that I have found and rescued Gwynneth, nor that something wonderfully lovely has happened on the Hall restoration, nor that I have been name the most Beloved Woman in England (after the royal family, of course).

I am writing because apparently I never told you how Quince died. I am horribly embarrassed that I never did so. You were so kind and patient (far more than I would have been) in waiting this long before even asking.

I will not argue that I am certain I told you everything, for I was taking a great deal of medicine for several weeks after it happened. It would seem that my memories of a fair portion of that time are not trustworthy.

I apologize for never having done so, and am only able to say in my own defence that I was certain I had.

It is clear you read the newspaper accounts, and the fact that you believed me innocent without hearing what I had to say about what happened – Susannah, you never cease to astonish me with the steadfastness of your loyalty. I am going to try even harder to find Gwynneth for you. I was to try as hard as I could regardless, but now my efforts will take on an Olympian and epic scope.

I suppose there is nothing left but to tell you about Quince.

It was the stupidest thing, really. Quince came upon the idea that stairways should not be the only option in going between floors. He was obsessed with the idea that dumbwaiters be enlarged – so they could hold people! He read about that lunatic French king arranging for something similar, where he was hauled up and down in a chair, and decided to try to re-create it indoors and with more ease.

Quince and his associate, Mr. Devon, were both enamored of this box-moving scheme, and spent enormous amounts of money on a contraption that could be put into a house and pull people up and down by some kind of winch, pulley and weight system. I did not presume to understand what they were doing at the time and I doubt anyone else does. Mr. Devon came to the wake, chalk-faced and embarrassed, thinking he could have averted the disaster. Of course, had he been here, he likely would have suffered the same fate as Quince.

The implementation of their idea, which occurred in our London house, was a disaster. The biggest difficulty was how to control both the rates of ascent and descent and the actual stopping of the aforementioned box. We lost two chambermaids and Quince's underbutler to the holes that had to be cut in the floors to make way for the box before Quince would put railings in around them. We lost a gardener and scullery maid discovering the box needed to have air holes, especially if the door problems had not been worked out prior to the experiment. I begged Quince to stop, for we were getting a horrible reputation from the deaths, but he would not be deterred. He said the fatalities would be in vain were he to give up prior to finding a solution.

Truth to tell, Susannah, I believe he remained diligent because he wanted a legacy of some kind, and unless I died and he remarried or he found a fertile mistress, it was not going to come from his name being carried on by sons. As he refused to divorce me and I was much younger than he, after Sarah he worked harder and longer than ever on his devices, which meant he had no time for a mistress. I used to tease him that his mistress was his work, and I wish had not, for in the end it was his work that killed him. In his posthumous defense, his other mechanical ventures were very successful. I am the owner of seven companies utilizing various contraptions to this day and, if my solicitors are correct, those alone shall spectacularly provide for me.

I found I have digressed from the point of my letter.

At the inquest it was found that the ropes used to pull the boxes up and down should be checked first to make sure they had not frayed or become weakened during prior tests. Or nibbled on by mice. We lost Quince, a stablehand, a parlor maid and a topiary expert who was there to meet with me and provide information regarding our garden, and part of Driver. We never did find Driver's leg.

Staying in the house where Quince died, especially when there was not much left to bury, was terrible. I remember the last words Quince ever said to me. Actually, they were the last words he ever said at all, said as I came into the foyer to meet the topiary expert. "Move aside, dear, I just want to make sure the box is lined up properly. . ." I turned and the topiary expert followed me to the drawing room doors.

I wish Quince's Last Words had been more memorable.

The house was a shambles – you would NOT BELIEVE the mess a ten-foot square box makes when it falls from the servants' quarters to the foyer. In my dreams I sometimes still hear the screaming . . .

The authorities said the sole reason I was not killed was because I was nearly through the door to the drawing room when it happened.

You do not wish to know the details of the aftermath, for a fair amount of the screaming was mine. Once I began I found I could not stop. As well as swooning and getting sick on the floor. Taylor did as well, when he arrived and saw everything.

I did manage to drag Driver away from the mess. One of the things that weighed in my favor at the inquest was that I used my skirts to try to staunch Driver's bleeding, even with my left arm broken. I did not inform anyone that my behaviour was neither heroic nor noble; I did not know my arm was broken until later, and the only thing I remember about Driver was him saying he was sorry he was ruining my dress.

Quince – well, I would rather not discuss that. Suffice it to say that there was good reason why a casket was not possible.

There are not words enough to fully describe it, I suppose, which is a wonder given the size and number of dictionaries available.

That is a good thing, I think.

I will close for now, as I have accomplished what I set out to. I apologize for not having told you before; perhaps now you understand why I may have decided there was no need.

I will away and lift my spirits with walking through the Hall to see how the work is progressing. The fact that I have little idea what constitutes finished work and that which has only begun will not serve as a deterrent, and my presence will perhaps spur the workmen to stop from falling off of, through and over things.

I will write again soon, and in the meantime, I remain

Your Loving Friend,
Annabella

Base Impulses

28 October, 1820

Dearest Susannah,

You need not apologize for asking about Quince. I would have done were it you, and I am still startled I had never told you before now. I do believe that country life suits me, for after my letter to you I did not have nightmares, which is a marked improvement from the first few months after the accident.

Relieved to be done with the aforementioned subject, I read the rest of your letter with a great deal of curiosity and actually read it through twice more whilst I made new notes. And a sketch or two. Thank you for being so patient with me and, yes, I keep all of your letters locked up where no one can get at them. I am also very grateful you do the same with mine.

Your explanations about Romance were very helpful, and I now understand what you tried to explain when I saw you: I may spend time with any man I please, in any way I please, but must be very careful to not Fall in Love, and if I begin to have strong feelings toward a particular man, should immediately break it off to protect my heart from hurt, and ought never dally with anyone who could either ruin my reputation or believe I am interested in a more formal or legal relationship. It is only when there is strong romantic feeling that it is a problem, for nothing can come of it but heartbreak and loss, and I am far too acquainted with both to be consumed by them again.

That makes much more sense than spending time with someone of whom I am not fond, for it seems it would be difficult to enjoy myself. I shall keep your advice in mind, but at present feel neither out of sorts or strange, so do not feel like trying anything new.

I hate to disappoint you, but I looked through those strange books of Quince's, but there is no bookstore stamp in the books, nor any indication of how they came into his possession, so I know not where they were purchased.

At least now I understand why I keep receiving letters from men in our class. I was embarrassed to tell you before now, for I thought those men thought me a harlot. I do not understand why they should, I was faithful to Quince. However, since my formal mourning period has ended I receive at least two letters every week asking if I might wish to become better acquainted with them, and perhaps spend time together alone. I found myself offended at their offers (some of which were horrifyingly specific and called to mind Those Books) and did not understand why I was suddenly the focus of this type of attention. Most of the men are already known to me and have never behaved with anything but decorum in the past, but are now shockingly interested in pursuing an intimate relationship.

And the offers! Of an apartment (which I do not need), furs (which I already have), jewels (I have a mountain of those) and some offered me <u>money</u>! I thought perhaps they misunderstood the meaning of the phrase "possible murderess."

I have not answered any of the letters, of course, dignifying them with a response was outrageous. At first I thought they did not realize the conditions of Quince's will.

A few of the letters rectified that: my services as a mistress are considered noteworthy, due to my scandalous reputation.

What I do not understand is why any of them might think I would be interested in a formal or restrictive (alarmingly, some implied that literally as well as metaphorically) relationship with any of them. I think some of them are in possession of books similar to those of Quince's I found.

Thanks to Quince I am ridiculously wealthy and have no need of the comparative pittances offered. If I find myself in a unique position it will be because I wish to be in it, not because someone paid to have me thusly arranged. It was all quite bewildering until your clarification. Now I understand and will refuse each one until they stop asking.

Your concern over my lack of prior romantic experience is sweet but unwarranted. I am happy, all in all, save for the death, sadness and suspicion in my life, and cannot miss something only experienced in a perfunctory fashion. When I said I did not mind when Quince did not come near me much after Sarah I was truthful, not self-pitying. It was part of my duty as a good wife and did not bother me overmuch, for it did not take a great deal of time and Quince was always so happy afterward. I find it amusing that you and I have such differing viewpoints on the matter and the subject itself has only been raised when it is unlikely to be of any use. I am rather behind everyone else, it seems, when it comes to such things.

In terms of how my time is now spent, Wetmoor itself is occupying all of it, as well as the correspondence and newspapers to which I must attend. The London staff has been augmented with applicants from town, which were in somewhat short supply until I did as Mr. Wicklestaff suggested and increased the salaries. The "haunting" of the Hall, so providential in keeping away vandals during its long vacancy, also made it difficult to find servants willing to work here. However, with the new salaries offered we finally received several suitable applicants. Offers were made to four girls and two boys, and more will be needed as different parts of the Hall are completed. I look forward to days when fires will be lit and grates are clean again! One of the posts was for another footman, for the demands of the Hall are more than Taylor alone can handle. He is hardly ever here, he is always going to the post or running back and forth between Mr. Wicklestaff and myself, and never has time to attend me. Prudence accompanies me as much as possible, but that means she can never arrange flowers for my rooms, make up my bed properly or attend to my wardrobe. It does not help that she also keeps getting lost. That girl's sense of direction is poorer than mine own.

It is quite an ever-changing sea of workers here: There are men who work in wood, those who work in stone, others that plaster, some that paint, and I do not like being unattended, for they are of the lower classes. Such men see a woman alone and think her a harlot who may welcome their coarse advances. That has not happened, but it could, and I do not wish to find myself smacking a stonemason for not being able to control himself. The trials and hangings alone would take up so much time.

I spent one thoroughly enjoyable morning in the library interviewing the prospective additional footman, which is the most restored of any of the public rooms. They were all suitable, and each came with impeccable references. I found I did not know which one would be the best choice. Without thinking I asked Taylor's opinion on the matter. He very nearly fell over with the shock of it. I decided to act as if there were nothing unusual about it, even though I mentally smacked myself for being too careless. When he realized my query was not rhetorical he recovered himself, proffered a name, and glowed when I told him to call the young man back so we could agree upon terms. Mr. Foxx is a lovely young man who will make a fine addition to the Hall. He is nothing like Taylor in aspect: where Taylor is dark-haired and fair-skinned, Foxx is blond and ruddy. Where Taylor is slight, Foxx is sturdy-framed. They shall nicely contrast each other. I know it is the style to have matching footmen but I find it rather alarming, as if one were being watched by puppets. I also cannot tell them apart, not that that matters, but it does seem rude, even to a servant, to call them by the wrong name.

I believe Wetmoor Hall is very agreeable to me, Susannah. Although the only rooms complete are mine and the kitchens, I find I do not mind, for the Hall will be a marvel when complete. Cook announced the kitchens are finally in satisfactory order, which I hope means meals shall soon reach her former high standards. My sleep has improved, as has my waking state of mind, save for one embarrassing moment.

Driver lives over the stables, where there is a cozy bedroom. He likes to be near the horses. However, the original stairs leading to it were too narrow to navigate with his wooden leg. When Mr. Wicklestaff proffered that a kind of chair lift on ropes might be more serviceable and require far less work, Driver and I both fainted dead away. Mr. Wicklestaff must be the only man in England who does not know how Quince died.

After the fainting debacle – Driver fainted onto me and I, also unconscious, had to be rescued from being smothered by him. I still have a bruise on my leg from his wooden one smashing into mine. With such dramatic reactions all talk of a chair on ropes stopped. There is now a very shallow, wide stairway in the stables, which now must be enlarged, for two stalls had to be knocked down to complete it.

By the way, there are still no ghosts in sight, which relieves me. I know not what I might have done had an apparition appeared, clanking its Hell chains and breathing foul odours. I would likely die of fright. It is also helpful to staff, for they are far more superstitious than I. I have not yet heard how the story of ghosts began but am looking forward to learning it.

Mr. Wicklestaff and I have finally reached a schedule for the Hall, which is quite comprehensive, and agreed on the budgets. He was surprised at how well I could do sums on my own, and his budgets accordingly became somewhat more rational. The first budgets submitted indicated we were building a Hall, not restoring one. As the roof and chimneys are mostly repaired, we have decided to begin inside with the public rooms, of course, for the few callers I have received have had to be met in the library. Luckily there have only been a few, for I shall have to visit each in return. I will try to choose a time when they will not be home, for I do not care to spend a morning or afternoon dodging thinly veiled questions about murder or hauntings. I would prefer for time to take care of both. It makes me a social coward, but I find that does not bother me overmuch.

Although the grounds will mostly wait until spring, it is imperative that the drive and front of the Hall are at least cleared away and beds prepared for fall planting. I would like to see everything bloom gloriously come spring. I am especially excited to see how the formal gardens in the back will look. There are formal gardens and beyond they and the pond and boathouse, through a gate, there is a private forest. It is quite small of course, but Sir Manfredson apparently enjoyed Nature a great deal and mine own grounds (not the cottagers') are quite varied and interesting.

I also must find a new land steward, for the man currently holding the position appears to do nothing but collect rents, steal some of the monies for his own purse, and drink himself into a stupor. I will also have to meet the cottagers.

Yes, I have cottagers. It is quite dreadful, really. Mr. Sinclair, my darling solicitor from London, has informed me it is the custom, although it shall not be necessary for me to know anything about farming beforehand. They also must be given something for Twelfth Night. There are over twelve families back there somewhere, scraping their living from my grounds. No one thought it important to inform me that that Wetmoor does not end at the thick wall bordering my private grounds. It goes on behind it for quite some time, acres and acres, and families live there growing food. That took me aback, I do not mind saying. There is a house garden and farm next to the Hall for our use, with chickens, cows and such for eggs, butter and cream, but that is different, it is for my convenience. I know I am trying to make a life for myself but feel most adamant that I not become some sort of farmer. I asked Mr. Sinclair to meet with the land steward and oversee him, to stem the tide of theft and to find out about these people. I do not wish to meet them until he has determined they are fit to come to the Hall.

Although I was quite annoyed that Quince had bought a Hall without consulting me or doing the courtesy of telling me afterward, I am very pleased he did it. I suppose it is an indication of how successful his mechanical ventures were that he could buy a Hall such as this and suffer no noticeable financial repercussions. And it was kind of him to have helped poor Sir Manfredson that way. I am told the designer and former master of Wetmoor is very comfortable with his son and grandchildren, even if he does refer to them as various members of the royal family, and rarely the same one twice.

Perhaps the rumours of ghosts began when Sir Manfredson went mad here. Or perhaps there are ghosts and they drove him mad, but I do not like to think of that possibility, so I shall not. I am grateful for Wetmoor itself.

Sir Manfredson did a beautiful job with the Hall, which is only proper, as it did cost him his mind. It is a folly, and a lovely one: each public room has a different theme drawn from Nature. The drawing room theme is flowers and ivy; the grand staircase is a forest, with each stair rail hand-carved as a tree, its branches reaching upward to twine together and form the handrail. The ceiling buttresses are carved to appear as branches as well. The dining room theme is the sky, with constellations peeking out through carved clouds and planets whirling about the chandelier, whose crystals are star. The games room theme is of the sea, with fish and other sea creatures gamboling about the fireplace and carved into the door lintels and mouldings. The morning room is done up as a marsh, the wainscoting carved into tall grasses from which storks, cranes and herons peer. It took two days to gain entry to the chapel; there were so many locks and barriers to it that I near despaired. I am glad I did not, for the chapel, although dusty and in considerable disrepair, is a jewel unto itself. The theme is butterflies, and they are carved into the wood everywhere. Mr. Wicklestaff believes that twenty different kinds of wood were used to create the wings of these creatures, and I will be soon visited by a trio of Italian woodcarvers who will set to restoring them. I believe when it is finished it will be awe-inspiring, a most fitting response in a room dedicated to God. It is very small, for contemplation only, but lovely. I understood why Sir Manfredson had locked it so securely, it would be a simple thing to destroy if one had a mind for such things. The gallery is the only disappointment so far, and only to me. The theme there is insects, or rather, insects I do not find charming, although the bees are tolerable. Mr. Wicklestaff thought it glorious, especially the spiders and their webs carved into corners. But if any room must be less than stellar it may as well be the gallery. Between Quince and I there are not enough family portraits to take up one wall, let alone an entire gallery. I have resolved to use it for the things Quince collected on our travels. They are all so odd and I should not like to put them where they could be seen, people might think me mad. What else am I to do with a suit of armor? Or those horrible, indiscreet statues he got on that dig in Italy? Where does one put a stuffed alligator? I would dispose of it but it would not burn. Well, it did, but slowly and the stench was unbearable. We dragged it out and left the horrible thing in the corner of the gallery.

The theme in the music room seems to be songbirds, which makes sense, but is now more a guess than anything. The plaster and woodwork is badly damaged by rain coming in through inexplicably broken windows, which were never replaced by the land steward.

The crowning glory, above all the rest, is the ballroom. It is the only room without a Nature theme, instead being a small but perfect replica of the Hall of Mirrors at Versailles. I near fainted when first I beheld it, and immediately saw in my mind's eye the Opening Ball I shall host when the renovations are complete: a glittering crowd dancing past the veranda doors flung open wide on a glorious evening. Each day I find something new in a room that escaped my notice prior. It is tremendous fun, for each day I rise wondering what new secret I will uncover.

A lovely surprise was the tennis courtyard. There is a tennis courtyard at Wetmoor! We only gained entrance yesterday, for the door leading to it was very stout and rain had caused the wood to swell in the frame. A woodworker was able to do something to it so we could open it without destroying the door completely. Imagine our surprise to find ourselves standing in a tennis courtyard, as riotous as the conservatory, grass near high as my waist, roses tumbling over the top wall and spilling down the side. It was like a fairyland. That is, until a mouse ran from the court into the Hall. That resulted in much screaming on my part – I cannot stand mice and rats – and a rather grisly chase by Mr. Wicklestaff and Taylor to catch the thing before it could burrow somewhere and begin to breed.

We cannot tell if the courtyard itself has a theme but it is a public area in its own way, so likely will. There is another door in one of the walls leading to the rest of the near grounds, which we did not see because it is currently overrun with roses. I was quite thrilled – Sir Manfredson spared no expense or luxury on Wetmoor. I shall have to learn how to play once it is restored. I plan to engage Mr. Ploughgoode's services to make up for his humiliation at Sumwattle, if he knows how to play. It is not very common anymore. Do you see why I am pleased I moved here?

The only thing I miss about London thus far is the entertainments and that the cemetery is no longer nearby. Of course maybe by summer people may want to visit and with their arrival will come diversions, so that part does not matter at present, but I feel strange that I cannot go to the cemetery anymore. During my mourning period I must confess that more than once I donned a cloak and went regardless of what the etiquette books said was allowed. I went there the day I left for Wetmoor, so I could say good-bye to Quince and

Sarah, for it may be many months before I return. It seemed wrong to leave them behind, even if they are far away enjoying Heaven.

It seems so long ago that Sarah was born. Quince was so proud of me, for it had been a difficult time. Do you remember how you used to come and visit me and we would play chess during my lying-in? That was such a nice thing for you to do. I was so excited that I was finally going to have a child – especially after so many disappointments and failures – and thought I would go mad when she slipped away. I might have were you not there to comfort me. It is strange I still pine for Sarah when I only got to see and hold her the one time. Right after that everything went so terribly wrong. By the time I regained my senses Sarah had been called to Heaven and had been given a proper Christian burial. Quince tried to wait, but my recovery was slow. He arranged the services, funeral and wake all alone.

Sometimes I still cry for Sarah, which is very silly, for we all know Heaven is the best place to be. And Quince is with her, so it is for myself that I am crying, which is selfish. That thought usually stops my tears, but sometimes it does not.

I believe I cry because with the loss of Sarah came the loss of being able to have any other children, and the twin losses at once were almost more than I could bear. I wondered if Quince would divorce me at the time, for the physician and surgeon were both quite certain and he would have been well within his rights to do so, but Quince was very kind. I have sometimes wondered if he did not because my parents were already dead, so where would I have gone? He merely said that it was all right, he did not mind, and as he patted my hand he told me I should not think on such things. So I do not, for there is nothing to be done about it. I try to remember that there is a plan for each of us, even if we cannot make out the form of it, and trust it will all be fine in the end. At least that is what the vicars say.

Well, that was certainly maudlin, was it not? I could not understand why I meandered to such a morose subject until I looked at the calendar: these thoughts always come upon me at this time of year; it was six years ago this week that Sarah came into and left my life. Please accept my apologies for such a doleful letter, and I promise the next one will be filled with cheer and fun. I have no one to whom I can pour out my heart, Susannah, at least not anyone that understands.

I will away for now and busy myself with choosing colours for the drawing room. The old rugs were taken up and sold to an antique store in London for a very good price, in spite of how ugly they were, but the paper must be stripped, etc., etc. Everything must be right, for I need to have tea with a baroness. Someday.

I will write again soon, my dear, and in the meantime please know, I am

Your Improving Friend,
Annabella

☙ Depraved Offers ❧

7 November, 1820

Dearest Susannah,

I just received your letter and to answer your very pointed question? No, I do not care to provide the names of the men who have made offers to me. It is quite annoying already. I know that normally a friend is supposed to act as a second in these arrangements – the parts about money and apartments and such – but they must not know who can be approached, so have undertaken to ask me directly. Since you insist, I shall not reply to their letters, even if it is so they will perhaps attempt to strike up a relationship with someone who is remotely interested in such arrangements. However, I hope that if I ever find myself in a situation where such contemplation is warranted I have the strength to go and find some kind of employment instead. Yes, it is always nice to be asked, but really, Susannah. How would you feel if you received letters that start quite prettily and end by asking if you would take a cold bath and pretend you are dead whilst they have relations with themselves in a corner? And the man in question is someone you have sat next to in Church! Yet that is the sort of thing being offered. Well, not all of them, but the array of offers is bewildering and occasionally upsetting. I have no idea why being hit with a switch would be remotely erotic in a romantic setting – and I have absolutely no interest in finding out. I think some of these men are seriously deranged. Now that you understand the scope of their interests I am sure you are shocked as I. All I know is the Regent – I am sorry, I am still getting used to the change – King George IV is setting a terrible example for our set. Things have become decidedly less circumspect since he took the throne, which I did not think possible. I cannot help but think he is the cause – I have heard about the parties he hosts and am thankful I have never been extended an invitation, for then I should have to pretend to have the pox or something dangerous and disgusting. Is that treasonous to say?

But since you are so very adamant, and although I find the letters I receive distasteful, I shall leave them unanswered and lock them away. You give very odd advice sometimes, Susannah.

I shall also trust that, as you said rather pointedly, my lack of "correct" experience in romantic matters is something to be mourned, not ignored. At the moment the only men with whom I could attempt to remedy the situation are unbathed, illiterate and coarse, so there is nothing to be done about it now. As the letters I receive seem to be interested in encounters rather more exotic than I find comfortable, those are avenues I have no desire to pursue.

Given these odd offers and stranger advice my pleasure in having Wetmoor to oversee grows every day.

The front grounds work has yielded gigantic bushes that are very itchy. We have been instructed to not to wander about by ourselves until they are removed, as apparently just coming near to them will land us in our sickbeds. This has vexed me terribly, for I moved to Wetmoor to no longer feel like a prisoner in my own house, only to find myself prisoner again.

The back of the Hall has been simpler: the roses running riot over nearly the entire wall surrounding the tennis courtyard was trimmed back into a semblance of control, the courtyard itself dug up and re-planted, although I left the roses spilling over the top of the wall, albeit with the door to the grounds uncovered and refinished. In its protected area Mr. Wicklestaff believes the grass will be lovely come spring.

I was thrilled to find the tennis courtyard has its own Nature theme, and it is of deep forest. The inside walls of the stone courtyard are carved with rabbits, foxes, cats, mice (adorable mice, nothing like real mice), all manner of little woodland creatures who appear to be hunting, chasing and hiding from each other through trees, bushes and glades. Trees have been carved in bas-relief that reach up to the upper edge of the walls. Soaring above the trees, carved into funny angled upper walls are eagles, falcons and other birds of prey swooping and circling, each appearing to have a little animal in mind for supper. There is even a lovely fountain in one wall, carved as if it were a tiny waterfall. It will be so beautiful come spring. It is open to the sky and I believe I shall greatly enjoy spending time there.

Oh, dear, I have gone on again for too long. Accept my apologies for such ramblings, there is no one to talk to here, but I must away and see to the work schedule for the rest of the week.

I hope you are well, and I will write again soon. Until then I remain

Your Mysterious Friend,
Annabella

15 November, 1820

Dear Susannah,

First, welcome back from Provence. I trust your sabbatical was restful, and staff was able to meet your needs and properly look after you. Of course, I know Randy was also available to fill in, as it were, and trust this arrangement was satisfactory as well. You have apparently much better luck with the men in your circle than I.

Mr. Sinclair and Constable Pukeston are both terrible ideas for me to begin my romantic education, Susannah, and you should put those thoughts completely from your mind. Mr. Sinclair is too young, works for me, and would have a failure of the heart were I to suggest any such thing, and Constable Pukeston is entirely too proper to even entertain such an idea. He is the type of man who properly and carefully courts and woos a woman and then proposes. He may already be married! I also refuse to proposition a man at Church merely to make my letters more salacious. How exactly would one make such a request: between hymns? During the sermon? In the line to greet the vicar? Before you say anything, an offer will never be made to the vicar, he is eighty if he is a day.

By the end of this letter you shall see that your suggestions, although kind and meant for the best, are all for naught. I found someone already. All by myself. Now you will have to read to discover the particulars – you cannot jump to the end! Let the tale unfold in its own good time.

The inimitable Lady Shardley Shardley, having apparently met again with her housekeeper and reviewing our initial meeting, undertook it to invite me to tea this past week. It took the better part of a day to choose the best outfit for such an occasion, especially as I would be attending alone, instead of as part of a crowd. It seemed Lady Shardley wanted to begin again with me, now that she believes I am good friend to a baroness and can destroy the reputation of her house. I also wondered if I might glean any information about Gwynneth, although I was not sure how to do such a thing.

Regardless of my own motivations, I looked forward to her attempt at reparations, for a discomfited hostess can be such fun, and she deserved to be uneasy, for it was terrible the way she treated me, whom she had never before met. I believe she has been catered to and cosseted for so long that she has forgotten that she is merely a lady, the same as I.

The day arrived, and with my invitation safely held in my new silk reticule, I donned my light mourning bonnet – drat these mourning requirements – arranged myself properly in my best carriage, and set off for Sumwattle Estate.

This time no one exploded through the front door and threw a fit in front of me. Instead a footman helped me from the carriage and the butler welcomed me into the house. The other arrival was much more fun, I must say.

All too quickly I was brought to the front parlour where Lady Shardley awaited. I was announced and the butler withdrew.

I nodded to Lady Shardley and commented on the beautiful décor. Lies are perfectly acceptable when discussing clothing or decorations, I feel, for honesty in those instances will only lead to hurt feelings on the part of those without taste. It is bad enough they are burdened by such a lack without adding further pain.

Lady Shardley gestured for me to sit down. We did not speak of the awful events I had witnessed during my last visit, but rather discussed gardening, of all things, a subject in which she is far more interested.

As we sipped and supped I was plied with a great deal of claret, for Lady Shardley has a fondness for spirits that is near alarming. Our conversation was so far removed from that of household scandals – including the one I had witnessed myself – that as the afternoon wore on it almost seemed it had not occurred. She was trying mightily to correct her earlier behaviour at the hunt, I must credit her for that, Susannah, even if the attempt rendered me almost incoherent from the spirits poured down my throat.

The "tea" was all too soon finished, and we shared a rather nice silence. Lady Shardley seemed to be carefully weighing something, as she stroked the mole on her right cheek with a hand so jewel-encrusted I marvelled at her ability to hold it up. Finally she seemed to have made up her mind.

"I shall send a footman with your carriage on your return, my dear."

I was surprised, to say the least. "Your generosity is quite welcome, however, no such gesture is required."

"Oh, but it is," she replied. She paused, and a look that may have been an attempt at shrewdness crossed her face. "Some servants – discharged for stealing or sloth – have been making sport of me. They have been making no end of mischief for my house."

Imagine my shock at this turn of events. She was trying to pretend that Gwynneth was a mere prankster. She must think people have hours to spend thinking up ways to embarrass her. However, as I write this, she has behaved badly enough in my own presence that perhaps they might.

Also, might she actually believe Gwynneth was lying? Even with my wits dulled I realized it was likely true: such claims are often made but are generally without merit. Lady Shardley might have no idea of the truth of the matter. Or perhaps Gwynneth was lying, and the father was a stableboy or footman. I realized it did not necessarily matter who put her in such a bad way, but I had been given the opening I had not been able to devise on my own.

"That is horrible," I said with as much sympathy in my voice as I could muster. "Some people are without shame." She needed to believe I was absolutely on her side.

"Utterly," Lady Shardley pounced. "They are wanton, degenerate and depraved."

"Thank goodness such a one is gone from here." I managed to keep from patting her on the hand, as it may have been a trifle too much, and because the growth on the back of her hand looked hideous.

"If only that were the case, Lady Upton-Church," Lady Shardley sighed. I tensed, sensing I might get information that was useful.

"She has not gone away?" I feigned horror.

"She lives in town," Lady Shardley said with great sadness.

"The nerve of her!" I exclaimed. Luckily it was assumed I was outraged.

"It is awful. I have tried to make certain she will stop with her ridiculous claims, but it galls me to have to pay for silence to one who is not telling the truth." She stopped to catch her breath.

So Gwynneth is still in Wimbish, somewhere, but has ceased her public claim that Lord Shardley is the one who has wronged her. Finally, information that will help me find her! All I needed now was to know where Wimbish actually was. Somewhere east of Wetmoor, I thought. I have not gone there, it is just a collection of tumbled shoppes and raggedy establishments. I send Cook instead.

"You were very wise," I finally said. Loathe though I am to admit it, Lady Shardley was clever to have done such a thing. Gwynneth's claims may be true or not, but money is something she will need, and silence paid for is better than silence given. Which was why I was asked to tea.

Lady Shardley would have been better off to leave the entire mess alone – she must have been aware that I had held my tongue regarding the issue – but she was well into her own claret at that point. She continued with a sigh, "She is not the only one." I tucked that away to consider later. "These creatures are always making mischief. I am concerned that their tricks, although tiresome and unimaginative at present, may escalate to something more frightening. You know how violent the masses have become. I believe you would be well served for my footman to accompany you home. He will ensure your safety."

"If you feel it best," I demurred. Why would I protest a footman? He could help me to stay steady while I walked to my carriage, something likely to be difficult considering the amount of spirits I had imbibed. I am somewhat chagrined to admit that I still have bad dreams about being chased by Luddites who want to hit me with wooden spoons.

"He speaks almost no English," she continued. "We believe he is from one of the northern countries, perhaps Sweden. Being of that land he is very tall and broad and none will dare approach you with him present. His full name cannot be pronounced, so we have shortened it. He is known to be Hughe."

"I beg your pardon?" I gasped, this was not quite what I expected, and she clarified.

"Hughe," she replied. "Unlike the English 'Hugh,' the 'g' in his name is not silent. He is simply Hughe."

Although I was not completely successful in keeping up with Lady Shardley's prodigious drinking I was nonetheless completely inebriated by the time I was escorted to my carriage, under the disapproving eye of Driver, whom I ignored. He was sitting as usual on top of the carriage, for he is quite self-conscious about how clumsily he ascends and descends with the wooden leg. I would think he would not glare at me, for anyone else would have let him go. He is shy one leg, after all. I have decided to lay in a supply of extras for, regardless of how often I ask, he has become quite fond of using them to practise his whittling, until they grow so slender they snap in half, usually at an inopportune time, and out in the country I have found one does not find legs lying about for the asking. I do not wish for the wood carvers to spend all their time making legs from wood meant for stair rails until the body carpenter can fashion a new leg, which is why his current leg is made of mahogany, a rather luxurious leg for a coachman.

I am going on about Driver because I am not sure how to explain the ride home, Susannah, but suffice to say that I am no longer out of sorts. I think some of the blame might be lain at your feet, Susannah, were I remotely vexed. Were it not for your enlightenment I should have never contemplated such a thing. Suffice it to say that you were correct, Susannah. About everything. I have indeed been living a sparse life.

Also, Hughe is spectacularly well-named.

I slept very soundly that night, no longer out of sorts, and tripled my church tithe that week. What would I have done had you not counselled me? Actually I am well aware of the answer to that question: Nothing. I would never have known what I have been missing, and I have been missing a great deal, Susannah. A great deal.

I must end my missive here – I want it to be in today's post, and I would so like you to have this as soon as possible. So in haste, I remain,

Your Scandalous Friend,
Annabella

꧁ Accidental Discoveries ꧂

19 November, 1820

Dearest Susannah,

I am writing back to you posthaste per your extremely strict and surprisingly annoyed letter. In my apparently meagre defence, I had no idea you wanted details of any trysts; I believed you would be thrilled I had one at all, and would likely be far more interested in what I learnt about Gwynneth.

Finally, to address your most pressing concern, such a thing will never happen again. I did not know that under no circumstances should a tryst be undertaken with any kind of servant. You really should have made that clear. I will avoid Hughe from this day forward and only look to gentlemen worthy of my attentions. But he secured mine for a short time. Normally I would absolutely refuse to divulge any details whatsoever, but as you are the reason I have any details in my possession, I will oblige as best I can.

As you know, I left Sumwattle Estate in a rather addled state (which was caused by Lady Shardley's alarming capacity for drink) and under the care of Hughe, should Luddite vandals overtake us on the ride home.

I am not completely sure how it happened, but it may have begun when I fell over on my seat from the swaying of the carriage and far too much drink.

Fear not, Hughe did not take liberties, Susannah, for it is not a liberty when you are offered something. As I fell right into Hughe's lap it was not unwarranted for him to think his lap was the intended recipient of my attentions. It was when I landed there your advice suddenly came to mind. So to speak.

It seemed impolite to correct him at the time, for he does not speak much English and I did not know how to act out, "I am terribly sorry that I fell upon you, I assure you, quite accidentally. Oh, look where my hand is, and oh, my, that is rather different than what I remember, and it would be an incorrect assumption to think you may kiss me even though your kiss is absolutely lovely – is that your tongue? – that feels absolutely divine and goodness, you are pulling me up on top of you and my skirts seem to have floated out of the way and however did your flies come undone while you were burying your head between my breasts? That tongue – what made you think of doing that with it? And my goodness, that really is nothing like I remember and seems so very happy to be getting some air. It is nearly waving at me. It feels lovely, I must admit, but never mind, if you would just put me back on my seat we will pretend it never happened." That is quite a lot to explain, Susannah. So I did not, as I was taught to always be polite and that was never discussed at Miss Penelope's. Had it been I am sure I would have paid attention.

His kisses were very different than kisses in my past, so much so that everything else rather followed of its own accord, as I hope is clear from what I have managed to scribble in a rather defensive hand.

In the end, and simply put, I rode Hughe home. It was the first scandalous thing I have ever done in my life. It was wonderful! I feel quite certain that no repercussions could ensue. Hughe is not stupid enough to divulge similar details to his friends or to Lady Shardley – who would credit him? He is a foreigner, after all. If he is indiscreet I shall tell everyone who the father of Gwynneth's child is and destroy the reputation of Sumwattle. Although she is not incredibly intelligent, I believe Lady Shardley understands that any public denunciation of myself or my house will result in the equal destruction of her own, and that ought to be enough to stay her tongue.

I hope that satisfies your unseemly curiosity.

The other reason for my letter is due to excitement of a different, albeit no less surprising, kind. I am feeling extremely smug, for I am the discoverer of new secrets here at Wetmoor. It is most thrilling!

Let me explain. Just yesterday it was pouring down rain all day, which left me miserable and out of sorts, for I had hoped to go riding in my private forest – there is one, we found it a few days ago. Those plans were dashed by rain, rain, and yet more rain. The workmen had to be sent home early in the day, for the road was already becoming impassable, and Mr. Wicklestaff himself had to leave for London for a few days, which left me with only staff for company, and they are company in the same way a cat is company, pleasant enough, but still inferior. I could not abide playing another hand of cards with Prudence, and Taylor is hopeless at chess, even after reading the books I gave him in hopes of improving the games.

I wandered about for a time looking at some of the supposed work, only to find plaster still not repaired, sections of wainscoting and paneling torn out, and the like. I counted the number of stair rails in the grand staircase that have to be replaced (29!), finished my correspondence, read the newspapers, did everything I could think of, and it was only eleven o'clock.

I finally found myself in the library to look for something to read but all of the books bored me. With nothing else to do I decided to root around in the library cupboards, for once my own books were on the shelves I did not really pay any further attention. Since it also serves as a study for me in some ways staff does not poke around overmuch.

The cupboards were mostly what I expected: some empty, some with old pamphlets and magazines stacked on the shelves, stationery tucked away and bottles of ink long turned solid in their glass jars. It was rather sad, and I began making piles of things to be discarded and things to be saved. It was not until I got to the last cupboard, which is tucked into a corner and rather difficult to get at, that I found it.

Plans. Drawings. Of Wetmoor! I was quite pleased to have found them, for perhaps I could review and improve the schedule. Something to do! I pulled them all out and spread them on the table in the middle of the room.

As I poured over the drawings, which were simultaneously rather more and less detailed than Mr. Wicklestaff's more up-to-date set, I began to be confused.

The drawings seemed not to be exact copies of the ones being used for the renovations, but instead those from an earlier date. A number of drawings were of specific rooms, showing how Sir Manfredson had envisioned them when complete, and a few even had notations of colours or finishes he thought would be appropriate. The man had dreadful decorating taste, I am sorry to say. There was a drawing of the music room, which I was happy to see is the theme of songbirds, although far more originally than the few that remain. That room is going to take longer to restore than planned. Which is true of near every room in this Hall. When

Quince bought it I don't think he cared about what happened to it, a most unusual decision for a man so fond of precision.

I was putting the drawings into some semblance of order when I noticed something odd. I am no architect, but it seemed that a few walls in the Hall are thicker than others. In three areas, actually, and in those areas the seemed are very thick indeed. I sat back to think.

I wondered if perhaps it was so the rooms would be properly proportioned, but Sir Manfredson was known for his excellent work, and I though it unlikely he would have made such a mistake on his own home. Then I thought it was space for chimneys, closets or storage that had been installed later, but a quick mental review showed that that did not seem to be the case. Two of the thick walls were opposing walls in the library where I sat, and the third was between the bedroom and dressing room in my suite.

Holding my breath I spun my chair around. And was faced with a regular wall. I was rather disappointed. I peered harder and it remained a simple wall. Well, not simple, for the linen-cut paneling is lovely, but a wall just the same. But on the other side of this wall was the conservatory . . .

I decided to be thorough, for it tickled my imagination to find secrets, so off I went down the hallway and through the big doors into the conservatory. I must get that place cleared out. It is very jungle-like in there, and I nearly ruined a pair of shoes clomping around in dirt to get near the wall in question. That wall was more disappointing than the first, for it was a sheer expanse of solid plaster.

I went back into the library and slumped in the chair, staring at the vexed wall. I had been so sure the strange architecture would yield something. Something like a secret room filled with riches, but I was sorely disappointed.

As there was nothing else to do I kept staring at the library wall. Then I was lost in daydreams of finding pirate gold or jewels and running away from roguish men who would try to steal it from me, or something similarly exciting. I have many such daydreams lately, sadly, there are no roguish men in sight. I was just dreaming of being chased through the forest by a dashing masked brigand when I saw it: a crack in the paneling. It was very hard to see, looking for all the world to be a part of the paneling itself, but it was there. I stood up and took a hairpin out of my hair, thinking it would be fun to see just how far the crack ran, so I could upbraid Mr. Wicklestaff for not having found the flaw. Using the hairpin as a guide, I found it went all the way to the ground, and way up high. Oh, he would receive a severe talking-to! My day was finally brightening!

Then the crack turned.

I have never heard of cracks running at right angles, and continued my hairpin investigation. The lengthwise crack could not be seen, for it was where the panelling met the moulding, but was most definitely there, and seemed to be a few feet wide. Then it turned again. Down. I was very excited now, for when I looked very, very closely, there was another seam.

Just then my hairpin was stopped by something. I peered at it and saw nothing, but the hairpin was truly halted. I took it out and looked closer but could see nothing.

I stood back from the wall and looked very carefully. From just a few inches away there was nothing to see at all. But if I had gauged correctly, the cracks I found seemed very nearly the same size as a door. A secret door.

Oh, this was very exciting! I ran to the wall and knocked on it, the way we have seen them do in plays, but could not hear any difference in sound. I looked all along the paneling to see if there was some kind of latch, but found none. I wondered if perhaps my mind was playing tricks on me, for I was very bored when I had begun. So I sat down to think, the same way they say you should in books. There was a door shaped-seam in the wall. The hairpin had caught near the top of the left side seam, which might indicate a hinge. So that meant, if it truly was a door, it opened on the right side.

Since it was closed, there must be a latch. I went to the library door proper and opened it. I have never really looked at a doorknob, Susannah, as I so rarely touch them. They are actually rather interesting. I jiggled the knob this way and that until I thought I understood the principle. Something must be manipulated to make the catch work.

I closed and locked that door and went back to the wall. If the catch in this possible secret door were there, it would have to be on the right. And it should not be too far away from the door itself. I looked at the level of where a doorknob normally was and then started examining the paneling to the right of the door.

It was perfectly normal. I kept going, right to the shelves that began, but of course they were all filled with books, so I began to pull the books down. What musty things they are! Soon they were piled up everywhere, and I could properly continue my examination. To my growing dismay everything still looked normal. The shelves were very sturdy, for they had braces beneath them, pieces of wood that ran the length of the shelf underneath and on each side to provide extra support.

I had gotten exactly nowhere and now the library was a mess. My day was proving a ruin. I leaned over to pick one of the books up and at that exact moment a bird smashed into one of the windows the way they keep doing, stupid things. These dratted skirts are awful, for the crash made me start and I fell over. I felt most ungraceful, Susannah, and was just about to get to my feet when I saw a gleam on the underside of one of the shelves. If I moved my head even slightly it was gone, but if I moved it back, there it was.

I must have looked a mad sight, crawling across the library floor over books so I would not lose sight of that little gleam. And I did not. When I got to it, it seemed to be part of a tiny hinge. I tugged and tugged on the brace but nothing happened. I finally got so annoyed that I smacked it for refusing to work properly for me. And that is when the magic click happened, and the brace swung open to reveal a latch! I am afraid I squealed and clapped my hands. I was not mad! I was clever!

I looked at the latch, which seemed a simple enough mechanism, took a deep breath, and pulled it. There was the softest click imaginable, and a door-sized piece of the library wall swung inward to an unknown place. I near fainted, Susannah. What had been a terrible and boring and awful day was suddenly like one of those stories with great and fantastic things popping up out of nowhere. I looked at the latch and closed the brace over it. I ran to the windows and closed the curtains, and checked that the door to the hallway was still locked. I then lit a lamp and stuck my head through the door, followed by the rest of me, and found myself standing at the top of a stairway leading down, if my eyes saw rightly, for I stayed near the door itself, holding the lamp up to peer about.

Susannah, it was a <u>tunnel</u>! A secret tunnel in my Hall! I was going to go dashing down it when I realized that I did not know where it led and if I closed the secret door I might get locked out and then starve to death before anyone found me.

That idea made me think of the ghosts. They are part of Wetmoor lore. What if that is what had happened to others and there were skeletons or, even worse, not-yet-completely-skeleton bodies in the tunnel and the ghosts were their owners? What if I tripped over one or stepped on it? What if rats were eating them? I ran back through the secret door and closed it, for mouldering bodies and rats were rather more than I could stand thinking about in any serious way. It is one thing when they are purely hypothetical, quite another when they may be tucked into the walls of your own home.

I tried to calm myself by putting the books back on the shelves. I know it was labour but I did not want Taylor to accidentally find the door and I do not believe he can properly alphabetize. When I was done I sat at the desk and listed all the reasons why leaving the tunnel alone was the sensible thing to do. At my back, the idea of it loomed over me.

It took less than five minutes before my curiosity completely vanquished my practicality and I was opening the door again.

I did pay homage to sensibility in that I spent some time examining the latch in the door, satisfying myself that I could not be locked in, but all would be locked out. I even went in the tunnel and closed the door, and was able to easily re-open the door and regain entry to the library. I also, and it is disgusting to say it, sniffed the air. There was no foul odour I could discern, so if there were bodies, they were long turned to dust or at least bare bone.

Finally I descended the stairway. They are quite sturdy, covered with some kind of materiel, for my shoes made no noise. It did not go down very far, perhaps 12 feet or so, and I was standing in a narrow passageway that curved away to my left so the end could not be seen.

I checked that the lamp had plenty of oil, took a deep breath and began to tiptoe down the tunnel. It was rather odd, for although I had gone down far enough to be underground the ground beneath my feet was wood, as were the walls and ceiling. There was some grit leaking through the gaps in the wood, but the ceiling seemed to be well braced. And not a body, bone or rat in sight, thank goodness!

It was only a moment or two before I found myself going up another stairway and facing another door. It seemed to function the same as the one in the library. I was about to open it when I wondered where I would be when I opened it. What if it were the stables? Or the veranda? What if someone saw me? I stood for the longest time, veering between discretion and curiosity.

Finally I realized that if I had come this far I should have the courage to see it through. If someone was there or saw me I could instruct Mr. Wicklestaff to wall it off and perhaps sack him for not finding it in the first place. Oh, how I long to properly sack someone!

I took a deep breath and opened the door, only to find myself in a darkened room. The low ceiling told me it was not a room in the Hall. I cast about for some kind of clue. It seemed to be a bedroom. Perhaps Sir Manfredson had tarty women meet him there. Oh, that was a disgusting thought! He is very old, nearly 70, and must be terribly wrinkled.

I could see the outline of a closed door across the room, so I went through that and found myself in a comfortable sitting room. I was in someone's home! What if I was in one of the cottagers' homes? I cancelled that thought as soon as it entered my mind; there was an actual floor, not swept dirt, under my feet, and it did not smell of goat. But I was clearly in <u>some</u> kind of home. If the owners came back they could have me arrested as an intruder and then what would everyone think?

That Lady Upton-Church went mad in the Hall just like Sir Manfredson and I would wind up in a lunatic asylum, wearing horribly unfashionable and filthy clothes, using my body as currency to gain some bread!

I was going to run right back and never go through the tunnel again when I realized that no one had yet leapt out and denounced me, so perhaps if the owners arrived I could claim I had gotten caught in the rain. I would pay them for the use of their home, for I always carry at least five pounds sterling in my pocket. That made me feel better. The room did look familiar in the dim light, however, which gave me an idea. Peering out the window past the drawn curtains confirmed it: I was in my own boathouse! The tunnel led here, although for what reason I could not fathom. It was so curious and I was enormously pleased, for no one could denounce me or think me mad for being on my own property.

I could not decide what to do. I had left the door to the tunnel in the wall behind me open and realized I should find the surely-hidden latch for this one, in case some dire emergency arose and it was imperative that I go back to the Hall through the tunnel instead of walking there like a normal person, though the direct walk seems to my unschooled eye to be shorter.

As I knew what to look for, finding the latch was a very simple matter. In a trice I had checked and tested it, and since there were no riches beyond imagining or bodies with knives still stuck in their chests, no ghosts careening through the air to frighten my hair white, I decided to go back to the Hall. I was closing the door carefully behind me when I noticed it: a little shelf to the left of the tunnel door. It had an oil lamp sitting on it alongside a tinderbox and box of brimstone matches. That seemed very practical to me.

As quick as anything I was back in the Hall, the need for caution no longer an impediment. Next to the door to the library was another shelf, similarly supplied, that I overlooked in my initial excitement. Sir Manfredson was apparently not only debauched but organized as well.

I put my ear to the door and heard reassuring silence. The interior latch sprang smoothly and I was back in my library, closing the door behind me, the wall once again looking solid and formidable. I looked around to see if anything seemed out of place. As it turned out the only thing out of place was myself, for in the looking glass I saw streaks of dust and sweat everywhere. I looked down at my skirts and found them similarly disheveled. I could not have staff see me like this, but could not think what to do.

I really am clever, Susannah, for with the sound of thunder came inspiration. I swept as much dust out of my hair as possible, then pulled the curtains back and opened a window, for it was still raining. It was a quick thing to wipe my face and arms clean with rainwater, using a curtain for a facecloth.

Slaps at my skirts and spinning put my gown mostly to rights; I looked perfectly presentable again. The only thing out of place was the smug smile that would not seem to leave my face. I have a secret tunnel! I do not care if it is without clear purpose, it is exciting!

I have not investigated the other areas yet, for my investigation took longer than I thought possible, and after I had put myself back together Taylor arrived for instructions. The rest of the day was taken with menu-making and direction to staff for the rest of the week. But I do think I soon will have sussed out another one or two secrets.

Which is why I put pen to paper to write you immediately, for I knew you would enjoy knowing the secret as much as I. You must promise to keep your counsel on the matter, however, for it may not be safe if it were to become general knowledge that there are ways into the Hall beyond the doors.

I have nothing else to add to my tale but had to share it with someone. That is the worst thing about living in the country; there is no one to talk to but myself, which is how I think Sir Manfredson may have gone mad.

I will write soon with actual news, darling, and know that until then I remain

Your Investigating Friend,

Annabella

☙ Funeral Arrangements ❧

22 November, 1820

Dear Susannah,

I just received your lovely card and gift to commemorate Quince's birthday. It was very sweet of you to have remembered.

I agree with you, it is better to remember Quince as he was, not as he ended, especially as his end was so very grisly.

I know I told you at the time that the funeral arrangements were well-received, but that was not true. Forgive me for the fabrication, but at the time I could not put into words what happened. I would like to correct that now, if you do not mind, for it has much weighed on my mind that I did not tell my dearest friend the truth regarding Quince's funeral. As I apparently did not tell you how Quince died I shall tell you the whole of it, and you should simply disregard any portion you already know.

I spared no expense, of course, hiring the best mourning-shoppe in London. Their employees draped the entire house and its surviving occupants in black, arranged for mutes, straw, black horses, etc., etc. They were also able to refer a company that could clean up enough to hold a proper viewing, although there was nothing to view.. One of those workers vomited when they saw the foyer, which I thought quite rude, as well as unexpected from a person who makes their living from death.

It was difficult to find a proper burial container for Quince. I was told a casket would not be appropriate, as what was left of him could leak through the bottom (causing another swoon on my part). As ever more macabre suggestions were proffered (using waxed fabric to prevent stains, etc.) I finally gave instructions to put Quince in a pretty jar and be done with it. Did I not have enough problems without having to worry that my dead husband was seeping into the floor during the wake?

Everyone we know came, but it was horrible instead of comforting, for some were overtaken with giggles when there was not the expected casket. In my defence it was a beautiful silver jar, chased with moons and stars, which was the closest thing to a Heavenly setting as I could find with no notice.

Most of the supposed mourners came to satisfy their curiosity, seeming to believe the newspapers without even doing me the courtesy of asking me what happened. They peered about the foyer where it occurred, leaning over the barriers where it was still unsafe, ogling as if they were at one of those awful freak shows instead of a house in mourning. When Mrs. Cotterwood came she told me people were looking for morbid evidence of the accident: Driver's leg lying about or an eye rolling across the floor. As if I would have allowed people in my house whilst gore still stained the floors!

At the funeral service even Vicar Drambert seemed callous. Along with the usual platitudes, he had the temerity to cast a doleful eye in my direction as he said, "Quince in the end became much like his namesake: jellied." To call my husband jelly in the eulogy was inexcusable and in very poor taste. The tittering from the congregation was proof. It was dreadful as I sat alone in the front pew, no family to surround me, no children to comfort me. I remember wishing the box had fallen on me as well, such was the nightmare of my life.

So now you have the truth, dear friend. I hope you understand if I did not speak of it before: it was all too awful to relive.

I am sure you are now breathing a sigh of relief at having been able to miss the entire thing, Susannah. I would have given much to have been able to do the same. It all turned out all right in the end, for I was found innocent of any wrongdoing and I inherited everything. That was rather startling, for you and I both know I would not have gotten through the simple math lessons at Miss Penelope's without your assistance. I am now in charge of an entire estate. Until I die or remarry I am responsible for myself. I wonder why Quince set up the will so if or when either happenstance occurs Oxford and Cambridge will be equal beneficiaries. He thought both to be populated by dandies. Quince was very odd, was he not?

I will away now and talk to Cook about how many girls we need to make sure Wetmoor is properly tended even during this renovation. I have the distinct feeling it will be more than I imagined and less than will be needed when complete. Such is the life of a lady, I suppose.

Please give my best to your family and know that I remain

Your Property-Owning Friend,
Annabella

☙ When in Wimbish. . . ❧

8 December, 1820

My Dear Susannah,

Please know that I have not forgotten my promise to determine if Gwynneth is all right. I was pleased to learn that she is in town from Lady Shardley, but with such terrible weather and so many things happening here at Wetmoor I have not had the opportunity.

Oh, Susannah, I cannot lie to you. I did not want to go to town. It is ridiculous, I know, but I am accustomed to London, a civilized city, and dreaded going to that claptrap collection of buildings masquerading as a place worthy of a visit. I go to Church, of course, every Sunday, sitting piously in a pew, much space on each side of me, for my fellow Christians are apparently terrified I may kill them. It is most un-Christian. Afterward I thank the vicar for his sermon, usually managing to quote a Bible verse it reminded me of, to demonstrate that I am not Evil. The first time I did it the people behind me gasped. You would think they expected me to be struck dead for venturing into a Church. Hardly anyone talks to me, even though the vicar is always kind (he should be, my tithe is <u>huge</u>). I also worried that if I went to town on my own, without God's protection in His House, I would be denounced in the streets. People love to denounce others, have you noticed?

However, I made a promise to you and, although lax in its pursuit, knew I would have to go to town to find Gwynneth.

So when yesterday dawned clear and bright I told Prudence to have Driver prepare the carriage so she and I could go to town.

It was a pleasant enough ride, and Prudence seemed excited to be getting out of the house. I was a trifle anxious, but soothed myself that I was doing a Good Thing on behalf of my friend. By the time we arrived I was quite sanguine.

Until we began walking down what passes for the High Street. Some people turned their backs when they saw me, others had the gall to gather their children closer, going silent as Prudence and I strolled past. I tried to think of it as hushed awe, but it was rather difficult. In London they were more subtle about their dislike, and I wondered if perhaps I should not have stayed at Wetmoor.

Things improved when we went into the sweets shoppe. The proprietor, Mr. Calloway, was effusive in his welcome and I was so grateful that I arranged to have sweets delivered to the Hall every week. He plied me with samples of his wares, which were surprisingly palatable, and bustled and cosseted me until I felt that my earlier discomfiture had been premature, and the people who seemed so put out by my arrival were merely unnerved by a member of the Ton (I *think* I still am, I have not been formally cut in public) walking down their meagre street.

Prudence and I left the shoppe in much better spirits, munching on some candied almonds Mr. Calloway pressed on us.

Then we went to the dressmaker. It was just a few doors down from Mr. Calloway's, and we entered Mrs. Greyback's shoppe with a *frisson* of pleasure, for the gowns arrayed in the windows were quite fetching. I am bored with my current mourning gowns and realized I might be able to find perfectly suitable day gowns here, when I can abandon all of this black and grey.

The shoppe was a little jewel and no other customers were about. The bell tinkled at the door as we entered and Mrs. Greyback popped out of the back room with a lovely welcoming smile on her face. Until she saw mine clearly.

"Welcome to Greyback's." Her voice could have frozen brandy.

"This is a lovely shoppe," I said brightly. "Are you Mrs. Greyback?"

"Yes, I am. You are Lady Upton-Church?" Her lip seemed to curl a bit on my name.

"Yes, I am. I am looking for – "

"There's nothing for you here, Lady. I am very sorry." She did not look sorry at all.

"What do you mean?" I tried to appear gently confused, and drew nearer the counter.

"We don't have the gowns you are looking for, Lady. I do not make mourning clothes." She stood firm behind the counter.

I thought I understood her ire. "Oh, I am not looking for mourning clothes, but my mourning is ending soon and I – "

The woman dared interrupt me, and Prudence's little intake of breath at the gall was audible. "I am afraid I cannot help you, Lady Upton-Church. Good day." With that she turned her back on me – can you credit it! – to go back into her likely smelly and filth-ridden private rooms.

"Excuse me, Mrs. Greyback, I should like to inquire about uniforms." I was not, but her behaviour could not be tolerated.

She snapped, "I am fully booked with other commissions, Lady. Perhaps you should go to London for your needs."

What had I done? I only wished to inquire about gowns, but her manner was so rude I could not keep myself from continuing to engage her. "Yes, it is clear from the throngs clamouring outside for entrance that you are overwhelmed with eager customers –"

"My niece was one of your maids, Lady Upton-Church. When you killed your husband you killed her, too."

My mouth dropped open. "What?"

"You killed my niece and did not even care, so long as it got you what you wanted: your big estate and your big pile of money. Gown yourself in that." She whirled and disappeared, leaving Prudence and I standing in the empty shoppe.

Rage suddenly eclipsed mortification. How dare she treat me like a criminal, like a murderess, when I had been cleared!

I stormed around the back of the counter and into her private rooms. She leapt to her feet and glared.

"How dare you –" she began.

I had had enough of her. "How dare I? How dare you! I was declared innocent, I had nothing to do with it, it was an accident, a horrible accident. He was my husband and I loved him, and did everything I could for everyone else that was there that day. I am sorry about your niece, I truly am, even though her relatives are awful, if you are indication of the quality of her family. You are a terrible, nasty woman, and your gowns would not be fit to be worn by a star-gazer in London!"

I turned on my heel and left the shoppe ahead of Prudence, so eager was I to be shut of the place, blinking back tears of anger and humiliation. I ought not have come to town, I thought, I should stay at Wetmoor in hiding forever.

I was having trouble seeing between my tear-filled eyes and the bright sunshine, which is why I walked right into someone.

I was so surprised that I near fell, and only a strong arm grabbing my waist prevented it. I looked up and saw to my shock that it was Mr. Ploughgoode.

"Hello there," he smiled. "We meet again." He looked a little closer at me while I blinked furiously to stop from crying right in the street. "Are you all right?"

I was horrified. It was apparently clear I was upset in public, which would not do at all. Suddenly a firm little voice piped up.

"That shoppe is filthy," Prudence declared. "Filthy, dusty – I sneezed six times in five minutes! Poor Lady Upton-Church picked up a piece of fabric and dust flew up and it all got in her eyes! We had to leave – she does not frequent such poorly-kept places."

I was astonished at her lie but quite grateful for it. Suddenly Mr. Ploughgoode was pressing a snowy kerchief into my hand. "Here you go, then."

I dabbed at my eyes and flicked the kerchief about my face and neck, pretending to bat dust away. "Thank you, Mr. Ploughgoode."

"You remembered," he smiled. Prudence looked intrigued.

"Of course I remembered, I might still be in a ravine were it not for you." Prudence looked very intrigued.

"Are you recovered?" He completely ignored Prudence, which I found I rather liked.

"Yes, it was nothing. I should like to extend my apologies for that day. I should have said something when Lady Shardley dismissed you. It was unfair." Prudence near goggled, but instead looked into Mrs. Greyback's and made faces through the glass.

Mr. Ploughgoode gave a slight bow. "That's very kind of you, Ladyship." He leaned in slightly. "Don't fret yourself. She'd have fired me before the day was out for something. You saved me a full day's work."

I could not help it, I smiled, my humiliation receding. Mr. Ploughgoode does not think me a murderess, or if he does, should give up his current occupation and take to the stage. And he is stunning. "If you insist."

"I do."

I was suddenly aware that I was standing in the middle of the town, chatting with a workingman. My reputation cannot sink much lower, but that might well scuttle it for all time. I folded the kerchief with care and returned it to him.

"My thanks, Mr. Ploughgoode."

"It was my pleasure." He tucked it back into a pocket.

"Good day, Mr. Ploughgoode." I had to quickly take my leave, and Prudence was going to be catching flies if her mouth hung open any longer.

"Good day, Lady Upton-Church." He gave a short bow, I nodded, and took Prudence's arm as we walked down the street. The moment we were a decent distance away she gave my arm a little squeeze.

"Who was <u>that</u>?"

"I met him at the Shardleys' when I was nearly shot by Baron Theosophus and fell into a ravine." I looked about, determined to put awful Mrs. Greyback's face behind me.

"Someone tried to shoot you?" Prudence was alarmed.

"It was an accident, Prudence." Prudence began looking about us as if we might be shot at any moment. "It was a baron, Prudence. I do not believe I will be shot here." Although I am weary of all this blame, Susannah, I do not mind admitting.

"Lady, that woman was terrible to you."

"Yes, she was."

"Do you feel better now?" We walked along for a moment while I considered her question.

"Prudence, do you think I should move back to London?"

"We just arrived here."

"Perhaps it was the wrong decision." I did notice that people were not cringing quite so much as we walked along, and one man tipped his hat to me.

"London is wonderful, it is, milady, but the house there is very sad." Prudence cast down her eyes, waiting to be reprimanded.

I sighed. "I know. It is why I wanted to move here."

"I don't think they're all like Mrs. Greyback, Lady. Mr. Calloway was very nice. The vicar is, too, and people are starting to be . . . better at Church."

"Do you think?"

"It would be the same in London, and, if you'll forgive me saying, the Ton, well, they'll likely not take you back unless you marry into the ranks again."

"I know." We paused at the stall of a greengrocer. He smiled and patiently waited as we mused over his offerings. I bought some dried figs and cherries, and he beamed as we completed the transaction.

I suddenly remembered that I was not there to dither about whether or not I should return to London and how many people might still think me a murderess. I was here to find Gwynneth. As we moved away from the greengrocer I decided to ask Prudence.

"Prudence, if you needed to find someone, but could not tell anyone you wanted to find them, and they did not know you were looking for them, how would you do it?"

She brightened. "You want to find someone? A husband?"

"No, not a husband."

"Oh . . . OH!" Her confusion changed to shock.

"NO, Prudence, not a lover. Goodness! Just a person I need to find."

"You're still young enough, Lady." She abandoned that train of thought at the look on my face. "You could – well, you could take out an advertisement?"

"Then everyone would know I was looking for that person. Really, Prudence, think." We were near the edge of town – it is so small it only took a few moments to reach it – and stood near a public house, the Rooster & Mussel, as we both thought hard.

I was sorting through different ideas, all of them poor, when the sound of yells broke my concentration. I looked about, wondering where such a row was occurring. It was from the back of the pub. Prudence and I looked at each other and immediately walked back down the street toward our carriage. Suddenly a girl ran past us toward the grocer, nearly knocking Prudence down in her rush, and she did not even pause to apologize. We both glared at her back as she ran to the greengrocer. I kept on musing as we passed her, as she begged for potatoes from the man, for the Rooster and Mussel had run out. I was wondering if I could send Taylor there to spy out gossip for me when the greengrocer's voice reached me.

"There you go, Gwynneth," were his highly welcome words.

I stopped and turned. Gwynneth was turning back to the Rooster and Mussel, but I would recognize that nose anywhere. It was her. Gwynneth! I found her! I realized the greengrocer was staring at me and I gave him a quick smile.

"Lovely figs, sir. Simply lovely."

He looked pleased. "Thank you, Lady Upton-Church. Very glad to be of service."

I turned back to Prudence, inwardly jumping for joy. Of course it was simple to find the girl, the town is so small, but I was still thrilled. I have found her! She is apparently employed at the Rooster and Mussel, Susannah, so shall not starve. If she is clever and careful she may avoid total ruin.

Prudence was still pondering the problem I had presented when we reached the carriage.

"You could maybe – who is it, Lady? If I knew that I could help."

"And old friend," I lied smoothly.

"You could write to their house and see if it's returned with a new address," she mused.

"That is a wonderful idea, Prudence. Thank you so much, I would not have thought of it."

Driver limped to the carriage and opened the door for us and we set off for Wetmoor, munching happily on dried cherries and having a spot of the claret hidden in the seat cushions.

That is my happy news, Susannah, although I had to suffer being castigated by a wicked dressmaker and buy figs when I do not like them.

Gwynneth is employed and living in town. She should be fine.

I will close for now, content in the knowledge that I have done my duty by you, and found How It All Turned Out for Gwynneth. I feel quite smug about the entire thing, save that now all my gowns will have to be ordered from my old dressmaker in London.

I will write soon, but in the meantime I remain

Your Clever Friend,

Annabella

☙ Secret of the Season ❧

15 January, 1820

My Dear Susannah,

How pleased I was to receive your letter yesterday! I have oft thought of you in the past few weeks, and as I was in the midst of grievous difficulties with the Hall, a missive from you was just the thing to brighten my day! Christmas in Paris! It sounds divine. I would have loved to been at your ball for the New Year, and cannot imagine anything more delicious. You are such a wonderful hostess, I am sure it will be the talk of France for many weeks.

I too have news, and it is rather scandalous.

First of all, I was most pleased you were happy that I found Gwynneth. She did indeed appear to be well, no sign of impending starvation about her. You may rest your mind knowing that all of your Lordship's children are fine, including her.

The holidays were quiet again this year, as it was not possible to leave the Hall for London as I had originally planned, which saddened us all a great deal. I had looked forward to holiday invitations and staff had their hearts set on seeing family while we were there, but it was too difficult to move everyone to London for just a few days, and of course I could not stay here alone. I would starve to death or freeze! My greedy staff were somewhat mollified by the bonuses they received, and meals began to improve after they received another bonus for the New Year. I hated doing it, but Cook's meals can vary as greatly as her moods. When London was denied for Christmas she must have been truly sad, for meals became inedible.

I thought bonuses would improve their spirits, as well as extra spirit rations until the New Year passes and I was correct in my assessment. Work halted on the Hall until after Boxing Day, as the workmen were spending time with their families. We went to Church in town for Christmas services, and I found myself to be the only titled personage in attendance; everyone else was in London. That depressed me, for although being singular is normally something greatly to be enjoyed, being surrounded by those of lesser standing is rather lonely.

In order to try to improve all of our spirits somewhat we did put up a tree and decorate it. I had to ask staff to join me, as there is no family to help trim.

Foxx will be fine, although I did scold him for not holding tightly enough to the ladder as he climbed to put a star atop the tree. Also, screaming will not mend a broken arm, and is certainly not reminiscent of the sounds of Christmas. However, Mr. Gibberwilly, the local surgeon, must have been able to gift his family handsomely this year; he must be wealthy from the fees I so frequently pay. After Driver returned to Wetmoor with a bandaged and plastered Foxx we sang songs and drank more spirits. Foxx finally stopped moaning, which was a relief.

For Twelfth Night I sent gifts out to the cottagers, since that is what one with cottagers is supposed to do. Mr. Sinclair and I dithered over what to do for them; they are the most dishevelled lot, which is embarrassing. I do not want people to think my cottagers are indicative of my own standards, so along with two laying hens, a pig and an iron plough blade per family, they each received fabric from which to make some decent clothing. And their rents for the month were forgiven. I am hoping they use it to purchase soap.

Mr. Sinclair and I clearly overestimated what is the norm for farmers, and I spent an entire day being called upon by one family after another, each one wanting to thank me for my kindness and generosity. I now have enough people praying for me that I could live the murderous and debauched life I am thought to be living and still be given a special place in Heaven. It was annoying, for they were insistent about meeting with me instead of sending along a message through Taylor or Foxx. The children were rather cute. I had not seen them before, the only people who ever came to the Hall before were the adults. The little ones were ragamuffins, to be sure, but there is something about the huge eyes in a child's face that makes one forgive their leaking noses and dirt-stained faces.

When all was said and done I spent a fortune on the holidays. It is astonishing to me how expensive it is to be wealthy.

The real news is that over the holidays I pried another secret from Wetmoor. I do love living here, Susannah, for it seems there is a new surprise every day.

As you know, I already found the tunnel through the library to the boathouse. Although I cannot fathom its purpose, it is still a delicious secret.

The weather had been most unfortunate, however, cold, snowy and wind-swept, and the views from the myriad windows uniformly dreary.

With the holidays complete things were settled into a routine that has been positively dull. I woke, ate, bathed, dressed, read and answered my correspondence, ate lunch, met with Mr. Wicklestaff to try to negotiate what should be done next, had tea, avoided the cottagers, determined menus, took care of the Hall, ate supper alone in the morning room because the dining room was filled with scaffolding and tools, and then read books until my eyes were tired and it was time for bed. It is why I have not written you; there has been nothing to write. Were it not for my accidental tryst with Hughe I would feel quite the spinster. I know that is silly, for it is how I expected to live my life, but now that I have tasted other pleasures I find myself quite unsatisfied and vexed.

It is even more unsatisfying to find I am unsatisfied out of choice as opposed to circumstance. One day you must explain how I could become desperate so quickly for companionship when I went virtually my entire life without it.

Mr. Wicklestaff made an overture to me. Although I am not the sort of woman that assumes every man in sight is pitching woo, it was an overture not to be mistaken for anything else.

We were going over the renovations, discussing various options in the library, where we normally meet. Taylor does not attend me during our meetings, for they involve business and it is certainly not any of Taylor's.

As we went through the drawings of the conservatory I suddenly found Mr. Wicklestaff's lips upon mine. Even more alarming, his tongue was in my mouth. The man is in my employ! I have no idea what made him think he could take such a liberty – surely he deals with women in his profession – he works on houses, which are a woman's responsibility!

I knew not what to do, for it was entirely unexpected. I thought if I could just push his tongue out of my mouth I could separate myself from him without the added humiliation of slobbering on each other.

This immediately proved to be the wrong course, for I found my tongue sucked into his mouth and played with, even as he bent me backwards and we near fell over. It was most alarming. I leapt back from him, slobber be d______, and wiped my mouth with the back of my hand.

"Mr. Wicklestaff," I said shakily, and found I could not think of what to say.

"Call me Ryan, Annabella," he murmured, mistaking the shaking in my voice, caused by horror, for passion.

"Oh, no, no, no," I dithered, even as I ran to the other side of the table. He began to give chase and I snapped, "Mr. Wicklestaff! Stop where you are!"

He did but seemed confused. "Lady, I was kissing you at your invitation."

"Invitations come in the post, Mr. Wicklestaff. Not in my eyes. Or mouth." I glared at him. "What were you thinking?"

"Oh. Oh, no," he said, realizing his horrible breach. "Lady Upton-Church – my deepest, most sincere – "

The worst part was that Mr. Wicklestaff had to be carefully handled. That did not come out quite right, for I had no intention of handling him at all. I would have sacked him outright, but he is the best renovations expert that would condescend to renovating a country house. I had to make sure he understood that I am completely out of bounds but leave him enough pride that he could continue his work. Thank God he is staying in town during the renovations! Were we under the same roof, even in another wing of Wetmoor, I would have had no choice but to let him go.

As he babbled out increasingly odd adjectives to frame his apology I had a flash of inspiration.

"Mr. Wicklestaff. Please stop speaking." Thankfully he did. "Your attentions are as flattering as they are unwelcome. It is unfortunate that the eggnog Cook has been serving to everyone who wanders through the kitchens should have so debased your normal decorum and equilibrium. I am sure it is that, coupled with not being able to be in London to pursue more appropriate women, who are not in mourning, or half-mourning, that has caused this . . . incident."

He peered carefully at me. "Yes," he said slowly, realizing I was giving him an excuse and he would be stupid if he did not use it. "I have been in the kitchens four times today."

"You should not go to the kitchens anymore, I think."

"I am so –"

"Of course you are, you have always behaved as a gentleman, and I trust – quite literally – that you will never do anything so untoward again. Should you I will have no choice but to let you go. The Hall will be completed and full credit given to someone else. Do we have an understanding?"

"I thought you –"

I kept my tone firm. "We have already established that your assumptions regarding myself were utterly incorrect. What I am asking is if you can restrain yourself in the future?"

"Of course, Lady."

"Then let us put the entire episode behind us."

"Thank you, Lady."

"You are welcome. But I believe it would be best to continue this meeting tomorrow so you might recover yourself."

He took his leave with gratitude and I went to my bath to rinse out my mouth. Brandy was an excellent choice.

I know you will say that I should have let the man go, but I could not bear the idea of finding another man to oversee these workmen. It was also nice to know I am still thought to be attractive.

Mr. Wicklestaff has behaved perfectly since that day, but I have felt cross, for I had the opportunity to dally with someone and not only let it pass by, but my vehemence ensured that no further opportunities will ever present themselves. His embarrassment has had a fortunate benefit: he has nearly worked the men to death in recent days and the last of the roof and outer wall repairs are complete, which is a relief. Now I do not have to skirt puddles, and I was growing tired of the screaming and injuries from workmen falling from the roof into bushes and seeing straw piled around the perimeter of the Hall for just such accidents.

But that encounter was not the most startling thing that has happened in recent days. I only detailed it because you have been so strict that I keep you apprised of the details of my romantic life, even if there are no details to divulge in a way that you might find interesting.

Then yesterday I jumped from my chair as if I had been poked with a stick, for I remembered! The plans, Sir Manfredson's plans! I had found the tunnel to the boathouse, and even though it is a pointless tunnel it somehow slipped my mind that it did not appear to be the only one! Something to do! I could look for the others! I pulled out the plans and studied them again. It appeared there might be a tunnel in my very rooms, although I could not tell to where it went.

All I needed was an excuse to go to my rooms during the day. I wanted to run up the stairway and start pulling everything apart, but knew prudence (not my maid Prudence, but the act of being cautious) should rule. I waited until after lunch and announced that I would withdraw to my rooms, victim of a headache. I picked up my correspondence and papers and asked to not be disturbed. As soon as the door was locked behind me I tossed my correspondence to the side and looked at all of the panelling, realizing that Sir

Manfredson's fondness for complex woodwork may not have been solely an aesthetic decision. The linen-cut has so many lines as part of the pattern that, try as I might, I could not find a joint or seam. At first.

According to the drawings a tunnel, if indeed there was one, had to be set in the outside wall.

It was devilishly difficult to see and I very nearly got the headache I had complained of from staring, but I finally found a straight line. As a hairpin had provided such success before, I used one again. And again, there was a door-shaped seam. All I had to do was find the latch.

I shall not bore you with the details of my search, but I found the latch cunningly hidden in the window frame. I looked about, suddenly certain that someone would leap out and scream "Aha!" at me, a most silly flight of fancy. When that did not occur I pulled the latch, there was that soft click and the door swung inward to reveal darkness. Once again, there was a small shelf to the left with a lamp and the means to light it. With a murmur of thanks to Sir Manfredson I added new oil to it and lit it, closed the door, and looked around.

Before me was a stairway, this one circular, going down, down, and down. It was somewhat cramped and dizzying, but in a moment I found myself standing at the bottom, looking down another tunnel.

Off I went. Who knew where this one would lead? It went on forever, it seemed, and suddenly I found myself standing in front of a door. Not a secret door, for there was no shelf and no odd latch. Just a door, but no knob. I put my ear up to it and listened: no sound came from the other side. I was not sure how to proceed, for the other doors had knobs. I finally pushed on it. With a soft click it opened.

I held my breath from anticipation, Susannah, and very glad I did, for the odour that assaulted my nose was foul! I near screamed, thinking that perhaps there was a dead body rotting away, when I realized that as awful as the smell was, it was rather familiar, and I have never been in the habit of smelling dead people. I assured myself it was likely not a body, and when I adjusted to the stench I peered in.

It was another room, Susannah. And not just a room – a bedroom! It was completely furnished, down to a wardrobe against the wall and a chamber-pot under the bed! The smell was coming from the bed, where a long-abandoned goose-down mattress was rotting away. It was mouldering and disgusting, but I was so fascinated that I ignored both it and the accompanying scent. On the table next to the bed there was a book, but it was the kind of book that Quince apparently liked to read in private. Some of the sketches were interesting, albeit likely physically impossible except to a mistress. Those women must do special exercises. It was when perusing the book that I realized I had stumbled into an assignation room. This, not the boathouse, was where Sir Manfredson must have met fallen women! I must say I actually enjoyed the scandalousness of it. I held my breath and opened the wardrobe and found clothing hanging there. There were padded silk robes and women's clothing, although that is a generous description. The women's clothing appeared to be for the women he brought here: stockings and corselets, all quite vulgar and not the kind of thing a lady would wear, but also a riding habit, complete with boots and hat and several riding crops. I suppose Sir Manfredson dreamt of being a jockey in his youth.

He must also have brought his dogs through from time to time, for there were leashes, collars and large muzzles for them. I understand he loved his dogs and was always ordering new things for them from London.

The walls were bare save for two large hooks screwed into the wall where I suppose he must have hung paintings, although they seemed rather high from the ground to be seen properly and the hooks are so large and sturdy one could hang a side of beef from them. There were two more near the ground where I think he must have tied up the dogs if they became unruly. All in all, a very strange room! It is wicked, do you not agree?

There was another door in the opposite wall, except it looked like a regular door, not hidden away. I looked at the door I had just come through and realized that when closed it would be impossible to see, for it melted into the panelling. I checked and found the latch for that door cleverly hidden in the top of the moulding of the wardrobe, which was part of the wall. Pulling down the moulding springs the latch and the door opens. When the moulding is pushed back up it catches and stays in place. I was becoming more impressed with Sir Manfredson's ingenuity every moment!

When I finished my inspection of the tiny room, I decided to go through the next door – perhaps there was something even more strange than the bedroom.

It opened to another tunnel. At that point I left both doors open behind me and went down this new tunnel for quite some time – I felt I might find myself in France at the end. Instead I found another stairway, circular as well, and I climbed it to the door at the top, putting the lamp down on the ever-present little shelf next to it, which had yet another oil lamp and the means to light it.

I took a deep, steadying breath, for I knew I was likely off the grounds with the distance I had covered and opened the door. It was heavy and I had to pull on it with all my might.

Susannah, the tunnel opens a portion of the wall of my grounds! That is why it opened so slowly; it is made of rock! I nearly fainted! It is in the south wall of my private forest, near the very back gate. I looked to see if anyone was about and was thankful to find that all of the huge old trees blocked a direct view of the wall from the Hall. Sir Manfredson must have planned it that way.

This door was different than the others in more than just materiels, Susannah. First of all, it began to close slowly on its own. I had to grab it and use a nearby rock to keep it propped open, for I had not found the latch to let me back in and did not want to tromp across my grounds back to the Hall. Second, unlike the other doors, the latch was not at the height of a doorknob. It was in a rock. I found it was because it was the only one that stuck out a bit from the others. It looked like rose quartz and the mortar was cracked all the way around, the only one so loose. Rather more accustomed to Sir Manfredson's ways I yanked on the rock and nothing happened. I pushed it and it swung up, hinged somehow. It was set high, and like the door tried to close itself. I had to hold it up with one hand and feel around for the latch with the other.

Then it was time for the test. I let the door close and examined the wall. You could not tell it was there. With the rock self-closing as well, you could not see anything at all. Holding my breath and beginning to shiver – I was outside, Susannah! – I pushed the rock up, found the latch and pulled it. The door swung inward. I let go of the rock, and as it slowly returned to its original place I dashed through the door for the relative warmth of the tunnel.

I was absolutely beside myself with happiness, for this is a far more interesting tunnel than the boathouse! It is for immoral purposes! I am the luckiest woman in England to

☙ Gwynneth Speaks ❧

14 January, 1821

Dear Susannah,

I wrote to you the moment I could, for I have new information about Gwynneth. I know we both thought the matter properly resolved, but unfortunately everything has changed in the most dreadful way. Not only that, I am very sorry to tell you, it is already too late.

It began last week when, in a moment of weakness and boredom, I joined the local theatrical troupe. I did not even know this poor excuse for civilization would have such a thing.

Baron Theosophus arrived at my door just one day after the New Year and would not be put off from seeing me. I was concerned he might try to pitch woo but was happily disappointed in that regard. In Wimbish there is a group that puts on a musicale once a year and everyone who is anyone provides assistance. It is the brainchild of Baron Theosophus and Duke Twitwhistle, who oversee everything. As I am from London it is believed I have some sophistication about the theatre. My obligations with the Hall have meant I have not met many of my neighbours except at Church, and then we are all very proper and kind, which is rather dull. Given that, his offer seemed to be just the thing: It would get me out of the Hall, allow me to mingle in circumstances not quite as constrained as Church and drive boredom away, for there is only so much fascination to be found in paint and plaster. I accepted.

It has been a lark for me thus far although I was dismayed to learn that Hughe, that Austrian rascal (or wherever he is from), is part of our merry band of players. Lady Shardley has become impatient with his poor attempts at English and hopes the theatrical society may help him improve his vocabulary, so he can take more specific and correct direction in his work. He attends every rehearsal and is learning every line, as well as providing assistance with the sets and heavier furniture we are using, as Duke Twitwhistle and Baron Theosophus have both proven their inability to lift anything heavier than a pair of dice, hand of cards or glass of port.

Pardon my uncharitable description, but Baron Theosophus is not what one would expect of a gentlemen. That wandering eye – I mean that literally – is quite discomfiting. When he speaks to me, his right eye remains fixed on my bosom and his left rolls in its socket like a Brussels sprout dropped on an uneven floor. Add to that startling picture the stoop to his thin shoulders, swollen, gout-ridden right leg and uneven pate, and one has a picture that lacks somewhat in the "dashing" area. As a final aesthetic insult, he has terrible nasal difficulties.

Our troupe is a varied crowd and I have met many different people thus far. I was saddened to find that Baroness Gurthwant is not among them, but her duties are far too pressing to devote so much time to a simple diversion.

It is not the rehearsals that are germane to my tale, but where we retire after rehearsals, it being far too cold in recent days to attempt a long carriage ride without prior fortification. It is the Rooster & Mussel public house.

Normally I would never allow myself to be seen in such a place, nor any of the women involved, but for the musicale the rules are a bit more relaxed, and the Rooster & Mussel has a private room that allows us to stay just inside the bounds of etiquette. In London it would be an outrage, but in Wimbish, with its paucity of choices for a meal, blind eyes are turned on occasion. However, in the guise of becoming a contributing member of the Wimbish community I could see Gwynneth there and make sure she was all right, had not lost a post again now that her condition must be showing. There are always a few of our ilk in attendance on rehearsal nights, and Prudence came with me to the first few rehearsals.

I abandoned bringing Prudence when it seemed she was the subject of much interest from the boys who work in other houses, which unnerved her. Instead I sit with Mrs. Frankwell. She has been the nicest to me at Church, and does not seem to mind my reputation.

The Rooster & Mussel is quite a charming establishment. The floor is swept clean, the fireplace cheerful and inviting and the spirits are top-drawer. The proprietor, Mr. Bargesniffle, is thrilled to have personages such as ourselves grace his threshold, treating us with great deference and not a little fuss. I enjoy this more than I should, but it has been such a chilly winter thus far. Mr. Bargesniffle's attempts at providing appropriate service to a lady of my station are inept and very, very charming.

But I digress again. I am sure you are dying to know how our theatrical troupe could shine any light on Gwynneth's – or your Lordship's – history. It is not something I ever expected myself, and I thank Heaven every day I have come to this county!

The first few visits Gwynneth was nowhere in sight, and I began to worry that she had been turned out, and was starving and freezing somewhere, huddled in a hedge. That is most silly, for she has funds, but I was still bothered that she had not been swabbing or serving or whatever it is she does.

Last night we were waiting for the snow to abate somewhat before attempting to negotiate the poor roads home. Were my own carriage to become stuck in such weather it could be calamity. Driver is less than vigourous, and may not survive walking for help should anything untoward happen, especially with his leg. I would not put it past Driver to use it as firewood in an emergency, and there would go yet another leg.

However. I digress. Again.

Last night we were all gathered around the fire, discussing the musicale and some of the difficulties being encountered, as the rest of the patrons slowly dispersed to their homes. They are mostly of the working classes, and as such are forced to retire early so they can provide appropriate services in the early morning hours.

However, last night my eye spied Gwynneth working behind the long wooden counter. She seemed to notice my gaze, and to shrink into herself a bit at the attention. That hair, and the hook nose peeking out through those bedraggled locks, confirmed what I knew to be true. She looked miserable, even though in her state she ought to be thrilled she was employed.

I sipped my drink and kept flicking my eyes over toward her. Mrs. Frankwell noticed. “Do you know her?”

“She looks familiar,” I said. “I’ve no idea why.”

“Poor thing,” Mrs. Frankwell said.

First of all, I must remind you that although I was properly appalled at the idea of 1) a woman in a delicate condition being seen in public and 2) the “public” was actually a serving house and 3) she was not wed when last I saw her, but the bump I had hoped might be a third and sagging bosom was actually more than three months along and 4) she was not out of her head about being with child when being turned out of Sumwattle so perhaps she was not out of her head about other things, it was clear to me that apprising Hughe of any of this was, well, pointless. So I decided to try to glean more information instead.

"Why is she here?" I whispered, pointing at the floor. "Here, in this place?" Was it my imagination, or was Gwynneth blushing?

"She lives here," Mrs. Frankwell said. "She married Rufus Bargesniffle three weeks ago." Her voice dropped. "Rumor has it they needed to get married quickly."

I thought I has misheard. "She is married?"

Susannah, if she is married she has lost her holdings, for you know the laws as well as I do. She must love Rufus very much, for even a small sum deposited for her 17 years ago would have increased handsomely over time. Perhaps Rufus was the father and we were wrong about everything.

Whatever the truth is, Gwynneth is wed to the son of the owner of the Rooster and Mussel and with child (and not in that order, God save her).

Before I could approach the poor wretch she scurried into the back room and Mr. Bargesniffle shooed us out into the cold.

However, next time neither rain nor snow nor night shall keep me from an appointment with the new Mrs. Bargesniffle.

I will write again when time permits, my dear. Until then I remain

So Very Fondly,

Annabella

18 January, 1821

Dear Susannah,

My mind has also rested much easier regarding Gwynneth. She is married and her child will not be a known bastard. The Rooster & Mussel is hardly the lap of luxury, but better than living in a hedge. The dowry of her trust will raise the family's standing in Wimbish. I believe she will be fine.

I write to you today to update you on my secret hideaway. It is adorable! I have spent the last several days sneaking the mattress out of the strange room by the sackful, to be burnt every night in my fireplace, as well the clothes that were ruined by moths or just too tarty to contemplate keeping. What a stench!

That left the dog collars and things that do not burn. I finally took them through the tunnel and off my private grounds, strewing them about the bog near the kitchens. I must have looked a mad sight, creeping about in the dark, flinging crops and such as far as I could. However, if anything turns up I will blame the ghosts.

Why should I not? Everyone else does. There have been new reports of the apparitions, heard late at night, pacing about and generally upsetting the entire staff. I remain blissfully unmolested and have given up trying to explain that if there are ghosts who are unhappy they would surely approach me first, as I am the only one who could change things to their satisfaction. At least I finally know the tale that began the rumours, and can share it with you.

After Quince purchased Wetmoor and Sir Manfredson had been taken away to live with his family the Hall went empty. Well, it had to, I did not even know Quince had done such a thing until he died. Grand and empty Halls are enticing to all sorts of people, Susannah: vagrants, thieves and drunks, mostly. That was what the land steward was engaged to do: keep people away from the Hall, and I suppose he did a good enough job. The damage we found when I moved here was not as bad as it could have been.

But Wetmoor was apparently very alluring to lovers.

Walker and Molly were both sixteen and promised to others upon reaching their majority. Then they met and of course fell hopelessly in love. They could not declare themselves, but apparently could not stay away from each other. They began to meet at Wetmoor in the boathouse next to the pond. The boathouse is like a house but with a space in the back for a rowboat. The front has a sitting room, kitchen, bedroom and small bath. It is quite charming.

One night, after a passionate reunion (they had been separated for two whole weeks!) Walker and Molly went for a stroll in the moonlight. Molly fell into the pond, which is far deeper than it appears. She could not swim, so Walker dove in to save her. This was chivalrous but, as it turned out, rather stupid. Walker was well named but swimming was not a skill in his possession.

The land steward discovered them the next morning as he performed his duties, both of them tangled in the plants that grow on one side of the pond. Unfortunately they had gone walking while nude. I am sure they thought it very wicked and erotic at the time, but in the end it was simply embarrassing for everyone. Perhaps that is why the steward drinks so much; he cannot forget the sight of those lifeless bodies, one of which had a turtle sitting on it when he found them.

Now everyone believes they haunt the Hall, which is silly, for they died in the pond. If they are here they should be lurking near the boathouse or in the water, not wandering about Wetmoor. There is also the question of why two lovers would choose to stay at the site of such undignified demises? They are likely either in Heaven or Hell. Before I moved to Wetmoor I would have said Hell, but since you have explained that romance does not automatically damn someone eternally I have not the vaguest notion of where they may have gone.

It does not matter what my ideas are: Walker and Molly are now firmly entrenched in the staff's thick skulls. However, they do serve a purpose now.

Susannah, do you have any idea how difficult it is to steal from oneself? I had no idea! But when creeping about late one night, gathering up down, cashmere blankets and pillows to put into my secret room, I realized they would be missed, for inventories are taken every month, and I was taking the best ones. I adore cashmere. I dithered for a moment, and then realized when it is brought to my attention I can blame it on Walker and Molly. Staff will be so relieved at not being accused of thievery they will immediately agree with me.

Servants are not the only ones who need someone to blame something on now and again.

My secret room is cozy and warm, whisper-soft blankets and throws piled high upon the bed, which is quite comfortable now that I have worked out how to tighten the ropes strung on the bed frame that hold the bedding off the floor. Two paintings now hang from the high hooks on the wall, for I could not remove the hooks no matter how I tugged at them. I used ribbon to get the paintings to hang at a normal height and tied great bows of it to cover the hooks themselves. It looks darling.

I am aware it sounds mad to be doing such things, but I have so little privacy. Servants are constantly in and out of my rooms, going through my clothing, etc., that I find I quite like the idea of something that is mine and mine alone. An added bonus is that if the social unrest continues and spreads to this county I can hide until the unwashed masses are done with their raping, looting and pillaging, so there is a practical aspect to making it comfortable.

I believe I am becoming quite eccentric, Susannah. Perhaps Manfredson was not mad after all. I find I am grateful for the diversions his folly has provided. An assignation room is no stranger than some of the brothels whispered about in London, and is certainly more discreet. I wish I could talk to Sir Manfredson about all of it, but he is mad, and I prefer for time to do its work and perhaps render him ignorant of his Hall and its specifics to my knowing everything. It is so delightful to make up reasons, which are all scandalous and exotic, than to know the truth, which is likely quite dull and prosaic. Except for the bit about the crops. I am beginning to wonder if Manfredson perhaps had no dreams of being a jockey, but instead had rather unusual inclinations.

Oh, that is silly, and shows how very bored I am out here in the country, with no equals about to amuse me.

I will close for now, for Mr. Sinclair will arrive soon with piles of papers, but wanted you to know of my project. I will write as soon as there is any more news, and until then I remain

Your Giddy Friend,
Annabella

♋ Gwynneth ♋

21 January, 1821

My dearest Susannah,

Oh, so much to tell you! More news on most every subject of interest!

Our theatrical troupe has become the focus of much news and excitement, with various romances springing up amongst the serving class, filled with passion and deceit. Of course I do not approve, but it is amusing to see various scenarios unfold in front of me, as if I were merely watching a play. Our after-rehearsal habit of retiring to the Rooster & Mussel, ostensibly to fortify ourselves against the cold trips home, has borne much rich and tasty fruit from the tree of gossip. I find that setting an example of appropriate moral character to the lesser classes in their own environment is gratifying on so many different levels. There is the most important gratification of lifting the level of discourse merely with one's own presence. I believe I may have ended a brawl before it began simply by clearing my throat. And whilst paying close attention for grammatical errors and flaws in education and breeding, one hears the tastiest tidbits. On any given evening, I am treated to a cornucopia of delightful news, as seen through the narrow prism of those who serve under stairs.

I would have never gone to the Rooster & Mussel without being involved in the musicale (which will be performed very soon, I know not how we will ever be ready), and would have never had the chance to speak with Gwynneth.

Yes, your eyes read right, on my most recent visit, Susannah, I dared speak to her.

I waited until Mrs. Frankwell (she seems quite excited to know a possible murderess) had gone outside to relieve herself, then watched as people passed the open door to the pub's main room. When Gwynneth passed it I called to her. She paused at the doorway and then entered, for customers are never to be kept waiting.

I asked for a port that I knew would not be available. She looked panicked and told me she had no knowledge of the cellars and it would be best to ask Mr. Bargesniffle. She said "mum" almost every other word, but I did not correct her regarding my station.

I told Gwynneth no harm was done, and that if the port did not exist, perhaps she could have a bottle of sherry brought to my table. She said she would, still hunched over, trying in vain to cover clear evidence of her condition. So much for falling into light conversation. I would, as it is always true with the lower classes, have to take the lead.

"Your name is Gwynneth, is it not?" I queried. Her head jerked up and she looked horrified.

"You know my name, mum?" she whispered.

"Only through mutual acquaintance, Gwynneth. I am Lady Upton-Church, and I am new to these parts. You and I have never been introduced."

"Oh. Hello, m'lady," she attempted an awkward curtsy.

"Hello." We stared at each other for a moment, and of course she looked away first.

"I understand felicitations are in order," I finally said, far too brightly.

"Lady?"

"On your marriage," I smiled in what I hoped was a warm way.

"Oh. That." She deflated even more, which I had not thought possible.

"Yes." She stood for a moment, and I was surprised to find myself pitying her. Obviously, she brought her dire straits upon herself, but it was rather sad. My own standards were coming dangerously close to becoming corrupted by too much time spent with inferiors.

Good evening then." Gwynneth turned away toward the door and an awful, quiet, forlorn snuffle issued from her.

"Are you all right?" I asked before I could stop myself.

"You're very kind, Lady," she sniffled. "It's the cold."

"Cold makes you weep?" I smiled at her feeble attempt to cover up her tears. "I think something else is making you weep. If you shared your burden with me, perhaps I could provide counsel. Sit down, and you can tell me what is wrong." She looked fearful but complied, and I found myself sitting at a table with Gwynneth, even as I watched with some amusement Mrs. Frankwell return, see her seat occupied and make a beeline for the table where Hughe sat.

"I remember you, Lady," she mumbled.

"We have never met, I am sure," I replied.

"You were there, Lady. My. . . my last day at Sumwattle. In your carriage."

I sipped my port and sighed. "My carriage was there, for I was invited. I would have been on time had we been given directions."

"So. . . you know."

"I am sure I do not, Mrs. Bargesniffle."

"You're bein' nice to me, even with that. You're a nice lady."

"Thank you. Now that we have that in the open, may I ask a question that may seem rude?"

"Why not? You know the worst already. 'Course I was lyin', the babe is Rufus'." Gwynneth was holding to her agreement with Lady Shardley, I was oddly glad to hear. She kept promises.

"You do not seem to have the happiness most of the newly married have," I said in a gentle tone.

"Oh. Well I'm lucky, I know that but me husband, Lady, 'e don't love me, only married me for the settlement."

"Settlement?"

"The settlement me husband is entitled to for marryin' me."

I was confused. She did not seem happy that Rufus Bargesniffle had her holdings, but she had married him. Of course, she was ruined, so perhaps had been grateful for a name to give her child.

"You have a dowry?" I finally queried.

"I guess, Lady, there was money to whoever'd marry me."

"You . . . you . . . you had means?" I could take to the stage, Susannah, I sounded truly surprised and confused.

"I did," she twisted her hands in her lap so much that I thought she would chap herself. But she did not seem happy.

"If you have means, Gwynneth, why did you marry a pub-keeper's son?"

Her whisper was filled with hurt and anger. "'Cuz I didn't know, Lady! I didn't, I swear! I didn't know 'til we was done and married, proper-like, at the church. It weren't 'til after that I found out, and then it's too late!"

I sat back, stunned. If this was true, then the picture has changed mightily, Susannah. We will know of a girl who could have been not one of our own, but at least hovering about the lesser end of the lower-middle class, robbed of her rightful inheritance and reduced to swabbing counters at the local serving house! For whatever reason Felicity must have never told her. She must have died before she could. I thought hard.

"Gwynneth, how did you learn of all this?"

"Mr. Bargesniffle, the owner, he used to work up at the Shardley place years 'n' years ago. He knew about it, said someone must have felt sorry me havin' such a rough start in life. He'd been waitin' for the chance to get his son around to marryin' me, but with me in such a state – " (here she gestured to her gently swollen stomach) " – it were easy, 'cuz who'd marry me when I ruint myself? When Rufus – that's me husband – asked I was so glad, and hungry and cold, it seemed a bargain, Lady. And now here I am with a babe on the way, a husband who don't love me and a father-in-law that just wanted me money."

She was right to be miserable; it is an awful situation. "And your own family?" I had a meagre hope she would tell me they were not who we think they are and then I could go on with my life without having to think about her anymore.

She dashed my hope. "Dead, mum. Me mum is. She died in a chimney sweepin' accident durin' the big spring thaw three years ago. Never thought she'd drown in a chimney, but there you go . . . Me father died before I was born. I never met him."

That explained why she did not know. Without that knowledge, she could not use it to leverage a proper match!

It would appear that regardless of this knowledge there is nothing to be done about it, for she is wed and the law is quite incontrovertible. I think.

I do feel badly that it has turned out like this, but wanted you to know that at least Gwynneth is not living in the streets, and although her circumstances do not appear to be happy, at least she does not appear to be abused, except by knowledge of her circumstances.

I must be off, and will write again when I have more news.

Your Snooping Friend,
Annabella

☙ Dithering ❧

17 February, 1821

My Dearest Susannah,

I fervently pray your trip to Lourdes was restorative, and that the baths proved to be as recuperative as rumoured. Pierre sounds a perfect concierge. How do you get them to attend to your every need without requiring instruction? It is an amazing talent, Susannah, and it seems that they always do exactly as you please.

You have been much missed as winter drags on and on. I wish I could come to Paris to visit! It is not possible, were I to leave for any period of time I am sure I would arrive home to find Wetmoor stripped bare and I would have to start all over again, except this time burdened with arrests and testimony and hangings of the men who stole from me on the first go. That is rather more than I wish to undertake, so I am staying until it is finished.

I am sorry to say the completion date has been pushed back again. I was first told the renovations would be done by May. I assumed given the general lack of focus and initiative in workingmen that it would instead be June. Now Mr. Wicklestaff is projecting a date in July! Can you credit it? If they fall as far behind schedule as they might, there may be no Opening Ball this year! There is nothing to be done about it now, and no point in worrying until it is warranted, but it was a blow all the same. I am not as strong in will as are you, Susannah, and confess that the news made me feel somewhat melancholy these last few days. I have been so excited about the completion, and now feel thwarted.

Do I sound terribly plaintive? I feel plaintive indeed, and apologize for bothering you with the trivial difficulties I have encountered. It is not from boredom; it has been bedlam lately, with the theatrical presentation, the Hall, and gossip, news and whispers all competing for my attention. Prior winters were complacent, but this one has kept me in a fair dither from morning until night.

I shall quickly dispense with the outcome of our little theatrical presentation: the musicale was presented to the public over two weekends with nary a fault. I was as proud of the performers as a goose is over her goslings, as they took to the stage before a quite excited audience. The singers and actors puffed up with pride at every outbreak of applause, and were quite overwhelmed at the response. It was more a diversion to keep them busy through the cold months, and I believe they almost forgot there was a point to all of the work, of which they were quickly reminded when the first sound of hands clapping sprang up from the darkened house of the town hall gathering room, which served as our theatre.

There is other news as well. During the final week before the "opening" and all the nights of performance I became a near fixture at the Rooster & Mussel, as the fortifying effects of their fare were more and more needed. I could also keep an eye on and ponder Gwynneth's situation, for I have found that although there is nothing to be done about her circumstances, it has been difficult to put her plight out of my mind. Clearly there is not enough to occupy it.

With every passing day Gwynneth's girth increases, as does her sorrow and general misery. I confess I have had more than one night of restless sleep, worrying about this creature. If her means have been swindled or tricked from her, it could happen to any of us. It nearly happened to me before I even knew I had lands and means! Of course, it could never happen to you, Susannah, as you are safely in the protection and care of your Lordship, but I, a woman making her meagre way alone in the world, could have had the same dire fate befall me!

Please do not think I compare my character with Gwynneth's in any way whatsoever. We may as well be from different continents, for all of our differences. What I mean is that I have mostly enjoyed the protection and decency of good men in my life, whilst Gwynneth seems to have suffered at less scrupulous hands (and definitely suffered from the effect other parts of their persons have had on her). If she has means, they should be hers, not tricked from her, using her unfortunate condition as a lever to lower her station even further! It galls me to think this may have happened.

That gall is what sped me to read through the old newspapers until I found the wedding announcement. I realized then that just because I read the rest of the newspapers I should not have stopped reading the announcements of births, deaths and marriages. It would have saved much time. I will avoid gossip, however, as I know from experience it is near all confabulation. Once I found the announcement I put pen to paper and wrote the Vicar Carthinston in Kingston Woods, who wed Gwynneth to Rufus Bargesniffle. I would like to hear the vicar's interpretation of events on that fateful wedding day, in hopes that Gwynneth is lying about having been swindled. If she is, then not only is she fallen but a liar as well, and I need not think on her anymore.

I am hoping to secure an appointment to meet with him (in the guise of adding my personage to his congregation, with the attendant tithes), to learn more.

But again, the clock speeds up whilst I am writing you! I must away for the weekend, once again leaving my tale undone! Please forgive the abrupt closure and know it is softened with the knowledge that I am

Your Fretting Friend,
Annabella

☙ A Very High Tea ❧

11 March, 1821

Dear Susannah,

I know you just received a letter from me, but I write to you today with delightful news: I just received my first guest to Wetmoor Hall. Of course I would have much preferred it be you, my oldest and dearest friend, but as you are in Paris it could not be helped. And my first guest may well have had to take precedence regardless, due to her title.

I have just received Baroness Gurthwant, Susannah. Can you credit it? I, a lowly lady (even more lowly when you consider I got my title from Quince, who was granted his in some secret ceremony by King George III, who may or may not have been in his right mind when he did it). Is that treasonous to say?

Never mind that. I received a baroness in my drawing room. I had promised Baroness Gurthwant I would invite her as soon as possible, for she was so very kind to me at the Shardley hunt.

In the interest of correctness, when I realized I could receive visitors, I sent an invitation to Baroness Gurthwant posthaste. I expected a refusal, for I was quite sure she had forgotten about having met me. Imagine my surprise when I received an immediate acceptance! Of course I turned staff nearly upside-down, for I wanted to make sure everything was as perfect as possible for her visit. I must say they outdid themselves: the parts of the Hall that are done were polished to a high gleam, Cook went mad in the kitchen preparing a perfect tea. I wore my best half-mourning gown and jewels, and drove staff near to distraction with re-checking everything throughout the morning. I was so very nervous! And then, when her grand carriage arrived, Taylor leaping to the door to help her down, I relaxed, for she greeted me with a huge smile and bussed me on both cheeks. She looked around at the foyer as Taylor took her cloak, and I realized that although I have become inured to the unfinished work, it must have looked awful to one such as she, and began to stammer out an explanation when she shushed me.

"Annabella – I may call you Annabella, mayn't I?"

"Of course, I would be most pleased."

"I understand the Hall is not finished. How could it be? Empty for years and you in it only seven months? I knew it would not be finished. I do not care. I want to see every inch."

"I would love to do exactly that. Shall I show you now, or would you prefer tea first?"

"Perhaps something to sip along the way. It actually appears larger from the inside, which I did not think possible." She peered up at the ceiling of the foyer, which echoed slightly from her words.

Constance was dispatched for champagne, as it seemed a celebratory moment. Crystal in hand, Taylor drifting behind in case we required anything, I provided Baroness Gurthwant with a tour of the public rooms of Wetmoor.

We had a most marvelous time, Susannah. Baroness Gurthwant is a delightful woman, and was so excited to the Hall. After she had seen everything we sat down in the drawing room to tea. The tennis courtyard, chapel and the ballroom impressed her greatly, and she explained that even the barony cannot boast tennis.

After Constance had served and withdrawn, Baroness Gurthwant lifted her crystal in a toast. "To your lovely home, Annabella."

"I am so pleased it meets with your approval."

"How could it not? It is a delight, a charm! Sir Manfredson never let anyone through the door, I know several people who tried to call in person. He referred to them as various members of royal families, thanked them for coming, and closed the door in their faces." We giggled at the idea. "So you can see, I have been waiting for literally years to see it."

"I was as astonished as you when first I saw it."

She put her cup down. "May I ask a personal question?"

"Of course, Baroness."

"Oh, please. When we are in private you must call me Sophia. 'Baroness' makes it sounds as if I am in my dotage."

"Of course, Sophia." I beamed to myself: I was asked to call a baroness by her Christian name!

"Why did you not come to Wetmoor before? I know it has an odd reputation, but I would have been wild to renovate it immediately."

This presented a conundrum. I did not want to appear ignorant, and the truth made me sound as if I were. Sophia sensed my hesitation and tilted her head meaningfully.

"Although you have no reason to credit me, I am incredibly discreet, Annabella. Not once has a secret entrusted to me found its way to the ears of another. Has my name ever been bandied about in your presence?"

"Of course not." I answered before thinking on it, of course, but on reflection I had spoken the truth.

"I love to keep secrets. Not tell them." She smiled so disarmingly that I was put at my ease, and realized that divulging the truth could not hurt me, even if it was discussed in larger circles.

"Sophia, I never came to Wetmoor because I did not know we – I – owned it."

She leaned forward. "Tell me everything."

So I did. I told her of how I found myself after Quince's death, the sole inheritor of the estate, including Wetmoor, which earned a gasp of admiration. I explained of Quince's long friendship with Sir Manfredson (beginning before Manfredson went mad, I was certain to emphasize), and his apparent decision to help an old friend in need by purchasing Wetmoor Hall which, being his folly, the land won in a terribly exciting hand of cards, was his own to buy or sell as he saw fit. The purchase ended Manfredson's by-then penniless state, but we had no need of the property; we had the London house, after all, so Quince had never told me. I only found out after he died.

Sophia was breathless. "You had a Hall and did not even know of it? How amazing! Tell me what happened next."

"Well, as you said yourself, I was astonished to find I owned a Hall and had never even laid eyes on it. So I decided to come here and see it for myself. I took one of my solicitors, and Taylor and Prudence, and Mr. Wicklestaff – he was there to make sure we did not fall through a stairway or somesuch – and I came to Wetmoor."

"What did you think?"

"At first the gray stone seemed gloomy and the gardens were long gone wild, so it seemed a foreboding appearance. I knew it was a folly, and was relieved to see no sign of whimsy – not a pineapple in sight."

Sophia leaned back and laughed. "Would that not have been awful? To find you owned a Hall and then find it to be ugly?"

"I was pleased to be incorrect. Then we went through –"

"What did it look like? When it was empty and abandoned?"

"It was filthy, of course, having stood empty so long. A great deal of woodwork had been torn out; for firewood, I suppose." I paused and sipped some of my own champagne.

"What are your rooms like?" I was surprised at the question, for I had only shown her the public rooms, but she was such a willing listener that I could not help myself.

"They are beautiful. They span the back of the Hall overlooking the property, the view from which is quite lovely. There is a bedroom, a sitting room – it seems to once have been an office for Manfredson, but is now a sitting room – a dressing room and a beautiful bath, complete with a huge copper bathing tub and an enclosed water closet. Those rooms do not have a Nature theme, which seems to be particular to the public rooms. They are paneled in linen-cut mahogany, and the plaster work is some kind of key design, according to Mr. Wicklestaff."

"But to leave London. . ." Sophia mused.

"I did not think I should ever leave London, I had lived there my entire life. But during mourning I came to hate the London house. Had I not moved to Wetmoor I would have to let a house somewhere else, and that seemed silly, for why let a house when you have a perfectly good Hall?"

"True enough," Sophia murmured. I poured out a bit more champagne before continuing.

"I asked Mr. Wicklestaff what it might take to become livable. He said it could be done, although the kind of workmen needed would sometimes have to come from London, there would be stops and starts that would be vexing, it would take the better part of a year to finish, and be expensive. It was sweet, for he seemed embarrassed to discuss the costs with me, a woman," at which Sophia and I both laughed. "Thankfully that was not a part of my considerations. I asked Mr. Sinclair to learn who the neighbours were, a simple enough matter, for I could not bear to find myself living amongst heathens or – dare I say it? – a lesser class of people."

Sophia laughed again. "Well, thank you! I have a house the next county over!"

I laughed with her as I poured her more champagne. "I did not know that then. I am dreadfully poor at geography, and Sir Manfredson is mad, so may have chosen to live in a horrible place."

"What were you told?"

"That this is one of the best counties in all of England and I was lucky to have a home here. It is fun, Sophia. I have an entire Hall to decorate and no reminders of the past."

"You miss your husband." She looked at me with pity.

I hate being pitied near as much as I hate being thought a murderess. I simply said, "I do. He was a good man."

Sophia sipped her champagne as she mulled something, then looked at me with an arched brow. "I imagine it is strange for you, being in charge of the entire estate."

This had to be handled carefully, for although I had no reason to doubt Sophia's assurances of discretion, there was also no reason to tell her everything. I sipped my champagne and then said, "Those were Quince's wishes."

"How do you do it? I would be at such a loss."

"I was. But I had a great deal of help, especially at first."

"And what of Mr. Sinclair?" Her eyes twinkled at me. "He comes here frequently. Is there a 'special' interest there?" I actually choked on my tea a bit.

"Oh, gracious no! Mr. Sinclair is, well, he is my solicitor. If I were to compare our relationship to any other, I would to liken it to having young brother. There is no 'special' interest between us. Nor shall there be." I almost shuddered at the thought of Mr. Sinclair as a suitor.

"And you cannot remarry."

"I can. I am not forbidden to do so."

"But if you do . . ." her voice trailed away and she raised a brow at me again.

This was beginning to border on the entirely-too-personal, in my mind, whether her purpose was mere curiosity or something more. "I am bound by the same laws as all women, Sophia. If I remarry the estate will go elsewhere." I thought it best not to say where, she may have been friends with the Bishop of Canterbury or the head of Cambridge.

Sophia tapped her fingernail on the side of her teacup as she considered this. "Were I in your position I would be disinclined to entertain remarriage as a possibility."

"I hope you are never in my position, Sophia. It came at great cost."

Sophia started and then looked down. When she looked up I was surprised, she seemed quite discomfited. "I am so sorry, I was not thinking."

"I know you were not being cruel." I wanted this part of the conversation to end. It reminded me too much of everything that I generally do not spend time thinking on: constraints, responsibility, all of the things that make life boring and occasionally vexing.

Sophia was not mollified. "Yet I was cruel. I was so carried away by the adventure you are living that I quite forgot it was preceded by much sadness. Please accept my apology."

"It is as accepted as it is unnecessary." I felt badly for her, she seemed genuinely distressed. We sat for a moment, for suddenly we were both rather embarrassed. Of course there is one very good solution to that problem. I picked up a bottle. "Would you like more champagne?" She smiled at me and leaned forward with her flute.

"I would love more champagne." I poured and we drifted to the dining room as the conversation drifted away from my situation to her own.

Sophia and her baron met in Austria, of all places, and she delighted in detailing to me their courtship and marriage, and said marriage was better on the second try. She absolutely adores the baron and considers herself very lucky to have found such a man. Do you know he does not keep mistresses? Given his rank and income it would be completely understandable, but he has told her she is more than enough for him. I credit he is likely the only baron in England to feel that way.

The afternoon waned and the sun was noticeably near the horizon before she took her leave. As we made our way to the foyer she glanced through the French doors in the ballroom leading to the veranda.

"You have not shown me the grounds, Annabella. I love gardens. Would you please show it me before I leave?"

"It is still wild, so we cannot walk about, but let me show you through the doors in the ballroom." I pointed out to her the boathouse, the formal gardens preceding the pond and the little forest beyond it. She was charmed by the patterns of fish laid into the stone of the veranda. The roses were of particular interest, and she asked many questions.

Finally Sophia had her fill of Nature and smiled. "I had a lovely time today, Annabella. You are a wonderful hostess." I thanked her for the compliment and then it was time for her to leave. She promised to invite me to her own home as soon as she returns to our little corner of England, for she will be returning to London with the baron until the middle of April.

I find I am looking forward to spending more time with Sophia, as we are very much alike, except for the part about her being happily married with four children and things having turned out properly for her. We are alike in our taste and sense of humor and enjoyment of life. I am enjoying my new life very much, Susannah. I did not think I would, and am sure there will be days in the future I long for my old life to be returned to me, but for now I find I am mostly content.

I say "mostly" because once again, correspondence and business decisions in the person of Mr. Sinclair await me. He finds it exciting to travel for business purposes, as it makes him feel worldly. We must meet with the cottagers again, but their requests have noticeably diminished since Christmas, and they seem to be getting on bit better. Their complaints are mostly the kind the lower classes always indulge in: accusations against each other of greed, theft, malingering, etc. It is quite dull, but they take it very seriously. Then, when they are gone, Mr. Sinclair offers his ideas, I offer mine, and we take turns in determining the appropriate decision. Neither of us wants sole responsibility, so it seemed the best thing to do, and no one has started screeching or keening when hearing decisions, so I suppose we must be doing all right.

One thing I am thankful for is that there is nothing sordid in the papers Mr. Sinclair brings. I still receive letters from lecherous men and amuse myself by filing them according to offers made, requirements expected, etc. It amuses me and makes it rather less tawdry. I think.

Write me as soon as you can, and in the meantime, I remain

Your Society Friend,

Annabella

☙ The Vicar of Kingston Woods ❧

17 March, 1821

Dearest Susannah,

I have news of my visit to Kingston Woods. News that changes everything. Again.

As you know, I had decided to visit the small parish where Gwynneth and Rufus' wedding took place, and had writ Vicar Carthinston to that effect – without of course, giving away the true purpose of my visit. He was thrilled to imagine additional tithes to his purse, and eagerly wrote back to welcome me any time I wished to visit, asking to be notified in advance so he could set aside time in his schedule to personally meet with me.

I set out to meet with him as soon as possible, which was last Saturday.

When meeting with the clergy it is best to put one's best foot forward, so I chose my apparel with great care within the limitations of light mourning protocol (I look forward to the day I can abandon grey and black!). I wore a silk gown which showed my bosom to great advantage, my hair was swept up in a new bonnet. I ordered it from Paris, Mme. Danielle's shoppe on the Rue di Rivoli. She has wonderful hats.

For my retinue I chose Taylor, as he has lately been much moping about. Still, he is young and easily distracted, so I decided the country would be just the thing to lift his spirits. I was surprised he did not think a visit to a parish in a far-flung corner of the county would be enjoyable, but Taylor has never really spent time with Nature. Cook packed lunch (I had no idea how long it would take to get to the town of Kingston Woods), as well as plenty of brandy and cognac. It still gets quite cold in the evenings here, as well you know, and I thought it would be good to maintain on hand as a medicinal.

I also selected Constance, my new parlour maid, instead of taking Prudence, which would be the norm. I wanted to get to know Constance a bit before she is turned loose in the better parts of the Hall. I know not how she may work out, although she was highly recommended by Duke Twitwhistle.

The duke, by all accounts, took an active interest in Constance's training. Regardless, she seems by any measure to be a bit of a flit. She shrieks if one walks up behind her, piles her furniture in front of her door before turning in for the night and her top is constantly coming undone. It seems the buttonholes are fair worn out, but until new ones arrive for her she has to make do with the uniform she has. Duke Twitwhistle has appalling taste in staff uniforms – I shudder to think what his house may look like. Constance is pudgy, unfortunately, which does not help when one's uniforms are poorly cut. That should be resolved when her new uniforms arrive, but for now she looks slightly dishevelled.

Despite these flaws Christian compassion demanded I at least try her out, for she does seem sweet. Happily the nervous nausea that first overcame her every morning when she entered my employ has ceased, and she seems to be settling in nicely.

Constance was apparently quite overwhelmed at being included in our travelling party, and Cook had to explain that I was not taking her to Church to test her prior religious instruction, nor to decry her as a harlot (where that idea came from I do not know).

Constance stayed in the carriage with me and Taylor rode next to Driver. Taylor found a pair of pistols from somewhere in case brigands overtook us on the road.

By the way, for all of my complaining, I adore Driver. He has the face of a raisin and a sense of humor to match: withered and shriveled and utterly without charm, but he is also an expert horseman. He is rather old, and although I was perfectly within my rights to let him go when he lost his leg in the accident, I keep him as a reminder of Quince. He reminds me of Quince in some ways: the tremor in his right hand, the rheumy cough, the squinty right eye and hunched-over appearance. If one's husband's name is the same as a shrub whose seeds are made into jelly, one should be wary about the external effect such a name might have upon their aspect. Quince's insatiable inquisitiveness could be amusing and his passion for tinkering did indeed increase his coffers almost ridiculously, but it was that passion that led to his death.

Where was I?

Oh, yes, going to Church.

It was a lovely day and I felt thoroughly jolly, as I always do when embarking on an adventure. I could hear Taylor chatting at Driver, who stayed silent save for the odd grunt or cough. Constance stared out the windows as we went along, answering my questions with a brevity and quietness that reminded me of Prudence. Once it was clear that light conversation was not going to occur I gave up and we each stared out the windows. It became a long ride. I would have taken a medicinal but wanted to remain sharp of thought when meeting with the vicar, so abstained.

The parish was nearly three hours' away and we had to go through the village of Kingston Woods first. I should be surprised to hear if you had any knowledge of the place, Susannah, as it was quite, well, unseemly is the only word that comes to mind. It is a collection of huts and shops, all with a general air of malaise and dissoluteness that I found quite startling, until I realized there were no members of nobility in the area. Then I understood. This is what happens when the lower classes congregate on their own, without the discerning eye of their betters to keep them on the straight and narrow.

Thankfully the village was very small and we travelled through it to the parish on the opposing outskirts in mere moments. Vicar Carthinston was waiting for us, a nervous smile on his face.

Taylor helped me exit, and Constance made her ungainly way out of the carriage while the vicar beamed in what I am sure he thought was a warm and welcoming way.

"Good day to you, Lady Upton-Church," he said, still beaming. It was difficult but I managed to beam back. Vicar Carthinston lacked the vicarly qualities I had expected. His waistcoat, although once presumably quite fine, was dingy and frayed, as were his cuffs. His hair blew about in the wind, as he was without wig or pomade. His mouth was crowded with teeth mismatched both in size and colour (much like the stones in the cemetery to the left) and I am certain he had not bathed since the last High Holy Day. I should have expected as much, given the parish he had been assigned and the state of whatever congregants happened to be in Kingston Woods, but since those were also unexpected, I remained startled.

I near stepped back from breath that would scare away the Devil himself and Constance cowered into her cloak under the too-bright gleam in Vicar's eye. Taylor seemed distressed that this man of the cloth was his better. In this case I must admit that this "gentleman" certainly seemed inferior to his inferiors.

We stood for a moment until Vicar remembered himself and invited us to the rectory. It was as miserly and dark as the rest of the parish and grounds. With Driver, Taylor and Constance safely stowed in the hallway, Vicar and I sat to tea brewed by a cook that appeared to be more of a "working" girl, especially since she appeared to be working for a vicar. As that could become fuel for our conversation, I declined comment. However, I did raise an eyebrow forcefully, as one cannot give the appearance of approval of everything. What would society become if the upper classes never commented on probable craven behaviour? So I raised my eyebrow, at which the vicar at least had the grace to look embarrassed.

We sipped our tea and Vicar asked from where I came, he was sure I was not from Kingston Woods proper. Of course I am not from Kingston Woods, only the last dregs of society that have been flung away from decent towns live in Kingston Woods! I bit my tongue (hard) to prevent myself from upbraiding him for placing myself and Kingston Woods together in a sentence, let alone his mind, and told him that we were from Wetmoor Hall. It is famous enough that he would know with whom he was dealing.

He was surprised and not a little suspicious that we should have come so far to see his Church, especially when my town has its own much more proper parish.

I allayed his suspicion by explaining that whilst my own Church is lovely, from time to time I enjoyed travelling to other towns in order to make my acquaintance with the clergy, as philanthropy combined with religious themes is my most favoured pastime (it is not, but he would not know that), and the clergy are such fonts of creative ideas for the beneficiaries of such philanthropy, as well as the form such a donation could take. As I own Wetmoor Hall, the vicar knew exactly what kind of donation I was capable of making.

I added that I heard specifically of his parish from a former maid who attended a "lovely" wedding there just a few weeks past, and that vicar had seemed to her so "kind, moral, upright, the very type of man a vicar should be." It was her charming endorsement that brought me to his door.

The balm of such ridiculous flattery laid his suspicions to rest and he smiled his snaggled best at me, while attempting (with virtually no success) to lift his eyes to mine, since they were firmly fixed upon my bosom.

Well, we ladies have so few advantages that I took that one by leaning further forward. "In fact, Vicar," I whispered, "I have been given to understand that from time to time you assist in . . . unusual matches."

"What mean you?" he queried. I heaved a great sigh and squeezed my hands together. This physical rearrangement had the effect I was hoping for: Vicar was besotted with my attributes.

"I understand that occasionally arrangements are made which are helpful to the married couple or their families, that may not, under scrutiny of gentlemen, give off the compassionate glow that was surely intended."

That seemed to confuse him. I decided to distract him even further, deliberately crossing my ankles in front of him, with my feet out from under my skirt. I pretended it was unthinking, but it was quite the opposite. Susannah, I felt like a common trollop. It was all Vicar could do not to faint as I continued to try to draw him out with a tale similar enough to what we fear Gwynneth's to be, that he might commiserate.

"If a girl had had a small dowry that could gain her a husband, then found herself in such condition that a suitable husband was quite . . . unlikely, and she was off the market. You see, the servant of friend of mine has. . ." I trailed off and wiped a faux tear from my eye. "The reputation of my friend's house could become tainted by a servant . . . They will do anything to prevent scandal." I trailed off, unable to think of anything else to say. It is more difficult to dissemble for a good reason as opposed to avoid social embarrassment. Luckily Vicar thought my silence was due to embarrassment over what I was describing.

"I had such a situation just a few months ago," Vicar murmured as I re-crossed my ankles.

"You did? I am astonished . . . " I dropped my voice as low as it would go and leaned so far toward Vicar that I was in danger of being betrothed myself by the time the meeting was over. "What happened?"

"There was a girl, a silly girl who'd gotten herself in trouble, lost her post, all alone in the world. You know, the sort of thing that happens to these silly girls all the time."

"Yes, go on . . ."

"Well, a man said his son would marry her all right. I was surprised because the man in question could have made a better match for his son. He's not nobility, but he's a hard-working man with an honest business. I was surprised he wanted his son to marry a ruined girl without any dowry."

"Really," I fanned my bosom, pantomiming fascination at the story. I would swear he twitched every time one of my fingers brushed my own skin. But I was getting what I wanted: confirmation.

"He said she had a dowry all right, and it was big enough to overlook the defect on her part."

"So you – helped – them?"

"Why not? The girl got a husband she'd not have otherwise, the son got a wife guaranteed to be properly grateful to him, the entire family would benefit. Everyone profits."

"Everyone save the girl, you mean," I could not help the retort. He snorted at the statement and sat up straight, shaking off my charms for the moment.

"Lady Upton-Church, you are naïve, as is appropriate for a lady of your station. A girl such as she – she's lucky, that's all I can say."

"What did she say about her dowry going to that family?"

"She said nothing. I do not believe she knew of it."

"You did not tell her?"

Vicar leaned forward and spoke kindly. "Lady, with the marriage came a generous contribution to our coffers, which was quite welcome, I'm sure you can imagine." He waved his hand around at our surroundings, and I near shuddered to think what it may have been like before the contribution. "With the family new members of my congregation, and this young thing Churchless herself, I realized their silence in the matter was Christian kindness, so she would not be burdened, as she has been with all other things, with the guilt that would come from finding out how far from her true station she has fallen, merely through her own failings and weaknesses. For me to go against her new family and perhaps create conflict or even cause the wedding to be cancelled – that was not something I believed to be in anyone's interest."

With that speech I had more information than I thought possible. Gwynneth was swindled! By Mr. Bargesniffle, no less, and I can no longer appear at the Rooster & Mussel, unless it is to speak to Gwynneth myself, but to be a patron and further line the purse of a man who would steal away a girl's means – I was incensed. But I was still with the vicar, so endeavored to hold my tongue. I am sure the blush that invaded my cheek was misinterpreted as interest of less than a noble kind (God save me!), but I could not help it. And there was the vicar, smiling with pride at the "great" match he had made, the only price being that of a young girl's future.

"Well, then," I leaned back so my décolletage would be less obvious, and put down my tea cup.

"Well, then, indeed," he stammered, confused by the abrupt change in my tone.

"You have an extraordinary parish, Vicar." He took that as a compliment, which was my intent. I rose as imperiously as I am able, which is considerable. "It is also clear that your coffers are far richer than other parishes in far more dire straits."

His smile faded as his brain began to process the actual meaning of my words. Which were brought on by his own.

"So I must take your leave, dear Vicar, and set out to find a parish in true need. Thank you ever so much for your time, it was quite educational." As I walked toward the door, Taylor, my ever-ready footman, pulled the door open from the other side. I swept past his murmured "I heard your heels clicking, Lady," brushed past Constance and with a nod to Driver, announced our immediate departure.

Vicar stood with his mouth agape as Driver clambered up the side of the carriage with his wooden leg tucked under his arm. I was surprised he was not waiting for us atop as he normally does – he does not like for people to see him clambering up and down, for he says he must remove his leg in order to accomplish it. Something about there not being a knee anymore. I suspect he is exaggerating, but the fact remains that Driver likes to only be seen on or off the carriage, not at some point in between. But sometimes I find him as I did that day, sitting on the carriage step, scratching his stump. I have spoken to him time and again about not taking his leg off in public no matter how severe the itch, but occasionally he forgets. This time I was rather glad of it. It certainly dismayed Vicar. Taylor opened the door and helped me in, and Constance clambered in behind me.

Taylor checked the door closures and climbed up next to Driver, and we pulled away and began the long journey home.

Like all returns, it seemed far longer than the travelling to. Once out of Kingston Woods Constance seemed relieved. She even offered that it was nice to be going back to Wetmoor.

Suffice it to say that I was so upset, with no one available to hear my tale, that I partook liberally of the brandy packed with our lunch. As I never partake alone if possible, I had Constance pour for herself as well. I could tell she was pleased by the honour, her blue eyes shining as she shyly raised her glass to my generosity (and then coughed with the first sip; she is not accustomed to decent brandy). We sat on opposite sides of the carriage, sipping quietly, each lost thought. I am sure mine were more complicated.

We each had another brandy and I was musing over what I should do next about Gwynneth when I was interrupted by the strangest sound.

Constance was asleep. It was completely inappropriate, she snoring away while sitting opposite me. I had heard she is fairly abstemious in her habits and frequently forgoes her wine ration, but a mere brandy or two should not have been enough to undo her. I cleared my throat loudly once or twice and even assayed a cough, but she was dead to the world.

The issue was settled when the carriage jerked out of a rut and she fell on the floor. I stifled a giggle as she peered about the confines of the carriage, clearly confused and then mortified. She leapt to her feet and hit the top of her head on the roof of the carriage, causing Driver to halt. I rapped on the roof of the carriage with my parasol and we began to move again. Then I must admit I did giggle. Shamelessly. Constance turned several shades of red, and I struggled to not let loose peals of laughter. Then she made it worse.

"Lady," she said, "I apologize mostly truly. I appear to have been overcome with . . . something."

"I think the word you are searching for is 'brandy', Constance." I tried to sound officious, and bit my lip hard to keep from smiling.

"I would beg your leave, Ladyship, to withdraw from the carriage in case it is . . . catching."

"Constance, I do not believe we should have to scoop you from the road each time you fall off the top of the carriage. You shall stay in here, for goodness' sake, and the next time I offer you brandy you are to say 'Kingston Woods' to remind me that you are sensitive. Oh, do sit down, you are going to fall on top of me if we hit another rut."

Her face flamed scarlet at the thought and she sat down quickly, now wide awake and still horrified.

"I do not often partake of spirits, Ladyship," she unnecessarily confessed.

"From now on you should stay with less powerful libations."

"I shall. I am so very sorry –"

Poor thing, she likely thought I might discharge her. "Oh, Constance, it is half my fault. I offered and you likely felt you could not refuse. Shall we leave it at that?"

"I would be grateful to," she sighed.

"But do try to stay awake for the rest of the ride home. It would not do at all."

"Of course. Thank you." She smiled at me and I was thankful the episode was ended, although it was quite amusing whilst it occurred.

The rest of the ride home was silent, and I whiled away the time watching Constance go from slightly inebriated to rather queasy to an awful headache to a terrible bout of drowsiness to full recovery, the entire time desperately trying not to show any of it on her face. I have decided she is a dear girl. Her inability to partake of spirits is a good sign. On our arrival at Wetmoor she fair leapt from the carriage (and only stumbled once).

The day was fruitful: Now I have the barest bones of this mystery, Susannah, but the principals (and principles) elude me. Gwynneth was not lying, but rather, was lied to. By everyone, from what I can tell. It seems in the near future I shall be poring over county records and Church notices or, more likely, paying someone else to do it for me discreetly. I cannot tolerate the thought that poor, horse-faced Gwynneth has been ill-used. Is not her life already sorely afflicted?

I shall write again soon, darling friend, but have realized the truly gargantuan proportions of this missive, and do not wish you to suffer eyestrain during the reading of it.

So adieu, and know I remain

Ever So Fondly,

Annabella

☙ A Disastrous Night ❧

22 April, 1821

Dear Susannah,

I know this missive has been slow to arrive, but have been so busy with financial decisions. I have also been busy with the cottagers, whose ire seems to have arrived with the spring flowers, so that their petitions took much longer than normal to sort out. They are now mollified, but were very annoying this month. I wish I could make them leave, but apparently it is not done, although it would be much easier if they did. Apparently as long as they pay their rents they can stay, or something like that; once it was clear I could not remove them from my lands I stopped paying attention to the reasons for such ridiculousness.

More importantly, I asked Mr. Sinclair to investigate Mr. Bargesniffle – discreetly, of course – as the man seems to have far more information regarding Gwynneth and her dowry than the owner of a pub should have gleaned from servants talking about their houses. It happened too long ago for it to be of any note now, I think, especially as servants in general do not have long tenures at Sumwattle. Mr. Sinclair has become accustomed to my odd requests, and promised to undertake the enterprise with the same discretion displayed in all other ventures.

All of that business left me, quiet vexedly, without time for personal correspondence! But now I can spend more than a few precious moments to compose a proper letter to you. I do not know how I shall fare in arranging my thoughts, and beg your forgiveness if this comes weighed down by ponderousness and gravitas, as I update you on the latest news from the country.

I was sorely disappointed to have missed you at Baron Gurthwant's birthday festivities two weeks ago. I accepted the invitation with alacrity, so pleased to have been included by Sophia. My time has been sorely taxed by the requirements of the Hall, and it had been far too long since I had spent time with my equals (the denizens of the Rooster & Mussel not even remotely counting as such), and I assumed rightly that Sophia's guest list would far exceed anything Lady Shardley may host. It was, I realized, the first event I have attended in longer than I care to admit. I know you had to stay in Paris with your Lordship, but sometimes I think the Crown may not understand how inconvenient its demands might be. Is that treasonous to say? However, you missed the most outrageous situation! Tragically, I was part of it.

One of the things which I was looking forward to doing with you was strolling through the Gurthwant gardens, as I am looking for new ideas for Wetmoor (if it is <u>ever</u> finished). My understanding is that Baroness Gurthwant has astonishing grounds.

It took longer than I thought it might to arrive at the barony, being one county over, and I was grateful to find my gown was appropriate to the event. It was very tight around the bodice, a deep gray – nearly black – covered with silver embroidery. My corselet was positively stifling in the warmth of the spring air, but I looked fantastic, which was all that mattered. As soon as I was announced, Baroness Gurthwant herself introduced me to a whirl of titles, all of whom seemed very interested in making my acquaintance. I must get out more. After that social requirement was fulfilled she turned to me.

"Exhausted?"

"Somewhat. I have not been to anything like this in a very long time."

She smiled and patted my arm. "You did beautifully, Annabella, and you look lovely tonight."

"Thank you."

"Would you like a turn around the grounds? Dinner will not be served for a while yet."

"You are very kind." I was grateful for the offer.

The grounds reflected the beauty of the house itself, being astounding (although a bit smaller than Wetmoor), and the variety of the gardens left me very impressed and not a little envious of Baroness Gurthwant's taste. I felt the amateur in comparison with her accomplishment in this area. She is almost Olympian in her interest. Of course, after meeting the baron for the first time I understood her desire to be out-of-doors, supervising herself into exhaustion.

Although the baron is, at first glance, the very picture of sophistication and dash, on closer inspection one becomes aware of an . . . well, I don't know any other way to put it but <u>aroma</u>. Were he not a baron I might use the word "stench." It is positively alarming. I thought perhaps he had just been dragged out of a bog, but that was not the case. It was him. Himself. That is when I understood Sophia's penchant for perfumes and colognes, which I had noticed at both the hunt and tea, and also explained why she had rose petals up her nose when she greeted me at the party. I thought the habit was a new French style, but it seems to be borne of necessity, as opposed to following fashion slavishly.

The baron was flawlessly turned out, his suit spotless, not a hair out of place – and thick, too, which is so rare. It was his person that is the difficulty.

Sophia clearly has thought her way around this issue, and occasionally a smidge of petal fluttered in her nostril when she smiled. She sounded a bit as if she had a cold, but her enunciation was marvelous considering the handicap under which she laboured. Dashing her husband might be, but I could only imagine dashing away from him.

We chatted of things inconsequential until other guests demanded his time. Sophia took my arm as we strolled away from the cluster on the veranda.

"I have never had the pleasure of meeting the baron before tonight, Sophia."

"Did you hear about the Beggars' Ball we had last spring?"

"I read about it in the newspaper."

Sophia giggled and quite un-self-consciously blew some loose rose petals into a dainty lace handkerchief. "It was a smashing success. Everyone had to come as guttersnipes and pickpockets and the lowest classes of people imaginable!" She then opened her purse, fished out a little packet and replaced the petals that had found their freedom.

"They did not!"

"Yes," she smiled at the memory. "The baron and I were the King and Queen of Thieves, the children were street urchins. Duke Twitwhistle and Baron Theosophus were common beggars!"

"What an original idea!"

"It was such fun! Everyone got into the spirit of it, after getting into the spirits a bit, of course, making believe they were Cockney or Dorsett or lower High Street."

"I am so sorry I missed it."

"As am I. You would have been a charming maid," and we both laughed merrily at the idea. "It was a very helpful façade, what with my husband's difficulty."

"Difficulty?"

"Oh, you are a dear woman, Annabella, but surely you noticed something about the baron is bit . . . off. The theme of Beggars was a perfect disguise."

"He seems a lovely man, Sophia."

"Oh, he is, and I love him dearly. But it can be difficult, especially when the flowers begin to fade in the face of oncoming winter. I understand his first wife had some sort of nasal abnormality, so his unfortunate condition was of no consequence. On the other hand, I have no such olfactory diminishment. So you see, the petals, they are very helpful."

"I understand."

"I have begun to plan a greenhouse. That way I can garden year-round."

"How brilliant!" We picked our way through the gardens as she led me to where the greenhouse is to be constructed. We were quite far from the house itself, the party itself receding as we walked. The site was behind a large hedgerow past the glorious gardens and a small pond, and as we walked along one side of the hedgerow we realized there were others on the opposite side. It was not until we were strolling right next to its imposing border that we even realized it.

"The cheek of you . . ." a voice said from the other side of the hedge. It was a man who clearly had breeding. Sophia put her finger to her lips, smiling impishly about the gossip we might overhear. We edged closer to the hedgerow, for there is nothing like a good bit of gossip to make a party memorable.

"The cheek of me!" said a girl's voice, which was clearly not well-bred. Sophia and I exchanged glances, eyes widening. "If you'd left the cheek alone or even left off at the cheek I wouldn't be in this mess!"

"How dare you –" the man sputtered. Sophia and I held our breaths – this was unbelievable. And delicious.

"They tol' me, didn't they," the girl hissed at him. "They said, 'Stay away from that one, girl, stay away. He likes 'em young and he likes 'em fetchin', that's why you got the job, but don't go into the wine cellars with 'im, don't go. We've lost so many that way, girl, if he asks you there you just faint or swoon, or say that missus needs something and get Cook to go,' but no, I were stupid, weren't I? I thought, sure he might be randy but 'e's old, and with that gout couldn't catch me if he tried. But then you were 'Try this brandy, girl, how's the cognac?' and sayin' all manner of nice things like you meant 'em. You seemed nice, but you weren't, were you, you were just like the boys down the pub but better-soundin', because all you wanted was a girl that'd make you feel young and you'd tell 'er anythin' to get what you's wanted."

"That is not true," the male voice said. "How can you say that after the kindnesses I've showered on you?!"

"I'll tell you how – what you've showered me with has got me up the spout!"

Although it was a near thing, after a moment it was clear that Sophia's and mine own gasps were masked by a similar gasp from the man. Sophia and I crept closer to the hedge, Sophia trying to keep the petals up her nose. ("Not as easy as it looks", she murmured, as we positioned ourselves to not miss a single word.)

"I'll have no girl in my house who has fallen," he said gravely.

"If that were true, SIR, then you'd have no women in your house at all, save your wife," she retorted.

"Have your things packed and be gone by morning," said the man. "You are dismissed."

"If you do I'll –"

Then the most unfortunate thing happened, Susannah. Sophia sneezed. Rose petals showered from her nose and silence issued from the other side of the hedge. But I was thinking quickly.

"Come here, Sophia," I said loudly, grabbing her hand. "Is this where the greenhouse is to be constructed?" After running a few feet back, I tromped as hard as my feet would allow back up to the hedgerow.

"Yes it is," Sophia replied, with volume to match, clapping softly at me to show her pleasure. "The hedge shall hide it."

"What will you do when it is complete?"

Her expression showed that the last thing she cared about in the world was her greenhouse. "I have not yet decided."

We then strolled along slowly, chatting and praying our ruse was not discovered, Sophia absent-mindedly brushing petals from her bodice. We reached the end of the hedgerow and looked at each other. Just as we stepped forward the very man in question came around from the other side.

"Lord Shardley," said Sophia, tilting her head at him coolly. When I saw him I gasped, for I could not credit my ears, Susannah! It was Lord Shardley! The same Lord Shardley of Sumwattle Estate! Unfortunately, when I gasped, I brought the sum total of my gasps in the last minute to two, which is more than my corselet, or the parts of me stuffed into the corselet, can bear. I swooned, quite to my vexation, right then and there next to the hedgerow.

As Sophia informed me later, I actually swooned into the hedgerow, but am assured the scratches shall fade in no time.

I awoke in a guest room, where a maid sat by to fan me. My corselet had been loosed and I looked around. The room was small but beautifully appointed. I lay on a feather bed, surrounded by four posts covered in blue damask. The furniture was cherry, from the Americas, and held a lovely sheen. The maid scurried to my side.

"You'll be fine, mum, you just had a little moment is all," she assured me, while helping me to sit up. "The baroness had you brought here for privacy."

"Thank you, girl. That was very kind." She handed me a cup of lemonade and pulled a summoning cord.

"Baroness didn't want you left alone a minute and I just let Pauline, the downstairs maid, mum, know you was awake so's she could tell the baroness." The maid glanced at the summoning cord. "Never got to pull that before, mum."

"Well, hurrah for you," I handed her the cup and leaned back on the pillows.

"Sort of interestin', isn't it?" she prattled on. "Pull a string and someone comes." I didn't respond and she thankfully fell into silence.

After a few moments, the swish of skirts and click of heels announced the arrival of Sophia. She entered the room and sat immediately by my side.

"Sophia, please accept my apologies – my new corselet – the measurements must have been wrong and it is ever so much more tight –" I began.

"I shall not hear another word on the subject, Annabella," she said, patting my hand. "You have helped make my party a smashing success. That corselet of yours should be knighted!"

"Whatever do you mean?" This was an unlikely turn of events.

"It happened after you lost your senses." Suddenly she realized there was a servant in the room. "You may take your leave," she told the girl, who scurried out like a mouse. "No need to provide more grist for their mill," she smiled. "How did you save my party? Well, let me tell you . . ."

According to Sophia, I swooned most dramatically into the hedgerow, where the decorative ribbons on my gown became hopelessly entangled. As she called for help, she eyed Lord Shardley suspiciously. He had the grace to be flustered, as footmen and others streamed from stables and the carriage lane down to where I would have lain were it not for the hedgerow, but instead to where I dangled.

Lord Shardley finally said, as the first of the servants neared, "Sophia, I have always understood your discretion to be absolute."

"As long as situations are correct I am absolute," she replied, tugging on my ribbons. "However, when a situation is patently unfair to one side or another I have less equilibrium, which makes discretion difficult." The first servant arrived and it was Hughe, who has been enslaved at Sumwattle Estate for several weeks. I have not seen him for ages and did not see him then, due to being unconscious.

"Lady!" he cried, knocking Lord Shardley over in his eagerness to help free me. As the Lord struggled to his feet, helped by less fleet-of-foot footmen, Hughe lifted me so the ribbons hung loose enough to be untangled from the hedge. Lord Shardley was sputtering with anger, which Sophia quickly smothered with courtesy.

"Thank you so very much, Hughe, I do not know what we should have done without your assistance," she cooed to him.

"I know this Lady," he said to her, holding me in his arms and still managing a fairly deep bow to Sophia. "Lady is good and nice. Who hurt Lady so?" He glared at Lord Shardley.

"Well, I never. . ." said Shardley, who appeared to be ready to draw his sword on Hughe. Suddenly guests began arriving to see what the tumult was about.

"Apparently you have. At least a few times," murmured Sophia, with a most pointed look in his direction, which caused Shardley to deflate.

Baron Gurthwant, most alarmed at the upset, pushed his way to the front of the crowd gathered at the hedgerow. As he stood near my head I began to sneeze and cough. However, Sophia took his arm and led him away, at which point I lapsed again into a faint. It was decided by Sophia that Hughe should carry me to the house, the servants would return their posts, and a gavotte be danced in my honour by the guests, with a champagne toast to celebrate the party overall. A drunken cheer arose from the guests, the servants returned to their duties, and Hughe carried me to the house, led by Sophia and the baron.

Having caught me up on the goings on Sophia smiled at me. "Hughe seems very fond of you, Annabella."

"He is very sweet," I agreed. "But I was really hanging from a hedgerow by my gown ribbons? In front of everyone?"

"It was tremendously exciting," Sophia said, confusing horror with pleasure. "The last time we had a really good swoon was at Duke Finchley's summer party, with that *faux* bull fight that turned out to be less faux and more fatal. And it happened very quickly, no one saw your person. The hedgerow kept you from ruining your gown as you would have if you swooned into the mud, so it is perfectly all right. You know as well as I, Annabella, that holding one's head high and continuing as if nothing were the matter is the major portion of maintaining a reputation in such a small corner of the Empire." She looked at me with a twinkle in her eye.

"Yes, that is true. I suppose." I fell silent, and suddenly the reason for my swoon came rushing back. "But what about the servant? And Lord Shardley? What shall happen?"

"Well, I admit I am more than somewhat intrigued by what we heard tonight. It shall be impossible for us to glean the truth of the matter from either party, but it may be possible to obtain that information from someone already in the house. I understand Hughe works as footman to Lady Shardley?"

"You are brilliant," I breathed.

"And you should not go home unattended, my dear." She made a great show of fluffing a pillow, but apparently had not ever done such a thing, and it wound up pushed up around my face. "Hughe will go with you. His devotion to you is charming, and Lord Shardley is in no position to refuse such a simple request from me. It is in his best interests to accede to my wishes."

"You are not just brilliant, Sophia, you are wicked as well."

"Thank you, dear," she smiled again. "How do you feel?"

"Ever so much better."

"The maid shall bring you a wrap – that corselet absolutely must not be re-laced, so the wrap shall properly cover you. Hughe will carry you down and get you settled in your carriage. He shall need to stay on at your stables overnight – it will be far too late for his return, and he will also be available should you need his services. I, on the other hand, must oversee the rest of the party, so must take your leave," she smoothed her skirts and stood.

"I am so grateful for your generosity, Sophia,"

"Oh, tosh," she shushed me. "As I have always said, it is not a successful party until someone has swooned. We shall meet again soon and can then take the time needed to ponder the things we have overheard tonight. But for now I must make sure the champagne is still chilled and the fireworks moved far enough away from the stables – we had a bit of difficulty last year with that. So adieu, and feel better soon."

"Thank you." With that Sophia swept from the room. As soon as she left the maid brought me a wrap and Hughe carried me down to my carriage. Thankfully the house was empty of guests – they were all assembling on the veranda for the fireworks display. Hughe settled me in the carriage very gently.

"I miss you Lady," he said simply. I suppose it was from my already overwrought condition that I found myself moved by his sincerity, for I have seen him only rarely since the musicale ended.

"Thank you, Hughe."

"I like your house better than Shardley house, Lady," he continued. "Thank you for letting Hughe come in your house."

"Thank you for taking care of me when I was indisposed."

"In what?"

"Ill." I leaned back, suddenly quite tired. Hughe was looking at me very worriedly. "I am fine, Hughe."

"Lady need bedding."

"Yes, I believe she does."

As the carriage trundled away from the Gurthwant barony the fireworks began. Although I was tired, I did peek out to see some of them. Small ones at first, barely eliciting an 'ooh' or 'ahh' from the gathered guests, they built as my ride home went on, culminating in a most fantastic display that lasted for what seemed like several minutes. In fact, one particular display was so impressive that I actually swooned again.

Thank goodness Hughe was there to catch me. And carry me into my Hall. And instruct the servants in how to properly care for me. And sleep in the stables.

On looking this over, I realize you must be as exhausted by the reading of this missive as I was at the end of that evening, so I shall close for now.

Please give my best to your Family, and know that I remain,

Fondly,
Annabella

☙ Mr. Gibberwilly ❧

27 April, 1821

Dearest Susannah,

As I proclaimed in my last letter, I was so looking forward to spending time with you at Baron Gurthwant's birthday party, but alas, the Crown once again interfered with your travel plans. It was likely all for the best, as I would not have seen you regardless, due to my unconsciousness. Of course, I am not normally one given to swooning, but I was shocked to hear of Lord Shardley's continued debauchery with the help. First Gwynneth's plight came to my attention, and then another girl claiming the same exact thing – well, where there is smoke there is a man doing something he should not, as Miriam Davis used to announce. I understand that Lord Shardley is hardly the first to be taken in by a casually displayed ankle or somesuch, but it seems that if no ankle is in evidence Lord Shardley tries to arrange events to speed that sort of thing along.

It is one thing for a man to be seduced by the wiles of the lower classes, another to chase after them like a schoolboy! Gentlemen of breeding should be over that sort of thing by 30 at the latest. Of course, I understand Lord Shardley received his title by virtue of inheritance as opposed to work on behalf of the Crown. I am sure that if what I think is true, it shall soon be found that he is not of noble blood at all, as a true Gentleman would never prefer the dubious charms of the peasantry, as opposed to the gracious company of real Ladies.

He does not even have the courtesy or generosity to maintain a mistress! Poor Lady Shardley. I fear she is not unaware of these developments.

Because, dearest Susannah, Sophia was entirely correct to send Hughe back to Wetmoor to insure my safety against more swooning after the birthday party and the attendant tumult. Hughe has been trapped at Sumwattle Estate – Lady Shardley rarely allows him to leave the house, let alone the grounds – but this has left him in the advantageous position of being witness to events there. With Hughe speaking so little proper English people are apparently inclined to speak as freely in front of him as they would in front of a chair.

I wrote Lady Shardley and asked if I could keep Hughe for a short time to help with my newest horse, who seems intractable and sullen. Of course, Lady Shardley has so many servants that I thought (quite rightly) her assent would be relatively simple to obtain. She acquiesced, but added that she was greatly in need of other services within her house, in the domestic area, so I dispatched Taylor to Sumwattle to assist her in whatever she may need for as long as she requires his services.

I believe Taylor may have allergies. When I called him to the drawing room to inform him of his new assignment he was standing next to a bouquet of hyacinths and peonies on a table. His pretty brown eyes began watering the moment he was given his assignment, and became more swollen and red the longer he stood there. He actually shifted his weight from one foot to another, and I realized I have been far too soft on him. He shall benefit from Lady Shardley's much stricter hand, and I told him as much. Then he began to sniffle and snuffle. It was terrible! Really, I would have expected that sort of thing from Duke Twitwhistle, but are not servants made from sterner stuff? Perhaps I never noticed prior because Taylor is most decidedly an indoor servant. I shall have to think on it whilst he is under Lady Shardley's instruction. I believe it is important that servants be flexible and stand erect in the face of any request from their betters. I confess that at times I think I am entirely too kind, and in other moments worry I have been too swift to punish the creatures in my employ. But servants should not have allergies. It is unseemly to think of them coughing and sneezing and snuffling and, oh my, I suddenly felt ill . . .

Thank goodness for Hughe! At the thought of the unclean possibilities rampant in my servants I swooned again! Most dreadful, really. Luckily, Hughe saw the tell-tale swaying that precedes the swoon. Swiftly he crossed the room and caught me before I could land on (I am most ashamed) the floor. He laid me gently on the now appropriately-named fainting couch and yelled for Prudence, who arrived immediately.

"Lady fall down," said Hughe, patting my hand. "Get something and fix Lady."

"Hughe, it is not for you to give orders to servants, especially as you are not even in my employ. Please, oh, drat!" The bewildered expression on his face made it clear he had not a clue as to what I was saying. I tried another tack.

"Prudence?"

"Yes, Lady." Her head bobbed up and down as she curtsied.

"Some spirits, please, Prudence. And cakes."

"Right away, Lady," she bobbed again and withdrew. I sighed as Hughe continued to pat my hand.

"Hughe?"

"Lady be well." He smiled nervously. "Lady be good."

"Hughe, let go of my hand." He continued to pat it, so I pulled it away. Dear thing actually looked crestfallen. I tried to push myself upright and, horror of horrors, Hughe tried to push me back down again! I do not know how they do things in Switzerland or wherever Hughe is from, but that was the limit! I swatted his hand away.

"Hughe! Take your hands off of me!" Hughe looked confused. "You must never attempt to impose your will upon your betters. Ever. If I wish to sit up, there is nothing for you to do about it except either help or stand by." I was feeling better with every word. "There is a reason for this and it is called –" I pushed myself up determinedly and promptly swooned again. My goodness, I must get new corselets.

When I awoke again, I was still on the fainting couch, now with a large bandage around my head, and time had clearly passed. Hughe stood by the window, while Prudence did needlework sitting in the chair that had been pulled up next to me. When my eyes fluttered open she dropped everything (literally, she is quite clumsy), jumped up and leaned over me.

"Don't move, Foxx has ridden for the surgeon."

"What happened? What time is it?" My head felt awful.

"You fainted again, Lady. We've called the surgeon."

"What happened to my head?" It felt like it was splitting.

"It hit the floor when you fainted. Hard, mum."

"My head touched the floor?"

"It more thumped the floor than touched, mum, but if you likc 'touched' better. . ."

"That's not what I meant, Prudence." I glared at Hughe. "How dare you let me fall on the floor?"

"Lady say Hughe must obey and help or stand by. Help to sit up wrong when Lady just fall down, so stood by. Hughe very sad about Lady head."

Just then the door opened and Constance poked her head in.

"Lady, the surgeon's here." Her lower lip quivered.

"Thank you, Constance. Why have we summoned a surgeon?" Both girls looked at each other, as if debating whether or not I should be informed of something. Prudence finally spoke.

"Lady, when you fell, you bumped your head –"

"I know all that, Prudence."

"When you bumped your head, well, it bled a bit."

My blood ran cold. And apparently also ran in great streaming rivers down the back of my head. You know how I feel about the sight of blood, Susannah, ever since the terrible riding accident at the fair we attended before graduating from Miss Penelope's school. I felt faint again.

"My head. It is bleeding?" Both girls nodded. "Send in the surgeon." Loathe though I am to run to a surgeon or any type of medical person for anything, I realized that the swooning was unusual and that I should be seen. I was . . . bleeding. From my <u>head</u>.

Constance opened the door for the surgeon and stood to the side as he swept past her, which is when I noticed that Constance has gained a good deal of weight. She is positively portly. I told myself to speak with Cook about her diet.

"Hello, my dear, I am Mr. Gibberwilly." He took my hand and shook it instead of bowing, which I found quite strange.

"Mr. Gibberwilly, how do you do? And I am not 'your dear'." At my mild rebuke he abruptly let go of my hand.

"My apologies, Ladyship, it is a habit to use endearments with my patients."

"How droll." There was an awkward pause and he looked around at my assembled staff.

"We should like some privacy, I think," he announced, placing his bag on an end table, snapping it open and beginning to rummage through it.

"I agree. Hughe, Constance, please take your leave. I shall speak with you later." They left the room. Prudence looked at me with some confusion, and I nodded at the chair next to me for her to sit down.

When Mr. Gibberwilly turned back from the bag through which he had so loudly rummaged, Prudence was in her chair once more and concentrating on her stitchwork. When he saw her he gave a "hrrmphh," held out a small hammer and dropped it. He nodded to her and waited for her to pick it up. She glanced at me out of the corner of her eye and I nodded "No." She is my servant, not his.

""You can go, girl," he groused as he picked up the hammer. He waved it at her to send her out of the room.

I was quite annoyed. Who did this man think he was, giving instruction to my servants? "She shall stay, Mr. Gibberwilly."

"What?" He looked flummoxed.

"I am always chaperoned while being medically attended."

"You are?"

"I would not go to a hatmaker without a proper chaperone, so cannot imagine why a surgeon's visit should be any different. In fact, it is even more important, to insure that both your reputation and mine remain unsullied in spite of our intimate relationship. Do you not agree?"

"No. I think it very odd." He was almost glaring at me.

"We women are prone to our whims and fancies, are we not? We are the weaker sex, after all. If you would indulge me. . ." I trailed off and tried to look helpless.

"Well . . ."

"I should hate to be overcome without my maid here and since that is my current affliction, I am not without cause to fear such a happenstance," I lowered my eyes, bit my lip ever so softly and stifled a sniffle.

"Oh." He looked down at his hammer. "I understand, your Ladyship, and apologize."

"It is all right." I am always magnanimous when I get my way. I have learnt, Susannah, that women have occasionally been mistreated by their physicians during private meetings and have always guarded against any such unwanted attentions.

He tried to regain authority. "You have been swooning?"

"Yes, just recently. It has never been an issue before, unless there was a duel or something similarly thrilling. But now I am swooning for no reason at all."

"Hmmm . . ." The surgeon looked at me and pronounced that my eyes and ears were clear, and I have fine teeth. He paced for moment, then peeked under the bandage on my head. "You're not bleeding anymore, and it seems to be clean." I felt rather sick at the thought. "Have you been engaging in strenuous activity?"

"Nothing that would induce a swoon."

"You only swoon when you are wearing a, um, a –" he pointed vaguely at my midsection.

"Yes, that is the only time."

"Then, Lady Upton-Church, that is the problem."

"Do you mean –"

"Yes, I do," he interrupted.

"I am the victim of a second-rate corset-maker!" I declared. Gibberwilly looked startled as I continued. "I have been swindled – the corsetiere used materiel that shrinks!"

"Well, I don't believe –"

"I cannot think what else it could be, sir."

"It does happen sometimes when women gain weight," he asserted. A dead and cold silence fell upon the room.

"Exactly what are you implying, sir?" My glare, even though from a comparatively disadvantaged height, was still formidable. He quickly began wiping his spectacles.

"I am implying nothing, Lady. Nothing at all."

"What am I to do? The dressmaker referred me to the corsetiere, which means my gowns have presumably also shrunk!"

"Of course." Gibberwilly was clearly out of his area of expertise. What would he know of dressmaking?

"I shall think upon this. Thank you." I lay back on the cushion. Prudence worked silently, but seemed to be quite cold. Her lips were pursed together and she was shaking slightly. My servants are all falling apart.

"Well, Ladyship, if you have any further need –"

"There is one thing further, sir," I smiled at him.

"Yes, Ladyship?"

"If you could speak to Cook and have her put Constance on a diet. She is becoming absolutely, well, fat, which reflects poorly on my house."

"Constance. Is that the girl that saw me in?"

"Well, she is not Prudence, so of course she is Constance."

"Lady, Constance is not fat. She is pregnant." Prudence yelped as she plunged the needle deep into her finger.

"I beg your pardon?" My eyes narrowed to slits.

Gibberwilly seemed utterly unaware of his insult, for he repeated it. "She is with child, Lady Upton-Church. Anyone can see. She needs to be turned out."

"How dare you impugn my Hall!" I rose to my full height, which is not tall, but still more intimidating than glaring from couch. I threw a bandage to Prudence. "Prudence, do not bleed on the furniture, dear."

"Yes, Lady," she managed to say around the finger she was sucking on and quickly wrapped the bandage around it.

"Lady Upton-Church, it is clear –"

"That you know nothing of the subject in which you claim expertise!" I finished for him. "You are a dangerously ill-educated man. You come to my Hall and tell me that I am fat and Constance is pregnant! Pregnant women do not work in great Halls such as this! Constance is working! It is that simple. You are disinclined to look with any decency on those with sturdy bones. I cannot help mine, I am part Welsh! Constance, well, Constance is all alone in the world and if she wants to spend her money on sweets who am I to deny her? She is a good girl, a kind girl and you have dared to not only cast aspersions on her, you have called me a wanton woman as well because, as we all know, the actions of servants reflect on their masters, well, mistresses, and you have called her a fallen woman so you must think me a trollop as well!" With that I lightly slapped him. I shall not tolerate such behaviour, Susannah, not at all.

Mr. Gibberwilly reared back and blinked at me very slowly while Prudence goggled at us both.

I stood my ground. "You should leave, sir. Our business is finished. See Cook for your <u>not</u> earned payment." He slowly picked up his bag and Prudence continued to gape at him like a blowfish. I whispered to her, "Stop staring and attend your needlework," which she promptly did. Mr. Gibberwilly walked to the door and turned back to me.

"You should have a care, Lady Upton-Church," he said gravely.

"Why ever should I wish to listen to anything you say?"

"Because I am a man and your better, titled or no. You are overwrought, unwell, and have clearly suffered from a severe head injury, else you would never have dared speak to me thusly. I shall forgive you your outburst, as it surely was caused more by outside influences and had nothing to do with reality. You could do with a good leeching to balance your spirits."

"You wish to put insects upon me?" I was appalled. "Where did you train, for goodness' sake? A bog?"

"Oxford, Ladyship. However, it is clear I cannot attend you further." As I stared, gaping even more than Prudence had been, he left. Prudence and I stared at each other.

"Well, Prudence, now you know firsthand how important it is to never see a physician or surgeon alone. They are not to be trusted."

"Yes, mum."

"Prudence?"

"Yes, mum."

"Tell Constance that when she goes out in the future she should wear a cloak, even if it is warm. At least until her diet begins to work. I shall not have people gossiping."

"Yes, mum."

"I am very tired, Prudence, and have apparently narrowly escaped a leeching. I believe I shall retire."

"Of course, mum." She stood and opened the door for me. "Do you need help?"

"I am fine. Bring me a tray with my dinner later."

"Yes, mum."

I made my way to my rooms and lay down, determined to get rest that did not involve unconsciousness. I was going to see Gwynneth the next day, in the lair of the Bargesniffles, at the Rooster & Mussel, so would need all of my strength.

I shall adjourn my tale for now, Susannah, as it seems that once again I have gone on for many pages without surcease. However, I will write again soon, for this brief respite from the cold and cruel world did not last – I am plunged in the thick of things again! But for now please know that I Remain,

Your Swooning Friend,
Annabella

☙ Gwynneth's Employment ❧

1 May, 1921

Darling Susannah,

From the alarmed tone of your letter I realize I ended my last letter to you rather abruptly and beg your forgiveness for the breach. I hope this finds you well and happy in your house, and that Lord Carollton is also faring well.

You shall be relieved to know I woke the morning after my unfortunate swooning with a mild headache and nothing more. I felt carefully at the bump on the back of my head, and was pleased to find the bleeding had stopped completely, so could leave the bandage off – I think Prudence used most of the linens in the Hall to fashion it. Mr. Sinclair was coming the next day, and I did not want to scare him to death with a gaping head wound. He would likely have carted me straight to London to be examined by the Royal College of Surgeons – the mere thought makes me shudder and feel rather ill. I was pleased at my rapid recovery, and bade Prudence to leave my corselet loose to make up for the shoddy and shrinking materiel. My bodice was uncomfortably snug, which confirmed that the dressmaker was using second-rate materiel in those as well. My bosom fair threatened to burst from my neckline. I hate tucking kerchiefs above one's bosom – it always looks more scandalous than to leave it alone – so left my neckline bare and resolved to breathe shallowly, lest I explode out of my gown in a most indiscreet fashion.

I hope I can rely on your discretion in this matter, Susannah. I would hate for it to get out that my gowns and corselets are not top-drawer.

However, I cannot take the time at this moment to have a new wardrobe made up – the fittings alone would take up every moment of my time. I am only in these light mourning clothes for another few months. It seems a waste to make up new gowns that shall be discarded come August.

With a (shallow) sigh I realized it would be best to make do with the wardrobe I have until then. However, until that day arrives I must circumscribe my normal habits, meaning no lovely breakfast in bed, as swooning all over the county shall not advance my cause one whit. However, I could have them altered . . . and suddenly I had a plan. A terribly clever plan.

Before I could enact it something needed to be remedied. Hughe's high-handedness with me during my spell could be neither excused nor condoned, and I realized it was past time for him to return to Sumwattle, as he has outlived his usefulness to me. In more ways than one, actually.

Truth to tell, I did not wish to romp with Hughe, enjoyable as the one time had been. Hughe may not know his station, is absolutely delightful in nonverbal pursuits, and quite solicitous of me in his own way, but we cannot talk, Susannah, except for strangled, taxing conversations wherein neither of us is certain what the other is saying, which makes me disinclined to engage in other activities with him. Especially now that he believes the unique position he held once in one area has endowed him with special standing at Wetmoor. That is one of the warning signs you detailed to me, so it was time for him to leave. I do not need him here, not with the staff I have.

Hughe took the news very well, only bowing slightly before leaving to pack. He clearly felt his behaviour to have been correct.

That done, it was time to enact my plan regarding Gwynneth. I told Prudence to have the carriage readied and nearly ran to it the moment it was pulled around. Foxx opened the door whilst Driver sat atop, whittling away at his leg, although he stopped when I glared at him. Once I was settled Foxx climbed to the top of the carriage alongside Driver.

Once we arrived I realized my terrible *faux pas*. I could not go into a public house alone in the middle of the day! I may as well strap a featherbed to my back and wander back alleys like a fallen woman! I sat there, biting my lip and feeling quite vexed with myself for not thinking ahead. Suddenly Foxx opened the door. When I did not disembark, he leaned into the carriage.

"Lady Upton-Church, are you all right?"

"I do not know what to do."

"What were you going to do, Lady?"

"I was going to – oh, for goodness' sake, Foxx, get in here. I do not wish for anyone to stare." Foxx looked startled but quickly obeyed. I have not spent much time with Foxx, Susannah, but he was the only person there and I needed help. "Foxx, I need to see Gwynneth, but I cannot go in such a place during the day, and unescorted. It is unacceptable."

"You have gone before, Lady," Foxx looked confused. Oh, I hoped he was not dim. I hate it when servants are dim. Naïve, yes. Dim is completely hopeless.

"That was different. It was winter, there were many people and it was evening, which is different than going alone in the middle of the day." We both sat and pondered. Suddenly Foxx looked up and smiled.

"I know what to do, Lady." He leapt from the carriage before I could say a word and ran to the pub. I wondered what Foxx had in mind. I would know soon enough if he was dim.

After a moment Foxx was rapping on the carriage door again. When I assented, he opened it and helped Gwynneth inside. He smiled at me as he closed the door. Gwynneth, now gargantuan in size, sat with her mouth hanging open, gaping at the curtains and upholstery. I whispered to Foxx through the window.

"How did you do that?"

"You could not go to Gwynneth, so I brought her to you." Perhaps he is not dim after all.

"Well, that should do." Gwynneth was now staring at both of us warily. We felt the carriage rock as Foxx took his seat alongside Driver and a moment later the carriage was swaying gently as we began to move.

Gwynneth finally thought to close her mouth, even as one hand gently stroked the velvet upholstery.

"Gwynneth?" She jumped and looked nervous, as well as anywhere but at me. "Gwynneth, do you remember me?"

"Mum, yes mum. You're Lady Upton-Church, mum."

"Yes, Gwynneth. How are you?"

"Right huge I am, mum. But well. I'm . . . umm . . . good."

"That is lovely." We sat for a moment while I tried to gather my thoughts. When I saw how distressed Gwynneth was becoming with silence I abandoned constructing a delicate discourse that would reveal to me what I needed to know and decided to be blunt in a way that I never would with my equals, telling myself that as Gwynneth does not know right from wrong in general (hence her embarrassing state), the finer points of etiquette would be lost on her as well.

"Gwynneth, are you happy?"

"Happy?" She sounded confused.

I tried not to sound impatient. "Are you happy in your life, Gwynneth? Are you glad of your husband and the life that you have with him?"

"The younger Mr. Bargesniffle is a fine, upstanding, God-fearin' man any girl'd be lucky to have, mum." She spoke very quickly in a flat voice. It sounded quite rote.

"I am sure he is, Gwynneth. But you did not answer my question."

"Me's lucky that a man such as he took me in, mum . . . an' 'e deserves my 'ternal grat – garti – thanks for all he done for such as me." Again, a flat (and somewhat memorized) statement.

"Gwynneth, please look at me." I was about to embark on a truly dangerous enterprise. Gwynneth turned those mousy brown eyes to me, and I saw that they were tearing.

"Gwynneth, if a Lady asks you a question, you know you must answer honestly, do you not?" The tears in her eyes grew larger but did not fall. "You worked for Lady Shardley, Gwynneth, and were properly trained." She gulped, and the tears floated in her eyes, a quite spectacular display of levitation. I swear, that girl would have cut off her own head before weeping in front of a Lady, for which I was grateful. Who knew how much she remember of proper behaviour? "Please answer me, Gwynneth. Are you happy?"

Gwynneth's words gushed out in such a torrent I near regretted asking the question. "I know I should be, mum, I know I could be out on the streets right now were it not for the Bargesniffles and all, and Rufus ain't a bad man, really he ain't. He ain't always goin' at me but 'at's only 'cuz he says I'm so fat and so I'm lucky in that. I know I am. But I ain't. Happy, I mean. Mrs. Bargesniffle, she lets me know what kind of nasty girl I am every day and Mr. Bargesniffle, he let go o' two o' the other girls, 'cuz I can work more hours since we live over the public house. It wouldn't be so bad if Rufus weren't out like a tomcat most ever' night but 'e is so no I ain't happy, mum. But I got no hope o' anythin' better, 'ave I? I'm lucky for the little I got and I know it. The baby'll 'ave a name an' a dad an' all. I know it could be worse. So's I don't mind I ain't happy, Ladyship. I got more 'n' I deserve, I reckon."

"I see." I sat there for a moment. My question was answered. I must continue in this enterprise. Had Gwynneth been happy it would have been different. But she is not, which gives me a small hope that – dare I say it? – intelligence lurks somewhere in that head of hers.

"Thank you for your honesty, Gwynneth." I looked out the window, scheming as to what should be done next.

"Don't tell no one, Lady, please . . . I mean, I know I couldn't ever tell a Lady what to do –"

"You may trust me, Gwynneth." She looked uncertain. I leaned forward and patted her grimy hand. "I shall not break your confidence." She sighed hugely and closed her eyes. Of course, I am breaking the promise simply by writing you, Susannah, but that cannot be helped. I embarked on this course in order to find out the truth of Gwynneth's parentage and prevent scandal from coming to your house, which I believe supersedes the wishes of a serving girl with "one up the spout," as they apparently so charmingly say.

Suddenly Gwynneth looked alarmed.

"Lady? Can we go back t'the pub now, Lady?"

"I beg your pardon?"

"I have to . . . I have to go back t' the pub now."

"Why?"

"Because . . ." She twisted her hands in what was left of her lap. Suddenly Driver's voice growled from above us."

"Because of her delicate condition, Lady. She shouldn't be bounced about in a carriage."

"Thank you, Driver. Please return to the Rooster and Mussel." The carriage was turning as I spoke the words. I tried not to think about the fact that Driver could hear what we were saying, but resolved to henceforth use a quiet tone when travelling.

Gwynneth gave a small smile. "Thank you, Lady."

"Do you sew, Gwynneth?"

"Yes, Lady."

"I have several things that require the deft work of a seamstress but done quietly. Not by my normal dressmaker."

"I've done piecework –"

"But you can use a needle and thread?"

"Yes, Lady."

"You shall henceforth come to Wetmoor on Mondays, Wednesdays and Thursdays, where you shall be employed as a seamstress."

"Lady?"

"You shall work for me."

"But Mr. Bargesniffle –"

I had already thought about that problem. "Tell him I have need of you. If he refuses to give you leave then you are to give word to Foxx. He shall be at the Rooster and Mussel on those days in the morning. A carriage shall come and fetch you and bring you home each day you work for me."

"Lady, you are too kind –"

"I am <u>not</u> kind, Gwynneth. I need discreet sewing done and discretion would be undone by your walking to and fro in your state. I am making these arrangements for my convenience, not yours." These poor things believe the least comfort is a kindness. How appalling.

"Yes, Lady."

"You shall start tomorrow."

"Yes, Lady." We rode in silence, but I noticed that Gwynneth's hands no longer plucked at the upholstery. We arrived back at the pub and Foxx, completely confusing protocols, opened the carriage door and helped Gwynneth down. She turned and looked back at me, her visage like the reflection of the full moon on a still lake.

"Thank you, Lady."

"I shall see you on the morrow, Gwynneth."

The ride home went quickly as I pondered and discarded several ideas of where to expend my efforts next. All too soon we were in front of my own front door, with Foxx helping me out and opening the front door.

I handed my cape and hat to Constance – wait, that wasn't Constance! It was Prudence!

"Where is Constance?"

"Cook knows, mum." Prudence took my things, then shooed me into my own drawing room.

"Are you implying that Constance is not here?" I kept trying to look at Prudence while she settled me on the settee and fluffed some pillows, but she has the most amazing ability to look directly at one without looking at them at all.

"All I know is that Cook knows, mum."

"Then fetch Cook. And tea. And some of those little cakes." The fabric of my gown was far too tight around my arms, which gave me pause. "Well, perhaps not the cakes, Prudence."

"Yes, mum," she bobbed and left the room. I sighed. Would this madness never end? It took longer than I would have liked, but Cook finally came into the room carrying a tray of tea and brandy.

"Where is Constance, Cook?"

"Lady needs some tea and brandy after such a chill day, mark my words," Cook growled and handed me a cup.

"It is not chilly, but . . . thank you." Who was I to reject such an offer? I took a sip. It was rather more brandy than tea, not bad at all. "Where is Constance?"

"Her sister took ill, milady, and Constance needed to tend her." Cook did not seem embarrassed by this admission, although she should have been. Perhaps her knee was bothering her again, she was favouring it. Actually, as I think on it, Cook leans the opposite of Driver. Perhaps if I could get them to stand together they would both stand upright. But that was for another time.

"Tend to her sister? What are you talking about? And sit down, Cook, you're alarming me with that altogether untoward list of yours." Cook sat in a small chair.

"Constance's sister, milady. She is with child and widowed. Her husband was killed at Manchester. The Peterloo massacre."

Oh, my. Well, that puts a different colour on things, does it not, Susannah? I mean, what happened in Manchester was the final event that decided me to move to Wetmoor. It was so horrible and so many people died including, apparently, Constance's brother-in-law. It was all so shocking.

"He was there?" I queried, more casually than I felt.

Cook nodded. "Yes, mum. So was Constance's sister. She survived. Her husband covered her with himself, which was how he died. A horse stepped on them."

"Oh, my," I breathed. "They were trampled?"

"She stayed under him until it were over, which must have been awful, between you and me, but the constable said it likely saved her life in the end."

"How many people died that day, Cook?"

"I believe it were eleven, mum, but some say far more. And one of them was our dear Constance's brother-in-law. A few months later her sister learnt she was pregnant, and there you are. She's all alone now and needs tending."

"But who shall tend to me?" The words were out of my mouth before I could stop them. "I mean, of course. Constance's sister – what is her name?"

"Laura, milady."

"How long shall Constance be gone?"

"Three weeks, milady. Maybe four."

"Three weeks! How am I supposed to manage without a parlour maid for three weeks?"

"Constance can be replaced, milady." She looked at me rather slyly, I thought.

"Oh, and how would that look? Letting go a girl who was helping the widow of a man who was killed at Peterloo? I would seem positively heartless!"

"We thought that Constance would be let go, Lady. She would have written you a letter resigning her post save the bit about her not being able to write."

"She cannot write?"

"Oh, no, milady."

"How does she finish my lists?"

"I read them to her and she memorizes them. We didn't want to bother you, and it seemed to work all right."

"This conversation is becoming more and more surprising. What secret lives you all have! Is there anything else going on I should know of? This is my Hall, after all."

Cook grinned, a rather alarming sight. "No, Lady. That's all you need know."

"Which does not answer the question, which is still going begging, of what to do whilst Constance is gone." We sat. I pondered, and then decided. "Have Prudence send for that sister of hers."

"Hortense?"

"Whatever her name is. She shall fill in until Constance returns."

"But Hortense is not a maid."

"How difficult can it be, Cook? Everything a maid does she is told to do, so as long as Hortense does as she is told we should be able to struggle along for three weeks. She shall be paid half wages. Make sure she is kept out of sight. It would not do for people to see that my Hall is in complete disarray."

"Hortense is eleven, milady."

"Is she in school?"

"No, Lady."

"Then this shall keep her busy and out of trouble. Given her age, she shall get one-quarter wages, since she may not be able to dust the higher ledges and shelves, and shall presumably need a nap during the day."

"Yes, milady." Cook looked oddly pleased.

"And no sweets!" I added.

"No sweets."

"Well, what are you waiting for? Send word to Constance that she is to return here immediately once her family obligations have been met."

"Yes, milady." Cook stood, which took a moment or two. I re-arranged my skirts while she was hoisting herself back up and finished my tea and brandy. It really is delicious with more brandy in it, Susannah. You must try it someday. In fact, I had two more that very afternoon, and slept so very soundly.

But now I realize that I have prattled on far too long about the mundane goings-on in my Hall. But you shall see, Susannah, that all of this has a bearing on the situation we are solving for yours.

I wish I had time to tell you of my next visitors, Susannah, for one has a bearing on your own house and the other . . . well, I should like that visitor to bear down on me. Is that titillating enough for you?

But I must away for now, and attend the Ladies' Auxiliary Fellowship dinner at the parish. It is one's Christian duty, after all, and I do so want to wear my new bonnet . . .

Fondly,

Annabella

☙ Mr. Ploughgoode ❧

8 May, 1821

Dear Susannah,

Greetings and felicitations! It has been so long since I have been able to write you! It has been quite a time here, and I have news from Mr. Sinclair regarding Mr. Bargesniffle.

Mr. Sinclair may have a career as an investigator for the Crown; he obtained fascinating information on our behalf.

Mr. Bargesniffle did not stay long at Sumwattle after your husband's departure, Susannah. His next post, obtained by way of a stellar reference from Lord Shardley, was at White's, where your husband stayed after leaving Sumwattle himself. Just two years later Mr. Bargesniffle purchased the Rooster & Mussel. On his salary, even including gratuities from members, there should not have been enough to even approach the previous owner. Further inquiry determined that Mr. Bargesniffle had not come into an inheritance or anything else in the normal sense of the word.

It is Mr. Sinclair's belief that Mr. Bargesniffle used information overheard at the club to bolster his own coffers, and I agree. Additional inquiries revealed a number of members who were glad to be shut of Mr. Bargesniffle, once they had recovered from sudden anxiety at hearing his name, and one muttered, "Good riddance to bad rubbish."

Mr. Bargesniffle seems to be similar to a lamprey eel – fastening himself to his betters to drain them of what he can before letting go in search of larger prey. It explains why he did not bandy about Gwynneth's provenance, and how he suddenly had enough money to purchase a thriving business outright, where the servants of great houses might loose their tongues with the help of his wares. He may not be guilty of outright blackmail (it seems not to be the case with Gwynneth) but he appears to be, at best, a shameless profiteer in information.

I was thrilled with what Mr. Sinclair had discovered and he blushed at my compliments of his skills. He was also reassured to know that I had decided not to approach Mr. Bargesniffle for any business enterprise (my excuse for the investigation), for he was as unsettled by the information he found as I was.

At Wetmoor things were not so pleasing. As you are well aware from my last letter, the Hall is in an uproar. How did things come to this? I am sure that I am not sure. I believe that I have gotten too mixed up and inquisitive in general, as opposed to specific inquisitiveness on your behalf. I have resolved to remain aloof from the goings-on below stairs and expend my energies where they might do the most good.

With that in mind I ignored Constance's 11-year old stand-in, Hortense, even with that foot of hers, and was abrupt with Prudence and Cook. I had begun a letter to Lady Shardley asking for Taylor to be returned to me. The previous two requests had gone unanswered, which showed further poor manners on her part.

There were bright spots in my day. Gwynneth was coming in the morning and my tennis lessons were to begin that afternoon. I have resolved to exercise and diet, as I am forced to make do with shoddy gown materiel for the near future. I queried amongst the ladies at the Auxiliary Fellowship Dinner last week and Mr. Ploughgoode received glowing references, even with his dismissal from the hunt. All of the ladies recommended him, although no one knows if he can play tennis. I may have the only court in the county. I wrote to secure Mr. Ploughgoode's services so I may enjoy fresh air and exercise. His reply affirmed he is able to provide instruction and has equipment to use until I procure my own. I was pleased I could engage his services, as I was the reason he was let go from the hunt.

Gwynneth arrived at 10:00, brought by Driver in an old carriage, the one we use to ferry workmen to hospital. It would not do for her to go into labour whilst walking the six miles to and from the Hall. I needed her to be rested, for she was there for more than sewing. She was there to provide information.

Alas, no information was forthcoming on her first visit. She was so terrified that conversation was impossible. She gaped at everything: the drawing room, the crystal, the dining room, Hortense, and blurted "Yes, mum, thank you, mum," at every turn. Of course, that was only appropriate, for every moment spent in my genteel Hall is one less moment spent swabbing spilled ale from the counters and fending off the advances of drunken louts from the fields. I turned her meagre attention to the gown I intended to wear for my tennis lesson. The skirts were fine, but the bodice needed work, as did the sleeves, and my corselet needed attention at the waist. I told her there would be an extra farthing for her if she finished by two o'clock. Mr. Ploughgoode was coming at three. I had a horrible fear that I might move my arm and the fabric would split, which would have forced me to kill myself.

She went to work with a will, wielding needle and thread with a skill I have not oft seen. I sat by, keeping a gentle eye on her as I finished my correspondence and had a light lunch.

It was remarkable what clever things she accomplished with a needle, thread and thimble. In fact, her entire demeanor changed. She seemed sure of herself and of what she was doing in a way that surprised me. She let seams out, trimmed materiel from unknown places and set tiny plackets and darts. After a time I simply watched her. Before I knew it the gown was done. She looked up and started when she saw I had been watching her.

Once I calmed her fears I took the gown and corselet. She explained shyly that she made adjustments based on what she believed would be the most flattering and hoped it would be passable. I assured her that it was only for a tennis lesson, which seemed to relieve her. I dismissed her for the day and went to my dressing room to change.

Susannah! I have a secret weapon in Gwynneth, all unknown! Gwynneth turned an every-day gown into the most charming gown I have in my possession! And the corselet – my figure is divine once I am stuffed into it! The work she did showed off my figure to its full advantage, each little dart and placket serving to exemplify the best and disguise the less attractive features. I could not believe how lovely I looked! I actually clapped my hands in delight as I spun in front of the looking glass. No matter the angle, I was absolutely adorable! The only reservation I had was that she set the bodice tighter and low-cut than the neckline I normally favour. I do not know how she did it, for it appeared a feature of the dress' design. It was too late to do anything about that, for even as I admired myself in the looking-glass Constance breathlessly announced the arrival of Mr. Ploughgoode.

Mr. Ploughgoode was waiting in the library, looking with seeming interest at the books on the shelves. Constance announced me and left slowly, backing through the door. I understood her odd behaviour when I saw him. I had forgotten how attractive he is. He is beautiful.

I was surprised he had again eschewed the kilt of his countrymen in favour of normal attire, for kilts are all the rage now. Although I have never understood why a man would wear a skirt, Mr. Ploughgoode would look fantastic in a kilt, Susannah. How can I put it elegantly? He is relentlessly impressive: broad-shouldered, perfectly proportioned even at his height, which is quite tall. That would be enough, but his face is lovely, which sounds an odd description of a man, but you know what I mean. When he helped me at the hunt, until his accent gave him away, I thought him a Gentleman. Most of the Scots I have seen appear to have been bashed about a great deal.

Mr. Ploughgoode appears to never have been bashed. His skin is near as fair as mine own, the planes of his face strong and clear, and his straight, elegant nose tops a lovely mouth. His hair is so dark a brown it is nearly black, with a curl that is neither a horrible frizz nor a meagre wave. That would be quite enough I think, but his eyes are truly stunning. Fringed by long, thick lashes, they are the most unusual color: grey. Dark grey flecked with bits of green and blue.

I betrayed no hint of being impressed, of course, instead greeting him with the appropriate amount of reserve and warmth one has with servants and hired help. "Mr. Ploughgoode, it is a pleasure to meet with you again."

He smiled as he bowed. "For myself as well." The burr in his voice made my spine tingle. He remembered me! It is nice to know one is unforgettable, and I could not help smiling.

"You seem to have not suffered from Lady Shardley's dismissal. Again, I am sorry for what happened to you that day, it was because of my fall."

He looked mildly startled. “No apology is necessary. I don’t think I can count the number of times I’ve been dismissed from Sumwattle.”

Why Lady Shardley would toss him from her estate was beyond me, for I was wondering if I could take lessons daily. Perhaps instruction in shooting, croquet, riding . . . oh, riding!

I cast about for what to say, for proper words had fled my mind in favour of other, less Ladylike, musings. Finally I said, “I am pleased you did not suffer any repercussions.”

He smiled at me with a slight twinkle in his eyes. Oh, drat! I should never have said anything or apologized. This was not going the way I had planned. It was all very discomfiting. He was there to provide instruction, so I began again and ignored the awkward staring at one other. The sharing of any memory, even a slight one, might cause him to think I find him attractive, which I do, but he did not need to know such a thing. He is a tennis instructor, for goodness’ sake. And a Scot! I cleared my throat. “I am afraid I am a novice, Mr. Ploughgoode. I have no idea how to play tennis at all.

He frowned slightly. “I am to instruct yourself? I thought you were engaging me to teach your son –”

“I do not have a son, Mr. Ploughgoode. The lessons are for me.”

He seemed quite confused, and I realized God does not give with both hands, Mr. Ploughgoode was beautiful but was also apparently stupid. I spoke slowly so he would understand. “I have a beautiful court going to waste.”

He stammered. “Lady Upton-Church – I – you –”

This was getting exasperating. “Mr. Ploughgoode, what is the matter? You said you can provide instruction. Were you exaggerating your abilities?”

"Of course I can play, and provide instruction . . . " He pursed his lips adorably. "Do you know anythin' about tennis?"

"There is a net and people swat a ball across it at each other. The upper classes play, at least they used to, before it stopped being the done thing." Would he not teach me if I did not know about the game? What an odd instructor!

He seemed embarrassed. "Lady Upton-Church, beggin' your pardon, and with all due respect, tennis is not a game women play. It would be, well, not wrong, I don' think, but not done – please know, I don't wish to anger you, but –"

I interrupted him. "Tennis is only played by men?"

"Yes."

"So your concern regarding lessons – you are afraid for my reputation?"

He appeared relieved. "Yes."

I thought that sweet, for he was willing to risk losing a client in order to preserve her reputation. He is not the barbarian I thought a Scot would be, but I set aside consideration of that idea in favour of working out a solution to the problem.

"May I be quite blunt, Mr. Ploughgoode?"

"Of course, Lady." He braced himself for a barrage of umbrage.

"In spite of always behaving properly I have a horrible reputation, as I am sure you have heard. Given that, I find I do not care what is done and not done. I do as I please, at least here at Wetmoor. The courtyard is enclosed, no one would see us, and it seems a waste to not play tennis because of my sex. I have two arms, legs and eyes, they all work fairly well, so I do not see why, if it is not too horrible a thought for you to contemplate, that you should not instruct me in how to use my court. If you are concerned about your own reputation, you may tell others you are teaching me something less scandalous. My staff is utterly discrete and they do not leave here often."

Mr. Ploughgoode's mouth was hanging open at the end of my little speech, but he quickly recovered.

"I'd of course be delighted to instruct you, Lady, but did no' wish your reputation to suffer from unfamiliarity with the game's general traditions. Are you certain?"

I was certain. I was very certain. I itched for lessons from Mr. Ploughgoode. I veritably panted for them. Tennis may be a far more enthralling pastime than I imagined.

The issue of my sex settled to our mutual satisfaction, Mr. Ploughgoode gathered the equipment I had instructed him to bring and I led him down the hallway to the tennis courtyard. Taylor opened the door with a flourish and I preceded Mr. Ploughgoode through it to the courtyard. He entered and looked shocked, for it is so lovely: the grass is like velvet, and I had furniture brought out – a little table and chairs – in case I need to rest. The carved walls give the feeling of being in a stone forest, the roses bloom in a beautiful tangle over the top of the south wall, and the fountain in the wall burbles happily.

He turned to me. "This is beautiful, Lady Upton-Church."

"Thank you."

"May I?" He gestured at the court and I nodded. He walked around the outside edge of the court, vaulting with ease over the net stretched to each side, noting the animals carved into the walls, running a hand over the grass, appraising the windows and angles of the upper walls. When he had completed his examination of the court he was smiling broadly. "I've not seen a court like this outside o' London. I can see why you don' want it to go to waste. It's extraordinary."

"Thank you." I was pleased an expert thought the same as I.

Mr. Ploughgoode gave me a racquet of my own and I walked to one side of the net, not realizing he had not moved from his place on the side of the court. There I was, standing in the full sun, and he was standing in the shade!

"Mr. Ploughgoode?" I called. "Why are you not on your side of the court?"

"Lady Upton-Church, please come back into the shade." I was rather embarrassed and walked back with all the confidence I could muster. "In order to learn to play properly, it's necessary to be familiar wi' the equipment involved."

Which of course makes sense, I suppose, when one thinks of it. I thought lessons would involve myself standing charmingly on one side of the net, with Mr. Ploughgoode hitting balls to me, which I may or may not hit back, as my mood dictated.

I was grievously wrong in this assumption, Susannah. Anyone with an arm can play tennis, but not everyone can play well, as Mr. Ploughgoode informed me. I began to suspect that Mr. Ploughgoode was a strict taskmaster, Susannah. I know tennis is a sport of the upper classes, apparently of men only, but had not thought it would require quite as much awe. Of course, I am the only person I know with a court, so perhaps I should be more impressed with the game.

First he explained what the different parts of the court were named, as well as a general idea of how the game was played. I began to become confused about hitting the ball off penthouses (the funny angled things atop the walls) and through the high windows and how it worked for winning, so once he was assured I at least knew the names of everything we moved on to my grip. Did you know there is a proper grip for a racquet? Not too firm, nor too slack. If you hold it too hard your swing is strangled, and if you hold it too loosely it works not at all for hitting the ball back. I hope I did not appear a complete fool, for I kept smiling at him. I think he believes I am completely enamored of the game.

Mr. Ploughgoode of course was extremely patient in explaining everything to me before selecting a shaft appropriate for my hand. He then spent a considerable amount of time testing and adjusting my grip, including the exact placement of hand to shaft, watching and then adjusting again.

The shaft was much thicker and longer than I had imagined it would be. When I asked, for it was so heavy in my hand, Mr. Ploughgoode said it was necessary to withstand the vigours of play.

I would have become bored, I think, except that he seemed to feel passionately that my grip be exemplary before progressing to the balls. We spent the entire lesson on the edge of the court, shaded from the sun by a fall of roses and the high stone wall around us, whilst I gripped in as many ways possible, and swung it about. I was concerned about my bodice, for with the lower neckline I thought my bosom might pop out from the exertion, but Gwynneth is quite cunning. For all of my twisting and turning it stayed firmly in place. My breath was coming quite quickly. Tennis, properly played, is excellent exercise! It was exhausting for me, I do not mind saying, and Mr. Ploughgoode nary had to exert himself at all, even though he was perspiring and appeared slightly unfocused by the end of the lesson. It is quite warm in the court, for the high walls prevent pleasant breezes.

Given that he was wearing a suit I understood why he seemed overheated.

Far too soon my first lesson was over. I believe that I shall enjoy my tutelage under Mr. Ploughgoode very much, Susannah. Now that I have mastered the grip, perhaps next time I shall be able to play with the balls.

After gathering the equipment, he gave a short bow and took his leave, and I immediately called for Hortense to draw me a bath. The athletic life is exhausting, but so very rewarding.

I must away – a carriage has just pulled up, and I have no appointments today. It is quite shabby, oh, my – it is

I must go. I Remain,

Your Frightened Friend,
Annabella

☙ *Taylor Unmade* ❧

15 May, 1821

Dearest Susannah,

So much news! I scarce know where to begin. I warn you now that this letter shall be Olympian in size (as I am sure the weight of it foretold) and Greek in scope and nature. In fact, I was concerned that the meagre weight of this letter might prove more than Taylor could carry, but since you are reading it at this moment, I may have been over-reacting.

I suppose since I have already begun, I shall begin with Taylor. He is, after all, at the root of all I have discovered.

Taylor has been damaged by Lady Shardley! Susannah, if she ever asks to borrow one of your servants, especially Paolo, you must refuse her request! If any other than those in permanent standing in her house become aware of what is going on it will be the ruin of her reputation!

It began the day after my tennis lesson.

Which reminds me, the details I provided you were about the actual lesson. Susannah, you have a most alarming imagination. I cannot recall exactly what I wrote, but if you think I would molest my tennis instructor whilst standing on my own court you must think me a terrible harlot. It was a lesson, Susannah, and the racquet was not a metaphor for Mr. Ploughgoode's personal equipment. Really, what do you think of me?

Where was I? Oh, telling you about what happened the very next day. I was planning to spend the day arranging flowers and attending to correspondence. Foxx was in the drawing room, standing like a soldier at attention. Hortense was attempting to dust and occasionally Foxx was forced to lift her so she could reach the tops of shelves, etc. Prudence was working with Cook and Driver was doing whatever it is that Driver does when not driving. I think something to do with tackling, and bashing the stable boys about, as they tend to mimic his listing gait.

So began a normal morning. I had begun to write you, in the drawing room to take full advantage of the sun, when I heard a carriage approaching. Foxx put Hortense down, waved her out of the room and peered out of the window past me. I, of course, was already there, curious to see who would have come to Wetmoor without prior notice, as I had no appointments that day.

The carriage was old and extremely shabby. I thought it might be brigands or Luddites come to kill us all in broad daylight, and told Foxx to go and get Quince's duelling pistols so he could save us from the certain tortures and murders we were about have committed on our persons. Foxx did not move, and before I could remonstrate him the carriage stopped and the door opened from the interior. Hughe emerged holding a large sack in his arms, and strode to the front door. He did not even use the servants' entrance! I was very glad I had sent him back to Sumwattle.

Foxx and I ran to the foyer and Foxx opened the door. I gasped. Hughe was not carrying a sack, he was carrying Taylor!

"There was accident," Hughe said, quite unnecessarily, in my mind. "Lady Shardley send back."

Taylor was swaddled from head to toe in bandages, a letter tied around his wrist by a ribbon. He was unconscious and no amount of shaking by Foxx would rouse him. I had no idea what to do, Susannah. This sort of thing was not taught at Miss Penelope's, as well you know. I plucked the letter from Taylor's wrist and told Hughe to take Taylor to his room and Foxx to ride for the apothecary. Again. The fact that this time the injury had not occurred at Wetmoor was poor consolation. Prudence appeared from the hall leading to the kitchens as Hughe walked toward the grand staircase. I was going to remonstrate him for not using the servants' staircase when I realized it is rather narrow, and Taylor would have his skull banging against the walls all the way up, so I remained silent. Prudence gasped when Hughe said to her, "Taylor broke."

"What happened, Lady?" she cried, as if I were already in possession of the facts. It is charming how our servants see us as all-knowing, is it not? I glared at her and sent her back to the kitchen, then ran to the library room to read the letter. I copy it out here for you to read for yourself, Susannah:

Dear Lady Upton-Church,

I am returning Taylor to you forthwith, as he has proven to be Deficient in his Post. My Position in this County dictates that I speak Bluntly when I see the Standards of the Nobility Lacking, and I must say Discreetly to you, that if Taylor's Behaviour is any Indication of the General Quality of your House Staff, I am Fearful of your Position within our Fair Society. He is a Confabulator, and not to be Trusted! The Lies that fell from his Sweetly Pouting lips were Appalling! You should not listen to Anything he says, Lady Upton-Church, and were it in my Power I would have Dismissed him on the spot. However, it was not in my Power, but it is in Yours.

I look forward to lunching with you again at the earliest opportunity, when Taylor has been Replaced by a more Suitable Servant.

Yours in Spirits,

Lady Shardley

Sumwattle Estate

I was astounded! Susannah, you have met Taylor and found him to be excellent in all of the positions he has held within a house, even when he was just beginning his career in service and did not know how to do anything. And never, ever, not once, have I known him to lie! I knew Lady Shardley was mistaken in her assessment of Taylor's character.

Just then Hughe came bounding back down the stairway. Taylor's bandages had been removed and they were more for cushioning than for the prevention of blood spilling on the carpets. Hughe bade me sit, as what he had to tell me was difficult and scandalous, and would be mixed in with his own observations about Sumwattle Estate. I asked if Taylor would be all right and he said that the apothecary would have to make such a determination. Actually he said, "Doctor know better if too much crushing."

I sat down and asked for a *précis* of Taylor's injuries. According to Hughe, Taylor has two or three broken or crushed ribs, bruised lungs, and several other general contusions. Most alarming is his state of mind, as he screamed when waking, stopped only by Hughe's large hand and assurances in the most broken of English that he was home and safe. Then Taylor managed to gasp out his brief but terrifying tale, before lapsing into unconsciousness again.

By that point I was furious, Susannah. Lady Shardley not only cast aspersions on my house and my servants, she has materielly damaged one of them! This is not a matter taken lightly and I said as much to Hughe. Sometimes I forget that he is only a servant, as he is so very tall, and also because I know he does not understand much of what I say to him. I have the feeling that makes him absolutely indispensable at Sumwattle Estate. However, that is a matter for another day.

Hughe then told me the sad tale of the Shardley house.

Since Gwynneth's dismissal, the disagreements and arguments between Lady Shardley and Lord Shardley have become more and more frequent and intense.

You see, the reason for the ruin that came upon the maids in her own house had never been brought to Lady Shardley's attention. She simply believed that good help was hard to find and keep, which is true, so an understandable assumption for her to make. She had no idea that the stream of girls in and out were indicative of a much more difficult and personal problem.

But Gwynneth's situation, in her own house, hearing from her housekeeper what was screamed from Gwynneth's own snaggle-toothed mouth, gave Lady Shardley pause. A rift was born between the Shardleys. Until that fateful day, the Fateful Day I went to Sumwattle Estate and was nearly murdered, Lady Shardley had dismissed the rumours regarding her husband's pursuits as the ramblings of the envious and small-minded of our set. However, after that day she began to review everything she knew about her servants and her husband's histories. In this review, certain patterns began to emerge which were not only devastating to her as a Lady, but humiliating to her as a Woman.

That is when her consumption of spirits, surely intended initially to boost her own, began to increase rather alarmingly.

Then she stopped getting out of bed.

Now, this was extracted from Hughe, who works for Lady Shardley, and I have been forced to expand on his sparse rendering of the tale. What Hughe managed to say was, "Lady Shardley angry at Lord Shardley for chasing girls with his spout up. She drinks now. And sleeps. And cries." I thanked the Good Lord that Hughe is from a place where servants are not bound to secrecy as to the goings-on in their houses. However, I realized that that trait may reflect poorly on my own Hall, if Hughe were to discuss with others various goings-on . . . and I said as much. He smiled at me.

"Lady nice. Nice Lady always speak with good meaning." Which I think meant I ought not worry. But back to my tale.

At that moment the apothecary arrived at the servants' entrance and required instruction. He has been to Wetmoor so often that when told one of my footmen had been crushed by a large, soft, heavy thing, there was not even a blink of surprise. Hughe waited to continue until the apothecary had gone. I did not know what to do with myself and thought of perhaps having a few cakes, but remembered that I am not eating cakes at present in order to prevent further clothing costs. I picked up the racquet Mr. Ploughgoode had thoughtfully left with me and began to practise my grip. Hughe looked out the window, perhaps in case any other of my servants were trundled back to Wetmoor by lunatic members of my class.

Presently the apothecary returned from his examination of Taylor. Cook conferred with him in low tones, which for all my straining I could not overhear. I put the racquet aside and waited for someone to tell me what was going on under my own roof.

Finally, after the apothecary had spoken with Cook, Cook spent a rather longer time with Hughe. Then Hughe came back into the parlour and bowed briefly.

I told him to tell me all that he could and quickly, else I would be forced to ask Cook or even the apothecary himself, as my servant was rather mangled at present and in need of care.

Hughe coughed and turned away, staring at the ceiling. He then explained, in blunt and coarse terms, what had transpired to put our poor Taylor into such a state. I will couch it in terms that will hopefully not render you a victim of the swooning to which I have so recently become accustomed.

It appears that Lady Shardley, through grief, humiliation and an overabundance of compensatory spirits to improve her own, has become melancholic. Any woman would feel the same way were we in her unfortunate position. However, her malady has manifest in confusion between servants and those of breeding.

In spite of his peasant blood, Taylor has always had a refined air about him, as you know. Given his delicate features, beautiful brown eyes and hair, both of which shine with health and vigour, it is not inconceivable that he be taken for another, especially when one's eyes have been compromised by bitter tears and strong brandy for several days.

Which is what Lady Shardley did, mistaking Taylor for a suitor from her youth, Susannah. She began addressing him with endearments and frequently referred to him as "Sailor." It is my understanding that Lady Shardley's first love was in the Royal Navy, a commodore, whom she was forbidden to marry due to an unfortunate confluence of family lineage.

I believe she was retreating into a kinder, gentler past, to avoid facing a present, and possible future, bleak both in terms of private affection at home and public standing.

Regardless, Lady Shardley was constantly summoning poor Taylor, requesting cakes, more brandy, more kerchiefs, all the while calling him Sailor. She was so undone she could not even remember his name! "Sailor, bring me more brandy." That sort of thing.

Taylor, who has been of course properly trained by myself, always responded promptly and perfectly to each request.

It was then that Lady Shardley made an error in judgment. She requested that he join her for brandy, Susannah. In her rooms!

Taylor rose to the occasion and remembered he was there to serve, not to question, and joined her. Taylor is unaccustomed to strong spirits, Susannah. He may have a pint at the pub to bolster his thin frame against the cold, but cannot not be described as a serious drinker by any but the wildest stretch of imagination. More than a thimbleful is likely more than he can tolerate.

Lady Shardley, on the other hand, has made a determined effort in recent weeks to turn a pleasant pastime into an avocation. In other words, Taylor was no match for her. Pound for pound, Lady Shardley trumped Taylor.

I believe Taylor felt he could not refuse; we may never know. Regardless, he began to match her, drink for drink.

It is difficult to ascertain what happened next, Susannah, but I have thought on it, and believe the reconstruction that follows may fall somewhere in the vicinity of the Truth.

After drinking far more than he is accustomed to, Taylor passed out. It has happened to better and more experienced men than he, as we both well know. But Taylor passed out on Lady Shardley's bed. If that fact ever gets out she shall never need be concerned about what her husband's reputation is doing to her house, it will be irreparably damaged by her own behaviour.

Lady Shardley was of course certain that Taylor was dead. She had to undo parts of his uniform to check for his pulse. He was not dead, but also could not be roused.

Realizing help was required, Lady Shardley climbed across the bed to ring the summoning bell, unfortunately breaking at least three of Taylor's ribs in the process, as she failed to notice that she was climbing over my poor slight servant as well. Having pulled the bell she realized, from her precarious position, that she too had imbibed more spirits than her present exertions allowed. That is what I believe led to her collapsing on top of Taylor in a dead faint.

It is the only explanation for how she wound up atop of a half-dressed servant, both unconscious.

What is of concern to everyone is the smothering effect that Lady Shardley may have had on Taylor. Literally. At first Lady Shardley's maid did not realize anyone was beneath her. It was not until she summoned help and rolled Lady Shardley over that Taylor was discovered.

We did not know what effect the lack of air may have on Taylor, Susannah. He was heavily sedated by the apothecary and Hughe only heard, "Lady Shardley was on top," from Taylor before the draught took him to slumber.

This left me in a quandary.

That my servant has been physically damaged there is no doubt. That his intellectual capabilities possibly were as well, meagre as they may be, was more alarming. One cannot have a servant who cannot obey simple instructions or remember his station. I had a horrible vision of Taylor, wandering the Hall during the Opening Ball, thinking he was Thomas Aquinas or perhaps a dog, lifting his leg as he pleased.

This would not do, but I could not think of a proper resolution. I thanked Hughe for returning Taylor and he returned to Sumwattle. The rest of us waited. Night fell, and after a cold supper Hortense was tucked into bed by Prudence. Foxx walked the hall outside of Taylor's room and Cook stirred a pot of soup for when and if Taylor awoke.

I fell asleep in the parlour in front of the fire, my racquet still in my hands. It was after midnight when I heard Foxx cry out happily from the top of the grand staircase.

"Taylor is hungry!" I leapt up and promptly fell over: both of my feet were asleep. Cook ran through the front hall with a tureen, calling in her raspy voice for Prudence to awaken. Foxx saw me struggling to my feet. Dear that he is, he ran down, helped get me up and we both ran up to the servant's quarters where Taylor lay, pale and wan but wide awake. Everyone else had already arrived, drat these skirts of mine! Cook was pinching Taylor's cheeks and checking his eyes, Prudence was patting his hand and Hortense stood in the doorway, rubbing the sleep from her eyes and looking confused. I approached Taylor's bed.

"Taylor, are you all right?"

He looked pained. "No, mum. Not quite." Well, he was aware of his physical state.

"Do you know who I am?"

"Lady Upton-Church. Don't you know who you are?"

"Taylor, we have been terribly worried." I smiled at him, for he did not look in the least bit dim-witted.

"Why?"

"After what happened to you." I did not know what else to say in front of the rest of the servants.

"Don't know what you mean, mum." Foxx, Cook, Prudence, Hortense and I exchanged looks over Taylor's bandaged head, although Hortense seemed confused.

"After what happened to you," I said again, as we stared at him. He lay there mute, scarce making a lump under the covers. He finally looked away from me, but that made him look at Foxx, which he seemed to find uncomfortable, at which point he glanced at Prudence, winced, looked at Cook, tried to smile at Hortense and failed, and finally, bereft of a place to look that did not involve looking into our faces, closed his eyes.

"So tired, mum."

Of course he was. So I took my leave, Cook leaving the soup with strict instructions to Prudence to make sure she fed Taylor and not the coverlet. Foxx wished him well, forgetting his damaged state for a moment and clapping him on the shoulder to emphasize his sympathy. Then he apologized. Hortense leaned over, kissed him on the cheek and tucked her rag doll next to him. We departed save for Prudence, who sat holding a spoon and waiting for our patient to voice hunger or thirst.

I went to bed exhausted, Susannah, and slept until almost noon. The household was in chaos, as Prudence, Hortense or Foxx frequently needed to leave their stations to attend to Taylor. They informed me he was doing well and had been able to sit up to eat. I made certain they sent my regards. Going to a servants' quarters is one thing when they may have been felled by mortal injury, but quite another when they shall live.

However, I still had the matter of Lady Shardley to resolve. It took several hours for me to decide on the appropriate course, and I hope my resolution meets with your approval.

After several attempts, some of which were quite severe, I completed a letter back to Lady Shardley, and had it delivered by Foxx posthaste. I have copied it out here for you:

Dear Lady Shardley,

Thank you for your letter and concerns regarding my servants. It is most appreciated by one of your standing.

I have taken your advice to heart and would like you to know that upon full review of all the salient facts, I do not believe the situation regarding Taylor is hopeless. I shall keep him under my tutelage and insure that any inadequacies in performance are correctly resolved. He has been in my employ for a very long time and is the son of one of Quince's favourite footmen, so there is a sentimental as well as practical aspect to my decision.

I understand you have not been feeling yourself in recent days, and do hope and pray that your former spirits return to you with all speed, and your back is restored, preventing further falls or unfortunate incidents.

Yours Very Kindly,
Lady Upton-Church

That should settle the matter, Susannah. Imagine the gall of that woman, her own house in a complete uproar and her poor history of the proper care and tending of servants, lecturing me on one of mine! It was completely out of bounds, but I am aware of her social standing, so endeavored to tacitly make her aware that I am Aware of What Happened, as opposed to merely aware of what happened, and the matter shall stay between the two of us, as long as she no longer attempts to control her own reputation with the ruination of mine.

But I now must away, for in the last three days I have spent entirely too much time trying to put my house to rights. I have not had time to tell you of the Dreadful Injury I received – but I promise I shall write again soon with the details, and until that time please know that I remain

Your Distracted Friend,

Annabella

☙ A Dreadful Injury ❧

22 May, 1821

Dearest Susannah,

I hope this letter finds you well and enjoying the springtime air. The garden shows of Paris sound lovely and I hope that you find a great deal of enjoyment in the selection of vegetables that may soon grace your own gardens and table.

I shall not be able to travel to London for another few months, which vexes me. I have business interests there that require my presence, as opposed to letters, etc. But the renovations work requires my presence as well, for if I am gone the workmen shall begin lolling about, looking for things to steal and importuning Cook for extra rations of stout.

I have sad purpose in writing you today, Susannah, and hope you are sitting whilst reading this. If you are not, please take a moment now and find a comfortable spot.

Baron Gurthwant is no longer with us.

I am as shocked to write those words as you must be to read them, as he was in the prime of his life, the very picture of health. Let me relate how I came to hear the news myself.

It was last Tuesday, the day of my next tennis lesson. I was looking forward to Mr. Ploughgoode's visit, hoping it would take my mind off of Taylor's injuries, Lady Shardley's insult and of how to extricate Gwynneth from the quagmire into which her life seems to have degenerated, although I have not the faintest clue about how to accomplish such a feat. The only thing I can think to do is to keep her here at the Hall and make sure she is paid enough so she can run away if she wishes. It is a poor plan, but the best I have been able to think of on my own. Hopefully, in time, something better may spring to mind. Mr. Sinclair is researching lineages and marital law for me, but his information is rather hodge-podge, as I cannot divulge to him the information I want.

In order to prevent Mr. Sinclair sussing out the truth on his own, I was so vague in my instructions that I am now buried in books about forms of weddings that, thus far, have yielded nothing that can help. The general tenor of them indicates that Mr. Sinclair believes I am trying to break Quince's will. But I soldier on regardless. I cannot believe that there is nothing to be done for the poor wretch. I shall update you if I find anything that can help.

Speaking of the poor wretch, Gwynneth came to Wetmoor the day before my tennis lesson and altered another dress. I do not mind telling you, Susannah, in spite of her general misfortune, the girl is an absolute genius, for the second gown was even more flattering than the first! What Gwynneth can do with some lace and ribbon is beyond compare.

If Mr. Ploughgoode's initial (and I am sure inadvertently obvious) reaction was indicative of the overall success of Gwynneth's work, then it is a smashing improvement on the original design. He actually <u>gaped</u> at me, Susannah, before covering it up by pretending to cough.

He was delightfully prompt and, once recovered from his gratifying response to my appearance, inquired with solicitude after my health, including a concern that the first lesson may have been too taxing. It was not, but I did not see any harm in feigning overexertion so as not to set too high an expectation of future performance. He apologized, bowing deeply as he did so, that rough Scottish burr sending tingles up and down my spine. It is delicious when one's servants are delicious, is it not? Although Mr. Ploughgoode is not under me, he is close enough to it that there may as well be no difference at all.

As we walked through the ballroom toward the door to the courtyard Mr. Ploughgoode was startled to see Taylor, now unbandaged but still unsteady, being led around the near gardens by Prudence, who has been an attentive nurse. I explained that Taylor was the unfortunate victim of an accident, and instructed Prudence to take Taylor inside for his nap.

Mr. Ploughgoode remarked that our county seems to have a higher-than-normal number of accidents that render inhabitants deceased or maimed in some way, a point which could not be argued. I did not know at the time that his observation was merely foreshadowing the news I would soon receive.

The lesson began pleasantly. Mr. Ploughgoode reviewed the proper grip of the racquet with me and was pleased that I had practised on my own between lessons. Apparently my hand strength is wonderful for that sort of thing, not the limp and graceless grip that most Ladies of my station possess.

With that matter settled to our mutual satisfaction we moved on to the balls. Apparently it is just as important to have a thorough understanding of the balls' properties as it is to have a proper grip. Firmness, size, etc., are all reliable indicators of their performance and it is important to know how to gauge them properly, so one can compensate. Although I was hoping to get onto the court that day I realized that we would again be standing in the shade and discussing equipment properties, so I called for tea to be brought. It would not do to be swooning out in the heat. Hortense brought it out well, I must say. I think she shall make a lovely little maid one day, if she can stop limping. She even managed a quick bob of her head before withdrawing back into the Hall.

As Mr. Ploughgoode was perspiring somewhat and seemed breathless I offered him a cup of tea as well. He gratefully accepted and we sat for a short break. His large hands enveloped the china cup completely and he complimented the flavour of the tea expansively. I could have sat there all day and listened to him speak, Susannah!

But that was not to be, nor was the continuation of the lesson, for Hortense arrived with a letter. She was so in shock of something that she forgot to bob a curtsey and also forgot that I should address her first. She ran to me, thrust the letter in my hand and said, "It's an urgent letter, mum, you must read this right away," and ran back inside.

I stood, Mr. Ploughgoode scrambling to stand first (and almost succeeding) and stepped away. He offered to leave, but I could not see the sense in it, as Hortense thinks all courier correspondence is urgent. I did, however, move away from him to read the letter privately, and the news clipping that accompanied it. It was from Mr. Sinclair, which at first seemed quite normal, until I read the contents.

Sophia's darling husband has passed on.

It was a terrible thing. Baron Gurthwant found himself locked in a small wine cellar off of the first pantry, looking for the proper chardonnay to drink with the night's fish course. Their cook was shopping and had taken the scullery girls with her to help. The baron may have been trapped there for several hours, any cries for release unheeded. He decided to have a cigar whilst waiting.

As you know from my conversation with Sophia at the barons' birthday party, Baron Gurthwant's one failing was his personal aroma. Sophia had settled the issue for herself with the cultivation of her gardens, but neither had ever thought of the effect it might have in an enclosed space, if it accumulated.

The lighting of a match for his cigar seems to have been the precipitating event, and the baron's end was instantaneous. Of course the pantry and wine cellar were destroyed, and there is to be an inquest, surely a mere formality.

I was stunned. It seemed only yesterday that I was swooning into the bushes at their house and now the Sophia is the Widow Gurthwant. Mr. Sinclair had written without commenting that no one else would have told me, and without invitations to dinners I may not have heard. His solicitous nature (especially for a solicitor) was the final straw of kindness; he knows I am fond of Sophia. I began to weep. Mr. Ploughgoode was beside himself at my tears, as I was unable to elucidate the reason for them.

I wept not because of any particular fondness for the baron, nor did I weep from shock, nor from Mr. Sinclair's thoughtful nature. I knew the baron only slightly, and the number of inquests and funerals I have attended have made me more sanguine than most regarding an unexpected demise. If Quince taught me anything, it is this: When it is your time, it is your time, and our Lord shall bring you Home by whatever conveyance He deems appropriate, whether it be a metal box falling four stories and crushing you or exploding in a wine cellar. It is all one to Him. I was terribly sad for Sophia, of course. I am very fond of her in spite of the shortness of our acquaintance, but that also was not the reason for my tears.

What was causing me to weep was the large splinter from my tennis racquet which lodged in the palm of my hand, for I had squeezed it hard during the reading of my letter. Mr. Ploughgoode was alarmed that I was weeping, believing the letter to be bearing bad news. Of course it was, but that was also beside the point. He called for Prudence, but she did not come. As I found out later when planning to dismiss her for the breach, Taylor had grown faint on the final stairway to his room and Prudence had to sit below him to keep him from tumbling down and finishing what Lady Shardley began.

Mr. Ploughgoode ran to me, then stepped back, then came forward and without thinking I held out my poor wounded hand to him, dropping my racquet and sniffling.

He stepped forward again and took my hand as gently as if it were a small bird. He ran a thumb over the fleshier part of my palm, stopping when he sensed the splinter. I gasped not only at the additional pain he caused by doing so but also because his touch was unexpectedly intimate. It did stop my sniffling. Men only take your hand to kiss it, as you well know. This was different. Of course, he is a Scot, so his manners are coarser than those to which I am accustomed.

He swiftly led me back to my chair and sat me down. Then he requested leave to examine the wound, as the fault was surely his in not checking the equipment first.

I hesitated for a moment, assured myself that we were alone in the courtyard, no one was in sight who might misinterpret his ministrations, and gave him leave.

He first began by holding my hand in his and ran his fingers lightly over it, staying clear of the affected area. His touch was quite feathery, in spite of the calluses on his hands. The feel of them made me shiver, only because I have never had my hand taken by someone who uses his hands. It is a most unusual sensation. Mr. Ploughgoode assured me his touch was to determine no other "rebel bits o' racquet" were lurking elsewhere. Then he peered for the splinter itself. It felt quite large. He apologized profusely for lacking the proper tools and said he only knew the Highland way of finding and removing it, which was not proper for a Lady.

I thought for a moment about the fuss it would be to have Prudence find Foxx to ride for that awful surgeon, Gibberwilly, who would likely behave poorly again, and the wait I would have to endure while my hand throbbed. It had begun to feel warm during his examination, it could be hours before I was seen to, I could develop an infection!

That decided the issue. To preserve my health and avoid another interaction with Mr. Gibberwilly, who would likely want to use an axe to remove a splinter along with my entire arm, it would be best to submit to a Highland cure rather than a proper English procedure and I told Mr. Ploughgoode so. He asked if I was certain, looking nervous. I told him firmly that I knew my own mind and the Highland cure was the appropriate action given the circumstances. He nodded, still looking uncertain.

Well, the Highland cure is rather unusual, Susannah. With very little ado, Mr. Ploughgoode leaned over and put his open mouth on my hand! I gasped, for apparently he needed to use his tongue to locate the splinter and he began on the wrong side of my palm, then worked very, very slowly across it with little licks and nibbles. I do not know why he had to nibble on my fingers and admit that I did not care what the reason was – it was <u>fantastic</u>. Once he reached the splinter (which seemed to take not near enough time), he swiftly removed it with his teeth, spat it to the side and blotted the wound with his kerchief. I was quite unsettled, as I am sure you can imagine. Then he asked where the spirits were kept.

Fortunately life with Quince taught me the value of preparedness and there was a bottle of Scotch tucked into a bush next to us. One never knows when medicinals may be required. As you know, I have with foresight stocked various parts of the Hall in case of emergency. Given the number of emergencies that have arisen I feel justified in continuing the practise: there is a fine brandy in my carriage, cognac in my dressing room and a delightful port in the pantry, amongst others. When I pulled the bottle from the bush, seeming by magic, Mr. Ploughgoode smiled at the bottle, apologized for the additional "bit o' sting" I was about to feel and splashed Scotch onto my hand.

He was correct, Susannah, but I believe Scots stoicism led him to understate the level of sting that occurred. Tears sprang anew to my eyes while he poured more Scotch onto his kerchief, before gently wrapping it around my hand and, unaware of the breach, turned my hand over and gently kissed it.

"That should prevent infection, Lady," he murmured softly. Quite softly. He cleared his throat and when he spoke again it was in a less personal tone. "To be safe, a wee dram should be taken as well." He tossed what was left of my tea into the grass and poured the most generous wee dram I have ever had the pleasure of taking for my health. I nodded and drank half of it down in one gulp, which met with his approval. I then gestured to his teacup and the bottle. He swiftly poured a "dram" to match my own, and toasted me lightly before downing his in a single gulp. He paused and cocked his head to the side.

"Single malt, Lagavulin," he grinned.

I could not helping returning the grin. "You have an excellent palate."

"For Scotch, I do. If you like Lagavulin, you'd adore Oban. It has more smoke in it."

"I have not heard of it. Perhaps I shall have Cook send for some. Thank you for tending to my injury, Mr. Ploughgoode."

He smiled. "Please, call me by my Christian name. In Scotland it's customary when one has tended another's wounds."

"And what is your Christian name, pray tell, that I may call you that?" Oh, it is a devilish grin he has!

"William, my Lady. But most call me Will."

"Very well then, Will, from now on you shall be known by your Christian name in this Hall. But not in front of staff."

"Of course. Thank you, Lady." Then he poured more of the Scotch, as it was tacitly clear that the lesson, truncated by death and injury, was over. Instead I drank Scotch by my tennis court, explaining the explosion of Baron Gurthwant to Will and trying to think if there was any way I could get another splinter in my hand. Or my neck. Perhaps my. . .

I have just realized where the sun is (not) in the sky! So engrossed did I become in relating the tale that I lost all track of the time and there are instructions to write out for tomorrow. I also have to decide what to wear to the inquest, which is in three days' time.

In the meantime, please know that I believe Will Ploughgoode is perfectly named.

Your Rather Tingling Friend,

Annabella

☙ Quince's Letter ❧

25 May, 1821

My Dearest Susannah,

You shall be relieved to know I have regained my former high spirits and appreciate your kind note of sympathy and support. It was a lovely gesture and I thank you for it.

Your concern regarding my hand was most welcome. As you can tell by the improved handwriting in this letter, I am completely cured.

I do not believe in changing treatments for what ails one, so have continued the liquid portion of the Highland cure detailed in my letter, alternately soaking my wound with Scotch and taking a drink as a further preventative. I am delighted to say that there is not even a mark, so am pleased that I did not wait for the surgeon, but instead trusted Mr. Ploughgoode's abilities and my own instincts regarding the matter.

Once again I find I must correct a slight misunderstanding on your part, and must endeavor to re-read my letters to you in the future to make sure I have been clear. The details of the first part of my lesson with Will (as I now refer to him, at his request) were once again of the actual lesson, not a veiled attempt to describe a more personal encounter.

I cannot imagine myself standing on the tennis court, dropping my racquet in surprise when Will vaulted over the net and ran toward me, overcome by passion, kissing me so thoroughly that the grass on the tennis court beckoned us to become more comfortable, and suddenly we were tumbling down upon it and each other, my dressed being peeled off by his lovely hands even as I freed him from the ridiculous amount of clothing men are perforce to wear in polite society to find a staggering person buried beneath the deerskin breeches, waistcoat, cravat, boots, the grass soft beneath me . . . It was a tennis lesson, Susannah. That is all.

It would be inappropriate for me to have a liaison with Will, Susannah, although the thought did cross my mind. More than once, actually, although sometimes in my mind I vault over the net and run toward him. I pay the man for lessons, after all. Were I to approach him he may only acquiesce from a sense of obligation, which is a horrible thought, I would then have paid for a tryst, and there shall be other opportunities without having to pay for them. I fervently hope so. If it came to that I would lock myself in my rooms and never leave them again.

Once I had regained my equilibrium after the horrible shock of Baron Gurthwant's death I set about to a plan that had nothing to do with the dead. As I waited for the inquest – of course I shall attend, it shall be a relief to attend an inquest where I am not expected to give testimony – I realized it would be all too easy to fall into melancholy and reminiscence, so I deemed it best to focus on the living. On Gwynneth, in fact.

A plan for Gwynneth is what I have lacked thus far, Susannah, and it has caused my efforts to be unfocused.

I am rather at a loss to know what to do, Susannah. Finding a way to happy and titillating ending for all (and not in that order, either) may be impossible.

So although my idea was to conceive of an elegant and witty plan for a resolution that would be only slightly

But now it is time for you to grow up, those are the only words I can think of for it. And you must do something that is anathema (look it up, dear) to ladies of your station. You must educate yourself, Annabella, and you must do it soon. You know nothing of how the world works and there are many who would cheerfully defraud you and leave you with nothing.

As I do not wish for that to happen, you must begin a program of study. Begin here in the library. Read the books, Annabella, even if it is difficult, vexing, and gives you a headache. Use the dictionaries whenever you need (we have several), ask Mr. Weerly for help (he is discreet), whatever is required. You must also begin to read the newspapers every day, but not for gossip and society information. You must read it to understand the world that you now live in without protection. I promise, it will become easier as time goes by and you have a broader body of knowledge from which to draw.

You must promise to do this for me, Annabella.

When you have read the books you will understand why I am so very adamant on these issues, and you will know what you need to continue to investigate on your own. If you do not wish to be penniless, or perhaps forced to marry someone who will not treasure you as I did, you will do this last thing I ask of you.

Annabella, I am very sorry that I have died. Please let this thought comfort you: I am with Sarah again, and I will give her your love.

Your Husband,

Quince

As you can see, it expounded at length on my complete silliness, which is why I did not want to tell you of it. I hope you understand. Now when I read it I am bemused. I really was a girl, even though I was married. Thank goodness Quince thought it a virtue instead of a deficit of character.

That is how it all began, Susannah, with Quince's letter. Quince was in many ways a queer husband, but had he not foreseen it was likely he would precede me in death and plan accordingly I should be in dire straits today. But he did and I am not.

After I read his letter in London I looked at the books in the library with new eyes. What had seemed a cozy room suddenly seemed to have far more books than before I found out I had to read them. Far more. It was Quince's Last Request, however, and nearly an entire year stretched out before me with nothing to do except look out the window and watch London go by.

I think he would be pleased to know I actually read many of them – I read every single day. As there are hundreds of books a full year was not enough time to finish them all. I started with fiction, as it seemed simpler than something about mechanical devices, but it was a start. After a few weeks I moved on to history, philosophy, law and the like.

Quince was right: there was much I did not know, so much left out at Miss Penelope's School, which is perhaps why is was called her School of Charms and Whimsies instead of her School of Classical Education and Rational Thought.

Following Quince's Request I also began reading the newspapers every day. It was very confusing at first, for newspapers assume one has been reading them every day since birth. Quince was right: it became easier over time.

I did not understand why Quince had made such generous arrangements for me in his will, for his holdings – my holdings, I suppose – are vast and complicated. I decided to be flattered and honoured he thought me capable of managing them on my own, including Wetmoor Hall itself. Were it not for his purchase of this property I would be forced to stay in the London house or let a house in the country. Things have turned out so differently than I imagined they would when a young girl.

I am sure Gwynneth feels the same, but for opposite reasons. Perhaps now you might understand more why I have become so obsessed with her. All of the men in my life (only my Father and Quince, but bear with me) did everything they could to ensure I would always be taken care of. First Father (God rest his soul) married me off to Quince. I was not thrilled at the time, for Quince was so old, but I realize now Father was more concerned with Quince's character than his visage. Quince's care of me during our marriage and his arrangements for me after his death show that Father was correct. Had Father chosen someone else for me, or Quince been a less honourable man, I may have found myself cast out and divorced after losing Sarah, with no means of my own beyond the charity and kindness of those who showed little of either characteristic after Quince's death.

I know Gwynneth and I have nothing in common – she is common, and I am not – but I feel someone should do something about her, even if it is only to try to assure she has a bit of money of her own. Everything else has been taken from her.

My goodness, I seem to have cast myself in the role of champion, have I not? Next I shall be ordering suits of armor and tilting at windmills or taking up arms against tyranny.

For now I believe I shall instead make up some fresh flower arrangements. Hopefully their lovely scent shall inspire me to something absolutely elegant in regard to Gwynneth.

I must away now, for there are other situations going on, but I have blathered on again, and did not even tell you about the inquest. I carried myself quite well until the end.

Your Quixotic Friend,
Annabella

ꕥ Another Inquest ꕥ

31 May, 1821

Dearest Susannah,

Greetings and Felicitations, spring is finally in full bloom! As Life springs forth with glorious riot, there was an inquest to attend. It seems that there is always a balance that must be struck. Even as eggs are laid lovingly in nests and buds begin to open themselves to sunny skies, there is yet another dead member of the peerage lying about, with all the attendant protocols.

For inquest attire, I wore a lovely grey gown, the same one I wore during the dreadful situation regarding Sir Herbert's death. No one from this county attended that inquest, so it seemed the best course given the short amount of time I had to prepare.

As the inquest was the most interesting thing to happen in our county in weeks, I knew the entire staff would want to attend. The workmen had all gone missing for the day, so I decided we should all go together.

Two carriages were prepared, one carrying myself and Cook, the latter bringing Taylor, Prudence, Hortense and Foxx. Taylor is faring quite well: he only limps slightly now.

The inquest was held at the Church, it being the largest building in town, and was filled to bursting with the curious and bored. Since I was a bit of both I decided not to cast aspersions on the rest of the crowd.

Such a crowd it was! There were Baron Theosophus and Duke Twitwhistle, both enthroned in the first pew, peering over spectacles and monocle respectively, leering at the women and frowning at the men. Lady Shardley was there but Lord Shardley was not. I was going to approach and inquire after her health, but she was buried behind a fan, avoiding all interaction. When Taylor saw her he yelped and Foxx steered him to the other side of the Church and out of her sight and more importantly, I think, she out of his.

Also in attendance were Gwynneth and the Bargesniffles, although I could not see why. It is well-known that the day of an inquest is greatly anticipated by serving houses, as after an inquest everyone wants to discuss what they heard and saw.

Then I saw most of the workmen who were supposed to be working on my Hall. I was going to upbraid the lazy creatures and order them to return to their work when Cook mentioned that work done resentfully is rarely done well. Although her statement was correct, I was angry that she presumed to say this to me, and told her so. She said that perhaps recent "conks" to my head had knocked some of the sense out of it.

Can you believe it! Cook dared say that to me! In public, no less, where anyone could have overheard her impertinence! We have known each other for years, it is true, but she had gone too far, and I told her so. She quickly withdrew, belatedly remembering that it was not her place to such an observation.

Driver leaned against the wall, staring impassively at the scene before him. I realized the last inquest he attended was the one for my darling Quince and the others, poor fellow. Driver carried himself brilliantly that day. He had to be brought from hospital on a pallet, but was the only one who could tell what happened other than me and, as you know, my word was rather suspect. It was decided his testimony was needed, so he was put in a wagon and brought him to the inquest.

Driver was the primary reason I was found innocent, for he confirmed everything I said, and told how I had tried to care for him. He only started crying the one time, when he told how hard everyone had looked for his leg, and that he missed it. Sometimes I forget he used to have two legs. He has adapted very well to the wooden one. He is on his sixth leg now, although the one that caught fire should not be counted against him, as he did not notice it was in flames in time to save it, and saved the stables with the burden of having to hop.

Also in attendance at the present inquest were the Gurthwants' servants and several other titles and peerages in various stages of conversation and intrigue, as so often happens when those of our ilk gather in any number.

The hubbub continued for a time, with Gwynneth approaching me shyly and eyeing my dress, asking if it pleased. I said it did very much and her services were still required. We set a date for two days hence. Hughe approached next and inquired after Taylor on Lady Shardley's behalf – the woman did not have the grace to approach me herself! I informed him that with time we hope Taylor shall be restored, but was still frail. Will Ploughgoode then drew near and inquired after my health, which was appropriate. I told him I was recovered and thanked him again for his efforts. He appeared pleased at my rapid recuperation and very pleased that our next lesson would be in four days' time. I was pleased myself. Just as Duke Twitwhistle was wheezing toward me we were all startled by the gavel banging the long table set before the altar, bringing the inquest to order. I made my way toward the seat that Foxx had secured for me which, to my dismay, was next to Baron Theosophus, but as I cast my eye about, there were no other seats left. With an inward sigh of resignation I sat down, and watched as the crowd sorted itself between the working class and their betters. Then Constable Pukeston entered. The inquest had begun.

First the coroner was summoned to present his opinion regarding the cause of death, which in the Baron Gurthwant's case, meant he had exploded. Constable Pukeston requested as a formality that more testimony be heard to ascertain the reason for such an event, as if we all did not know what caused such a huge conflagration.

The kitchen staff were summoned to vouch that they were not in the house and so could not have heard the Baron's cries for help.

The rest of the Gurthwants' staff were brought forward to describe their whereabouts at the time of the incident. Those that were out of hospital, that is. Two still remain, but they are expected to make full recoveries.

Then darling Sophia was called, Susannah. She had not been in the Church proper, of course, instead choosing to wait in the small anteroom where the vicar prepares himself for services. She entered, her black mourning gown making her appear haggard. I remembered how awful it was to testify at Quince's inquest and my heart went out to her. This was the second inquest at which she was forced to testify due to the death of a husband but, in this case, she actually loved him.

She was sworn in and sat down. After a moment the local barrister, pressed into service as the inquisitor on behalf of the Crown, began to ask her questions.

Yes, she was very happy with the baron.

No, there was no one who wished him ill.

Yes, she had information that could shed light on his death.

Not a sound could be heard.

Haltingly, with great embarrassment and a lowered voice, she explained the baron's unusual aromatic condition. She detailed his love of a fine cigar and the great relaxation he found when spending time in the wine cellar.

Utter silence ruled the Church. Constable Pukeston leaned forward. "Is it your belief, Baroness Gurthwant, that Baron Gurthwant expired as a result of the importune interaction of those three . . . characteristics of his?"

"Yes, sir, I do," she replied, tears springing to her eyes. She fished in her reticule for a kerchief and when she lifted it, rose petals drifted down to the floor. With that she was undone. Her weeping would have turned a stone heart to butter, Susannah. Constable Pukeston was alarmed, as was the inquisitor. As were we all, actually. This was not the stiff upper lip we have been trained to employ during difficult times. It reminded me of when Countess Vinkle discovered her son had gotten his mistress in trouble and eloped with her to Gretna Green instead of making arrangements and marrying a suitable woman. I thought Countess Vinkle would drown herself in the punch bowl at Almack's when the news was delivered by nasty Mrs. Farrel-Stone. Drowning was preferable to the scene she caused that day.

Sophia apologized even as she continued to weep, her head down, mortified at her lack of backbone. Constable Pukeston of course forgave and quickly excused her. She fair ran back to the anteroom. Silence ruled until the door closed fully behind her, at which point the silence turned to excited whispers about her testimony. Constable Pukeston let it go on for a moment and then banged his gavel for quiet. As we are all well versed in inquest etiquette, we immediately silenced ourselves.

After a moment Constable Pukeston ruled, as expected, that the baron had died as natural a death as possible given his unusual constitution. Then he stammered that the death was unnatural, but not in a legal and murdering sense. More in the sense of the rarity of citizens exploding in their shoes, which caused some tittering. Looking relieved, he banged his gavel and ended the inquest. The working class was pouring out of Church, all headed toward the Bargesniffle pub, the family itself barely outpacing them to be at the ready for the windfall they would receive from another's misfortunes.

Which is what they seem to be quite fond of doing, Susannah. Taking advantage of the misfortunes of others. There they were, doing it again, this time benefiting from Baroness Gurthwant's pain! It is appalling what people with no breeding are capable of doing for a few pounds. As we trailed the hordes running for the pub, Foxx walked behind me. I felt oddly out of sorts and simply wanted to return to the Hall. Then Foxx spoke up.

"Gwynneth will be at the pub today, Lady."

"Yes, Foxx, I know."

He was not deterred. "Gwynneth is very . . . big now. Do you think she should be working so much?"

I tried to suppress my irritation but was not successful. "What am I supposed to do about it? I am not her mother, nor am I her keeper, and I am certainly not going to a serving house in the middle of the day." We stopped near our carriages.

Foxx was not deterred. "You could send us and we'll watch Gwynneth."

"It is not enough that you spend the day lolling about at inquests? You now want leave to spend the rest of the day in a pub as part of your duties." Foxx reared back at my ill-tempered response. "My life is spent dealing with everyone's problems, Foxx. Constance has to take care of her sister, so I am left with a midget for a maid. Taylor is crushed, Prudence spends most of her time tending him and does not come when I call her! Driver is, well, he is Driver, but he is an odd driver, and I keep him because no one else would hire him, and I am sure I run the worst house in the county –"

"Lady Upton-Church –"

"How dare you interrupt me!" I was in a rage without the slightest notion why, but it seemed Foxx would suffice as an object upon which to vent myself. "I do not remember where you trained but if you ever interrupt me again I shall send you to Lady Shardley's and she can crush you as well." I turned and walked to the carriage. At that moment Will approached Foxx.

"Are ye all comin' to the pub today? They're serving lamb with quince jelly." To my great horror I began to cry.

"Quince," was all I could squeak. Will looked horrified as again I wept in his presence. Foxx walked me to my carriage and I fair fell into the back of it the second the door was opened. Will stood with his mouth hanging open, a perfectly reasonable response to my unbelievable behaviour.

Suddenly I knew why I was so out of sorts, Susannah. I had not been to an inquest since Quince's, and the memories of that day were swirling in my head.

It was a terrible day. The whispers, titters and smirks of those in attendance, just as there were for the baron's death. People had gathered outside the court and were calling the most terrible things to me. I do not think I would have managed to walk in on my own without Prudence's assistance.

I thought my broken arm might have netted some sympathy, along with cuts and bruises courtesy of flying bits of box and people, but there was none. At least the authorities realized I could not be so clever as to have arranged such a horrible deed on my own and at the same time be stupid enough to be there when it occurred. They were correct in that.

As I wept in my carriage out of sheer self-pity I could hear Foxx and Mr. Ploughgoode murmuring to each other as the rest of the staff went to the other carriage and got ready for the ride home. It was clear no one from Wetmoor would be going to the Rooster and Mussel. I was too embarrassed at my behaviour to do anything but be carted home, Mr. Ploughgoode standing forlornly in the road, watching us leave.

It was a quiet ride back and Foxx was at the door with alacrity to help me down the steps of the carriage. Taylor limped to get the front door and everyone else looked down. I went straight to my rooms. Even after I had changed and curled up in bed, veritably buried under the bedcovers, I could not stop thinking of my dear, departed, disintegrated husband.

Quince had his faults, Susannah, as all men do, but he was my husband. In his own way he cared for me deeply and did his best to make sure I was taken care of properly, which is more than most can say for their husbands. Sometimes I miss him.

Life with Quince could be difficult, exasperating, and very, very strange. When not buried in his work there was always something happening: an inquest, an archaeological dig, a summer party, a scandal. Quince enjoyed inquests best of all,

Susannah. He would attend those of strangers, as he loved the idea of a life and death examined. Afterward we would go to the nearest serving house and sit in a corner, drinking sherry and eavesdropping. With him gone, I realized that chaperones and servants or no, I would not be able to indulge in that petty pastime in the same way. And those days were memorable.

It is ironic that his inquest was one of the best-attended and most explosive in recent memory, as you heard from others in attendance. I like to think he is laughing in Heaven that he was able to be the subject of that which interested him so much, but it is sometimes cold comfort.

Perhaps that is why I have been enjoying the mystery of Gwynneth and the goings-on in the county. It has been fun.

Please do not mistake me: I am not pining away for Quince by any stretch, for with the fun oft came loneliness and tears. He worked very hard, which left me alone much of the time.

I suddenly realized how unattractive all my self-pity was. There are likely hundreds of people who would trade places with me and consider themselves lucky to have such difficulties.

What difference does it make that I have a complicated reputation? Most people in London do as well. I can remarry if I wish, so cannot curse Quince if I decide not to pursue such a course. My new life is a fine one. I have servants aplenty, amusements galore, delightful diversions, your wonderful friendship and a beautiful Hall that may someday be finished. But until I came to this county fun was in scarce supply on my own. Suddenly there is fun again. There is a purpose. There is a reason beyond mere protocol for visiting people, talking with them and writing letters, and I am enjoying it immensely.

This realization was followed by another: huddling in my bed sobbing for all that is lost is more than self-pity, it is pathetic. So I got out of bed (it was only noon, after all) and decided to write you instead.

After all, I have to set an example for others.

Your Dear Recovering Friend,
Annabella

☙ Mr. Ploughgoode Resigns ❧

2 June, 1821

Dear Susannah,

I must confess your congratulations on my "pluck" were a trifle premature. It turns out I have not much nerve at all.

The next morning I did manage to climb out of bed and stop my horrible self-pity, but wound up back in it, after I had eaten breakfast and begun to prepare for the day.

We were in my dressing room and Prudence had just finished helping me into a gown when she asked permission to speak, a most rare request. I gave her leave and sat down, for whatever it was, it was difficult for her to frame.

"I don't think you should read the newspapers today, Lady." She blurted it out even as she stared at the floor, twisting her apron in her hands.

"That is silly, Prudence, although kind, but I read them every day. Why should this day be any different?"

Prudence went scarlet. "The baron's in a jar."

I felt as she had hit me over the head with a book, and was glad I was seated. "What do you mean?"

"He exploded, didn't he? Blew up, and there wasn't much of him left. They're using a jar. Like Lord Church."

I felt dizzy. Had I begun an awful trend? I saw in my mind's eye rows of jars on the shelves of a mourning shoppe.

"I did not know that." I finally said. "A jar?"

"Yes, and I'm so sorry, but you should know, because Lord Church is in a jar and I was afraid if you read about it. . . Well, you've been through enough, haven't you? I think you have. It was so awful last time and you were so brave, but what if you didn't know and then read about it –"

"Thank you, Prudence." I found tears welling in my eyes. "It was very kind of you to tell me."

"Taylor overheard at the inquest. He thought it would be better if I told you."

"That was kind of him as well." I sat there while she stood and I looked up at her. She really is a sweet girl.

I am a grown woman, however, able to handle difficult circumstances, like newspapers. I began to stand, but my knees gave away and I plopped back into the chair. "Oh, that was clumsy."

Prudence ran to me. "Are you all right?"

My breath was coming short, I am afraid, but I did not want to appear frail. "These new shoes –" I began to stand again and found myself fading back into my chair.

"I'll get you a brandy, Lady." She was rooting through my armoire even as I thanked her. The first sip was difficult, for my teeth chattered on the glass. The second went down a bit better and I took a deep breath.

"I am not feeling well, Prudence."

"Of course not, Lady."

I proved I was not lying almost immediately by vomiting my breakfast and brandy onto the floor. "Oh, I am sorry, Prudence!" Some had got on her uniform. "I shall buy you another uniform, oh, oh, no," and I did it again. I was glad she leapt back in time.

"Lady, you're quite unwell. You should lay down."

I had broken out into a sweat and felt very strange indeed. "I made such a mess –"

"I'll have in cleaned up in a trice. You need to get back in bed right now." Suddenly she was clucking over me even as the hem of my gown dragged through a bit of egg.

My voice sounded odd to me. "I did not even do that when it happened to Quince. Well, not at first."

Prudence patted my arm. "It's that corselet, Lady. That terrible fabric. I'll look at it and see what I can do."

"That must be it." I felt better knowing it was my corselet and not my nerves causing such a mess.

I submitted to being put back into my nightdress and tucked into bed, Prudence bustling about like a housekeeper.

"I'll get some dry toast for you with tea to settle your stomach, get your dressing room taken care of, and let the household know you're not to be disturbed."

"All right." As it was the first time Prudence had ever shown the slightest bit of spine I decided to acquiesce.

After she left I laid there wondering what I should do. The moment she said I should not leave my rooms I felt myself again, although I would not admit that to anyone but you. It seems I am not as brave as I would wish. It was the thought of another jar, Susannah, although why it should be upsetting I do not know. It would not be a glass jar.

Prudence was back only moments later, bustling in with a tray, bustling out, bustling back in with rags and buckets, disappearing into my dressing room and I began to feel more and more embarrassed. I chewed on some toast, drank some tea and my stomach began to feel better. Then I laid there again. I did not even have a book at hand. What was I supposed to do, lay there all day? If I did the workmen would laze about, the servants would slack in their work, and the

Hall would not be the slightest bit improved by the end of the day. Prudence finally came out of my dressing room and smiled at me.

"Good as new, Ladyship," she smiled.

"Thank you, Prudence." She left and I flung the covers back. I could at least get dressed and read in the library, I thought. I felt much steadier so I put on my pellise robe, rinsed my mouth and chewed mint leaves to get rid of the taste.

As I came down the stairway Prudence nearly frowned at me. When I told her my intention to read books in the library instead of attempting to face the newspapers she fussed me down the hallway, settled me onto the settee, tucked a throw around me, brought me more tea and piled books nearby so I would not have to move.

I was reading an engrossing passage from William Blake's Innocence and Experience (I still do not understand it) when Prudence entered to disapprovingly announce the arrival of Mr. Ploughgoode, who was waiting in the drawing room. I checked my appointment book, which confirmed the fact that I had not gone dotty, but Will had, in fact, arrived for a purpose unknown. After considering the situation for a moment, I decided I would meet with him. It was not as if I were going anywhere else.

I do not believe in rewarding uninvited callers (especially from a lower class) by sweeping into the drawing room as if expected. It could encourage more of the same behaviour. I finished the chapter I was reading, went up the back stairway to my suite and chose an appropriate gown for meeting an unexpected but ridiculously handsome caller that one shall never dally with (which is more difficult than one would think), had another cup of tea, and <u>then</u> swept into the drawing room. As Taylor opened the door Will scrambled to his feet, looking embarrassed. I nodded to him and sat, but let him stand. There are standards to uphold, after all. Taylor raised a querying brow and I nodded for him to withdraw.

Will began by apologizing for the unannounced visit, which was a correct beginning. I accepted but did not reciprocate for the two hours it took me to greet him. Again, there are standards to uphold. I asked him the purpose of his visit.

It took him what he may have thought of as a "wee" bit of time to tell me, going in looping circles of logic in order to arrive at a most vexing point.

He had come to resign his post! When I inquired the reason for this development he felt the need to look up the chimney whilst clearing his throat, so I began to question him.

It was not my skills at tennis which, although embryonic, Will felt could blossom beautifully.

It was not the times or dates set for lessons.

It was not the state of my tennis court.

It was my tears, Susannah. My tears. This was finally stated as he stared fixedly over my shoulder at the wall.

Apparently Will has an aversion to tears to rival mine own to blood. He noted that of the three times we have ever met I was undone twice by tears of his making, and the only appropriate thing to do was to remove the thing I found so upsetting, which appeared to be him, himself.

I was not sure how to proceed, for I have looked forward to my lessons and here was my instructor, resigning his post! To say nothing of the embarrassment I should face if it became common knowledge that I am too frail for a simple game of whatever it was Will told everyone I was learning. If people thought I could not play croquet or something similarly untaxing I would be a laughingstock!

His resignation would not do and I told him so, which gave him pause. I believe he thought I would shakily acquiesce and perhaps swoon once he had departed.

He explained that his Scots constitution is unsuited to tears as, in Scotland, when a woman weeps the man causing the offence either recites a poem, kills something for her or proposes marriage, of which only two are acceptable in England, but neither of them were appropriate to the situation involving me. Without these options he had been reduced to drinking copious quantities of Scotch whilst attempting to determine the proper course, which had eluded him. Thus he was tendering his resignation, which seemed to be the only thing to do.

I had no idea Scots were both so sentimental and coarse simultaneously, Susannah. Of course, God knows what they get up to there with their kilts and cabers, but I had no idea that simple tears undid them. Englishmen respond to tears properly: by either bursting into tears with you or telling you to pull yourself together, which I suppose is another reason why Scotland is part of our Empire instead of the other way around.

That realization did not resolve the issue. I wanted tennis lessons and I wanted them with Will. I realized the truth, as prosaic and unrequired with hired help as it normally is, would be the best approach.

I explained that the splinter should not count, as it was from injury, and the remedy was more than satisfactory (my hand tingled at the thought of the Highland cure), and that "quince" was more than jelly, it was my late husband, both as a namesake and a state of being. I then informed him that if he followed through on what I considered to be a very cruel threat of ending my lessons I would promptly do the one thing that he appeared to abhor above all, which would be to cry. Great gulping sobs, complete with a swoon or two for good measure, the likes of which he would not forget for the rest of his life.

That rendered him speechless, as intended. As we regarded each other in silence it appeared we were at an impasse. I did not feel it necessary to inform him that I was mortified by my tears after the inquest and had resolved to pretend it had never happened, which I have used to great advantage in the past.

After the silence had stretched to a breaking point I told him I would do everything in my power to prevent further upset to his sensitive nature (at which he bristled, as intended again) by weeping, as long as he promised to not take any future tears so personally, which would suit us both.

He pondered both the slight to his masculinity and my promise for a moment, before smiling and agreeing. He confessed that he had greatly regretted tendering his resignation, for he enjoys our lessons very much, unusual as they are, but had seen no other way around the knotty issue of tears and etiquette.

With that finally resolved, he took my leave, but not before forgetting his station and kissing my hand. I was going to upbraid him, but it was charming in a way, and I also believe he was subtly inspecting my hand, as it was the same one so wounded during our last lesson.

The rest of the day was spent indoors, determining menus for the coming week, overseeing Hortense's cleaning and the like. Cook was also out of my good graces with her high-handedness at the inquest. I realized all my servants were thinking themselves above their stations, so I spent the rest of the day writing out lists of things that needed proper attention in the Hall, guaranteeing that all and sundry would be kept busy from sunup until sundown. Except for Taylor, who still requires naps in the afternoon, and whose previously flawless carriage had been marred by a slight list to the right, which brings the sum total of listing servants under my roof to three. For the Opening Ball temporary help can be brought in from London but I must begin hiring more before then so they are all trained properly. It is ridiculous how much time properly staffing my home is taking. And Constance has been gone forever. I shall have to speak to Cook about that.

In the meantime I shall concentrate on the games room. I have sent for samples of silks and brocades from London for the furniture, which shall give me something to look forward to, and if that does not brighten my spirits, then nothing shall.

Well, I suddenly have dozens of things to do, Susannah, and I am behind on business matters. Mr. Sinclair arrives tomorrow and is such a dear boy. He copies my manners and such – I believe he is attempting to improve himself through mimicry. He is looking for a wife, and has confided to me that he has had precious little luck in that regard, for he is not yet established. I am hoping that at the Opening Ball he shall have the opportunity to more widely cast his net. And we have to meet with the cottagers. I heard an ominous rumour: a goat is ill. I am sure the afternoon will be spent hearing about goat death-curses and similar nonsense. Well, there is nothing to be done about that now.

Give my best to your darling family, and give me all of the best bits of gossip from Paris.

Your Very Busy Friend,

Annabella

☙ Baroness Gurthwant's Grief ❧

4 June, 1821

Dear Susannah,

Your letter was so very sweet and yes, I have recovered from my upset about the inquest, although my shame did continue for a time. After Will left I realized the only thing to do for it would be to visit Sophia. I am not a close friend and perhaps would be refused, but on rising the next morning I wrote out a note and gave instructions to Prudence.

Before the morning was out we were on our way to the Gurthwant barony. It is so pretty there, Susannah, and I smiled as we passed the Fateful Hedgerow. All the trappings of mourning were on display, right down to mutes standing on each side of the door. I walked over straw and used the knocker wrapped in black. It was as if I had returned to my own life such a short time ago, although Sophia's mutes were likely real.

The butler opened the door and stared in astonishment that I myself had knocked. He recovered and explained that Baroness Gurthwant was not seeing anyone.

I smiled as prettily as I could manage. "I know this is unusual, but would you please take this letter to her? I shall wait in my carriage for her reply."

The butler was nonplussed, for this was out of order – the wishes of the grieving are always obeyed – but took my letter and card and closed the door in my face. I returned to the carriage under the eye of the startled mutes and waited, pleased that I had a bottle of port and glasses brought along. Prudence and I each had a glass while we waited. She was curious, and I told her I knew Baroness Gurthwant's situation too well and wanted to help.

It was a short time before the butler returned to the door, nodding that I would be allowed in. Everyone was surprised except I.

I was brought to the drawing room and left alone to wait for Sophia. It is an exquisite house, of course, but on this visit I saw that most of the objects were seeming of sentimental value. A short time later the door opened and Sophia entered.

"Hello, Annabella." Sophia looked terrible, her mourning gown highlighting the pallor in her cheeks and dark circles under her eyes, which were red and puffy from weeping. I immediately embraced her.

"I am so very sorry, Sophia."

To my surprise she began weeping against my shoulder, her voice ragged and broken. "It is awful, it is terrible!"

"I know," I soothed her, patting her back as one would a child.

"I had to bury him in a jar, Annabella."

"As did I."

Sophia interrupted me by gasping and sitting down. "Oh, goodness, that is where I got the idea. From you."

I was astonished. "From me?"

She blew her nose and waved at me to sit next to her. "Well, there were so many problems with a casket, and there was not very much of him, and I remembered reading somewhere about someone with a similar problem – it was you."

As I do not know of anyone else dying so gruesomely that a normal casket would not suffice, I nodded. "It must have been."

"I never thought to think where I thought of it. It was in the newspapers when your poor Quince went – do you realize both of our husbands have exploded?"

I thought it best not to discuss the difference between crushed to bits and exploded husbands, as the end result was exactly the same.

"It is why I came today. It is much more difficult than if they simply died. Or died simply. I used to wish that Quince had pitched into his soup at dinner or died in his sleep." I thought it best to change the subject somewhat. "How are the children?"

My pathetic attempt at steering the subject to something more cheerful failed, for she began to weep once more. "I was with the children outside and there was a horrible bang, I could not imagine what it was, even if I had been able to imagine something I would not have imagined <u>that</u>. Christian – he's the oldest, he found one of Stephan's fingers a few days after everything and has not spoken since, no matter how we beg him."

"Oh, no." I remembered finding Quince's foot. I did not exactly find it, I tripped over it when the physician was leading me out the door for hospital and I do not remember anything more until I woke up with my arm in plaster and a terrible headache. "He will be all right, he is upset, and justifiably so."

"I cannot believe I am telling you all this, I know it is completely out-of-bounds –"

"Nonsense. If you cannot tell me about your husband exploding, who can you?"

"Thank you." She sniffled into her kerchief.

The drawing room door opened and one of the servants brought in tea. After it had been poured out and the servant had withdrawn Sophia's tears had stopped.

She sighed. "I do not know what to do, Annabella."

"What do you mean?"

"Stephan's will. He left everything to Christian of course, but until he reaches his majority I am in charge of the estate."

"You are?"

"Yes, he did not leave it to solicitors or trustees. I mean, I am the trustee. If I wish."

"What do you mean?"

"Well, the will was very specific, but there is so much of an estate, so many things that Stephen took care of, and I do not know anything about it."

I sighed. She was in the same exact position as I was such a short time ago. "But you can give it up if you wish?"

"Yes. That was not in the will, but the solicitor explained that I could have others take care of it for me. They will give me an allowance for clothes and things for the children, but solicitors can take care of the rest."

"I see." I stifled another sigh so she would not think me bored. I was not, I was resigned to find she was in more of a similar situation to mine than she knew. "What does your father think of their suggestion?"

"He is in America, he does not even know Stephan is dead. It shall be months before I hear from him, and I cannot wait that long."

"Have you brothers?"

"Two. They are with father, doing something with land there – I do not know anything of their business, Annabella – except that they are buying land for something."

"Cousins?" I coaxed. She looked at me strangely. "Uncles?"

"Of course I have those, Annabella, but we are not close. Why do you ask?"

"Did these men have papers for you to sign?"

"Yes, but I was upset and then Christian began screaming – they left them and are coming back. I have to sign, Annabella. I know nothing of business."

"May I give you a piece of advice, Sophia?"

"I would love advice from someone."

"Do not sign."

She looked shocked. "What do you mean?"

"Exactly as I said. Did you read the papers?"

"Yes, but I did not understand them. There were pages of them. But they are such kind men. They were Stephan's friends, you see."

"May I see them?"

"Of course." She summoned the butler to fetch them. When he was gone she looked anxious. "Why do you wish to see them?"

"I received a set of papers when Quince died. I would like to see how similar they are to yours." I hoped she would leave it at that.

"Did you sign?"

This was a difficult moment. I did not want to frighten her, but it was important for her to know that not everyone in the world was kind, thoughtful and acting purely out of the goodness of their hearts.

I know you were shocked that I did not turn over the care of Quince's estate to anyone, but the circumstances were so strange, and I realized how vulnerable I am in the World now. You are in Paris, with a busy and complicated life of your own. I did not wish to add to your responsibilities, nor to believe I was only writing so that your darling husband would intervene. Why is it that when one is in the gravest need it is most difficult to ask for assistance?

I worried that if I told you what was going on you would grow to dread seeing a letter from me, and it was important that I keep your friendship. I had lost so much, and became quite irrational that I could lose you as well, which shows how disjointed my thinking had become. My physician said I was horribly traumatized, which I thought silly at the time, but perhaps that is a symptom of trauma – one thinks one is fine.

And since I have told Baroness Gurthwant my Pitiful Tale, I should tell you as well, you, who know me better than anyone in the world.

After everything was over – the inquest, the funeral, the wake – staff and I were at sixes and sevens. Of the servants that survived almost all resigned their posts, some of them without any other prospects, for the scandal and whispers made them objects of curiosity, and they were occasionally censured when they ventured into the London streets. Even our beloved housekeeper, Miss Abblesham, left me. She had not been able to get around much since the accident with the chandelier, but she could not stay on after what happened; she had known Quince for decades and was too heartbroken to stay. Quince had established an annuity for her in his will, and the last I saw of her she was being hauled down the sidewalk in that contraption Quince designed for her, headed for a cottage near her sons. In the end I found myself with only three and a three-quarters proper servants left. Driver was in hospital for two months before being brought back to the house, when he did not die.

Once the coroner had declared Quince's death a Horrible Accident and cleared anyone else of responsibility (most importantly, me), the solicitors arrived. A group of them, clustered in the foyer like a flock of fat and glossy pigeons. They were from the firm that handled Quince's business dealings and legal papers. As it pertained to Quince's estate they were allowed to visit, even though they were clearly loathe to set foot in such an unlucky house. But a visit was required, because there were things that needed to be discussed.

I was still in shock, at a loss for what to do, for Quince always took care of those things. I just looked pretty and ran the house, and Miss Abblesham took care of most of that.

You see, the purpose of the solicitors' visit was to discuss what was to be done. About me.

You remember that Quince was the only child of only children, the same as I. His first wife had died in a bizarre boating incident before having children, and you know what happened with me. Quince was entailed, but it assumed he would have children, something clearly expected by his own father when he created the entailment, forcing the family property to go to the closest male heir. As there were no heirs at all Quince's inheritance was simply that: his own, and could with it what he wished.

I was astonished to find that Quince had made a will. Clearly after what happened with Sarah he foresaw that it was necessary. It was unlikely he would survive me, being 42 years my senior, although I am sure he did not envision such a dramatic end for himself, but children were no longer a possibility. And he understood the Law.

The men had come to discuss the will, for I inherited all. Everything. No annuity set aside to be parsed out by lawyers, no trust set up with the bulk going to Good Works or any such thing. I received everything. If I remarried everything would go to Oxford and Cambridge Universities in equal portions, and the same shall happen when I die. But if I remain unmarried, I can do as I please with every asset in the estate.

This was vexing to the solicitors and I may have found it amusing except for the fact that it was me they were vexed by, and their diligence was in service to making sure a man got the estate, any man, as opposed to my poor excuse for a person (in their eyes). But they could not avoid it: I was the sole inheritor of Quince's holdings.

I am sure they were suspicious that I knew of the arrangements, for they had read the newspapers that said (along with everyone else in London) that I had hastened Quince to his Reward so I could enjoy rewards of my own. Of course I did not know of any of it. I had no idea Quince considered such things. I never had. I also thought I would be the mother to at least five beautiful children who adored me.

I had no idea Quince's tinkering was so profitable! I thought he was merely clever with money.

At the first meeting my head swam with confusion and fear. The solicitors anticipated that, and had prepared several papers for my signature that would solve everything. They were soothing and calm, save for the youngest one, who seemed distressed.

I had taken pen in hand to sign the papers so thoughtfully brought by Quince's friends when I remembered something Quince said a few years before his death. It was at a dinner party, and someone asked him what he thought was the most important thing in business dealings, for his acumen was much admired. He stated very sternly that the most important thing was to Never Sign Anything You Have Not Read or Do Not Understand. He said that was the ruin of most people. He said it mattered not if it was a bill for five pence of paper, Everything Must Be Read and Understood.

As I sat at the writing desk with the papers I could almost hear his voice again. I had not read the papers, did not know what they contained. It would be a dreadful slap at Quince's memory to ignore something he felt so strongly about. Especially since he was dead.

So I put the pen down and told the men I appreciated their care and concern but was exhausted with everything that had happened, so exhausted I thought I might faint, which alarmed them, and could we please finish another time?

They could not do anything but acquiesce to me, but promised to return in a few days, when I felt more myself.

Although I was exhausted, lonely, and so much wishing for advice and counsel, I knew no one would come, except for perhaps Vicar Drambert, for I was as much an only child as Quince, our parents both long in their graves.

So I read the papers. It was hard, Susannah, harder than almost anything I have ever done, for there were fancy words, convoluted logic, and a great number of pages. I spent the next three days in the library with a dictionary, slowly but surely translating the papers into something I could understand. It was queerly satisfying, for the time passed without weight upon it, unlike the days before the funeral, and I knew that someone would return for the papers, so could not dally. On the third day someone did return, but I had Prudence send them away with the excuse that I could not see anyone and too distraught to speak. As my behaviour was not normal it was not difficult to believe that I was distraught, and my ruse gave me another day.

It took four whole days, Susannah, but in the end I was very glad I had listened to Quince and had taken the time, for signing the papers would have surely been ruinous.

The papers gave control of the estate to the care of those same seemingly solicitous solicitors who stood in my own drawing room and plotted to steal from me. The entire estate would be handled by them, and they in turn would give me a suitable (but unnervingly undefined) allowance on which to live, and would be "allowed" to stay in my own London house. On my death everything would pass to the institutes of higher learning, but in the meantime those same gentlemen who asked so kindly after me would have the authorization to do anything that they wished with everything, in order to "maintain the estate properly." There were enormous fees for these services, and a percentage of any gains would go into their coffers for services rendered.

I was not good with sums at the time. (Do you remember how poorly I fared in arithmetic at Miss Penelope's? I would have utterly failed were it not for your help.) Given the poor state of my skills I re-did them at least ten times, but it appeared by my calculations that the estate would be gone in less than ten years, and I would be widowed, barren and penniless.

This was a terrible mess in which to find myself, for the men were imposing, and I was nervous about discussing this with them. They might talk in great circles until I signed from mere exhaustion. They were not as easy to deal with as normal servants, who do as bidden, do not try to explain to you why you are wrong and if they do, you can sack them.

I sat up most of the night, pondering how best to handle them. It was near dawn when I realized I knew what to do.

I would behave like a Lady.

When the men reappeared the next day I found I looked forward to their visit, for it at least took my mind off the mess in the foyer. The most senior of the five men, a Mr. Beecham, asked if I had signed the papers. I said sweetly that I had not and would not and would anyone like tea?

I was enjoying myself, for they all seemed nonplussed. I sat and indicated they could do the same. They did awkwardly, and Prudence brought in tea. After she had served and left Mr. Beecham leaned forward.

Was it because I could not write, he asked as he patted my hand. It was an awful presumption, but I did not say so.

I smiled cheerily and said I was sorry for wasting their time, but after discussing it with a friend of Quince's had decided not to sign. Of the five, four looked angry. The distressed young one from the day before, Mr. Sinclair, looked pleased.

One of the other old ones, Mr. Newsome, said that such papers were confidential and should not have been divulged to anyone, as such arrangements were considered sacred.

I looked wide-eyed and a frightened and said they should have made that clear, for I was only a woman, and could not have been expected to know that, and why would they find any such divulgence problematic, as they were trying to help me.

That caused a dread silence, so I munched on a biscuit and waited. Mr. Newsome finally spoke, and it was a long, stultifying speech. The points were all ones I am sure you have guessed: I was only a woman and of course allowed to request assistance. The arrangements were for my own good, so I would not have to be "bothered" about thinking about my future, as it would be taken care of for me. These men had handled Quince's legal affairs for a years and considered taking care of me a salute to his memory. They would be happy to take as long as necessary to explain why signing would be the best thing for me, as it was my best interests in which they were interested.

I cocked my head and pretended to consider the notion for a moment and then said no thank you, I would somehow struggle on without signing. Mr. Sinclair was almost smiling, which I noted with interest. He did not seem to be the same as the others.

Mr. Beecham sighed and said in his gravelly voice that he was afraid he would have to insist, for my own good, that I sign. This annoyed me, as he was imperious and arrogant, so I told him he had perhaps confused his role somewhat, for he was neither my husband nor my father and could not order me about.

Mr. Newsome then said I was overtired and he himself would come back in a few days' time, if I did not mind, and we could discuss everything again. He was apparently the most charming one of the group. I said I would be more than glad to, which seemed to relieve everyone but Mr. Sinclair, and they stood to leave. I had Taylor show them out, and almost clapped my hands in glee at their discomfiture.

Then I wrote to Thornton Weerly, an old friend of Quince's, asking to meet with him on a business matter as soon as possible. Quince spoke highly of his character and intelligence and I knew he might be able to help. He was also a solicitor, albeit at a smaller firm than the ones Quince used. I had Taylor take the letter immediately.

Mr. Weerly came the very next day, read the papers and confirmed what I had suspected: they were near-blatant theft. I asked him if he would be my solicitor and he said he would be honoured, except he could not handle all of the work Quince's – my – estate would require on his own, and knew little about patents and such. I asked him if he would handle them for a short period of time, until I could find other solicitors, as I did not like having any dealings with these men at all. He agreed, and we drew up the papers together. He was much better than those other men, for he explained what everything meant and encouraged me to look up words myself so I would be comfortable with them. This was the kind of person I needed.

When we finished the new papers he took them to be copied out, promising to return on the morrow, for I wanted them in place before Mr. Newsome returned. The next day Mr. Weerly and I signed in front of a notary he had thoughtfully brought, and I felt much better about everything.

Again I was left sitting in the house with nothing to do, so I read more of Quince's papers. It was still difficult, I had to go slowly, but focused only on correspondence between himself and his solicitors, and had a gleam of understanding from my prior study. It was very helpful. And I waited.

In just two days' time Mr. Newsome was again knocking on my door. Mr. Sinclair was with him, and he appeared nervous.

Susannah, Mr. Newsome behaved like a besotted suitor, inquiring after my health, admiring the house (even though entire parts of it were still unsafe). I think he may have pitched woo had I not been recently widowed. Mr. Sinclair was to act as witness and notary, so sure was Mr. Newsome of winning my signature. I retrieved his papers and he went through them point by point, blurring explanations here and there, skipping over entire portions in other places. In his interpretation I would be fortunate indeed to sign.

I asked him if only my and his signatures' were required to make everything legal and aboveboard, for I did not want to find myself receiving visits from each of the other men in turn to sign things, as it was all too complicated for me. He assured me he had authority to act for all, and Mr. Sinclair nodded sadly that it was true.

I nodded and smiled in all the right places and when he was done he handed me the pen. I then brought out my own set of papers. I told him they had been prepared by a friend, would clarify the relationship between us very much to their advantage, and he only needed to sign, for they were very complicated and he need not bother himself with the details. I was only acting in all of our best interests.

He was brought up short, and took the papers from me. As he read and comprehended their meaning his face darkened. He threw the papers on the writing desk and said they were ridiculous, I was out of my head, and he would not sign them. Mr. Sinclair looked confused. I told him it was best that he did, for the papers severed the business relationship between the estate and his firm completely, which I was allowed to do. Quince was their client, and as I had inherited everything, including his business, had also the same rights as Quince, to dissolve the relationship at any time, for any reason, as spelled out in contracts signed long ago. That I had in my possession. Mr. Sinclair looked shocked and then pleased.

Mr. Newsome barked that I could not do such a thing. His raised voice brought Taylor through the door even though it was a business meeting, and Mr. Newsome quieted.

I replied that I could, and would, and there was nothing to be done about it, unless he wished to find himself and his colleagues dealing with other, surely less charitable and noble, solicitors, who would fight like dogs for the right to represent me and all that I had.

I asked again that he sign the papers, knowing his signature would cover the other solicitors as well, which ended the relationship between us and transferred authorization to Mr. Thornton Weerly. It was lovely, for Mr. Newsome knew he must, there was no recourse for him, that indeed had been the relationship. They could not refuse my request without severe damage to their reputations, as trying to swindle a widow out of her own house and living would be looked poorly on, for all solicitors have mothers and wives and sisters.

As Taylor impassively looked on Mr. Newsome stared at the papers. I turned and asked Mr. Sinclair if I had the facts in order. He froze for a moment, stammered, and then said I did. Mr. Newsome glared at him and told him to keep his tongue. Then Newsome picked up the pen. He said I would be sorry one day for this, and I told him I appreciated his concern.

He signed, then I did, and Mr. Sinclair notarized each set. It was done.

Mr. Newsome left in a huff, and Mr. Sinclair smiled at me as he followed. He seemed happy with the outcome, which should not have been the case. I told Mr. Sinclair he was welcome back if there were any questions, but the other men should stay away, for I did not wish to argue through my mourning. He said he would arrange it.

The next day Mr. Weerly came back and we began to go through all of Quince's business papers. He is a very kind man, Susannah, and were it not for his heart condition Quince would have made all of his arrangements through Thornton, I am sure of it. But he tires easily, and I believe sooner rather than later Quince may be greeting an old friend in Heaven.

I received the outcome I wanted: I, and I alone, would watch over the estate. I believed it is what Quince would have wanted, and was the least I could do with him gone.

Over the next few weeks Mr. Weerly helped me to find a firm of the size and reputation needed to handle the estate. Of course there was no shortage of interested firms, but Mr. Weerly helped me to find one that was populated with decent men, most of whom had either heard of Quince or had dealings with him from the opposite side of the table, and respected his skills. Mr. Weerly was lovely and helped with the contracts and to understand the scope of my holdings, of which the word "vast" springs to mind.

At the end of my tale Sophia was pale and ashen. "Do you think that is what my solicitors will do? Steal the estate?"

"Anything is possible when there is much at stake, Sophia."

"What shall I do?" Her voice rose to a wail and she burst into tears again. "I am not brave, I know not what to do –"

"How much money do you have? Actual money." I needed to shock her out of bursting into tears again.

"Stephan kept three hundred pounds sterling in a safe, in case there was more unrest and we needed to flee."

I was glad he had a brain. Until it exploded. "That can keep the house running properly until your father or brothers can come. Send for them, and until they come, sign nothing."

"But those men said time was of the essence –"

"Tosh. A signature can be made at any time, but once made it cannot be so easily undone. You need to protect your children, Sophia. They need you to do that."

"But the men will be angry."

"And I say 'tosh' again. Whether they are upset or not is unimportant. You are the widow, Sophia. If anyone should be upset, it is you. Your children need you to be strong now, so strong you must be. You may cry yourself to sleep every single night, and you shall for a long time, but during the day your duty is to keep the Gurthwant future safe."

"You are right." She was sitting straighter in her chair.

"When a relative returns you can decide what to do. Until then I can recommend a very good firm, should your solicitors turn out to be deceitful, for the men I now deal with are rather accustomed to a woman in charge of an estate and it shall not be so strange to them. They can at least review the papers to see if you shall suffer financially by inaction and make a recommendation. They are good men, Sophia, and if you are uncertain of anything, send for me and I will come immediately."

Sophia sat for a moment. I was relieved to see her tears had dried and not sprung anew. Then she smiled at me. "Everyone else has just come or written and said how sorry they are. You have done much more."

I was feeling oddly pleased with myself. "I am fond of you, Sophia, and believed perhaps you could use help."

Sophia finally straightened in her chair. "It would seem I suddenly have a great deal to consider."

"I am sorry, but you are right. You do."

"So if you do not mind . . ." I did not, I was in fact pleased that my visit had the intended effect. Sophia was going to begin making a new life, much as I had over a year ago. She called for the papers to be brought in and I reviewed them quickly, marking passages of concern – it seemed her solicitors were hoping to care for her and her family in much the same way as mine had planned. Sophia watched with interest as I skimmed the pages. When I was done I gave them to her and she took them with no small amount of trepidation. We both stood, and she suddenly grabbed and hugged me.

"Thank you, Annabella. Thank you very much."

With that I felt I had done a good thing, and was glad she felt the same. I took my leave and she promised to write me and tell me how it turned out. When I got in the carriage she was standing at the window of the drawing room and gave a little wave and a tiny brave smile. I waved back and suppressed a shudder. She would be locked up in there for an entire year. I hope she has a library. There is only so much needlework and Bible-reading one can do without going completely mad.

So I have done what I could for Sophia, Susannah. I do not know how it shall turn out for her – how could I? – but I hope I have found her some time. Those first days are the worst, I know too well from experience, and her family shall be far more careful with her holdings than strangers might.

Luckily Sophia did not think to ask about Mr. Sinclair. You see, the near-theft of my estate was how I met my solicitor at all. He was the same one who worked for those awful men.

And how, you must be asking, did one of the awful men come to be my principal conduit for business dealings? It is because I am soft-hearted and, in my defence, rather a mess at the time. If something awful happened to anyone that they had not caused I found myself overcome with sympathy, as I knew all too well the feeling. I had to stop myself from sending donations to every charitable organization in London.

But that does not answer how Mr. Sinclair has come to visit Wetmoor every month.

It was one week after everything was settled with those thieving solicitors that Taylor announced a caller. I thought it was Vicar Drambert, come to stare at me again, tell me time heals all wounds and look about for proof of my guilt. It is difficult to be counselled in spiritual matters by one who thinks you are guilty.

Imagine my surprise at finding Mr. Sinclair in the drawing room. He seemed anxious and I asked why he had come. He said he wanted to make sure that everything turned out all right for me. I told him I had engaged new solicitors and thanked him for his concern. I wondered how his colleagues had taken the news.

He said they took it badly, but was glad I was pleased with the outcome. I asked how he was getting on and he looked down in embarrassment.

Those men discharged him without references not two days after he had been in my house! When I asked the reason he said he could not say. I asked him to please tell me, for he had seemed a fine young man when I had met him, and if it were not too personal nor embarrassing, I wished to know the cause.

Mr. Newsome told his colleagues Mr. Sinclair was the reason they had not been able to maintain control of Quince's estate, for he would not admit it was their doing. As they were eager to lay blame at feet not their own, he was discharged.

I was appalled. All Mr. Sinclair did was tell me that I understood the facts, which was twisted into cause for ruining his livelihood. He tried to explain that he did not mind, that those men were different than he thought solicitors were, and in the end it was best, for he did not seem suited to the way they handled business matters. In spite of his words he looked glum.

I asked him if he thought I had done the right thing, and told him the names of new solicitors. He said I had been clever indeed, and he was glad I made the decision I had, it would have been his own had he found himself widowed, at which point he got a bit confused, finally adding that my new solicitors were some of the best in London, and one day he hoped he would qualify to work with such gentlemen.

That settled it. I bade him to wait a moment and have some tea while I wrote out a quick note to my new solicitors. I asked him if he would do me the favour of taking it to them and waiting for the response. He said he had no other engagements and would be happy for a reason to go to their offices. I told him I was sorry my situation had caused his ruin, and hoped one day everything would turn out all right. He took his leave and I said a quick prayer.

I went to the library to escape from the silence that hung about the house, and it was then that I found Quince's letter to me with his Last Request. That same day I began my course of studies.

The next morning I was finishing breakfast when Taylor announced a caller. I was surprised, and told him I would see them in the drawing room.

When I entered I was facing a huge bouquet of flowers, but the person holding them could not be seen, so large were the blooms. Taylor stood off to the side, looking decidedly displeased.

Then the bouquet was brought down and placed into my arms by Mr. Sinclair. Before I could say a word, he said he did not know what the proper etiquette was and had decided he did not care, his visit was acceptable as it pertained to business – his face fair shone at the word "business." I was going to inquire when he blurted out that he had delivered my message to my new solicitors the day before as requested. He was awaiting the response when one of the senior partners recognized him, although from where he did not know. They sat and talked for a while, and he was offered a post with the firm! Without a recommendation! He was over the moon with happiness and suspected it had something to do with my note, and wished to thank me, and flowers were a poor symbol of his gratitude but the only thing he could think of, and hoped it was not an insult with my mourning and all. He also handed me the "response" sent back by the firm.

I do so hate it when people believe they are astonishingly clever, Susannah, and hate it even more when they actually are.

I smiled and gently told him I did not know what he was talking about. He faltered for a moment, and then said he was sure it had to have been my note which had started everything, for he knew he had never met the man who hired him, I must have told them to meet with him.

I told him that the note was merely authorization to transfer funds from one account to another, and if he found a post for himself it was due to his suitability, not the intercession of a lady, although I appreciated he thought I had the authority to get such a thing done.

This was not the response he expected. I told him his gesture was lovely, and only inappropriate due to my situation, and perhaps there was a young lady he would prefer to see holding them.

He said he was horribly sorry for the error, and seemed about the start bashing himself about the head with the flowers when I interrupted him.

I told him I thought his instincts and obvious kindness were admirable traits in his profession, and was sure we would meet again some other day, as he was now working for the firm I employed for my dealings, and was glad indeed of it. Of course, I said it in such a way that he would not think I had a romantic inclination toward him, for men are easily encouraged, even when there is no encouragement in the first place. He smiled and said he hoped for it as well, and I would always be a prized client, for if it were not for me he would have not lost his post nor gone to the new firm with my message and therefore would have been working with awful men until his very soul was sucked dry by corruption.

I told him I was glad I could help.

With that he took his leave, almost falling down the front steps as he could not see past the bouquet he held, and I ignored Taylor's inquisitive look as I swept past him to the library where I could read the "response":

Dear Lady Upton-Church,

Thank you for sending Mr. Sinclair to us. We agree with your assessment and believe he will make a fine addition to our staff.

Yours Very Sincerely,

Michael Hallowell, Q.C.

That is what really happened, Susannah, and I am glad I told you of it. It was so strange but it turned out well in the end. I told Sophia the tale not to scare her out of her wits but because I was afraid she may have had similarly amoral solicitors, and she has four children to raise. Losing everything would be more disastrous for her than for I, which is why I broke with etiquette and visited her. It is important that she be careful, as during the first days of grief one can make decisions that can have devastating consequences.

Well, I have whiled the day away once again, Susannah, lost in reminiscence and rudely shoving my nose into the business of others. I can now write at a speed I dared not dream of at Miss Penelope's and I may have made the stationer in London quite wealthy.

It is a comfort finally telling you these things now that they are over and nothing but a rather dismal memory. It all turned out well in the end, I have Wetmoor and my new life. Well, I shall have a new life as soon as I have time to fashion one. Perhaps after the ball. . .

I hope you are similarly content, Susannah, and I look forward to hearing from you soon. When your letters arrive I fair clap my hands in glee – with Sophia locked away you are the only source of sophistication in my life. So quick write and tell me everything, and while waiting to receive it know that I Remain,

Your Independent Friend,
Annabella

More Surprises

9 June, 1821

Dearest Susannah,

It was wonderful to get your letter so quickly. Paris this time of year is lovely, even with rain, and I wish I could have been a guest at your dinner party, but I have been so busy myself. I am in a constant whirl of decisions and obligations.

I was dismayed at the disappointed tone of your letter, and promise that I shall never, ever again NOT tell you everything that is going on in my life. I am pleased you do not care if the news is good or bad, as long as I tell the truth of it. It is the mark of true friendship.

In that vein, I shall update you on my tennis lessons, although there is nothing to report. You seemed cross that I have not written about Will recently, but so many other things have been going on. My lessons have been enjoyable but we do not yet play, for Will refuses until I am some sort of expert with the equipment. I have spent hours with my hand either gripping a shaft or balls, sometimes both at once as I get used to dealing with them at the same time, so there has been nothing to tell. He and I usually sit to tea afterward, as we are both quite overheated from the lesson. I enjoy his company a great deal. He is an excellent conversationalist and surprisingly well-educated. It is nice to have someone with whom I can visit, as callers are so rare, and they generally only want to discuss the Bible. With Will I discuss history, philosophy, all manner of subjects. He is a very nice man.

I do have other, far more important news than that of my tennis lessons.

Gwynneth is now a mother.

Gwynneth went into labour at the serving house, as that family of hers has no understanding that pregnant women should not work in public. Luckily she realized what was happening and hiked herself up to her room, screaming for someone to help. As the Bargesniffles were too squeamish to tend to Gwynneth herself, the family got a midwife and a healthy girl was born just ten hours later. Gwynneth survived the birth, and I am told that both are resting comfortably, but the family is chafing for Gwynneth to get back to her place behind the counter. That family is barbaric.

A name has not yet been chosen, as Gwynneth does not like the names Rufus has proffered, and he lost all interest as soon as he found out that he is the "father" of a girl. In fact, he was heard muttering that if he had known it would be a girl he would have never gone through with "any of it," presumably because he shall now be responsible for providing a suitable dowry for a child not his own.

This is exactly what Rufus and the Bargesniffle lot deserve, and I would not waste tears on any other calamities that may befall them, including rashes or bouts of dropsy. Gwynneth has to rest for now, but I will bring her back to the Hall when she is back on her feet. She can bring the child, as I do not trust the Bargesniffles she is manacled to by law to take proper care of it.

The information came to me courtesy of Driver, who was dispatched to get Gwynneth for her work here at Wetmoor. I decided it was all right that he sat and had a few pints as the information was bandied about the room, since he reported to me the moment he returned.

In other news, Sophia wrote me. She did as I instructed and read the papers for herself, and sent word to her father and brothers, who I am sure shall return from the Americas with immediate haste. She feels so much safer now. I was glad to hear from her, she is such a lovely woman.

And that is not all, and the next is the most important reason for this letter. I found another secret in the Hall, Susannah.

I found it when I realized that there were more windows on the outside of the north wall than there were to be counted on the inside. It was then that I realized there was one strange portion of the old drawings I had never investigated. I was embarrassed when I realized it – what have I been doing all these months?

I examined the old plans again, and there seemed to be another unnoted passageway, which was between the games room and the library. After tearing apart the library and having to put it back together again myself I realized if there was another door it would be in the games room, for who would have two secret doors in one room?

In the games room I found a door latch set in a carving (of a walrus, no less), and stepped inside another tunnel. Another small shelf was to my left with a lamp and tinderbox to light my way. I was not as nervous about setting off down yet another dim passage, as the others proved to be safe and clean, wondering only what surprises might be in store. It was a short tunnel and I found myself in front of a normal door, not like the ones before. I tried the knob, but it was locked. I tugged on it with all my might, but the lock would not yield to me. For the moment the way was barred.

I was stymied, and realized that there was no way in for the moment. I returned to the games room and, after determining that the workmen were still at lunch, let myself out and hurried to the library. How could I get past that locked door? I actually gnawed on my thumbnail as I pondered. I have had great good luck with a hairpin in the past and resolved to use this method again, but on my return to the games room found workmen returned and labouring in it. Why is it that workmen are only on time when one does not want them about? It is one of the great ironies of life. I comforted myself that at the end of the day they would leave and I could steal away to "check their work" or some other subterfuge, and make the lock yield to me.

Dinner was a quiet affair, Hortense and Prudence taking turns at serving me in the morning room. I look forward to the dining room being completed, but the morning room is cozier, with the fireplace crackling merrily away, its light dancing along the wainscoting that has been so beautifully restored. I shall have to remember to mention it to Mr. Wicklestaff. His staff may be slow, and surely lackadaisical, but the result is worth the wait even though it chafes me to admit it.

When supper was complete I dismissed Hortense, who was unsuccessfully stifling yawns behind her tiny hand. She bobbed a curtsy and took my leave. Then, my hand grasping the hairpin in my pocket, I left to "see what work had been completed."

In a trice I was back in the games room. I waited a moment to make sure no one was about, and then slipped back through the secret doorway, closing it softly behind me. I trotted down the corridor and found myself in front of the door. My hairpin did not work! I do not take kindly to being denied, Susannah, as you well know. But there I was, standing like a fool in front of a locked door. I finally gave it up and made my way back to the games room, and went to my rooms and prepared for bed. I was exhausted and none too cheerful, but knew that a good night's sleep could put much to rights.

I must take your leave now, Susannah. It is some days hence since the events I just described took place, and there are plasterers here to begin work on the music room. It is in poor shape, indeed, and much of the moulding shall have to be repaired or replaced, and I must accompany Mr. Wicklestaff while he instructs them.

Oh, goodness, I have not told you about Constance . . . There is not enough time now.

I shall write again soon, and remain still

Your Vexed Friend,

Annabella

☙ Walker & Molly Return ❧

12 June, 1821

Dearest Susannah,

It is a few days since I received your last letter, and I have scarce had a moment to breathe! So much going on, and so little time to set it down on paper for you. The swirl of activity in my Hall may now rival the activities in much-missed London.

First, and once again, I must read my letters carefully before sending them to you. I know not how many times I shall have to say it, but there is nothing going on with Will. I am describing tennis lessons, not erotic encounters. You must think, Susannah. Were there anything going on I think I should be describing things he might do to me. He has not done anything of the sort, he is very respectful. I am learning how to use tennis equipment properly, that is ALL.

In a less tawdry vein, renovations proceed apace, and I am beginning to think about the Opening Ball. It shall be a glittering affair, and you and your husband must make your way here for it, Paris obligations and the Crown or no. Is that treasonous to say? It would not be the same without you here, Susannah, so you must promise me you shall attend, even if the date is not yet set.

I have spent an inordinate amount of time trying to open the door in the games room passageway, and remain thwarted. It is difficult enough to enter the passageway without being noticed, yet my efforts have been rebuffed time and again. I have tried every key in the Hall on the lock, all to no avail.

The staff is in an absolute state. After a lovely caesura in their superstitious ways, suddenly everyone believes the Hall is haunted again. It is tiresome how superstitious these people are, Susannah. They claim to hear footsteps at all hours of the day and night, doors opening and closing, and all of these mysteries are the work of the ghosts, Walker and Molly, who cannot rest. I do not know what they are going on about, Susannah, for I have never heard any such things, and do not appreciate the continued insistence that such occurrences are happening, but only when I am not present. Hortense actually began crying while pouring my tea the other day! Thank goodness Constance has finally returned to her post.

However, that too has not happened without an equal and most upsetting situation: Constance returned with a baby!

Luckily Cook warned me before their actual return, via the gossip that travels about below stairs. Apparently Constance's sister died in childbirth and there was no one else to take up for the poor baby, so Constance became its de facto "mother." I do not see any family resemblance whatsoever.

Its name is Hope. I had no idea what to do when Cook told me the news. The child is somewhat famous, being the offspring of one of the victims of Peterloo, so I did not believe I could let Constance go without facing additional unpleasant talk about me. It is one thing to be considered a murderess, but to be considered thoughtless and cruel is completely unacceptable.

But a baby! Apparently Constance was the only sibling, their parents are dead, all of the usual things you find in the lower classes, so I sat down and thought and came up with a perfect plan, which was ready by the time Constance returned.

The nursery. There is a nursery in the Hall, of course, a large one, and since I shall never have need of its services it can be easily turned over to use by an actual child without any inconvenience to me. I had not decided what to do with the room – I have more rooms already than I know what to do with – so it matters not a whit to me what is done with a nursery, as long as staff do not all get it into their heads to bring all the children of the world to the Hall for safekeeping. And there were the children's clothes and bedding that were given to Quince and I by my family, in the hopes that the accoutrements of offspring would hasten the actuality of them. I put them away after Sarah, for I could not bear to discard them, but it seemed nice that they might actually be used, even if by an orphan.

I told Prudence to send Constance to me on her return, without the child in evidence. I did not need to see it, after all. The next day I looked up from my reading to see Constance standing in front me of me, twisting her gloves in her hands, shaking like a leaf. I was going to chastise her for being so bold as to bring a baby home, but she surprised me: she resigned her post. She said she returned because it was the least she could do for having put me out so very much with her family problems, but she could not be a proper maid and raise a child, which was her responsibility now that her poor sister had succumbed to some sort of post-birth dilemma, as I nearly had.

I was pleased to see that Constance has learnt her place so well, and realized my earlier decision, made in a weak and sentimental moment, was correct. However, that was the second time someone has tried to resign a position in which I wish them to be, which annoyed me. I put my book down and stared at her for a moment. She has slimmed down marvelously while at her sister's, she looks quite herself again!

I told her the child could stay as long as I was never burdened by so much as a peep out of it, and led Constance to the nursery.

Cleaning and repainting the nursery was nothing for Mr. Wicklestaff to arrange, even in secret, as I did not need the staff to see it before I knew if I was going to allow the child to stay.

I had Constance's bed put in there, of course, since the babe is sure to cry, and had some old curtains put up that were not going to be used anywhere else, ones I thought might look nice with the linens. Constance needed a soft chair so she could sit with the baby, and I did not care for that old chintz thing that used to be in the attic in London. I was also not fond of the dresser from the guest room in the London house, and there had to be somewhere to put all the things babies need. When all was said and done it looked rather nice, if I do say so myself.

Of course, I would have never done any of it had I known how Constance would respond. She collapsed at my feet, sobbing that I was the kindest, most wonderful, loveliest lady anyone could ever work for, and be in her prayers for the rest of her and the child's life for my generosity. It was quite embarrassing and my kid shoes got spotted from her tears.

I informed Constance that she and the child could stay as long as I never had a hint that there is an actual child living here, with a slight reduction in wages, as it shall be eating food at some point, which will come out of my kitchens. Hortense would also stay, both as a maid-in-training and to look after the child when Constance was looking after me. Constance agreed, of course, as was proper, mopping her red eyes with her gloves and snivelling all over the room as she patted the drapes and furniture. The cradle is the only new thing, made by the woodworkers. I could not bear to give her Sarah's, which is in the attic, covered and safe.

It did seem the easiest thing to do, Susannah. This way I get my properly trained maid back and a maid-in-training, for the same expense as one maid. All it cost me were some out-of-style curtains and a chair I would not put in a mud room.

With that good deed done, I went about my day, which turned out to be difficult, as I suddenly had staff unceasingly underfoot: bringing me tea, asking if I needed anything, on and on. Taylor managed to pull the doors open to the veranda for me, which has been beyond him during his convalescence, but he seemed to feel strongly that he accomplish it without Prudence's help. Prudence went about her duties with a silly smile on her face that I had to tell her more than twice was out of place. These people! It is a miracle I ever get anything done.

The rest of the day was spent choosing colours for the music room and working with Mr. Wicklestaff on deciding what should come next: the cutting room or the wrapping room. But I made sure that I turned in early, for my next tennis lesson was the next day, and wanted to make sure I was properly rested, refreshed and without tears for Mr. Ploughgoode. I had, after all, promised that I would not burden him with tears ever again, and I did want to keep my promise. I shall tell you all about it in my next letter, darling. It was simply divine. With that tantalizing morsel I shall take your leave. Until next I write, I remain,

Your Philanthropic Friend,

Annabella

20 June, 1821

Dearest Susannah,

The speed of your reply was astonishing! For a moment I thought our letters had crossed in the post. You must have written the moment you finished my letter.

Many thanks for your compliments on my handling of the Constance issue, and set your fears to rest: there is no indication that a child is in the Hall. Occasionally Hortense answers a bell for Constance, but other than that, things have returned to normal. My meals have improved somewhat, I suppose because Cook no longer has to instruct Hortense.

But you do not care about that. You want more news of Will. I had no idea Lord Carollton enjoys shooting to the point of taking lessons. Is it not a small world? Although perhaps not that small, you do have a home in this county as well. It is truly your loss that you have not met Will yourself. That must be your punishment for eschewing England for Paris.

Please assure yourself I am not angry that you keep wondering if I am having a liaison with Will, I am bewildered. He is a good and proper man with whom I enjoying talking. No one else comes here, Susannah. He has almost become a friend, in a way.

Now that I have finished explaining that nothing has ever happened with Will, I shall have to describe our most recent lesson, during which something did happen, but not in the way you have implied, although I can now confirm that his body is magnificent. Is that tantalizing enough for you?

On the delightful day in question my tennis lesson was scheduled for immediately after lunch. Normally Will and I meet in the late afternoon, but he was off teaching someone in another county how to play golf, so I was without lessons for a full week.

After a quick review of my facility with the equipment, and after all this time, we were going to play. I was quite excited. We went to the court and each stood on our own side. Mine was with my back to the sun, which was only proper. Exercise is important, but not at the expense of the fairness of my skin! Will began without a racquet, merely tossing the balls over the net for me to hit. I did hit a few, but had trouble with balls that did not come directly to me. My skirts make it difficult. Will apologized and adjusted his throws so I could hit them back and get used to the feel of it. I was doing well, but much time was wasted with Will running around getting the balls, although it did seem to be excellent exercise for him.

This had continued for some time when I noticed Will was pinking up alarmingly. He was also moving slowly to get the balls, and when one that I returned hit him in the head, he seemed not to notice. I was about to inquire if anything was the matter when he collapsed on the court! I screamed for help and ran to the net, remembering the times Quince had collapsed during our marriage, and the instructions the physician had given me for such occurrences.

No one came, Will continued to lie there, and I realized he could be dead or dying. With a muttered curse I ran to the net and began to climb over it in the middle where it hangs lowest. As you know, I had dreamt of doing such a thing (albeit for a completely different reason) and thought it would be simple enough to accomplish.

Do not ever make such an attempt, Susannah, it does not work. I found myself hanging over the net with one shoe trapped in the net. So focused was I on freeing it that I stopped paying attention to the rest of myself.

Fortunately when I fell I landed on the other side. I scrambled to my feet as if I had not just nearly landed on my head and comforted myself with the thought that the only person who might have seen me perform such an unladylike act was, in fact, dead to the world. I ran to Will with only a mild limp.

He was breathing, but red in the face and hands and unconscious. I again called for help, literally yelling for someone to come immediately and checked his forehead, which felt as if it were on fire. I set aside my annoyance at his thoughtlessness in conducting a lesson while ill, for that could cause me to become ill, and bellowed for someone to please come. Of course the workmen were sawing and hammering away in the ballroom, so my cries went unheeded. It was then that Will began to move a bit, although he was still shockingly red. He opened his eyes and looked confused, as the last thing he knew he was standing on the tennis court, not lying upon it. I told him not to move. By then I realized what had happened to him.

I waited while Will managed to sit up, and inquired after him. He was greatly embarrassed, still pink in the face and hands, which concerned me, but I thought it best not to mention it. Men are such children about any perceived infirmity and he was already quite weak.

It was the sun. Our lesson took place while the sun was high in the sky, so there was no shade on the court, and the high walls prevent fresh air from blowing around, so it is warmer on the court than if we were in the open air.

Scots are bred to live under dark and rainy skies, not in sunshine. It would take less time for a Scot to succumb to the heat than an Englishwoman, and I told him so. He was about to argue the point and thought better of it. He was, after all, the one collapsed on the tennis court.

The only thing to do was to get him out of the sunshine before he expired of it. I looked at the net and realized it was impossible to go back into the Hall: I could and would not repeat my earlier climbing feat in front of him, he would think me a complete harlot, and I thought he would not do much better in his weakened state. I pointed him to the other door, the one leading to the grounds, and told him to go to the boathouse and lie down until he had certainty of his consciousness. When he tried to rise up it was clear he could not manage such a meagre task on his own so I helped him to his feet. Then, my arm on his to steady him, we walked to the boathouse. I even had to open the courtyard door for him, for he kept missing the knob with his hand!

Once at the boathouse he tottered across the threshold and looked surprised at the cozy room he found himself in and said so. I replied that he should be thankful for it and to lie down as I opened the windows and closed the curtains, which he did.

That done, I found the claret stashed behind the works of Shakespeare on the shelves lining the longest wall and poured one for him as a restorative. I gave it him and realized I needed one as well, so poured to match his. He downed his claret in one gulp and held out his glass for another, quite forgetting his position, as well as mine. I found it amusing as opposed to insulting – a great Scot like that brought to his knees (well, his back, actually) by the sun!

I sat down and sipped my claret while he stood and paced the room, draining the second glass in as many minutes. I asked if he was feeling better, and he was, but was still very pink, and also suddenly streaming . . . well, the only word I know for it is sweat, Susannah. Forgive my language, but the man looked for all the world as if he had just leapt into the pond, not dropped on the tennis court. He poured a third claret, muttering that he was thirsty, and re-filled my glass as well. I proffered that perhaps he should drink water instead, at which he scoffed. At me!

Men. I forgot how very important it is to them to seem in complete possession of themselves, but especially when they are hardly in possession of themselves at all.

After he downed his third claret he began looking for water. He grabbed a pitcher and quickly filled it from the hand pump on the counter, which comes straight from the well. He drank right from the pitcher, gulping so quickly that the liquid overflowed the lip of it, splashed down his throat and onto his chitterling, making it stick to his skin. I was finding this very interesting, Susannah. I have never before seen a man act so completely as if I were not there. Of course, he was out of his head, which explained the lack of any attention being paid me. And he was gasping and sweating . . . it was very thrilling. I was enjoying his distress more than was strictly appropriate.

Then things took an even more interesting turn. Gulping huge lungfuls of air, sweating and altogether overheated, Will tore off his frock coat and loosened his cravat. I decided to stay quiet as a mouse to see what transpired next. I was not disappointed.

First he rolled up the sleeves of his linen, revealing those fantastic hands and beautiful forearms, which I had not truly appreciated until then. He then tore off his cravat and dropped it unceremoniously on the floor next to his frock coat. Still he streamed and boiled, flicking his sweaty hair back and wiping his eyes. He had some trouble with the buttons on his waistcoat and finally yanked it open, buttons flying every which way. I should be glad it came undone with his back to me, as the buttons zinging through the air may well have cost me an eye. When he peeled his linen off I was pleased to see that his shoulders are broad not through clever tailoring, but because they are muscular. Exceedingly muscular. As is his back. When his linen and chitterling came off, flying past my head and landing on the settee next to me, I was almost undone. There is something about a half-dressed, magnificently fashioned and sweaty man standing in front of one that is purely fabulous. I do not mind admitting, Susannah, I had rather forgotten where I was and who I was with, I was that mesmerized.

When he began to undo his flies I inadvertently squeaked. I am sure I was alarmed, but my shock was so great he was half done before I made a sound. At my gasp he jumped, looked around and turned, if possible, even more scarlet than he was prior. He apologized and tried to pick up his clothing but it was clear that such a simple task was beyond him, so I told him to stop and sit down, looking away lest I stare. He promptly did and held his linen in front of him which, while rather adorable, quite ruined a spectacular view. He apologized (again), resigned (again) and pitched face-first into my lap.

That was unexpected, if I do say so myself. It was still daylight and I there I was, pinned to the boathouse settee by a near-naked and unconscious Scot, which was not how I had envisioned my day. I tried to push him up and off of me but found that although I have strong hands, my arms are not and gave it up. I patted his poor wet head, noting that the damp had made it curl even more, and realized there were worse ways to spend an afternoon.

Far worse. So I stayed, drinking claret and waiting for him to recover himself. I must have been affected by the sun as well, Susannah, for I became drowsy. Will rolled over, head now startlingly near my bosom, and I found myself tracing the outline of his mouth with my finger to pass the time and to stop myself from staring at his breeches, which were mostly undone, but not on purpose, so it seemed rude to peek. He has a very nice mouth, and seems to have all his teeth. I know this because he caught my finger gently in his teeth, nibbling it ever so slightly, kissing it as well. Of course, he was unconscious when he did this. It was an echo of the Highland cure.

I must have drowsed myself for a while, for when I next opened my eyes the sun had dropped considerably in the sky, I was curled up on the settee, and Will was sadly as dressed as possible given his button-less state, sitting at rigid attention on the other side of the room. I sat up quickly – my ankles were showing! I felt quite the tart.

His face had returned to its normal pale hue, so he had clearly recovered from his mishap. He immediately stood and made a small speech. First he thanked me for saving his life, which I thought slightly hyperbolic, but held my tongue. He apologized for drinking all my excellent claret. He had not, but I did not want to bother him with details. He apologized for his clothes apparently falling off, going rather pink again as he did. There was no need to apologize for that, but again, I did not want to burden him with clarification. He then resigned. Again. Which is getting to be an annoying habit.

I rejected his resignation, brushed off his "near-nudity" (and I am quoting him, Susannah). I reminded him I had been a married woman, after all, not a spinster, my husband frequently required care and I was not going to have another person in my employ become damaged. I would get Lady Shardley's reputation, for goodness' sake. It was in my own best interest (unstated was the fact that more than one interest of mine was satisfied) to make sure he remained well when teaching me, and to continue to be my instructor, for even though I knew little about the game of tennis, the lessons were extremely interesting. He was again surprised. I believe he has taught many weak-hearted and weepy types of ladies, most of whom would faint at every little thing. I did tell him that in the future, to prevent such a recurrence, he would be allowed to remove both his frock coat and waistcoat and also roll up his shirtsleeves during lessons. It is normally not done, but in for a penny, in for a pound in terms of societal conventions, Quince always used to say, and it is better to have a tennis instructor who is slightly undone and conscious than one that is correctly swaddled in the ridiculous amount of clothing that is de rigueur in our society, but unconscious in the middle of the court. No one would see it, after all. Except for myself.

He could not fault my logic in that regard, and was appropriately appreciative, for he enjoys our lessons as well.

There was one concern he could not quite quash, and that was that matter of my reputation. What would everyone say when we both came out of the boathouse, whether at the same time or not, having been in there alone for what appeared to be hours? It could cause gossip of an "unseemly nature." I was pleased he was concerned.

I had no such concerns, and told him all he need do was leave and walk slowly back to the Hall on his own, and ask for me when he arrived. I could see in his eyes he was fighting the inclination to ask what was going on, and also his realization that it was not his place to do so, which meant he had recovered himself. He bowed lopsidedly and left moving slowly.

As soon as I was certain he was on his way back to the Hall, it was a simple matter to set off through the tunnel back to the Hall. In just a moment I was back in the library, snuffing the lamp that lit my way. I quickly touched my curls, shook out my skirts and checked in the looking glass to make sure I had not inadvertently gotten any colour during my lesson, nor dust on my gown, before sitting on the divan near the windows with a book. At that moment Taylor arrived at the doorway, announcing "Mr. Ploughgoode." I thanked him and had Will sent in.

I thought he was going to faint again. He did not, but the start and the goggle-eyed stare he gave made me smile. As Taylor was in the room practicing standing quietly, neither one of us were able to say anything about what had transpired in the boathouse. Which was nothing, but it still would not do to gabble about it. He finally cleared his throat and said carefully that he wanted to thank me for cutting the lesson short, and to confess that he had gone to the boathouse for some water, and then became ill. Taylor faltered in his training for a moment, for he raised an eyebrow. I replied in a snapping tone that I was aware of where he had gone, as I was left standing on the court for ten minutes before giving up and going to the library to spend my time more profitably, improving my mind. Will was taken aback, and then replied that he was sorry for the breach, it would not happen again, and begged my forgiveness, but there was a slight twinkle in his eye. I am sure there was an answering one in mine, for it was rather delightful to have the conversation in front of Taylor, who was completely unaware of the goings-on. I accepted his poor excuse of an apology and we agreed that he would return two days' hence to conduct a proper lesson.

That done, he apologized again, and kissed my hand before taking his leave. There was again the echo of the Highland cure in it, and lasted rather longer than entirely appropriate, which he made up for by leaving quickly.

That handled handily, I queried Taylor how his recuperation was progressing; without the bandages it is hard to tell. He smiled at the question, and said he was nearly mended, which pleased me. He has been so quiet since the incident, Susannah, none of his usual sweet sparkle. Lady Shardley is not a welcome subject in my Hall, and I am afraid may not be for some time.

As you can imagine, my tennis lesson took up most of my day when it was not supposed to, and in spite of my afternoon nap, I found myself ready for bed early. Excitement can do that to a person, as we learnt at Miss Penelope's, and so I retired for the evening. It was important that I get proper sleep, for the next few days were going to be very busy indeed.

I am afraid I must cut my missive short, Susannah, and prepare it for delivery, for Constance and Hortense are going into town and can post it for me.

I shall write again as soon as I am able, and until then, please remember me as

Your Life-Saving Friend,

Annabella

ꟾ A Most Difficult & Personal Conversation ꟾ

23 June, 1821

Dear Susannah,

I am so pleased your new gown designer is such a smashing success! It is so difficult to find one that can not only design a gown properly but be original as well. Do you remember the one that was all the rage just a few seasons ago, until the first big ball, when all of us found our gowns were identical save the colour? The only consolation we had was for it to become an amusing tale to tell those who were not in attendance.

I have decided that Gwynneth, once she has finished taking in my existing gowns, shall be given the ultimate test of her skills: to design and make my gown for the Opening Ball here at Wetmoor. I know you must think me mad, Susannah, but I do believe, based on what I have seen of what she can do with fabric, that my gown shall be the talk of the town, and not in a derogatory way. With that in mind, I summoned her to the Hall. She only gave birth a few weeks ago, but time was of the essence in more ways than one. We have a nursery now, for goodness' sake, so she could even bring the child with her. I must confess I have wanted to lay my own eyes on it, to see if it resembles Lord Shardley in any way. As it is a girl that would be regrettable, but there you are.

Mr. Sinclair had come from London for our regular meeting and was departing again when my carriage came up to the front door – Driver must have gotten mixed up again and thought Gwynneth was a guest instead of a hireling. They arrived early, and I was suddenly faced with a foyer full of people. Prudence and Constance appeared from nowhere to coo over the child, and Mr. Sinclair even proffered a kind word. I stood a bit off to the side for a moment and then asked that the child be brought to me. Gwynneth put her in my arms and pulled the blanket back from her face. And there she was, Susannah.

Of course, given her parentage, it was unlikely a lovely little babe would be looking at me, and sadly that was the case. She has the chin, nose and brow of her mother, and the cheeks, hair and mustache of her father. I felt sorry for the little thing, but sometimes these things pass and they can blossom. She is beginning somewhat behind the starting line, as it were, so shall have to work extra hard to just catch up. Poor little thing: all this at only three weeks old.

When I had completed my obligatory gushing over the beauty of the child, as these murmurings are required no matter what the station of the mother, I asked her name. Gwynneth said that at the moment she was called Baby, but her given name would likely be Gabrielle, which I thought a rather fancy name for one so plain, but refrained from saying anything aloud. Then Gabrielle was taken to the nursery by Prudence for more fussing and I completed my goodbyes to Mr. Sinclair. I had a suspicion that Cook was in the nursery, another opportunity to slack off on her kitchen duties. I suppose that as long as my meals were prompt, hot and delicious I should not complain, but it is difficult. I warned Gwynneth that with the work being done on the Hall it was unlikely the babe would sleep, which she barely heard, as she was staring off after the child with longing in her eyes. I had to actually say her name twice. Finally she tore her eyes away from the hallway and looked at me. I realized she had not been out of sight of the child since their first acquaintance. However, the discussion I was going to have with Gwynneth was not fit for ears so new, but I did not want to alarm her, as she has been so easily unnerved in the past. I was pleased to note she has a pleasant figure, when not distended by rampaging Lords.

We went to my dressing room, where I showed her the gowns that needed work. She patted them absent-mindedly, nodding that she could have them done within a fortnight. I added that more work was going to be required, if that was convenient for her. I meant it facetiously, but she considered the question so carefully that I realized she thought I was asking her in earnest. I was curious as to what she would say, so waited whilst her brain slowly ground out an answer, which of course was in the affirmative. She is not a complete dolt, after all. I decided not to frighten her with the notion that I wanted her to design and make new dresses, for it was difficult enough for her to decide to continue the work she has been doing.

Which left only the difficult part of the conversation that needed to take place, Susannah, but a conversation that was crucial to Gwynneth ever finding happiness in life. How I could make that clear to her I did not know. She had picked up a gown and was examining its construction when I bade her sit. She began to sit in the sewing chair, and I told her she should sit in the chair near mine. A proper lady's chair, that is. She was startled, but I decided that the best chance for the conversation to result in the desired outcome was if I approached it as one woman to another, not mistress to servant. I know that sounds odd, but I have cultivated so many eccentricities of late that one more surely could do no harm. I poured us each a cup of tea, watching her eyes grow large and round at the sight. I handed her a cup, only spilling a bit, and then poured for myself. After a long draught to wet my suddenly parched throat and wishing there was something a bit more substantial than tea in the cup, I decided to be forthright.

I began by asking Gwynneth if Gabrielle had yet been baptized. I sighed with relief when she replied in the negative, but my spirits sank when she informed me the baptism was to take place the following Sunday. I then asked if she trusted me. She sat for a long time, and finally shook her head no, not without seeming embarrassed by the admission. I recount what I said next as best as I can recall:

"The fact that you do not trust me gives me hope for you, Gwynneth, for you do not know me at all, nor what my plans may be in regard to your life. You must realize by now that I have had another purpose for you than merely to have my gowns altered, although the result has been more than I could have hoped for. You sensed aright: I have had reason to seek you out and to become knowledgeable about your personal situation. Please be assured that although my reasons for doing so must for now remain shrouded in mystery, they are not in any way intended to distress your life, which has been distressed enough by the landed gentry in the last year. Do you understand what I am saying?"

Of course she did not. So I simplified: I could not tell her the reasons for my interest, but I wanted to help her, not plunge her life into even more misery than she was already mired. This she understood. I then continued that it was imperative that not only Gwynneth's but Gabrielle's very future lay in delaying the baptism. She paled and gasped.

My request led to a convoluted discussion of the state of a child's soul, the risk of eternal damnation that was being courted by Gabrielle's continued unbaptized state, and the dire risk the child was in every day of unconsecrated expiration, given the amount of filth to which she was subjected with her cradle in a room over a serving house.

I kept countering with the same statement: if Gabrielle (and Gwynneth) were to have any chance of happiness in this sphere, the baptism had to be postponed. Gwynneth finally realized my request was deadly serious, and the consequences, whichever way she chose, were equally serious, but only affecting one existence at a time: this one, or the next. I offered that she could have the vicar spill some holy water on Gabrielle to safeguard against the demons of Hell itself rushing in to destroy her until the baptism could be properly conducted. As Gwynneth is practical as well as resigned to the fact that her bastard child shall likely already go to Hell no matter how many good works she does, she finally agreed to delay the baptism.

I was relieved. I had no idea that Gwynneth had that kind of spine. They say all mothers are fiercely protective of their young, but I had not expected to see that sort of devotion from one whose station in life could hardly slip lower.

The next part was more delicate. I had to determine the status of relations between Gwynneth and her erstwhile husband, Rufus. She had said he was not always going after her before the birth, and that had led to the glimmer of an idea. I drank more tea, wishing that I had thought to fortify it before this discussion, as it would be unseemly, as well as unladylike, to pull out the brandy in my wardrobe and drink straight from it, but I did indulge in some wishful thinking for a moment. Then I plunged in, hoping her husband had not yet done the same.

I asked if relations had resumed between herself and Rufus. Everyone knows a new mother must be given time to recover from childbirth, but I had no idea how the lower classes handle the issue. Unfortunately my question did not pierce the thick veil of Gwynneth's incomprehension. She said his relations were fine, with mother, father and all siblings alive and well, although between she and I, there were better mothers-in-law in the world than Rufus'. She did not know to what I referred. We sat in silence as I tried to think of delicate yet clear wording of my question.

I asked if Rufus had been exercising his rights. Gwynneth said he had the same rights as any free man in the Empire. By now I was truly craving some brandy, but knew I had come this far, I must see the course through. I asked if he had resumed his place in her bed. She said he had never slept in her bed, it was only large enough for one, and as Gabrielle slept in a cradle next to her, there was no room.

We were getting nowhere and the day was slipping away. I finished my tea, took a very deep breath, and asked if he had resumed marital relations with her of the type that could result in a brother or sister for Gabrielle. She yelped and dropped her cup and saucer on the floor, where they smashed into pieces. She tried to pick up the shards with shaking hands, saying that it was none of my business no matter what my station. Which was true, unfortunately, so I could not even upbraid her. It vexes me when that happens. I told her to leave the pieces of china where they were and to forgive my intrusive questioning, but it had a great deal to do with her and Gabrielle's future. She shook her head, "no." I was relieved, but realized that she might be shaking her head less as an answer to my question than as a refusal to answer it. I sighed inwardly.

"Gwynneth, you could not possibly be more embarrassed by this conversation than I, but it is imperative that I know the answer to my question. It is not to humiliate you nor amuse myself that I seek the information. It is for your future, and I am afraid that we may sit here for hours whilst I await a response for, as much as you may wish to delay answering me, I shall sit here until Judgment Day if I must, although I would prefer it take rather less time. So if you please, simply answer yes or no: have you and Rufus resumed normal relations between husband and wife?"

She blurted out the answer. "How could we when there never were any to start?"

She dabbed at her eyes with the hem of her tatty skirt. I was concerned I had imagined this most perfect of answers, and asked her to repeat herself.

To my surprise, the younger Bargesniffle had not availed himself of Gwynneth's admittedly limited charms before the birth, due to what he referred to as her "fat self" being undesirable. Adding insult to what is likely a very slight injury, he has been spending time of a carnal nature with a girl from Kingston Woods that he met on his wedding day, and has nary a spare moment for his wife. So Gwynneth is a fallen, married spinster, three things I thought impossible to land together in one person, yet here it was accomplished quite handily.

When I had confirmed I understood her properly my heart went out to her. I do not think her life could get worse if she erupted in boils.

But it was also cause for relief on my part. It would make things ever so much easier. Of course, only if she followed my next request to the letter.

"Gwynneth, although I am sure you feel this conversation could not possibly become any more base, I must make ask something of you that you may find to be not only wildly intrusive and improper, but very, very odd." She was too bewildered to reply.

"Gwynneth, no matter what happens, if Mr. Bargesniffle decides that he would like to begin normal marital relations with you – do you know what I mean by that?"

"D'you mean if 'e wants to poke me?"

Her euphemism made me wince. "Yes. Well, if he wants that, you must not under any circumstances allow him to."

"What d'you mean?"

"You must not be <u>with</u> him, Gwynneth. Not for any reason."

"But 'e's me husband, mum. 'E's got rights."

"I understand, but you must put him off somehow. Tell him the midwife forbids it, or it could hurt you. What am I saying? He would not care about that. Tell him it is your time of the month, anything that would put him off. Stop bathing or brushing your teeth and hair, make yourself as unattractive as possible to him. If only you had a goiter, what a difference that would make!"

"A what?"

"Never mind. Just promise me that you absolutely shall not have relations with Rufus."

"Well, I never did want to anyway, mum. 'E's got that thing on his head." Which is true; it does look strange. "So I got ter make sure that even if 'e does start lookin' at me the way men can look, that if 'e does look at me I'm so disgustin' 'at 'e'll look somewhere else first?"

"That is exactly what I mean, Gwynneth." Thank God!

"But why? I mean, beggin' your pardon and all, mum, you've been nicer to me than I deserve, I know 'at, lettin' me come 'ere an' sit in a nice chair an' all, but I don' understan' why what 'appens to me makes any difference a' all."

I had so hoped she would not ask me that! "I cannot tell you now, Gwynneth, but be assured that I would have never undertaken this conversation with anyone, ever, unless it were of the utmost importance. All I can say is that it is truly for your own good, and for Gabrielle's as well."

"Yes, mum," she mumbled, realizing she could ask all day and I would not answer to her satisfaction, but perhaps invoke my ire.

"Will you do as I ask, Gwynneth?"

"I don' think I'll 'ave to do anythin', mum, given the way it's been so far, but I'll stop bathin' 'n' stuff, if it makes you 'appy." Which, I supposed, was the most I could hope for under the circumstances.

"Thank you, Gwynneth. One day Gabrielle shall also thank you." We sat for a moment, for although I had plotted out how the conversation was to go, I had not thought of how it should be concluded. The silence was long and awkward, and I was just thinking wistfully of the brandy bottle, so tantalizingly close, when she cleared her throat. I looked at her, and she suddenly seemed very young. I realized with a start that she was barely 17, just a bit younger than I was when I married Quince.

"Will 'at be all, mum?" She asked quietly.

"I believe it is, Gwynneth. Thank you." She stood and went to the gowns.

"I can take these home if you like, mum, and work on 'em there, and then send 'em back as they're done."

"Gwynneth, I assumed we would resume the same pattern as before, except every day of the week. God knows what slovenliness your husband's family lives in. I promise, we shall not have any more conversations like the one we had today." She looked crestfallen, and was fingering the fabric of my blue gown, when I realized the issue.

"You should bring Gabrielle with you. I do not think she should be left with your mother-in-law. And she must take sustenance."

"Could I?" How quickly her eyes went from dull to bright!

"I shall send a carriage every day save Sunday."

"Thank you, mum, thank you ever so!"

"Your work shall take most of your day every day, do you not agree? For many, many, many, many days?"

"Oh, mum, this, it ain't nuffin' for me to do, really, but . . . " she trailed off as she saw the look in my eye. "You know best, mum."

"A carriage shall pick you up at eight o'clock every morning and take you home at night. I shall send your wages with you, which you shall turn over to Mr. Bargesniffle, as he is losing money by allowing you to work here. Will that be satisfactory?" She grinned, realizing that this could be a great boon, for the difference between money paid and money paid out are two different things, which was my intent.

"Yes, mum, that will be lovely, mum. Thank you, mum." She actually bobbed a little curtsey.

"We shall see you on the morrow. Take care to not make too much noise, I am a light sleeper."

"Yes, mum." And that was that. I gave her leave and she fair ran from the room. I could hear those great feet of hers pounding down the stairway and running for the nursery.

Well, that is one hurdle overcome, although there are others in the way. I only hope and pray that the harlot from Kingston Woods is fetching and eager to please Rufus, so his attentions continue to not be on Gwynneth.

The next thing was to write Mr. Sinclair with some questions. He has been a great help to me thus far, and I am hoping he will continue an unsullied record in that regard. Once the letter was posted I finally had some time for myself.

That time was spent trying again to get into that room in the hidden passageway, the one off of the games room. The labourers had finished their work, and had not discovered the latching system for the panel, so cunningly hidden in the walrus carving. They were all in the ballroom, working on the plasterwork and stone, so it was a safe time. I went quietly down the stairway and made my way to the games room without being seen. It is much improved from the state I originally found it, the carvings gleaming from a new coat of wax, and the plasterwork finally restored. Of course, I have no idea why Sir Manfredson decided the trim should all be that of the sea, but it does make for an unusual look. I love that all of the doorknobs in the room are shaped like dolphins. Quick as anything I was back in the passageway, and soon standing in front of the door that had defied me so many times. This time I had a new hairpin I thought might fool the lock. For the longest time I jiggled it this way and that, until it became clear I would face defeat once again. It was infuriating.

You know how we women are, Susannah: curious to a fault and angry when thwarted. That is how Bluebeard wound up with dead wives. But I was becoming warm and rather weary of standing in front of a door that I owned yet still could not open. I sighed loudly and returned to the Hall proper. The room would keep its secrets for at least another day, but not forever. I shall find a way in on my own, for I cherish the secrets of this Hall, and shall not give them away to others, so if a way is to be found, it shall have to be by me.

When I returned to the library to attend my correspondence, I found instead Prudence sitting next to a tearful Hortense. They started at my entrance, and Prudence leapt to her feet.

I asked if there was something wrong, which they denied. This was contradicted by continued snivelling from Hortense. It was too much, and I said so, and demanded they tell me what was going on.

Hortense is now convinced she has heard Walker and Molly, the annoying Ghosts of Wetmoor. I sighed inwardly, sat down and asked her why she believed such a silly thing. She said she had heard something walk past her in the hallway sighing, but it could not be seen, and if that was not a ghost, then what was?

What I do not understand, Susannah, is why everyone hears and sees these ghosts save me. I live here, and not once have I heard a creak, groan or felt a cold breeze that could not be readily explained by a foot on a stair, another injured workman heading for hospital or a window not properly fastened. Why must everyone obsess themselves with spirits and goblins? I feel that if there are ghosts in this Hall and they want something, they shall make themselves known to me in no uncertain terms. I have far better things to do with my time than to unravel the riddles of what is beyond this existence. This existence is complicated enough, what with all the goings-on, and to ponder another would exhaust me.

I finally told Hortense that big houses make noises sometimes, especially ones that are having so much done to them, and she should not worry a whit about a ghost unless one walked up in front of her and shouted "Boo!" in her face.

That seemed to do the trick, for she stopped sniffling and tried to smile. I then dismissed them and turned to my correspondence. It takes two full hours each day to read all of the things that Quince felt so strongly I keep abreast of, and the sun was already high in the sky.

And my correspondence for today has just arrived, Susannah, and a more intimidating mountain of papers I have not seen in some time. I had no idea how much time it took to actually determine what happens to money. I must away and go through all of the papers, and this letter can be posted immediately.

I shall write again soon, my dear, and I remain

Your Relieved Friend,

Annabella

☙ Mr. Ploughgoode's Collapse ❧

27 June, 1821

My dearest Susannah,

I know that I moved to the country in order to have rest and quiet, but I believe the physician may have been sorely in error with that prescription, or else believed I am one of those Ladies who goes to the country and sits on a chair tatting lace. If so, he is a poor diagnostician indeed!

In spite of all of the obligations of which I find myself the sole owner, I love watching this Hall come back to life. I believe it shall be the talk of the county when unveiled at the Opening Ball.

It would appear from the patterns of disarray through the Hall that Sir Manfredson reduced his perambulations in the Hall more and more as he grew older. I think by the end he only used the drawing room, the nursery and the kitchen, the rest of the Hall being shut up tight. It took days to clear out the things he left behind as he reduced his life to a minimum.

The music room shall be especially charming, I think. I know from the secret drawings I found that the theme of the room is songbirds, which seems appropriate, and Mr. Wicklestaff agreed that songbirds are in keeping with the Nature theme of the Hall, the only break being the ballroom, a spectacular break in theme unless you believe that all of the doors leading to Nature itself somehow remedy the lapse. Mr. Wicklestaff believes the damp that pervaded the music room shall require most of the plastering to be replaced. I have instructed him to make sure that the renovation be as close to the original plasterwork as possible, as I find the songbirds flitting about the cornices to be quite charming. I adore the design liberties that Manfredson took when building his folly, Susannah, and Mr. Wicklestaff agrees with me in this instance. He says he knows just the man, and will have him sent for to begin the work as soon as possible. When the plasterwork is complete, I shall then have the curtains hung and furniture delivered, along with a glorious piano from London. I have already writ the proprietors, and am assured it can be delivered as soon as I give word. I do enjoy having money, Susannah, if that is not too craven a sentiment. I have found that many difficulties disappear if one waves enough money at them.

However, this is not true of every issue, and is what makes life so annoying at times. Like the fact that Taylor still has regained neither his stamina nor strength. He has to nap at least two hours in the afternoon or he begins to list again.

Gwynneth spends her days working on my dresses, of which each is more becoming than the last, although it took some time for her to learn to go more slowly, so that she shall be here longer. I have also asked her to look at my hats and bonnets to make sure they are still appropriate for the gowns, and to extend her "employment."

I also finally asked her to make my Opening Ball gown. She near fainted when I asked, and I had to repeat myself three times before she believed me. The smile that came over her face made her almost pretty, Susannah. I asked her to also design a gown for the day after, when I shall be receiving letters and visits from far and wide congratulating me on such a fine event.

We began discussing materiels and colours, and she asked if she could make some preparatory sketches for my approval.

I have decided that all of that should stay here, for what the Bargesniffles are not aware of can do them no harm, and I do not believe it necessary that they be aware of Gwynneth's skills, lest she find herself shackled to a loom somewhere, and her services cost me thrice what they do now. Once we have designs I approve, I shall send for materiel from London.

It is a good thing we can have it all sent for, as Gwynneth has taken my request to make herself unattractive very much to heart, and now resembles an overgrown chimney sweep. Were it not for Gabrielle in her arms when she arrives, I would not be sure it actually is Gwynneth. It is almost alarming, and I have found that we need to have the windows opened and rooms aired out after her departure. I cannot complain, as she is following my instructions, but I did not think she would deteriorate so quickly in terms of hygiene. Apparently it is effective, however, for Rufus now veers away whenever he sees her. Keep your fingers crossed!

Mr. Sinclair is now sending me books on contracts to augment those in my library, and I am quite pleased at how my plan is taking form. I shall not bore you with the details right now, as I am not certain of everything, and would hate to raise your hopes, only to see them dashed.

You shall be relieved to know that Mr. Ploughgoode suffered no deleterious effects from his collapse the other day, and I am glad I was able to provide details you enjoyed. And I did not peek down his breeches when he was unconscious, so your own imagination shall have to suffice for what appear to be quite depraved musings.

I have found that Will has a sly sense of humor to go with his inability to tolerate sunlight. When he arrived for my lesson yesterday I met him on the court, where Prudence had left water with lemon should we become thirsty. He bowed and resigned. I gave a start of surprise and he looked up, a bright twinkle in his eye, and said he would resign at the beginning of every lesson going forward, to save time later. I could not help but laugh, Susannah. I then told him I had cried for an hour in the morning, so to be ready and tear-free for him.

As agreed, he removed his frock coat and waistcoat, rolled up his sleeves, and the lesson was going quite well, I thought. Mr. Ploughgoode very much approves of how I handle the racquet and the balls, and I am able to return his serve more often than not. Soon I shall be able to angle my shots off walls and perhaps even through the windows, but for now I am getting used to hitting the ball with some regularity. I was just beginning to really enjoy myself when I realized that Mr. Ploughgoode was again looking unfocused. Then one of the balls hit him in the face, and down he went like Walker must have in the pond.

This time I was ready. Using my racquet I propped up an edge of the net. I got the water and lemon and crawled through the space, which I thought quite clever. I then poured the water and lemon over his head, which woke him immediately, although next time I shall take pains to avoid pouring the water up his nose. He sat up and (once he finished sputtering out the water) said he had no idea why this was happening to him, as it never had in the past. I poured him a glass of water and when he finished drinking it, he said he became dizzy at times in high summer, but never to the point he does at Wetmoor. Then he looked up, grey eyes wide, framed by their very long lashes: perhaps it was the ghosts, he thought.

Yes, Mr. Ploughgoode believes in the ghosts, Susannah, which was disappointing. He seemed more rational than that. I told him there are no ghosts at Wetmoor and he almost argued the point, until he saw the look in my eye and thought the better of it. I know not what they get up to in Scotland with their bog sprites, leprechauns and fairies, but they are not in my Hall, and that was all I would hear about the matter.

Wanting to change the subject, Will said he had regained himself and was ready to begin the lesson again if I wished. I made him turn away while I crawled back under the net.

It was a scarce fifteen minutes before he collapsed again. I know not how he keeps any clientele at this rate, but that is none of my affair. The man swoons more than I do. I crawled back under the net, checked that he was breathing, and sat next to him. I shivered, for there was a fierce nip in the air. As soon as clouds scudded across the sky Will came to himself again and sat up, looking around. He winced when he saw me and stood sheepishly, which I did not think possible. He took my hand and helped me to my feet, and insisted on lifting me over the net. He picked me up as if I weighed little more than a feather and deposited me with grace, before clambering over the net himself. He then apologized for the trouble he was causing.

I decided not to remonstrate him, he was already mortified by his inability to last an entire lesson whilst I was clambering around saving him, and the clambering was exercise, so not a complete waste of time. I gave him leave to sit and join me, then pulled the bottle of Scotch from the bush and poured us each a dram, and asked if he had seen an apothecary for his problem. He had not, for like all men he preferred his own diagnostic skills to that of a surgeon, although given the standard of care provided by surgeons in this county, I cannot fault him. He has never had this spate of collapsing in his life and cannot determine the cause. He feels hale and hearty at all other times, but somehow goes "funny all o'er," as he put it, when giving me my tennis lessons.

I told him he could stay in the boathouse for the day, as well as evening if he so desired, but I would be returning to the Hall for the rest of my day, as I had several pressing obligations. He seemed flattered by the offer, but demurred. He had other obligations as well, and would take my leave. He bowed and kissed my hand again, lingering even longer than he had before, which I found to be very pleasant, especially when his unsteady state caused him to gently tongue the space between two very happy fingers, and left.

The rest of the day was taken up with menus, lists of items to order from London, quarrels and conferences with Mr. Wicklestaff; all of the things that my life encompasses recently. Oh, and letters continue from men seeking my favours. One received today was of particular interest: a quite impressive offer of gifts, etc., on the condition that I be willing to dress as a shepherdess. That was new.

But there are things to which I look forward, Susannah. So with that in mind I bid you adieu for now, so that I may prepare for the excitement that I am sure lies just around the corner (and in this Hall, that is all too true!)

Fondly I remain,

Your Busy Friend,

Annabella

☙ A New Friend ❧

5 July, 1821

Dearest Susannah,

It was wonderful to hear from you so quickly, especially from Italy. What a lovely vacation for your Lordship and yourself! I hope Firenze lives up to your standards for a respite there, and the weather agrees with Lord Carollton's gout. It is a terrible ailment, and you are a wonderful and organized wife to have thought to have his favourite footstool brought along on your journey.

Things here at the Hall proceed apace and the workmen are busy as bees at a hive. There is an Opening Ball to plan and I would like for it to be held during my lifetime. It shall be wonderful to see all my peers again, especially you. Will is my most frequent visitor and although I consider him a friend, I cannot confide things to him the way I might to one who is not also working for me. The other most frequent visitor is Mr. Sinclair. He came and went again yesterday, arriving at the same time as Gwynneth. She is now brought to the servants' entrance, of course, but we all met in the hallway.

Mr. Sinclair has lovely manners. Gwynneth followed my directions with alarming determination, and is the most dishevelled creature I have seen since you and I attempted charitable works in our youth and went to visit the sick in hospital for the poor. Now I send money.

There are things stuck in Gwynneth's hair and I am not sure what exactly they are, but lack the courage to ask. However, when Mr. Sinclair saw her in the foyer he bowed as if she were a lady and inquired after her child. She managed to curtsey and pulled the blanket back so he could see for himself. He was effusive in his praise for Gabrielle, and Gwynneth blushed. It was quite sweet. After our meeting Mr. Sinclair dashed back to London, for he has met a young girl he fancies. He was taking her to the theatre that night, and asked me for advice on proper comportment for such an event. I was very happy to advise him on appropriate dress and manners – hopefully it goes well and I can meet her at the Opening Ball.

Petitions with the tenants were sped through at a breakneck pace and our solutions to the litanies of woe were dispatched in under two hours. We are getting better at all of this. Most tenants seem to want someone to simply listen to them. I should like the same thing, but there is no one to petition to except myself, which is most unsatisfactory.

There have been other events at the Hall that I believe shall arouse your curiosity.

Gwynneth has shown me several sketches for approval, but we have not yet settled on a final design for my Opening Ball gown. About half of my gowns are done, and she is working on the others while Gabrielle sleeps in the nursery with Hope. Everyone has taken my instructions to heart, Susannah, and I would never know that there are children about, which is the way I prefer it. Mr. Wicklestaff and I were quarrelling about what to do about the fireplace in the music room – he wants it changed completely, and I want it restored to its original state. As he lost the battle for the games room fireplace he seems to be doubly set on having his way in the music room. I think he is concerned that potential clients would see the games room fireplace, with its carved seals, otters and other sea creatures gamboling around a fire, and shall think it his idea and he might lose a commission. I think the games room is whimsical. With the rest of the room as it is, filled with carvings of seaweed and leviathans, a mantle supported by Doric columns would look even sillier. But winning the first battle has meant that he is twice as adamant about the music room. I like the carvings of musical instruments that make up the music room fireplace, especially the mantle, which is carved as a piano keyboard, whose keys can be struck, except there are bells hung from the keys inside the wall behind. One can play the fireplace! But to restore it means tearing out more of the wall and how many people play the keys on a fireplace? That was Mr. Wicklestaff's opinion. So the argument went round and round for seeming ever, and I was vexed when I realized I scarce had time to change into a gown for tennis, as Will was arriving at three o'clock for a late lesson. It seemed best to schedule lessons when the sun was lower in the sky.

Although he was on time, I was not, and we did not begin until four o'clock, although it seemed much later with the clouds so quickly coming in. He said he had no other pressing engagements and the delay was no inconvenience at all, which pleased me. I am getting rather facile in the game, and have managed to start hitting off the walls and return the same kind of shots, but that has brought dissatisfactions. There is a good deal of volleying back and forth between us, but neither of us is confident enough of the other to actually play. It almost seems Mr. Ploughgoode is concerned he shall overtake my ladylike sensibilities, and I am worried that if I attempt to truly play he will smash one back that will kill me, so we hit the ball back and forth, which is boring. I thought tennis would be more exciting, but it seemed not to be the case. I finally requested a rest, and we stopped for tea and water, which is set out on the little table for us. I asked him if tennis was generally so very dull, repetitive and unimaginative. He thought for a moment, and replied that the skill of the players has much to do with whether or not the game itself is exciting. I asked if he ever intended to test my skills further than the meagre bit he had to start and he said he would endeavor to challenge me more in the future. I then inquired about his other skills, for I understood from other clients that he had many. He choked a bit on his tea then, as thunder sounded far off in the distance. When he recovered, he explained that he also taught riding, shooting, archery, golf, hunting, any sporting skills in which a titled person may require instruction, and he also teaches children of the peerage.

The riding interested me a great deal, for I wish to establish a bridle path through my little forest beyond the formal gardens, and asked his opinion. He said he would have to walk the area before making any suggestion, but would be happy to undertake the venture for me. I did not want to wait, and asked if he would consider a quick perambulation right then, preparatory to a more thorough inspection of the possibilities.

He acquiesced quite prettily and was pleasantly flustered when I asked if I could accompany him, as I would like to understand the qualities of my new lands, and he could perhaps aid in that area. As it was more or less a business offer there would be nothing wrong with us walking together. We went through the Hall to the veranda and, once outside, he proffered his arm chivalrously. I took it with a smile and we walked to the gate separating the formal grounds from my forest. Will said a storm was on the way, and perhaps we should postpone the review, but Scots always think it is going to rain, as rain makes them so very happy, and I said so, so we continued. He pointed out areas of interest, certain ways that would be better for the horses while still affording the feeling of being in a real forest. I was having a lovely time, for once putting thoughts of plaster and wainscoting out of my head and enjoying my grounds, which I have woefully neglected.

Then the rain began. We both looked back and realized how very far we had walked. Will grinned and said rain did indeed make him happy, doffed his coat and held it over my head to prevent my curls from getting soaked. We began to walk back, but as the rain began to come down a little harder than was altogether pleasant, we began to trot.

When we reached the Hall he yanked the veranda door open and shooed me through ahead of him and we were both laughing. Prudence was there and looked shocked and we immediately put on serious faces. Will put his coat back on and, forgetting his station again, instructed Prudence to make sure I was given hot rum with butter to ward off a chill, before telling me I should immediately change into dry clothes. It was not his place to give any such instruction but it was for my own good so I let it pass. He is chivalrous without even knowing it. He was perfectly prepared to leave in the rain and ride his horse back to wherever he lives.

Were I to allow him to leave under such circumstances he would catch his death of cold, and I would be no better than Lady Shardley, so I told Constance to take him to Taylor and make sure he had a place to stay for the night, or until the rain passed, so I would not have to read about him succumbing to a fever three weeks hence. That settled, I went to my rooms, changed into dry clothing and warmed myself by the fire. Prudence brought a light dinner and the buttered rum (which was delicious, I might add), told me that Mr. Ploughgoode had been fed and was settled, and sent thanks for my thoughtfulness. I dismissed her, thinking no more of the matter, when she turned at the door.

"Lady, can I ask a question?" she said.

"You just have, Prudence." There was a silence, and I realized she was not going to be put off, even though her last attempt at initiating a conversation with me resulted in my vomiting all over the floor. It must be important to her. "Yes, Prudence, you may."

"Why are you nice to us?"

"I beg your pardon?"

"You're nice to us, Ladyship. Why?" I was confused. This was perhaps the last question I would have thought Prudence would ask, no matter how her previous employer may have behaved.

"I am not nice to you, and I resent the implication. I would prefer that my staff remain in working order, and that is all. How dare you make such an insinuation?"

"I'm sorry, Lady, my mistake."

"It most certainly is, Prudence, and I shall not have you bandying such notions about. I would be run over by every needy person in the county if it were, and then what would I do?"

"I don't know, Lady."

"Of course you do not, for you are not a lady."

"Beggin' your pardon, I meant no offense."

And of course she did not. These people think that proper maintenance is some sort of boon. It is ridiculous, is it not? I dismissed her again, and this time she had the sense to leave.

I finished my buttered rum and went to bed, hoping the morning would bring normalcy and sunshine.

My hopes were made real, and in the morning there was no sign of Will, Prudence was blessedly back to her taciturn self, Mr. Wicklestaff and I continued our rather heated debate regarding the music room fireplace, sun shining through the windows the entire time. The Hall echoed with sounds of sawing, hammering and the occasional scream, and all was right with my world after such an upsetting conversation, which came entirely too quickly on heels of a delightful walk of my grounds. Mr. Ploughgoode and I must complete it soon.

And I shall have to discontinue this letter immediately, no matter how incomplete, Susannah. Fabric samples have arrived from London for the ballroom, and I simply must see them at once. I shall write again soon, and know that I remain,

Your Dear Friend,

Annabella

☙ Acquiring Suitors ❧

13 July, 1821

Dearest Susannah,

I am pleased Siena and the surrounding areas were to your liking, but give my condolences to his Lordship on the mishap he suffered during the walking tour. I cannot believe the guide was so careless as to allow the path to come so close to the edge of a ravine. I am sure your husband shall make a speedy recovery. There is a poultice which may help the skin affliction that has blossomed upon his hands and face, and I enclose it in the hopes it may provide relief from the itching. Years ago Quince and I were at a friend's in the Country, and he was trying to flush a pheasant when he stumbled upon a new plant and picked a portion of it for analysis. Unfortunately it was a plant not friendly to him, and after burning it all, and I had chastised him for his insatiable curiosity about things, we found this poultice cut his recovery in half. I hope the same applies here. The ingredients can be found anywhere.

I am quite excited to report that I have gone to a dinner party. It was at the Plumwyther home, almost two full hours' from Wetmoor. They are from Church, and Mrs. Plumwyther has always been kind to me at meetings of the Ladies' Auxiliary League for the Church. Their home is lovely, although small, with cozy appointments throughout. Actually, it may not be small at all – the Hall may have altered my perceptions of scale, as it is so very large, that almost every other building seems cramped to me. I hope it does not end up overwhelming me, especially as Quince felt so strongly about it. Well, nothing to be done about that now.

The dinner was delicious – roasted game fowl, fish in a wine sauce, a lovely lemon ice for dessert, although the wines seemed to have been chosen haphazardly. I thought wistfully for a moment of your dinner parties, Susannah, as the wines are chosen with such great care in regard to the menu, but it was pleasant all the same.

I was quite the curiosity at the dinner, for I do not receive invitations, so have been absent from nearly all social events save Church, where the only conversation is spiritual and quiet in tone, when anyone bothers to speak to me at all.

At least I had already met most of the other guests or seen them, but Church conversation is not nearly the same as dinner conversation. In a social setting everyone's fear of me dissipated in direct relation to the amount of wine consumed. Suddenly everyone was addressing me, requesting details of the Hall and its progress, which I was more than happy to provide – save the really interesting progress, which is still a secret that remains between you and I.

The question of the famed ghosts arose, and everyone seemed both relieved and disappointed that I have not been faced with a screaming apparition in the dead of night. I believe I am the only one who does not believe in and does not wish there to be ghosts. I think they envision the Opening Ball complete with a hideous apparition showing up at midnight to terrify the guests. Most of the guests at the Plumwythers' shall be invited – as well as everyone who is anyone in the county, as well as a number of from London. I hope it is a smashing success, and from the interest expressed by my dinner companions, believe that is not too high a hope. One thing that heartened me is there were no mentions of jelly, dead husbands or anything smacking of reference to my life before coming to the country. Dare I believe that my move has actually accomplished a diminishment of the scandalous portion of my reputation? I shall keep praying so – it has been dreary being thought of as a murderess, regardless of how exciting others might imagine such a thing to be. I would rather be seen as myself.

The assembled guests were not many, although more appeared after dinner for the entertainments. At dinner were the Farthingtons, the Gintwists, the Herbathovers, Mr. Castleton, Miss Dover, Miss Paget, Miss Bryce and Mr. Gibberwilly, who attended me when I suffered the unfortunate bout of swooning some months ago. He virtually "hrmmpphed" when we saw each other, and I realized he had neither forgotten nor forgiven what he clearly saw as my poor behaviour when last he saw me. Of course I have no need to apologize – the man called me fat and my maid pregnant which, I was happy to note, was not mentioned by him at dinner. He would never bring up such a thing for, although a mere surgeon, he does have the sense God gave a goose, and knew he would suffer socially for such a breach of manners. Fortunately he was not seated next to me at dinner, but Mr. Castleton was.

I forget sometimes that most people are hoping I shall make another match now that Quince is gone, not knowing of course that it would take either a truly singular man or a leave of my senses before I marry again. It was clear that Mr. Castleton had been amply informed of my situation and my assets (financial, of course), as he was deeply fascinated by every word that dropped from my mouth. It was appalling, Susannah. I understand his income is quite impressive, as he has managed to profit from both the war just past and successful investments in speculative ventures, but he does not even have lands! Quince's holdings were not necessarily impressive when we wed, but I did not choose him, and he at least had a house, for goodness' sake! Mr. Castleton is good-looking, but his slavish devotion to me was quite transparent, although I shall withhold final judgment on his character, for I may merely be suspicious. A widow with holdings must be, lest she be taken in by an insincere but flattering visage. He was charming, I suppose, but not very interesting at first blush.

Titled personages were in short supply at the dinner, for of course Baroness Gurthwant is in deep mourning, but also because Duke Twitwhistle and Baron Theosophus have gone to Africa, of all places! They left two weeks ago, giant rifles at the ready, wide-brimmed hats on their nearly bare heads, bubbling over with excitement at the adventures to come and grand storytelling to follow on their return, and there was a great deal of discussion at dinner regarding Africa, about which no one seems to know anything. I know it is large, hot, filled with strange people and not considered important enough at Miss Penelope's to go into any detail about. Apparently there are beasts aplenty, the likes of which I hope never reach our fair shores – most of them sound terrible, with horns and fangs and great appetites for human flesh. I also hope we do not have to face another inquest before their sabbatical is complete, for although they are annoying, they are peers, and it would be a shame to see the population of our county dwindle any further.

Lady Shardley was also mentioned in passing, with great delicacy. The tenor of the conversation implied that she has become "nervous," and she has refused all invitations to events in the last two months, and stopped attending Church. Murmured sympathy was offered around the table, but I did notice a glimmer of smug satisfaction from a few less kind in attendance.

As you know, I am not pleased with what Lady Shardley has wrought in my own Hall, but certainly do not wish her ill. How I longed to proclaim to those guests the true cause of Lady Shardley's woes. I believe any number of the wives in attendance might have found an uncomfortable accord with her situation and, with that knowledge, been perhaps more charitable.

Mr. Castleton's interest continued after dinner, when other guests began to arrive for the entertainment, surprisingly provided by Miss Dover and Miss Paget. Miss Dover is quite an accomplished pianist, and Miss Paget fancies herself an accomplished singer. They were embellished by a violin player and a flutist for the music, and a number of dances were played, most of which found me hand in hand with Mr. Castleton who, if nothing else, is adept at ensuring he is in the right place and time to partner with a lady. In making his intentions known he nearly knocked Mr. Gibberwilly out of the way to partner with me in a gavotte. Whist was played by the younger ones, and I was pleased I was not dragged into a game, for I find it a bit boring – Quince loved it – but that did leave me in the position of dancing or sitting out, which I was not inclined to do.

I was able to get Mr. Castleton to leave my side for drinks, at which point Mr. Gibberwilly arrived at my side like an arrow shot from a bow.

I was surprised, he seemed disinclined to have a conversation with me earlier in the evening, but when I saw the flush on his cheeks and the perspiration on his brow (entirely unearned from dancing), I realized his determination was more a liquid form. I steeled myself for further (albeit whispered) remonstration, but was surprised.

He wanted to inquire after my health. I told him it was restored and thanked him for his concern. He then stammered that he was sorry for his poor behaviour at our last meeting, and wished to recant his cruel remarks on myself and on my house, that they had been, on reflection, hastily made and incorrect. This gave me pause, for he does not seem to be the type of man to either apologize to a woman nor to reflect on his own behaviour. I accepted his apology and he then he explained that his wife has been quite ill, which has been upsetting and affected his manners.

He continued that she has since become an invalid, he is struggling to manage his practise, his home and raise their eight children alone, adding that he believes his wife is not long for this world, pausing to wipe a poor excuse for a tear from a dry eye. This may have been more convincing had he not been staring at my bosom during his speech. Of course after eight children I myself would likely also be an invalid.

Another fortune hunter, I sighed to myself. They are everywhere. At least he was not asking me to become his mistress. Mr. Gibberwilly may fancy himself to be ahead in the race, as he has attended me medically, and has more of what he clearly believes to be an intimate claim on my affections.

I try to find these offers complimentary, Susannah, I do. But more often than not they make me feel like a horse on market. All of these men with their veiled and unveiled offers and invitations all assume I am a dullard and in dread need of a Man to come and take care of everything, including my fortune and properties, for me. However, when I find that I am becoming annoyed with such attentions, I remind myself that I am fortunate. Many women are not asked, fewer still are in a position to be able to refuse the attentions of a man based on his character rather than his purse, and even fewer in that number have had the good luck to marry a much older man who was the only child of only children, so there was no way for his estate to be entailed away, leaving the wife at the mercy of some cousin or brother, whose caretaking may well depend on a *quid pro quo* arrangement. We both know those who have been in those unenviable positions, Susannah, and I thank God I will not be one of them. In fact, I shall only suffer financially if I remarry, which I find to be the height of irony.

I thanked Gibberwilly prettily for his apology, and offered my sympathies on his personal woes, which made him beam. I believe a visit from the surgeon shall be coming soon. It was clear he had gleaned from the dinner conversation too well the opportunities I appear to present, and he shall likely visit under the guise of stewardship as opposed to romance. I find it appalling that he is casting about for another wife when his current spouse in not yet Gone, but there are eight(!) children in tow. Five are girls, he sadly informed me. The dowries alone will be crippling, especially on a surgeon's income. I shall have to ensure he is never shown the nursery, else I shall find him following me at every turn.

Fortunately Mr. Castleton returned with our drinks, something I had not anticipated finding pleasurable, but it is amazing how one's mind can change in these matters. Mr. Gibberwilly was flustered at being elbowed aside by the now-welcome attentions of Mr. Castleton, but there was nothing to be done. The Plumwythers appeared pleased with themselves at the match they believed they had made, and I smiled at them across the room while Mr. Castleton and Mr. Gibberwilly traded places. The drink was delicious though, very light and refreshing.

The dancing continued, and I found myself dancing with more than Mr. Castleton or Mr. Gibberwilly, as they were so oft attempting to place themselves properly against each other that I could easily place myself one off and dance with someone who would presumably not ask for my hand in marriage.

When the evening came an end I was pleased to see Driver and Taylor standing next to the carriage, glowering at Mr. Gibberwilly and Mr. Castleton as they hovered at my elbows as bookend escorts. It was a horrible breach and showed how lacking in manners both men are. I glared at them both, but neither was willing to cede the arm he held. I finally flapped my arms so that both were forced to let go of me. I walked to the carriage, both men trailing behind me like goslings behind a goose.

When they saw Driver they were both nonplussed by his expression, which I know is merely the way he looks, until reminded that it is frightening to those unaccustomed to him. They each faltered (which means bravery is not a trait either possesses) and I stepped forward, smiling warmly at Driver. Taylor, looking appalled at my escorts, opened the carriage door and took my hand to help me enter, which earned him a warm smile as well. He smiled back and looked implacably at Castleton and Gibberwilly. Both men drew back and I stared straight ahead while Taylor fastened the door and Driver began his long climb to the top of the carriage. Thank goodness he had not taken his leg off during the evening, as it would have undone both of my would-be suitors. On the other hand, perhaps they would not have walked me to the carriage at all.

Taylor bowed briefly to both men and climbed up next to Driver while I leaned back into the velvet upholstery, letting out a quiet sigh of relief. I had looked forward to a evening out with equals, but found none, and now it appeared I had two suitors. I know not what will happen with them next, but have no doubt I shall see both again, and sooner rather than later.

"Later" is when I shall have to continue my tale to you, Susannah, for the hour grows late (again!) and I must turn my attention to the menus for the week so that the orders are placed in time, lest I go hungry. I shall write again soon, dear friend, and know that I remain faithfully,

Your Popular Friend,
Annabella

☙ A Dark & Stormy Night ❧

15 July, 1821

Dearest Susannah,

Thank you for your sympathies regarding my suitors. There is nothing more awkward than knowing you are about to be pursued by those whose pursuit is not welcome, as you well remember from the Season you made your debut. What a whirl of suitcoats and swords there were around you, and Lord Carollton should be grateful forever your eye fell upon him with favour! I am pleased he is making a speedy recovery with the help of the poultice, and that your unexpectedly protracted stay in Siena has been somewhat enlivened by the presence of that Randy servant.

Things have been enlivened here as well, you shall be very glad to know, although in a different way than I would have ever imagined. What I am to relate is shocking, and you are the only person to whom I can fully pour out my heart, which I find myself needing very much. I am hoping that if I put everything down on paper for one who will receive it kindly I may be able to sort out for myself the various quandaries in which I have found myself mired. Of course now you are bursting to know of what I am referring, but be patient, all will unfold in this letter, with no rude severance before it is completely told, post or no.

It began two days after the dinner party I wrote of in my last letter. The day began promisingly, slightly overcast, which boded well for my tennis teacher remaining conscious for the entire lesson.

I spent the morning working on the guest list for the Opening Ball. I have to begin now because hundreds must be invited and it would be terrible to forget someone important. The menu must be chosen as well, as well as calculating the number of extra servants required for such a huge crowd. Cook and I spent hours together, finally coming to happy agreement on all of those issues, which earned me a toothy grin from the old woman who is rarely, if ever, pleased.

The planning lasted until late afternoon, and it was time for my tennis lesson. Prudence helped me change into a more appropriate gown, noting that the skies had become more overcast even as I wondered why it was necessary to change into a third gown of the day when I had not even left my own Hall. Sometimes such thoughts come into my head at the strangest times. It is a fact of life that one has different outfits for different occasions, and Prudence and I have become quite adept at getting me dressed. Having many gowns has been a boon in that it has kept Gwynneth working here for simply ever.

By the way, Gwynneth and I have chosen the designs for my Opening Ball gown and for the day after, and both are both stunning, if you do not mind my saying so. That girl is a gem of a find, even with her fallen status and bastard child. I intend to keep my knowledge of her skills to myself for the time being, as there will plenty of opportunities in the future to make them known, I believe. In the meantime she has worked miracles on my existing gowns. Constance has reported that Gwynneth can be heard to be humming tunes to herself at times and is often found working on a gown in the nursery as opposed to the sewing room, in order to be near her little Gabrielle.

Gwynneth has been successful in postponing the baptism, at least for the time being. She told the Bargesniffles she wants the baptism to occur on the same day as her departed mother's birthday, to honour her memory, which the family has accepted readily, so they may postpone the cost of a post-baptismal celebration. Thank God they are greedy! In terms of appearance she seems to have reached a point that cannot be further lowered, hovering at "slovenly." She tries to improve a bit when at the Hall, pinning her lank and filthy hair up neatly, and insists that my instructions or no, she will wash her hands clean before working on my gowns. She sits with an old sheet between herself and the rest of my wardrobe, stitching and tucking away. It is very satisfactory for all concerned.

But Gwynneth is not the point of this letter. I find I am delaying the rest as I can scarce believe it myself. I fear the act of telling you shall make it impossible to deny. I am so grateful for the vow we made at Miss Penelope's, when we pledged to be sisters in spirit to each other forever, and would remain always each other's staunch ally, regardless of the vagaries that Fate might deal out to each of us in turn.

I have done something terrible.

As I was making my way to the courtyard for my tennis lesson I was stopped by Taylor, who informed me that Walker and Molly had been heard again, Hortense was in the nursery crying, Gwynneth left because she was worried they would abduct her baby, and the workmen had also left for the day in fear.

This infuriated me, although the only person I could complain to at the moment was Mr. Wicklestaff. The workmen are already costing more than they should, as it has been difficult to find men who are not too frightened of ghosts or injury to work, and now they were leaving at the least little creak! Mr. Wicklestaff explained he had heard the sounds himself, and realized that any work the men did after that was bound to be dodgy and slapdash and the weather was turning, so he had released them early so they might get home and collect themselves. It was ridiculous, and I told him so.

In fact, I gathered my entire (although still slight) staff and told them I did not wish to hear any more about the ghosts and should never again be disturbed with wild stories and imaginings. If Walker and Molly themselves appeared and pinched someone I did not want to hear a word of it, no matter how convinced anyone might be of the experience. I also told them I would be going to my rooms directly after my lesson and to not disturb me for any reason, as I wanted to calm myself from these matters, which were vexing me more every day. A dinner should be left for me, and I did not want to see a single face until the next day, when I hoped I had recovered from this latest impudence. They all hung their heads and quietly left, now painfully clear about my views. I took a moment to collect myself, for the day had begun with such promise and I did not want the remainder of it to be marred by the fears of simple people. A small glass of port was helpful in that regard.

Once restored to my customary high spirits I met Will in the tennis courtyard, where tea, water and lemon stood waiting for us, although he did look over at the bush where the Scotch is hidden.

The skies at that point were dark, and I teased that he might actually stay upright for the entire lesson, which made him unaccountably blush and reply it was quite probable he would. With that we began, but once again we just hit the ball easily back and forth. I stopped the game and asked that since I knew his skills were more advanced than what were currently on display, to please make the game more interesting for me. As hobbled by my skirts as I am, I was still easily hitting all of them back. He looked a trifle surprised until I reminded him that I engaged his services for exercise and there was woefully little thus far. Then he began to play more in earnest. He is an excellent partner, for although it became much more difficult for me, it was never completely beyond my skills, which are still developing. He was quite pleased I was able to keep up with the higher level of play, even laughing when I managed to hit one (quite by accident) he could not return. It was by far the best lesson to date and when completed I was quite giddy and breathless. I had such terrific fun, and found I did not want to go back into the Hall to see work abandoned or servants trembling in fear, so I asked Will to join me for tea. He readily agreed, but his eye kept wandering to the bushes, until I asked him to pour me a "wee dram" and one for himself. As we drank we chatted, as we usually do, and he told me a bit more about how he finds life in England. He said that, as a Scot, it can be strange at times, but had felt the need to see more of the world than his beloved Scotland, and was able to do so while still discharging his family obligations. Our conversation then drifted to favourite books and music, that sort of thing.

Then I remembered the bridle path, and asked Will if he would continue his examination of the grounds for this purpose. As before he glanced at the sky and warned of impending rain, but I would not be deterred. I resolutely did not want to go back into the Hall and deal with anyone there. He said that as long as I did not mind getting wet he would be glad to act as an escort. In fact, he thought rain would make him more comfortable. So not as to ring for a servant who would come atremble, near weeping from supernatural fear, I fetched a light cloak and parasol from the mud room myself and we began to walk the grounds again. Rain began a moment after we left, but I did not mind – it was warm and rather refreshing, and my hair would not be ruined, for it was up in a simple twist.

As Will was not fazed, we did not let it dampen our spirits nor our pace, and we went to the "forest." It is dotted with copses and small hillocks, and as we wove our way around and over them Mr. Ploughgoode frequently turned back to the Hall to determine the distance travelled and the overall effect of a bridle path. It was all quite interesting, as he took care to explain to me what he was looking for, and I also learnt the names of some of the trees and plants growing there. He also informed me of any costs that might be incurred by more elaborate grounds work needed in order to make for a lovely and interesting path. The rain began to come down harder, but I was dry under my cloak and parasol and he said he was comfortable, even though he was becoming soaked. He said it reminded him of home. Then he took a small flask from his coat and offered me a sip of his favourite Scotch, the Oban, to "ward off a chill." He added that although it came from the Midlands, I might find it an interesting change, and certainly superior to Lagavulin.

I accepted his expertise in the matter, taking another sip in case it became colder, as we were now very from the Hall, and it would be some time before we could get all the way back. In fact, we were near the southern wall of the grounds, near the west end, so we had travelled some distance. After he took a medicinal drink for himself he restored the flask to his pocket, informing me that no Scot would be caught dead without the "water of life" on their person, and no inference should be drawn regarding any drinking difficulty on his part by the mere presence of it. That made sense to me, so we continued our perambulation.

Until the thunder began. Normally thunder begins a long way off, so one has time to take cover. It was not the case that day. The thunder cracked right over our heads and with it rain poured down alarmingly. We both flinched at the noise and Will advised that we turn back. I nodded, as it was difficult to hear, and we started back to the Hall. Then the thunder roared again and lightning struck close by. I could see it shoot up sparks and dirt on the other side of the wall! I had never seen lightning strike that close, and stood stock-still, the image of the lightning still dancing in front of my eyes, so it was difficult to see. Will plainly had the same reaction, for he kept shaking his head and blinking. It was the loudest sound I have ever heard. The rain then poured down in sheets, blown almost sideways by winds that seemed to come from nowhere, and my parasol was torn from my hand and blown away by the gale. It was the worst storm I have ever encountered and I was at Bath the year of the swimming race disaster. We both stood peering up at the sky for more lightning. Thunder rolled again, and when lightning came down once more Will turned my face into his coat to protect me. The wind was whipping the tree branches into a frenzy. We were in real danger.

Suddenly Will was shouting in my ear that we had to get away from the trees and to safety. We were nearly to a clearing when the dreaded thunder sounded again, and lightning came down right in front of us, striking a large oak not 60 feet away! It fairly exploded from the force of the strike. I froze as the lightning snaked down, and Mr. Ploughgoode flung me to the ground and covered me with himself which, although chivalrous, would not have helped had the tree had fallen upon us, except to make the inquest more scandalous.

When we looked up the wide trunk had been split in half, fortunately in the opposite direction to ourselves, and pieces of the tree were everywhere, including one which landed on Will. I tried to push him off me but he would not allow it, watching the sky and tree until he satisfied himself we were safe. Then he shoved away the branch that had pinned us down and helped me to my feet. With Will favouring his left leg, now holding my hand, we began to make our way over the branches which now stood (or lay, I should say) between ourselves and the Hall.

At first we were slowed only by the continuing gales of rain, which soaked us both through and made it difficult to see, but as we progressed my skirts and cloak became tangled in the split and fragmented pieces of tree until I found myself quite horribly trapped by them. This frightened me even more, as I was surrounded by other trees that might well be struck by lightning at any moment. I tried to pull the fabric free, as did Will, but it was impossible. Finally Will took me firmly by the waist and pulled me backwards whilst I yanked on my skirts. When they came free it was so unexpected that he fell on the ground and I landed atop him. The rain continued to pound down on us and, after taking a moment to catch his breath, Will yelled that he would never walk the grounds with me again if there was even a single cloud in the sky. Against all reason this observation made me laugh and he joined in, even as the thunder kept crashing down. Finally we stopped, for we were no better off than before.

In fact, it was worse, as our route back to the Hall seemed designed to confound us and the rain, if possible, had begun to come down even harder. I clambered to my feet again, Will helping me, my tattered and torn skirts now dragging on the ground, and took a good look around. I saw a stain spreading on the back of the leg of Will's breeches and realized he was bleeding, which normally would make me faint, but I did not have the luxury of swooning at that moment, although it was more than warranted. When I pointed it to it he said the branch that had fallen on him was rather nasty, but he was fine.

Then the hail began, which was too much. Why had I instructed staff to leave me alone? They would never realize we were out in the storm, so hope of rescue was pointless. I tore an already ruined bit of my skirts free and gave it to Will as a poor excuse for a bandage. It would not do to survive the storm and then expire from blood loss or infection. He tied it carefully around his leg. While he did that I turned my head and tried to think of something else, which was difficult considering the situation in which I found myself.

Then I remembered. In the terror of the proceeding moments I had forgotten that my Hall is no ordinary Hall. Will had begun to lead me back toward Wetmoor when I stopped him.

"Do you trust me?" I yelled, as we were both fair deaf from the thunder that continued to batter our ears. He looked confused, and then nodded that he did.

I took his hand and began to lead him in the opposite direction, back toward the wall. He pulled away at first, but I would not let go and would not be deterred. I resorted to ordering him. "You must follow me!" He stopped pulling away and allowed me to lead him to the wall. The thunder kept rolling every few seconds and the lightning was continuing, but at least seemed to be confined to outside of the grounds proper. The hail did hurt, however. I would advise that you avoid it if at all possible.

When we finally reached the wall, unimpeded by felled trees or huge branches, I looked back and forth, gauging where we were in relation to the back gate.

"What are you doin'?" he queried. "This wall is as dangerous as a tree, we must get to safety."

"Which is exactly where we are going. Please trust that I know what I am doing, Will." And I began to pace along the wall toward the gate, peering closely at the stones.

There it was. The rose-coloured quartz stone sticking out a bit from the others. I ran to it just as lightning took down another tree on the grounds not 100 feet from us, Will close behind. I asked him if he was discreet. His response was indignant. "I am a Scot. I take secrets to my grave. Why?"

I then pushed the stone up, so cleverly hinged, and reached for the latch. My fingers found it but it was too wet for me to get a good purchase, so I told Will what to do. The look on his face when part of the wall opened to us was almost worth everything that had happened. Almost.

I pushed him in ahead of me and down the steps to the tunnel, returning back up the steps to make sure the door had closed behind us. I fetched the candle and matches, located on the shelf to the left of the door, lit the candle and came carefully back down so he could not look up my dress. Thank goodness I had worn a cloak – without it I would have looked like Lady Fortenescue when she adopted that French custom of showing up everywhere in soaking wet and scandalously transparent gowns. It did net her a husband, however.

Which is beside the point. When I reached the bottom he was staring the other way, down the dark passage. It was not until I was down the steps that he turned back to me. He is a very gracious man.

"Wha' is this?" he finally asked.

I was close to collapse from everything that had just occurred but he seemed quite collected, only curious about our present circumstances, so I explained to him about follies.

He nodded and said he had heard of them in Scotland, but thought it meant the house looked strange. He sat on the ground and I sat on a step. In silence we listened to the storm.

"We're goin' to be here more than a momen' or two, Lady," he finally said. "It coul' be hours." That bothered me a bit. I was cold, drenched, wretched and shaking like a leaf. In fact, I had begun to feel quite faint. My face must have gone pale, for he stood and rubbed my hands in both of his to warm them, assured me that we were safe, took out his flask and handed it to me. I took a dram more Scot than English and he did the same. It was warming and I felt more myself. I like the Oban, Susannah. You should try it.

He was so kind when everything was my fault, when he would have been well within his rights to at least show annoyance.

"Will?"

"Yes?" He looked up, and I saw he was concerned for me.

"I should like to apologize. You were right about the storm. I should have listened to you. If I had, we would not be trapped in a wall."

He looked astonished. "There's no need for apology, Lady. If I'd not wanted to walk with you, I'd not have done. The storm's not your fault. And you found a safe place for us. I'm fine." He was looking at me oddly. "But thank you."

"I – thank you." I did not know what else to say. I can normally chatter like a magpie, as Quince was so fond of noting, but was suddenly speechless. I believe I was in shock.

Suddenly he reached out and brushed at my hair. I was quite startled and he smiled. "Hail," he explained.

"Oh." I was going to reach up and brush them away myself but did not. I could not remember the last time someone had touched my hair.

He flicked more of them and they clattered to the floor. "Rather a pity," he murmured, hand hovering near my ear.

"What?" I was having trouble thinking.

"They looked like diamonds. It looked pretty." He gave one more quick brush and sat back.

I had no idea what to say so I said nothing at all. We sat for a few more minutes, he glancing at me when I was not glancing at him.

The rain continued, and I realized that Will was right – it might go on for hours – do you remember the storm three years ago? It went on forever, and we all had to sleep at the Islingtons' that night. I had not planned to divulge anything else to him, but feared we would catch our death of cold waiting for the storm to abate, and the walls were beginning to seem close. I was worried I would become hysterical, for my trembling had begun again, and it was not from the chill in the air. One more bout of hysterics might cause Will to give up on my lessons. I stood.

"If you will follow me, please," I said as gracefully as possible, and led him down the passageway. In a trice we had arrived in the small room I had found so many months ago. I lit the lamps on the little table, which were low, but there was light enough to see the room. He was astonished.

"Wha' is this?" he finally queried.

I replied that as far as I could determine, it was what could be delicately described as an assignation room, built by Sir Manfredson. He looked at the paintings hanging from their ribbons, and then to the hooks in the wall.

"An assignation room?" He had no expression on his face, he did not even seem startled.

"Yes. I use it as a place read without being bothered. Sir Manfredson even had a place to tie his dogs." I pointed to the hooks near the floor.

"Dogs?" Will sounded dim, as if he did not understand what was so obvious.

"He had things for dogs that he kept here. Leashes and muzzles and things." I had to stop because Will started choking and coughing very hard. Perhaps he was fevered, I thought, and was having trouble thinking. When he had recovered himself I finished explaining. "They were in the armoire, but I got rid of them. I do not have dogs."

"Oh." He sounded quite odd and the look on his face was odder. He went to the armoire and opened the door. Then his wonderment was complete, for there were the clothes and dressing gowns I had left, the ones that were not all tarty and ruined.

I felt somewhat embarrassed. "There were others, but they were . . . not the kind of thing I wanted to keep."

"This is a folly if ever I heard of one," he finally murmured. He looked at paintings and the pretty bed. "Who did the decoratin'?"

"I did. I liked the idea of a secret hideaway, but it was austere and ugly and rather strict in the strangest way when I first found it. I wanted it to be nice, so I brought these things from the Hall."

"Oh." He seemed at a loss for something to say, but suddenly his face softened as he looked at me. "You made i' look ver' nice, Lady. It's very pretty."

"Thank you." I was pleased he thought it was nice, for he is the only person who has seen it since I took it over for myself. As we stood in silence I realized that I had gone from taking a nice walk to nearly being blown up by a tree, drowning in a storm, dragging my tennis instructor into a tunnel and leading him to a secret bedroom which, on balance, looked decidedly tarty. I decided to adopt an aloof manner.

"I hope I may rely on your silence," I said, striving for a cool tone in my voice to establish a semblance of normality. "It could be dangerous were anyone to know about this room, as it leads to the Hall." He pointed out that it only led to the gate, so I pulled on the top moulding of the armoire, which opened the door to the next passageway. I felt better talking about things that did not involve incipient lightning strikes and death. He sat down heavily in the small chair.

"You are, by far, the most surprisin' woman I've ever known," he finally said. I did not know how to reply, Susannah. I have become accustomed to the empty flattering of fortune-hunters and mistress-seekers, and unlike them, Will was utterly sincere. I finally stammered that I would leave him there for his own safety and return to the Hall to assuage the fears of my staff, which would be running rampant and increased by a storm such as this. He nodded absently, said he would be perfectly comfortable, let himself out in the morning and never breathe a word to anyone, for my safety was of utmost importance to him. I thanked him for his kindness and went through the passageway that led to my rooms.

When I was safely in my rooms I realized I had a slight problem. I could not call Prudence to help me change – I was soaked through and did not care to be asked any questions.

Have you ever tried to undress yourself? It is a horribly complicated process! My gown was ruined, so when I had to cut it from myself it was of no consequence. The corselet was more complicated, for I could not reach the laces. With the help of my looking-glass and a knitting needle I finally managed to untie it, noting to myself that perhaps Prudence should be given a raise. Finally I found myself in a dry pellise robe. I toweled my hair dry, stowing the destroyed gown in an old chest and left the corselet and other things near the fire to dry. My dinner was waiting as I had requested seemingly days ago but I did not eat, still feeling jangled from everything that happened and, once my ablutions were complete, found my teeth were chattering again. Suddenly there was a knock on the door. I called for them to enter and it was Prudence, asking if I was all right. I told her I was and thanked her for her concern. She replied that the storm had unnerved everyone, but she had wanted to make sure I had no further instructions and how had I gotten into my nightdress on my own.

I could not tell her what had happened so I told her I was capable of changing on my own and gave her leave before she saw my drenched clothing, and she withdrew.

I stared at the fire for a moment, exhausted but still shivering. My thoughts kept returning to the storm, to Will's courage and care for me. I felt altogether strange and then began to be concerned about Will. He had been injured protecting me and I left him in a cold, mean room with nothing to eat or drink. I was a poor excuse for a hostess!

I wrapped up the dinner and pulled a bottle of port from my armoire. Armed with those feeble excuses for thanks I returned to the small room where I had left him veritably trapped. At the end I realized I did not know the proper protocol for entering a secret room and simply knocked on the passage door with my foot, as my hands were full.

When Will opened the door I realized I may have made an error, for in the light of my lamp he appeared to be wearing only a padded dressing gown from the armoire, and the room was dark behind him. He apologized for his disarray and while inviting me in, tried to pull the robe fully closed, which I found chivalrous. I entered and gave him the food and drink, apologizing for leaving him without anything but a lamp in such a dark place. He said he did not mind, he had stayed in worse, which beggared my imagination. I inquired after his injury in case he needed bandages or (God help me) stitches. He gulped down the food and drink, barely stopping for breath, told me he had checked his leg and it seemed to be only a rough scrape and thanked me for my concern.

He finished the meal in a trice, drank deeply of the port and finished with one more swig of Oban from his flask ("to prevent infection," he grinned) and I had one as well when he proffered it. Then we sat and stared at each other.

I did not know what to do, that sort of thing is not covered in any etiquette books I have ever read. Finally I stood and said I was pleased he was well and his injury inconsequential, and begged his leave. He scrambled to his feet when I stood and thanked me for my kindness. He said he would find his way out in the morning and would leave the lamp where it had been should the tunnel ever be needed again. Still we stood. As I fidgeted, he said I had shown great bravery in such wild circumstances and thanked me for thinking of a safe place to weather the storm. I replied that his actions had likely saved my life, which they surely had, the wound in his leg lending gravity to my statement.

He bowed and I realized there was nothing to do but leave. If he proved indiscreet I would have the tunnel walled off. I turned to go, holding the lamp so I could see, when a small but sharp breeze gusted through the passageway and the lamp blew out. I stopped, for in the sudden and pitched darkness I could not tell where I was in the room. Will's voice behind me sounded nervous, asking what had happened, having just been introduced to strange and providential passageways and underground rooms. I was attempting to explain while I fumbled for the tinderbox on the little table. I managed to get the tinder lit but a breeze came through again and snuffed it before I could re-light the candle, which I am afraid renewed my fear so that my voice shook. There had never been breezes in the passageway before. In the dark I dropped the tinderbox and when I sensed something in front of me I grew alarmed.

Perhaps there were ghosts, I thought. Walker and Molly were real and angry with me for having denied their existence for so long. They would surely do something ghostly and awful, something that would turn my hair white from terror, and then everyone would think me old, which near turned my hair white from contemplation of such a hideous occurrence.

I put out a trembling hand to see if it was my imagination or truth, only to find corporeal silk covering an extremely corporeal torso. Will had moved closer to me in the darkness. I had not heard him move, perhaps my ears were still affected by the thunder, and was so astonished that my normal grace fled and I fell back with a squeak. Will tried to prevent my falling, but only succeeded in catching his hand on the sleeve of my robe and fell with me.

When I landed on the bed I was stunned; I had not realized I had gotten so turned around in the darkness. My imagination had taken such wild flight with visions of ghosts deciding to make themselves known during a storm and dark and lightning that I am ashamed to say I clung to Will and shook like a leaf. For the first time since Quince's death I was terribly afraid and wanted protection. For a moment there was silence. Then I realized Will was completely atop me, a most unseemly position and completely of my own making. I began to stammer out an apology for my weakness and frailty.

His mouth on mine stopped my words and nearly stopped my heart, for I have never had such a kiss before. Soft, sweet and very, very gentle. My mind, already reeling, apparently came unhinged, for I found myself kissing him back, tasting the faint flavour of Scotch on his tongue, feeling the rough stubble of his cheek on mine. Slowly, ever so slowly, his teeth tugged gently on my lower lip and his tongue licked at the corner of my mouth. It was completely unthinkable, wildly improper, yet I found myself helpless to pull away. I did the opposite, pulling him down to me so the kiss would not end. It did not, and when he became more insistent I blush to relate that I responded in kind. He began to taste his way down my neck, which made me near swoon. I am quite thankful I did not, sliding my hands inside his dressing gown instead. My hands were cold and he was so very warm.

Nuzzling his way back up to my mouth even as his hand slid around my waist he asked if I was all right. I was. Fear of ghosts and demons had fled and I told him so. I could almost see his smile in the dark and he whispered that the Highlands had cures to remedy whatever ailed one. He was very, very right.

I touched his face, for I still could not see him, tracing the outline of his mouth with my fingers, which were each extravagantly kissed before he abandoned them for my lips once again. I thought to demur, I thought to refrain, but to be kissed like that! As if he were slowly and surely tracing every part of my heart with his mouth, and I thought no more.

I woke the next morning in my room by sun shining brightly through the windows, nary a sign of the tumult of the night before. It all seemed to be a dream. Perhaps it was, I decided, for things would be much less complicated if only a dream.

I stretched luxuriously, my silk nightdress feeling lovely on my skin. I looked at the time and realized it was ten o'clock and no one had brought my breakfast. That was strange, and I pulled the summoning bell to find out why I had been so ignored. It was less than a minute before Constance entered with my breakfast, face wreathed in concern and fear, asking if I was all right. I told her I was fine, in fact, I was wonderful, but why did she ask? She then reminded me of my instructions the day before to not be disturbed under any circumstances. She hastened that I had been obeyed save Prudence's earlier breach to insure that I was safe, but I had refused to answer her knock that morning. Due to that the news of ghosts and everything else that had happened were kept from me, for everyone was well aware of my feelings regarding Walker and Molly, but the storm had disturbed them to new heights, which was why Prudence was not answering the bell, she was packing her things to go work in a house where one was not wary of ghosts. That soliloquy completed, Constance put my breakfast down in front of me and stood back.

My mind whirled. This was not the morning I had imagined for myself, I had imagined something, well, something very different, but one rarely receives what one wants in life, so I poured tea into my cup and asked Constance to please explain herself and everything else to me, for I had not been bothered by the storm at all.

Between you and I, I shall be grateful to that storm for the rest of my life.

Constance informed me that Prudence had resigned that very morning, as soon as the sun was fully risen, but resigned to Cook, as I had refused to answer the knock on my door. I sighed and told her to send Prudence to me.

Prudence entered fair wringing her hands. Before I could say a word she told me she had to resign in order to save her immortal soul. I was famished and, whilst munching a buttered scone, asked her to please tell whatever had happened to cause her to feel she had no recourse but resignation. She said she could not, as I had forbidden them all to mention the very thing that was causing her to leave. I took a deep, calming breath and released her from any such vow, so I might know what had happened to cause her such distress.

It was such a dark and stormy night, she finally related, and she had become unnerved by the sound of the hail on the roof, so decided to go down to the nursery and sleep there with Constance and Hope, thinking it might be quieter. She was making her way down the long hallway leading to those rooms when she heard it.

The thumping began softly at first. In fact, at first the rhythmic sound was so quiet and gentle that Prudence paid it no mind, until she realized she was alone in that part of the Hall. She thought to run, but knew she would be chastised for succumbing to her feverish imagination and so continued to make her way toward the nursery. Then the thumping, akin to a beating heart, began to increase in both volume and speed.

The rhythm was mesmerizing, and Prudence stopped in her tracks to listen. The muffled thumps continued without cease, increasing and decreasing in tempo, riding on a wave of otherworldly melody Prudence could not hear.

Then gooseflesh raised on her arms, for Walker and Molly, the dreaded ghosts, began to vocalize their anguish, which had never occurred before, crying out for blessed and sweet release. They were pounding the very walls for escape. This was no instance of a staccato burst of knocking, over in a moment and forgotten in less time than that. This was something on a level heretofore unknown and all the more frightening when compared to the paltry visitations previously experienced.

Prudence was too terrified to move. She was trembling so violently that her candle blew out, leaving her in the dark.

The thumping pace then slowed, which was almost more unbearable than the faster pace, but the groans continued to provide a staccato counterpoint to the unrelenting continuation of their need to finally come to their Reward.

Then there was a low, hoarse laugh and Prudence knew that Walker and Molly were being tormented by a demon, for what but that kind of creature could laugh at the sound of such torment? They surely were tormented, for the pounding continued without pause. Harsh gasps could be heard, for they seemed too exhausted at that point to even continue moaning as they strove to escape the bonds that held them to this sphere.

The pulsing rhythm again increased in volume and speed that seemed to become almost frantic in its pace, until suddenly there was a triumphant and hoarse cry from Walker. The thumping slowly ebbed away, and there was complete and utter silence.

Prudence did not know if the ghosts finally achieved release from this mortal coil, but was too afraid to tarry and attempt to ascertain the truth. When she could finally summon up her resolve some moments later she fled to the kitchens, where Cook heard her story sobbed out between cups of tea and (I will have to speak to Cook about this) some cakes.

Cook allayed Prudence's fears and told her the storm must have caused her to have a waking dream, and to collect herself and not wake anyone with such nonsense again. Prudence apologized as Cook grumped away and then sat for a time alone, drinking tea and trying to find some courage. On realizing she was alone in a near empty part of the Hall she decided that Cook was right, but wanted still to stay in the nursery, which was quieter than her own room.

Prudence went back down the hallway and was nearly to the nursery when a long, low moan pierced the silence. She froze where she was, wondering if it was a waking dream or if Walker and Molly had returned.

They had. And the moans were followed by groans. Then the thumping began again. It was overwhelming, it was inexorable, for as soon as she thought it could not go on any longer, it did. She sat down in the hallway and buried her face in her hands, praying to God for the poor creatures to be released and cause no further upset in the Hall, in which she was so happy to work. God did not respond or, if He did, the answer was No. The thumping continued, longer and with more abandon than the first time. Molly's cries matched the fury of the pounding, sounding to Prudence to be plaintive and desperate, which pierced Prudence's heart. She continued to pray. Finally she heard them both cry out to God Himself. There was then a complete cessation of noise. Prudence continued to pray, throwing the Lord's Prayer in for good measure and waited. Silence reigned. She ran into the nursery, threw herself into the chair there and prayed for the rest of the night. Perhaps they had been freed, she thought to herself. Perhaps they would bother the Hall no more.

It was with these thoughts that she finally drifted to sleep, with the corporeal sound of Constance's snoring in her ears, for Constance can apparently sleep through anything.

Then, just before dawn, it began again. Not groaning. Not moaning. Creaking. Prudence awoke to the sound of creaks, as if the very beams were being tested, followed by sighs. She held her breath. Let them be freed, she implored God. But they were not. Walker and Molly were still in the Hall, and although the third time the moaning, sighing and crying out were not as loud and the thumping did not go on as long as it had before, they were no dream. They happened.

Prudence realized that Walker and Molly were not only not free of the Hall, but had become bolder, no longer content to drift about knocking over objects and walking unseen about Wetmoor. For that reason she had to resign and promised she would never breathe a word of the real reason for her sudden departure, even to Constance, whom she loved, for Constance was not visited by the same terrors and would perhaps be safe.

Well, I inwardly sighed, at least I knew who the ghosts were, for her description of what she had heard was an unnervingly accurate, albeit completely misinterpreted, rendition of what I had experienced for myself. Actually, what I had participated in myself. Unless I was a ghost already, having died of ecstasy, except then Constance and Prudence should not have been able to see me and I would not have been able to eat scones.

Prudence had not had a waking dream and I had not had any kind of dream at all. It was Will and I. We were the ghosts, although much more enthusiastic, vigourous, passionate and loud than when Sir Manfredson was in residence. Clearly sounds made in the tunnels can be heard throughout the Hall.

For myself, knowing that it was not a dream I knew also guilt would soon follow, for I did not set out to seduce my tennis instructor in a secret assignation room in a hidden tunnel of the Hall during a storm and become besotted. I wanted to make sure he had food. I think. Oh, drat it all, I cannot not even plead drunkenness for my behaviour. I was fairly sober, and he is so delicious, had protected me during the storm, had not run off screaming like most men would have, and he is kind, and, oh, none of that mattered. I was sure he thought me a horrible harlot.

I know I should have crept away after that first time, really, but it seemed rude, and it is my Hall. Any creeping should have been done by him and he did not. Although the second time was his idea I must admit I did not refuse, for I thought perhaps I had imagined how spectacular the first time was, and if it was not it would be so much easier to pretend it never happened, or that with the lamp lit I could literally see why it was such a bad idea.

As it turned out, I had not imagined it how wonderful the first time was, I had underestimated it. Much to my surprise lamplight only improved everything. Then I was tired and fell asleep in his arms, which was the first time I had ever done that. Slept in a man's arms, for Quince had his own rooms, of course. It is a most lovely feeling, curled up together, strong arms wrapped around me and keeping me safe and warm.

When I woke he was still there, and on waking himself he began immediately to reach for me, murmuring lovely and longing things in that delightful burred voice of his, and I have no excuse whatsoever for my behaviour the third time. I climbed Will as if he were a tree. It was incredibly unladylike, which did not seem to concern him in the least, he more than met me halfway in enthusiasm. Afterward, when he had fallen asleep again, I stayed. I did not want to leave, I wanted to remain caught in a tangle of cashmere, silk and limbs, which was of course why I finally returned to my rooms. Wanting to watch him sleep was the first (or fourth, fifth or sixth) indication that I had not embarked on this course in the correct frame of mind.

I had closed my eyes while those thoughts ran through my head and then other thoughts began to intrude as well, ones not conducive to not being besotted. I shook my head hard and when I opened my eyes Prudence was staring at me. Poor thing. I tried to find the right tone with which to address my poor maid.

I finally told her I could not accept her resignation, not so close to the Opening Ball, but felt that Walker and Molly had perhaps been released from this mortal coil, by their repeated and valiant efforts to throw off the spectral chains that bound them, and gone to their richly deserved Reward. I did not tell her that I had several times.

I asked that she postpone her resignation after the Opening Ball, but if anything else occurred before then I would accept her resignation and also provide her with two months' pay instead of one, as long as she kept her tongue about the reason.

This was altogether too tempting for Prudence to refuse, although she did make a fair showing by biting her lower lip and peering up at the ceiling to contemplate the offer. Finally she said it was a fair request, and she would hate to miss the Opening Ball after everything that had happened, so would accept my generous offer. With the issue thus settled, she withdrew to unpack and return to her normal duties.

One of which included drawing my bath. I had the urge for a bath that was positively bacchanalian in scope and requested she prepare it as quickly as possible, and within the next hour I found myself up to my neck in hot and sudsy water, gently sponging sweat and dirt and everything away. When Prudence helped me dress there was an embarrassing moment. I apparently had a love bite on the inside of my knee. And one . . . well, that is not important. Fortunately Prudence is naïve and thought them bruises. I told her I fell out of bed during the storm and landed on my . . . Never mind, it is not relevant.

Trying to behave as if I had not just had the most wonderful night of my life I decided to see if everything was back to normal in the Hall. I felt incredibly well-rested and happy, in spite of the events of the day before, which should have rendered me immobile with remorse. I realized remorse should wait until I felt less sublime so it might count more and resolved to meet the day as the lady that I am.

As I descended the stairway I was pleased to hear the sounds of workmen going about their business, sawing and bashing away at things. Taylor appeared at the foot of the stairway. There was a caller waiting in the drawing room for me. His tone was disapproving. I could not think who might be visiting.

Imagine my surprise to find Mr. Castleton warming his hands at the fire. He beamed and took my hands in his as he told me how very beautiful I looked, which was a bit forward, if you ask me. I took my hands back and asked him to sit. We did and he said how very excited he was to see my famous Hall, it was a marvel. I thanked him for the compliment, relieved when Constance arrived with tea. After pouring she withdrew and we drank in silence. The last thing I wanted to do was sit with a craven suitor, but could think of nothing to truncate the visit.

Mr. Castleton looked with approval at the appointments of the drawing room and requested tour. I was trying to think of a polite way to decline when Constance entered. I had another visitor who required a moment. Thank God! I thought. The girl is worth the trouble; she has brains in her head. I begged Mr. Castleton's pardon and stepped out with her into the foyer. I was about to thank her when she informed me Mr. Gibberwilly was waiting for me in the morning room. That was completed unexpected. I told her to see me in and to ask Mr. Castleton to wait, for although his attentions were not wanted, they were preferable to the oilier intentions of Mr. Gibberwilly.

So I found myself in the morning room with Mr. Gibberwilly, a second cup of tea at my elbow, another scone on another plate. Mr. Gibberwilly said he wanted to inquire after my health, as our conversation had been so rudely interrupted at the dinner party. I said I had not suffered any more spells and thanked him. He remarked that I was glowing with good health, the pink in my cheeks and sparkle in my eye rendering his question moot, but wanted to be sure I understood how much concern he had regarding my well-being. It was awful, but I thanked him again and inquired after his wife.

Insensate, of course. Not long for this world. Very sad. Had he not been so very unmoved by her plight, it might have seemed he was a caring husband. He looked around the morning room, complimented me on my taste and asked if he might see the rest of the Hall. Another tour request! I felt suddenly as if I lived in a museum! I was explaining that the Hall was still unfinished, nothing worth seeing yet, when he interrupted and said perhaps he should wait for the Opening Ball.

I suppose he has to be invited, but the gall of the man!

Just then the morning room doors opened and Constance announced a visitor who begged a word as soon as possible. Mr. Castleton must have become impatient, expected or no, and I asked Mr. Gibberwilly to please wait a moment.

In the foyer I was turning to the drawing room door when Constance stopped me. I had an actual third visitor, it seemed. In the games room, as Constance did not know where else to put him, the regular receiving rooms already populated. Had I acquired yet another suitor? No, Constance whispered. It was Mr. Ploughgoode. On some sort of business matter.

Oh, my. Will. I had not thought he would reappear so soon, before I could think. I then realized he was only there to resign his post, for he could not spend another moment with me since I had the morals of a tomcat or some similarly wanton creature, which would be horribly embarrassing coming from a Scot. Then I could atone with a five-fold tithe, large donations to the poor and forget the entire thing.

I thanked Constance and bade her wait in the foyer, should either of the other gentlemen require anything, and went down the hallway to the games room. I stood outside the door for a moment, unaccountably nervous, and found myself shifting from foot to foot like a young girl. I had just begun to wonder if my hair looked pretty, if the gown I wore was fetching, when I stopped myself. What was I thinking? As I knew I had to face him sooner or later, although later was sounding better to me, I steeled myself and entered.

Apparently wantonness is not something Will considers a sin, for no sooner had the door closed on us when he was kissing me. In broad daylight! I scarce had time to register how marvelous he looked before he pulled me into his arms and drove the speech I was going to make out right from my head. Although it took some moments, I was able to disentangle myself from his embrace and stand back, trying to regain my composure, which was missing, for he was supposed to be cold and awful, not kissing me so thoroughly I nearly swooned and successfully unlacing my bodice. He then said he had only meant to come and see me, until he actually saw me and had to kiss me, for which he would not apologize. Then he kissed me again. With the window in full view – had the curtains been open we might have been seen!

This was not helping me to not feel besotted, which was what I was supposed to be trying to do. Or not do. Be besotted. Do you see? I am in a complete dither. I was instead thinking that there was a secret tunnel just to the left, we could go in there and we would have to remain standing, but that would be fine, in fact, it would be divine. What was I thinking?

Again I managed to pull away, keeping his hands in mine before they encircled my waist, to be followed by pinning me to the wall with his body, sliding his hand under my skirts as I unbuttoned his linen and ran my hands down his lovely chest to his deerskin breeches . . . Oh, my. I took a deep breath and while retying my bodice thanked him for his care, which was not the stern tone I meant to set. He smiled and said he would have not have been able to be kept from seeing me if his legs had been cut off in a carriage accident. That was a bit jarring until he explained it had happened to a friend of his.

Then he pushed me up against the wall, pinning me like I had just been imagining, burying his face in my neck, nibbling my collarbone, nuzzling my bodice and subtly sliding his hand under my skirts. We were both thinking the same thing, and I found myself pulling his linen from him, which did not work very well in actuality; his coat was still on, so he wound up flapping his arm around, trying to get his hand free of the cuff that trapped it. In my imagination I had been more skillful, in my fantasies his clothes had just fallen off of their own accord. Reality is so much more difficult.

Why do men wear so many clothes? He managed to get his arm out of his coat, his waistcoat was unbuttoned and his linen was as far off as it could be with everything else still on, and I began undoing his flies while he pulled my gown and underskirts up every which way, murmuring that I had enough materiel on my body to clothe half of London, to which I whispered in his ear that he was similarly clad, before gnawing gently on the lobe. In a marvelously commanding moment he grinned, lifted me clear off my feet and, as my legs wrapped themselves around him of their own tingling accord, he spun and set me on the edge of the billiards table, which I found a delightful notion. Kissing, giggling, tasting and having an utterly debauched time, we were very nearly indulging our mutual inclinations when there was a knock at the door.

I squeaked, Will jumped back from me and then stumbled back; his cuff had caught on my underskirts. As I worked to free it and scrambled off the table, calling for the person ruining my morning to wait a moment, he got his coat and waistcoat back on. As he re-tied my bodice I did up his flies, a rather difficult task at that exact moment. I made sure my gown was not over my head while he re-buttoned his waistcoat and stood behind a tall chair near the windows, striving to look as if he had not just nearly had me on my own billiards table. I am not sure how successful he was in that attempt.

Once I was assured we were more or less dressed and far apart from each other I called for whomever it was to enter (I was hoping I could sack them for the interruption). Constance entered and placed tea and scones on the cards table, which made me wonder how many scones Cook makes each morning. Constance seemed to grin as she turned and left. I am sure she found it amusing that I had three men in three rooms to see me. There are worse things that could happen to a person, I think.

But tea, as always, brought me to my senses. I could not leap upon my tennis instructor simply because I desperately desired to; I had a Hall to run, two other men waiting for me to re-join them, and a host of other things requiring my attention. Will meant to sweep me up once more but I sidestepped him and sat at the games table, pouring tea out with a hand that trembled. I had been trembling so much in the last twenty-four hours, perhaps I had palsy instead of being besotted. It was a comforting notion, for then I was mad with illness as opposed to being infatuated Will. My voice shook as I explained that although I would love to, I could not see him at that moment in time, there was so much going on, work to be done, storm damage to be evaluated and dealt with, did he understand?

He did not, the embarrassment he felt at having been so suddenly and bewilderingly rebuffed showing plainly on his face. Then I felt terrible. This was going terribly awry. The entire morning had not gone anything like I imagined and I found myself asking for forgiveness. Yes, I know, it was ridiculous. He was the one who was unannounced and kissing and touching and nibbling me and making my head spin. It is very difficult to think with all that going on. If only I could think! And feel at least some measure of regret.

Regret would be a good thing, and regret and time might bring me to my senses. I clearly needed to attend Church more often. And read my Bible. But instead I compounded my lack of spine by saying I would very much like to see him on the morrow. With that the hurt on his face changed to pleasure and he said it would be his honour to return the next day, for he had not thought of anything but seeing me, which was what had forced his unscheduled return. The candor of his words was undeniable. This was no fair-tongued swain seeking to spin a cloud of compliments around my head. It nearly brought tears to my eyes. It has been such a long time since anyone has spoken to me with such an open heart. I thought Scots did not have one at all.

He added that he had left the small room, taken his horse without anyone the wiser and returned to town, where he had spent the morning waiting to come back to the Hall. He stood, took my hand, bade me adieu until next we met, then turned my hand over and kissed my palm with his open mouth, an incredibly accurate recreation of the Highland cure, before stealing another kiss from my lips, which near landed me back on the billiards table. I nearly swooned from a total lack of remorse, which would have been a disaster, for Mr. Gibberwilly would have been called in for assistance. What a mess that would have made! Then Will departed, leaving me sitting at the games table, staring into my tea and trying to feel awful.

The problem is that I care for him, Susannah. I like him. Drat it all, I adore him. I know it is ridiculous, but I like him as a person just as much as I like him as a man. He is intelligent, kind and funny, does not think it strange that I read history and philosophy, or that I have no children but a full nursery. Quince treated me like a figurine, but Will likes me for myself, which makes me feel special. That is the one thing you were very stern about, that I not feel this way. I am sure you were able to tell from my earlier letters that I enjoyed his company more than I should but I never thought anything would come of it, so it seemed harmless enough. And now I was (and am, shamefully) completely besotted. In the light of day I realize what a disastrous idea it is and the reasons for it, but the besottedness has not stopped, regardless of your warnings.

I could only think on these things for a moment, as there were two more suitors to be dispatched, although certainly not as intimately.

I went to Mr. Gibberwilly and told him circumstances prevented my spending any further time with him, I was very sorry, could he forgive me? Etc., etc., which he of course was obliged to accept, having come uninvited. He was then seen out by Taylor, which left only Mr. Castleton.

Mr. Castleton proved more problematic. He had made himself comfortable in a chair, reading the book I had left on a table, and appeared to be prepared to stay the day if need be. In order to get him to leave I was forced to accept an invitation to a musicale in Clarington in a fortnight, of all things. We will attend as part of a group, of course, although it was clear he intends to be my primary conversation partner for the evening. I was so distracted that I did not realize I had accepted until he was leaving. He also had to temerity to kiss my hand, which was not remotely as welcome as the last kiss it received. In fact, I wanted to wash it immediately.

When all were gone I collapsed into a chair, trying to sort out what had happened to cause such a predicament. Prudence came in and set a bottle of brandy down next to me, along with my favourite cut-glass. I spent the next few hours trying to untangle everything into neat and clean portions, completely unsuccessfully, and realized I need counsel, as this is the strangest situation in which I have ever found myself.

I have two appropriate, completely forgettable suitors and one completely inappropriate, utterly unforgettable suitor and I do not feel the least bit of remorse though I should be feeling remorseful enough to throw myself out of a window. I should have never stayed with him, for I like him so very much. Which leads to this letter, which is being finished as night has moved in, and will be posted to you tomorrow.

So there you have it. The entire and unvarnished tale, Susannah. I hope you understand I was out of my head when everything occurred with Will, brought on by fear and lightning and everything else. I do not know what to do, for I adore him and he is a workingman! And a Scot! He is not a tryst, nor casual liaison, to be casually dismissed. He is wonderful.

Please respond as soon as possible with your answer; I will sleep nary a wink until I know your mind and heart in this matter. I will wait with bated breath and know that regardless of your answer, I remain,

Your Sister in Spirit,
Annabella

22 July, 1821

Dearest Susannah,

I am so happy to be writing to you once again! I was afraid you would have lost all respect for me. You must have written the moment you finished my letter and I thank you so much for your words and understanding.

Although I am pleased I was able to provide nearly the level of detail to satisfy you in regard to my activities, I am especially overjoyed that inaction is not your judgment, for the regret, remorse, sensibility, etc., that I was hoping would overtake me, leaving me lonely but correct, did not materialize. From your letter I realize it likely will not and, truth to tell, I did not want it to.

As you know, when I found myself weak from loneliness and spent time with a man I followed your instructions, for Hughe could not steal my heart, and increased my Church donation for a week or two, before neatly ending it. It succeeded with Hughe, for he was not a lover.

My plan was to await your response before taking any action, including inaction, if those were your instructions, for I am aware of the potential disaster in embarking on such a course. On Will's return I was going to send my apologies and continue to refuse to see him until I had heard from you.

The next day it seemed that my instructions to Will were not as clear as I believed when I told him to return to me, for he did not. Mr. Sinclair arrived for our regular meeting and I was distracted throughout. I could not concentrate on the business matters that required my attention and wished he would leave, for my mind kept drifting to activities that had nothing to do with business. When he told me the young girl he cared for had become betrothed to another I am afraid I did not show much interest, for I kept waiting for Taylor to announce Will's return. Which did not happen.

I finally managed to focus on my guest, and when Mr. Sinclair departed he seemed cheered in spite of his romantic debacle. But I must have still seemed distracted, for as he left he told me he hoped I felt better soon. I was embarrassed, for I had not realized how poorly I had hidden my feelings. When he was gone I returned to the library and wrote you of everything that happened during the storm, the remembrance of which made me quite tingle in anticipation. This longing was dreadful. Especially when Will did not return.

I was disheartened by his absence, and realized he knew the same thing as I: anything between us can only end in disaster. After spending the rest of the day and evening in the library writing to you, I realized I was poor excuse for a lady if I were to while away the hours waiting for an expected, supposedly eager, caller who had not the decency or courage to call.

I finished my letter to you, sealed it very well, gave it to Foxx to post and removed myself to my rooms with Prudence. She seemed startled and I realized it was scarcely dusk.

My feet sounded as heavy on the stairway as my heart felt in my chest. When I was in my nightdress I dismissed Prudence and had her dismiss everyone else for the evening as well. Once she was gone I locked the door, performed my ablutions and then sat in front of my vanity, staring at a visage that no longer seemed the cheerful and graceful reflection normally seen. At least I was finally feeling awful, but for all the wrong reasons. I was supposed to feel awful for what I had done, not because I could not do it again. I was quite sure that would not count, although it made me realize why your warnings were so adamant, so I chastised myself. This was no way for a lady to behave. I have a good life, a beautiful home that I actually own and a staff that may someday be exemplary, which was more than most can say. I counted my blessings and decided it was for the best, as there was nothing to be done about it. I was not going to pine away after my tennis instructor when I should have never done anything but take lessons, this was finally the remorse you had warned of, so I should be glad of feeling awful, for it meant I was not irredeemable, and had learnt a Very Good Lesson as well.

With that I took my Bible in hand and went to bed, intent on reading that Good Book in the hopes that sense would leech from it to me, restoring what had gone missing. I had not realized how tired I was from events of the last few days, but in mere moments my eyes closed of their own accord and the Bible grew heavy in my hand. Just as I was drifting off it seemed to slip away completely, and I found the solace of sleep.

The dream I had was wonderful but also dismaying, for in it Will had come to me and was with me once again, and it was not even remotely awful nor a disaster.

Imagine my surprise when I found that it was no dream at all – Will was in my room! I woke and he was sitting next to my bed watching me. I started and almost screamed, but he quickly shushed me with a finger to my lips. I clutched the bedclothes to myself and in the most indignant whisper I could conjure, asked him what he thought he was doing? How had he gained entry through a locked door? Was he out of his mind? I could have screamed, or clubbed him with something heavy, as he was an intruder, after all. To all of that he smiled and responded that I had wanted to see him on the morrow and, although late, he had kept his promise. Then he pointed to the door set into the panelling. He had come through the tunnel.

I told him it was extremely presumptuous of him to have done such a thing, I had meant he should come to the front door like a normal person, not gone sneaking about like a thief in the night and to compound it by kissing me when I was asleep and defenceless was very much not the behavior of a gentleman.

He was clearly bemused by the first and confused by the last. He swore he had not kissed me. He had not known the passage led directly to my rooms. He thought it would open into some lonely hallway, and it was only curiosity that caused him to contemplate such a stealthy entrance. He was astonished to find himself in my rooms, especially uninvited, and was going to leave, but could not help stealing a moment to watch me sweetly sleep when I roused myself, to both of our embarrassment.

Still in a whisper I asked him to not strain my credulity any further, I knew he had been kissing me; I could taste him on my lips. He slowly shook his head, eyes never leaving mine. No, he said. He had not, and never would, for that was a liberty even he dared not take without clear invitation. He had not kissed me. Then he smiled. Perhaps I had dreamt it?

No, I stammered, I had not.

He had dreamt of me often, perhaps I had done the same? He asked as he slowly drew closer to me, imperceptibly pulling the coverlet down from where it was pulled up to my chin.

I was quite sure I had not. I had been dreaming of . . . snakes. It was the first thing that came into my head. Great big snakes. Nothing like kissing. He drew even closer, not even a breath away, and whispered that snakes would do. Then he pulled back a little, which made me lean forward, and he said he would leave if I so desired it, though it would break his heart. I only had to tell him so and he would be gone like the mist in morning, with only his true and remorseful apology left hanging in the air, to bother me no more. Those damned Scots. They are supposed to be coarse so I could explain that nothing could ever happen between us again, with all the proper reasons for such a practical decision, then wall up the tunnel behind him and devote myself to Good Works and atonement. But my thoughts turned to smoke by his words. By the pulse I could see beating in his throat. The way his hair curls ever so slightly over his ears. The look in those stormy grey eyes. By his mouth.

I cannot claim that he kissed me for I moved to him, perhaps less than one-half breath of distance, not really very much at all, but I am equivocating, I know. Then he was taking my hair down and tangling his hands in it, I was kissing him just behind and below his left earlobe where it makes him shiver, he was tugging at the laces of my gown as I pulled him down to me, and I was undone.

Will has since come to me every night and I am without the spine to break it off. I should move to France where, according to your letters, these things happen every day. I have tried to feel nothing for him, completely without success. I go to Church more often, but I fall asleep, for it is almost the only time I sleep. I have told myself what a terrible idea this all is and forget the reasons why when I see him.

I requested that we discontinue our tennis lessons for a time, as maintaining my equilibrium in front of the staff is hopeless for now, and they cannot ever know, nor can anyone else. He readily agreed and assured me that his discretion is absolute and inviolable. I suppose it does not matter, for no one would ever believe him. I hope.

He always brings me some trinket when he comes: a pin, a kerchief, a comb for my hair, of which he is fond, especially when not bound in some complicated style. Although his gifts are small and simple, each one was clearly chosen with me in mind: the comb sets off my hair beautifully, the colour of the pin matches my eyes. The first night he brought me a small carved cat which he saw in a shoppe window and made him think of me. He gave it to me shyly as dawn broke upon tangled sheets, and was delighted at my delight with it. It now sits on my vanity and I smile at it when I brush my hair in the morning.

One thing that is helpful is that the walls of my rooms are far thicker than the ones in the tunnel. I checked the plans again, and the fortress-like thickness of the walls indicate that Sir Manfredson either had or planned to have very loud evenings in these rooms himself. Will and I do not have to speak in whispers, and when one evening things were less than the silence for which we had been striving (amongst other things) no one was the wiser, a welcome discovery. When I told him the truth about the famous Ghosts of Wetmoor he laughed so hard at the notion that we are Walker and Molly that he fell out of bed.

He is always gone at dawn, ghost-like in his own way, and I spend my days waiting for evening. What a strange reversal! I used to crave the days and nights were merely something to be whiled away.

I really should move to France.

So you can understand why your letter was a balm for my troubled yet unrepentant heart. I know it will all come to ruination and despair, tears and regret, and perhaps a move to the Americas to start anew under the name of Mildred Barrencold, for how else do these things ever end? I remember the sermons in Church during the days I could stay awake for them, but I continue in spite of it all. I can no longer look askance at Gwynneth, for I have Fallen far further than she ever could.

The heart wants what it wants, you are so very right, although I would never in a million years of pondering have thought mine would want a Scot.

I will end this letter here, for am I exhausted. I thank you again for your support and encouragement as I continue this course. What would I have done if I could not have told anyone! I believe I may have done a fair imitation of Baron Gurthwant.

I will write again soon, and know that I remain,

Your Soothed Friend,

Annabella

27 July, 1821

Dearest Susannah,

I strongly disagree with your last letter: your grace and understanding are the most wonderful things, for you are the only person in the world who knows of the affair I have found myself conducting with the licentiousness of a dance-hall girl, so I shall not have my gratitude brushed aside like crumbs from a table. It is sincere and true and you know what your accord in what I am doing means to me. We will say no more on that score, for you will never dissuade me that you have not given me the greatest boon, that of true friendship, which lasts through vagaries of Fate of which we could never have dreamt in our youth.

Although it does make me feel slightly self-conscious, I shall keep you apprised as you have requested. I am glad you keep these letters of mine locked away, for I would surely pitch myself off the cliffs at Dover should anyone ever discover what I am doing with my life.

You shall be quite pleased to know that my affair with Will continues unabated, and I have stopped waiting for remorse, regret, guilt, mortification, boredom or horror to descend upon me. If it has not yet, it will not. I really must be part French. It is certainly not English.

In light of my self-consciousness, and in reference to your alarmingly specific queries about Will's <u>personal</u> attributes, Susannah, I do not believe it any of your business, if that does not sound impertinent. Suffice it to say that he is perfectly capable of satisfying any need, requirement, whim or passing fancy I might have. In quite thorough measure. It is also clear he feels the same about my person as well, a most happy confluence of satisfaction.

One thing he did that I found rather strange stopped when I explained to him that I can never have a child. He was positively obsessed with the idea, and some of the things he did to prevent such an occurrence were bewildering to me (and rather messy). I am sure a person as sophisticated as you likely knows exactly to what I refer, but I am much more provincial and he had to be quite plain in the end so I might understand. I thought he would expire of embarrassment during the telling and I was just as embarrassed that I had been so unschooled. It was very sweet, for one would think after everything we have done with each other no such timidity could be possible, but I was wrong.

My mother kept a dreadful amount of information about Life from me, I think.

I feel the luckiest woman in the world to have found him, for as much as I enjoy every single portion of his person, my feelings for his mind and heart match are still greater. We talk long into the night, sometimes through the night, about everything and nothing all at once. We have read many of the same books, and he has taken to reading me a poem by Robert Burns every night he is here for, according to Will, Robert Burns is the greatest poet in all of history, the recitation giving him the opportunity to not only use a dialect dear to his heart, but teach me the odd Gaelic word or phrase.

I must confess to you that all of the Gaelic I have learnt sounds odd, and I am apparently hopeless at the pronunciation, but I adore drifting to sleep with words I do not understand murmured in my ear. He tends to slip into it when he is very tired. Sometimes he does not even notice and is startled when I ask him to please speak English. It is not something he allows himself to do often, for he says that too much of it can make him long for home terribly, and his life is in England now, but he will not say why.

And when long and ecstatic nights end, and sweet kisses and hurried good-byes meet the dawn, busy days begin.

My gowns are proceeding apace and Gwynneth is creating visions, as it would not do for me to be outshone by anyone else that evening, for it shall hopefully become the stuff of legend. She is also being kept very busy on my other gowns, for they all have to be taken in again. Between tennis lessons and everything else, I am shrinking along with the fabric that horrible dressmaker used, so Gwynneth's work must now be reversed. And yet she works miracles! It is astonishing to me the illusions to be spun with needle and thread.

I also ordered new underthings, for they no longer properly fit. It never hurts to have pretty things throughout one's wardrobe. They are coming from the shoppe you told me of in Paris.

I have had to take up tennis again, as staff began asking what had happened to Will, or Mr. Ploughgoode as he is always referred to in front of others. I worried they might draw an inference from his absence, so asked that we begin meeting at least twice a week during the day, in our previous fashion, to keep idle minds from construing anything near the truth. I am sure I am being overly cautious, but he was agreeable on the condition that he not receive payment, as it would make him feel quite unmanly. This was understandable, and I had not known how to broach that subject, so I was relieved by the request.

Our tennis lessons began again the next day, and we were both comfortable with the resumption. I did not blush, he did not faint, and the tea we sat to afterward was very companionable. It was far easier than I thought it would be. Then Prudence came out and told me I must take my leave, as I had to get ready. I had no idea to what she referred. Then she reminded me. The dratted musical revue with Mr. Castleton. It was that night. With everything else going on it slipped my mind. I could not cancel, it was unthinkable, but I accepted when everything was different, for at that time I was never going to see Will again. He was very quiet, and I thanked her and told her I would begin preparing in a moment.

When Prudence had left Will had a grim look on his face but said he understood I could not cancel without notice. He stood to depart, and then said if Mr. Castleton laid a single finger on me inappropriately, Mr. Castleton would find himself covered in plaster for months and be unable to chew his own food for the rest of his life.

I was pleased at his possessiveness and promised I would remain untouched. I added that it would be a very late night, for Clarington was some distance, although there would be four of us, and I would not be alone with Mr. Castleton. I felt awkward, and he asked if I wished that he not come to me that night. I did wish it, but felt odd going to a musicale with one man, only to come home to another warming my bed. I am not that French, and told him so. He laughed, and said he thought I was more French than I might like to admit. He made me promise I would not refuse him the next night, and departed.

I then had to fly to get ready for the evening. There was one gown Gwynneth had not yet improved and I donned that, seeking to make myself as unadorable as possible, which is not easy, but one must do what one can. I did not use face paint or do anything special to my hair, striving for a plain, tired look. At the last moment I added the pin Will gave me to my dress, which made me feel better. Just as I finished putting my things in my reticule Mr. Castleton was announced.

As I came down the stairway he beamed up at me. He had gone to great lengths on himself, I was dismayed to see: pomade, a new walking stick, the latest style of cloak and suit. He bowed extravagantly at my feet and kissed my hand, saying he had never had the pleasure of escorting such a beautiful woman and thanked me for the honour. I clearly had not achieved my goal of appearing haggard and old.

With that we left, climbing into his large new carriage, where we sat opposite his business partner from London, Harold Filson, and his wife Lorena. The men fell to talking and Lorena smiled limply at me, offering an even limper hand. We made our acquaintance, the men chatting away about business matters they assumed were far over our heads. Lorena and I spent an amiable enough time discussing the latest fashions from London and Paris, the upcoming Season, while I kept one ear open for anything that might prove beneficial in terms of my own business interests. The evening did not need to be a complete waste.

It was near six o'clock before we arrived in Clarington, and I had two interesting pieces of information regarding two companies in London, and knew more about Lorena's sisters and cousins than I thought could be relayed in such a short time. She has the ability to chatter on forever about nothing, which I suppose is a valuable trait in the wife of a prominent businessman. I tried to do the same, but sometimes it was difficult.

Clarington is a quaint little town, and Mr. Castleton promised the musicale would be exciting. He said he had heard of it from another businessman in London, and that he enjoyed doing things out of the ordinary. I believe that was supposed to interest me, but he had ignored me in favour of talking about prices of raw materiels and the like during the ride, so it did not. In truth he stood no chance for my affections. It was impossible. The evening stretched out long ahead of me.

However, it proved to be a very enlightening evening, and I believe you will find the details of it as interesting as the more personal ones related earlier.

We dined first at the establishment next door to the music hall, when Mr. Castleton's stratagem came into focus. Mr. Filson extolled his virtues, Lorena limply confirming, which include intelligence, honesty, a keen eye for business, piety, fidelity, thrift without parsimoniousness, perfection, good teeth, sobriety, on and on and on. At that rate I could have easily skipped Church that week, for I was surely in the presence of a God-like being. Every question, every story illuminated yet another perfect facet of a perfect man. It was so boring. That is unfair, I know. They are lovely people, and Mr. Castleton went to great lengths to make me aware that I would not find myself married to a drunken, wayward, pauper of man who would attach himself to me like a leech for the purpose of draining my finances and heart dry. It was simply that I have no interest in him, and would not even were I not otherwise enamored. I am sure he will make some woman very happy. I am not that woman, and the evening he had gone to such lengths to arrange was all for naught.

But I nodded and smiled and affirmed in all right places, wondering how I had gotten myself into this situation, for I wanted nothing but to be back in my Hall. Perhaps I was becoming a recluse, like Sir Manfredson before me, and I would over time lose all of my social graces, as well as invitations to things, until I was rattling around the Hall looking for Will, who would have left me for a suitable girl who could be seen with him in public, until I was found in the boathouse, sleeping on the floor, hair turned white, skin sagging over my bones. It was a horrifying thought. I could not allow this to happen. I have been obliged to refuse some of the few invitations I have begun receiving to dinners and the like in recent months, as the renovations are going on at breakneck speed, but I had to end my self-imposed isolation. I had just vowed this to myself when I realized a question had been put to me. Unfortunately I had no idea what the question was. The simplest thing to do was smile and nod and say, "Lovely," which is what I did. That is how I accepted an invitation to a ball with Mr. Castleton in London, in September, at the Filson home.

Blindly accepting invitations was not the way I had intended to reintroduce myself to London Society. The only comfort I had was that I had not accidentally accepted his hand in marriage because I was thinking of other things. Well, the ball would be punishment enough for that and taught me a lesson. It showed how much my social skills have atrophied. I would never have done such a thing before Quince's death, but being locked in a house for a year studying, then moving to near-exile in the country, had worn them away to a sliver. I made sure I paid attention to everything said for the rest of the dinner.

I will stay in my own house when in London. The trip needs to be undertaken regardless for some arrangements for the Opening Ball could not be accomplished by letters, now the dates were set for me. I decided it was all for the best and to practise my conversation skills with my dinner companions. It was difficult, for my sphere of late includes a rather impressive knowledge of plastering and stonework, but an unimpressive lack of knowledge of the goings-on in London. I allowed myself to be brought up to date on engagements, births, deaths and the like in a circle from which I have long been removed. I was surprised to find out how much had happened during this time, and noted everything I was told, so I might be better informed at the Opening Ball. And be more prepared for the Filson's ball. I consoled myself that it was a chance for Gwynneth to make me another gown. I do not have anything appropriate for such an event at present, styles change so often, and my wardrobe has been circumscribed by mourning. London is not as forgiving as the country, so she would have to provide at least three new gowns for my trip.

Soon it was time to go to the music hall and find our seats for the revue. Fortunately Mr. Castleton's and Mr. Filson's stations warranted a private box, so we were not crushed between our inferiors in rough and tumble seating, for it was very crowded. It was only a few moments before the meagre orchestra began to play, and the musciale began.

It was amusing, I suppose, but the last theatrical presentations I had attended were in London, so I am accustomed to a higher standard. In fact, I found I was paying more attention to the orchestra, as it was generously referred to in our programmes, than to the entertainments that accompanied them. There were songs, jokes and silly magic tricks, and then the main act was announced. Mr. Castleton informed me in a whisper that he had heard the singer was extraordinary. Her name was unusual: Lillienda Stonekup, which sounds German. That explained her aspect. She was not feminine at all, wearing a gown surely specially made for a rather unusual, spare frame, a scarf at her throat to match the one in her hand. Then she began to sing, and my mouth dropped open.

Her voice was lovely. It was low which, given her frame, somewhat surprised me. She reminded me of some of the opera divas I have seen in London. But it was the emotion she brought to the songs that was exquisite. The ovation she received after her first song was earned, as were the others that followed, but I became distracted, as she reminded me of someone, but I could not think of whom. It was yet another demonstration of how cloistered I have become, and I had had enough reminders of that for one evening.

The interval passed pleasantly, and the second act was much the same as the first: inconsequential talents running one after the other until the return of Miss Stonekup, who gifted us with more songs, sung even more beautifully than before, as the finale. It was altogether an enjoyable diversion, I must admit. However, after the performance was over and the patrons were streaming out, I realized I needed a moment to myself. I had not been out amongst such a press of people in a long time and found myself unnerved, which never happened to me in the past.

I begged a moment and went down a hall in the opposite direction of the clamorous throng to get some air, going through the first door I found and shutting it behind me. I had not thought to knock, I do swear it, Susannah.

I was not alone in the room. It was a dressing-room; I had gone further than I thought to escape the groundlings. And it was not just any dressing-room, it was Miss Stonekup's dressing room.

Normally I would have apologized for my error and removed myself, except that Miss Stonekup was in the midst of changing into her normal clothing. Her normal clothing was a suit. I did not know it was Miss Stonekup until I saw her reflection in the looking glass. Her makeup was still applied, and her hair in the revue was apparently a wig, for it was cut like a man's underneath. She, well, He, whirled around and stared at me.

"Leave my dressing room," he said. Or she. It was all very confusing.

"Why are you wearing a suit?" I blurted without thinking. Clearly I am nearly bereft of manners.

"Leave my dressing room immediately," Stonekup said, and pounded her, his, whatever, hand on the table she, oh never mind, stood at. She glared at me. I had, after all, completely invaded her privacy. I murmured an apology and turned to leave when I realized whom Lillienda reminded me of.

Daniella. Constable Daniella Pukeston. It was uncanny, really, now that I was closer, and since I was closer I also realized Lillienda was far less feminine than the somewhat unfeminine presence she had on stage.

There was only one way to find out. As I opened the door I said, "Thank you for a beautiful evening, Daniella."

He replied, "Thank you." I slammed the door and whirled to face what was now clearly a man, and we both gasped.

"You are Constable Pukeston," I accused.

"You are a trickster!" he said. Then he seemed to collapse in on himself, sitting down in a chair and covering his face with his hands. He did not weep. He sighed, which was worse.

"What are you <u>doing</u>?" I had to ask, Susannah. Would you not have done the same, if faced with a similar circumstance?

"You would not understand, Lady Upton-Church. A lady such as you could never understand what my life has become.

I shall resign my post in the morning, I swear before God Almighty. I will leave the county – I will leave England entirely if you so order me, so long as you do not divulge my secret. I will do anything you ask."

I was perhaps the only titled person in his acquaintance to whom his plea would find sympathy. What if I had to explain my life to a stranger? Would I find support? Decidedly no. I sat down next to him.

"I think you may find yourself surprised at what I am capable of understanding, sir. Perhaps you should unburden yourself to me. You must be quick, as I only have a moment, but you seem to have been waiting for something like this to happen. Now that it has, take the opportunity to explain to at least one person what is going on here."

To my great surprise, he did.

Constable Daniella Pukeston, whose parents had always wanted a girl, dreamt his entire life of being a singer. In his middle-class family the stage was unthinkable, perhaps more than divulging his fondness for women's clothing. A fondness he was helpless to fight. Over time it had become a more and more dominant part of his life. He had always had a beautiful singing voice, high for a man, but stirring to any that heard it.

The conflict within him grew after he became a constable, trapped in a stultifying and regimented existence. He had become two people: the upstanding and admirable Constable Daniella Pukeston in public, and a miserable, wretched fetishist in private. It was driving him mad. He was desperate, near suicide, and realized he must indulge the shameful part of himself in order to continue living. As suicide would damn him forever, he came upon a plan. He would have two lives, each separate, which allowed him to express both parts of himself harmlessly. And so Lillienda Stonekup was "born."

The fees he received for singing were donated to charity, and he took great care to only sing far away from the county where he was the constable, and had refused offers to sing in London for fear of discovery.

"But I knew," he closed. "I always knew that someday I would be found out, and it would all be over. I know my affliction means I can never marry, for what decent woman would have such a man? And I do love women, Lady. I have no other inclinations that would be considered unnatural. But this is something I cannot deny. I have tried to do as much good with it as possible, Lady, I have, but it does not erase the blemish on my soul." Then he buried his face in his hands again, and asked only that he be allowed to leave town quietly.

Had I discovered this a mere month before I may have remonstrated him. I may have uncloaked him. I may have held him in contempt. But there he sat, looking so small, so sad, and I realized that his affliction only hurts himself, and the hurt is so very great.

We all have secrets. Some are more shameful than others. Those that hurt others should be exposed, so the perpetrators can be punished. This was not one of those secrets. And I told him exactly that. I thanked him for a lovely evening, and to please send my regards to his sister, Lillienda, and her marvelous voice.

His shock was great, as was the relief, but I could see he did not trust my words. I understood that as well, and bade him goodnight. I joined the rest of the party in front of the music hall, where Mr. Castleton's carriage awaited. Everyone was solicitous and I realized that I could not attend the ball with Mr. Castleton. He is shallow and uninteresting but not a bad man, and it would not do to give him hope when there is none. To be in his company in public had already encouraged him and would in time make others think a match had been made, when the reality was that it was a waste of his time and purse. I asked if I might speak with him alone and we stepped away. I told him I was sorry for my disappearance, but had found that being out so in public was discomfiting for me (that part was true). I said I realized that I was not ready to re-enter society (true enough, at least escorted), and wished to withdraw my acceptance to the Filson's Ball, as my discomfiture at attending a simple musicale proved it was beyond me at that moment (not very true but kind).

Mr. Castleton was dismayed but instantly solicitous. He apologized for having rushed me and told me that of course I should not strain myself in any way. He offered me his arm and led me back to the carriage, patting my hand as if I were an invalid. He settled me with great care, and on the ride home made sure the conversation was such that I was not required to join in. He was not awful at all. Just lonely, I think, and wanting a wife. I felt badly that he had been misled in regards to myself. I will still have to go to London of course, to take care of legal matters, but now I would be unencumbered with a suitor who does not suit.

With such thoughts whirling in my head it was a great relief to see the outline of my Hall rise up in the moonlight. I wanted to be home. Taylor was waiting, and I thanked my hosts for a lovely evening. Mr. Castleton told me he looked forward to seeing me again and wished me well. I was grateful that he did not kiss my hand. Well, I did not offer it. I believe he thought I was tired as opposed to being opposed to that notion.

Taylor let me in, and after he took my wrap told me a light supper and wine were waiting for me in my rooms if I was hungry. I thanked him and dismissed him for the evening.

Prudence was waiting in my room and helped me change into my nightdress, clucking when I told her Mr. Sinclair would not likely be calling again.

"Seems a nice man," was what she said.

I smiled at her. "He is. He is simply not the man for me."

"Ummm, Lady?" She fidgeted.

"What is it, Prudence?"

"Your supper. It's, well . . . it's gone. I think the gho – something happened to it." She waited for remonstration. I knew where my dinner had gone and smiled.

"It is all right. I am not hungry."

She blinked in astonishment and smiled. Ghosts are very helpful, Susannah. You should get one or two.

I dismissed her for the night and once she was gone collapsed into a chair. What an evening! It was barely midnight, but I felt as if I had been awake for days. Then I dabbed on some scent, brushed out my hair and went in search of my supper.

When I reached my secret room Will was stretched out on the bed, reading a newspaper by candlelight. I decided to be as casual as he appeared, for he did not look up when I came through the door.

"Why are you here?" I asked, waving my hand at the room.

"The food is very good." He sounded a little cold and continued to read. He was more bothered by my evening out than he had let on, and I thought it might be a good idea to make clear exactly where my affections lie. I took the newspaper out of his hands, sat astride him deliberately and kissed him, gently tangling his tongue with mine.

"That is all?" I knew my voice was pleasingly husky.

His tone was still aloof. "I should think you would be grateful I waited here to keep from scaring Prudence to death."

"I am glad you returned. It was a boring, awful evening." I smiled at him, but he did not return it, as I had reminded him where I was.

Although he truly was bothered, he became distracted when I slid my hands inside his linen and gently ran my nails down his chest as I began nibbling and licking his ear, which he loves, but he still managed to say, "I knew you would look for the dinner. There are chocolates for dessert, and I very kindly saved them for you." He pulled back a little, picked up a chocolate treat and considered it for a moment, watching me watch him. It was adorable, for although he did wish to stay aloof, he still fed the chocolate to me.

"Thank you," I murmured. His coolness melted as I slowly licked the traces of chocolate from his fingers. He actually groaned a little. It was fun to tease him this way, so I still sounded casual, even as I pulled his linen from him. "I thought we agreed you would not come tonight," I murmured, kissing my way along his shoulder, moving down his chest and was quite gratified to notice his breathing change. I have never seduced anyone, Susannah. Normally he and I mutually ravish each other. Seduction is quite titillating. "Although," I paused, "I am very glad you did."

I looked up at him to see if he was assured. He saw the question in my eyes and settled me more pleasingly on his lap, his voice low as he wrapped his arms around me and tucked my legs around his waist. "I am sometimes incredibly contrary, Annabella. I do have a mind of my own, you know."

I kissed him slowly again and whispered, "Really? I did not know Scots had minds."

He smiled as his hands slid under my gown, brushing the backs of his fingers across my stomach as they moved higher, which caused my breathing to change as well. He murmured in my ear, "Funny, I heard the same thing about the English . . . You must be French after all." Finally all hope of pretense was dismissed and we rolled over so he was atop me, clearly planning to claim me then and there, but I remembered Walker and Molly and my promise to Prudence and said we would either have to be completely silent or go to my rooms. He thought for nary a second and said he would race me back to the Hall.

We tied for the finish.

I am sure your head is spinning from what I have told you, and trust that Constable Pukeston's secret is as safe with you as my own. I do not see the harm in it, except that which he does to himself. I have not told Will, for I made a promise, and I did not think he would be comfortable with the image of our chief law official wearing a gown and singing sweet love songs in a music hall.

I will close this letter now and write you again soon. It will be a whirlwind until I see you at the Ball. Perhaps you will be in London at midsummer! I would so love to see you! Please tell me you will have returned by then so we can see each other face-to-face.

In the meantime I shall write long letters to you so I might keep you informed on all of the news of my rather chaotic life, and you must continue to do the same for me. I remain

Your Secret-Keeping Friend,
Annabella

☙ Mourning Ends ❧

1 August, 1821

Dearest Susannah,

I found myself laughing aloud at your last letter, and wondering if I should be pleased or offended that you found the news about Constable Pukeston a scandal that should be exposed, given his official position in our county. Of course, you were obliged to set the scene using only my meagre words for accompaniment to your imagination, so perhaps the fault lies more with the tale as I presented it than with the reader.

I had the opportunity to reflect upon Daniella's predicament for a few days before I wrote you. I find it difficult in recent days to cast aspersions on the perceived failings of others' characters, as my own character is not what I always believed it to be. However, trust me when I say that Constable Pukeston will not sully the reputation of this county, or of England. Fear of discovery likely causes him to be more zealous in his public life. It is the way of these things, I believe.

I am so pleased you have been able to leave Siena, and that your Lordship is fully recovered from his accident, and even more pleased that you are at long last coming to London, even for a short time. I will be there at the same time to take care of business matters with Mr. Sinclair, so I can see you. I know you will be busy, but please promise that we will spend some time together, as I have missed you very much. These letters sustain our friendship, but in order for it to thrive we must see each other face-to-face, even if it is infrequent.

My gown for the Ball will be beautiful, Susannah. It will not have a speck of black or grey on it, for those are colours that have accompanied me every single day for two years. I know not why other widows decide to wear mourning clothes forever. It does make deciding what to wear very simple, and there is not the expense of replacing the staff uniforms and such back and forth, but it is so very dreary!

You know, it is odd. I just realized it is unlikely I shall ever wear mourning clothes again. I have no relatives at all, so shall not find myself packing away my lovely gowns and going to a mourning-shoppe. Is that not strange? I had not thought of it until just this minute.

Well, nothing to be done about that, I suppose.

In the meantime I find I am feeling quite content. I did not think when Quince died I should be able to get on by myself, but with his posthumous help it seems I have done exactly that.

The only thing left to do is to get into that confounded secret room in the Hall. I have not told Will of it – he only knows of the passageways from the boathouse and the wall. A quiet voice in my head told me to keep the information about the third tunnel between myself and you. I do not know why, but that voice seems wiser than I, so have heeded it in this instance. With my evenings of late very much occupied with other activities, I find that I am either unable to make further investigations or forget about them.

You will be amused to know that staff is concerned about my appetite. I always eat supper in the morning room – a horrible breach but the dining room really is too huge to eat in alone, but now have also asked that another, lighter supper be brought to my rooms in the evenings. Will eats like a proverbial horse, and is always happy to see something laid out for him. I find it pleasant to discuss the day's events while he fills his stomach. Also, although he always brings me something when he comes, I never have anything for him, for what would I buy him? He does not wear scent, nor jewelry, and I do not think he would enjoy baubles or such, so I make sure there is always food for him. I am turning into a most ridiculous creature. But staff cannot understand how I can eat all of the food – my breakfasts are ridiculous of late, I am now famished in the mornings – and still stay slender. It is the best diet I have ever embarked upon.

And now I must away, for a special delivery has arrived I think staff will find pleasing.

You may have noticed from the date of this letter that in less than one week my mourning has officially ended. Can you believe it will have been two years?

Regardless, new gowns, uniforms, everything, have arrived from London, courtesy of my old dressmaker, and next Tuesday every bit of black and grey will be banished from this house forever, for I am mourning no more.

Your Country Friend,

Annabella

☙ A Surprise Visitor ❧

4 September, 1821

Dear Susannah,

I know you have not heard from me in ages, but it has been one thing after another here in the country, but I am now assured that Wetmoor will be finished and spectacular for the Opening Ball. Mr. Sinclair was thrilled to know he would be invited, and when he left yesterday he almost skipped to the carriage. There will be many young ladies attending and he might meet someone who will properly value him. He reminds me of a puppy sometimes and I have become very fond of him.

I trust you received your invitation to the Opening Ball, as have nearly 350 others in recent days. Now I have to go through with it. Will was posted an invitation, of course, and he accepted in a most delightful and interesting manner, unlikely to be duplicated by any other in attendance. He thought I would not feel comfortable inviting him, which is ridiculous. If Mr. Gibberwilly can be invited, then Will can be as well. I do not know how I shall feel if girls twitter and swirl around him, hoping for a dance. I am most silly.

As you are dying to know, things are wonderful with Will. I am so happy in his company, and sometimes during a vexing day I have only to think of seeing him in order to improve my spirits. He seems to feel the same.

Will is at Wetmoor near every night. I believe I spend more time with him than I ever did with Quince, who frequently worked late into the night. Sometimes days would go by and we would only see each other at dinner and breakfast. I wondered if such constant proximity with Will would breed conflict, but that is mercifully absent. We almost never argue. We occasionally have a mild spat, brought on more by exhaustion than real conflict, which is quickly made up. We have also become much more comfortable and easy with each other. The more I learn of him, of his intelligence, integrity and kindness, the more enamored I become. He does not speak much of his past, save an occasional story or brief aside and I have a feeling that there has been great sadness in his life, so keeps to the present. It seemed strange at first until I thought upon it. I have been similarly reticent with him, for much of my life has been either utterly without note or terribly tragic and I do not feel the need to bring all of that into the present. I believe he feels the same. I feel so very lucky that we met, for we are very well-suited to each other.

Sometimes we simply curl up and fall asleep. I was concerned the first time it happened, I thought he was becoming bored, until dawn brought its own pleasures. Sometimes we sleep and, come the morning, he kisses me and leaves. The first time it happened I asked him when he returned if there was anything wrong, and was relieved at his answer. He said he was flattered, but if we tried to keep the pace with which we began we would die. He thought I should be pleased he enjoyed my mind as much as my other qualities, and noticed I was not waking him, I slept just as soundly at his side. He did note that we did not always need sleep, which begged the question of whether I was tired at that moment, as he backed me up against a wall with a wicked grin.

He calls me Bella when we are alone. It sounds nice, an Italian name rolling from a Scot tongue. He always returns, so I do not think I need be concerned. It is just strange. Most people only spend time together in public, private time is by arrangement and when the evening is complete, someone returns to their own room. That is what Quince always did. I am suddenly living the opposite.

I prefer this new way.

That aside, I had to write and tell you of what occurred not two days ago, for it is too much to keep to myself.

It began last Tuesday. I was finalizing what I need to have for my trip to London. Why do solicitors love papers so? I am near drowning in them: signatures for this and approvals for that. I know it is to protect us each from accusations of mismanagement but I have come to believe Mr. Shakespeare was correct: The first thing we should do is kill all the lawyers. Gwynneth was sewing in the nursery and staff were attending their normal duties. Hortense and Constance have devised an agreeable division of work: Hortense takes care of everything at her eyeline and below, and Constance is responsible for the rest. They make an amusing pair as they go about in tandem. Hortense will make a lovely full maid when she is grown, save for that foot of hers.

The public rooms of the Hall are finished, although the guest rooms and such are not, and the grounds are still barren and stern. Mr. Wicklestaff contracted a groundskeeper to clear away the storm damage. His name is Mr. Seaverton, and his knowledge is so great that I have asked him to bring the grounds up to snuff before the Hall is opened to the public.

I thought you would find it interesting to learn that the tree, that horrible tree that was struck by lightning during the storm, was the most damaged of everything on the grounds. Apparently it was over 100 years old, and only lightning could have brought it down. As Mr. Seaverton was detailing the damage, he said that had anyone been in the vicinity they might have been killed. He said the winds were so fierce that a parasol had actually sailed onto the grounds, wrenched from some poor hand. It was found under another branch. I coughed up my tea when he said that, and it was a moment before I was able to speak. I had forgotten that Will had flung it away at the height of the storm. Thank goodness it was an ordinary parasol and not one of the ones made for me in London, which would have been impossible to explain. Mr. Seaverton will also be laying out the new formal gardens and trim back my little forest for a bridle path, and met with Will to discuss it. I was inordinately pleased that Will's ideas were met with approval, and the two men reached accord quickly and easily. It was doubly helpful that Will is aware of what areas of the grounds the bridle path should not encompass, for fear of a horse crashing through the thin crust between the grounds and a secret tunnel. What they have agreed on will be lovely and winding, and beautifully frame my private forest, and Will has promised to take me riding through it as soon as it is complete.

I was not present at the meeting, but later Mr. Seaverton spoke highly of Will and, after seeing the remarkable work Mr. Seaverton has made with the grounds in such a short time and with Will's recommendation, I have decided to extend Mr. Seaverton an offer of full employment as the new land steward. He seems to be personally acquainted with every leaf and blade contained in the grounds, as well as every single person in the County who knows the name of any leaf or blade anywhere. I have shamefully ignored that part of Wetmoor, Susannah, for there has not been time.

I do not even know the name of the current steward – Mr. Sinclair handles everything to do with him. I knew the situation needed addressing, but have not had the will until the storm forced the issue for me. Under Mr. Seaverton's excellent instruction, the damage has been cleared away, with new bushes and young saplings taking root, and other plants and flowers are tucked into beds and along the drive. The Fateful Tree is now firewood. Will occasionally tosses another log on the fire in the evening and says, "Take that," while prodding it with a poker, even though his injury is healed.

I find that discussing things about the Hall with Will is helpful, Susannah. I have been making decisions alone about everything for so long. Before his death Quince made decisions in regard to business and financial matters. I had neither the need nor the opportunity to discuss such issues with anyone before, and I find it reassuring. I do not discuss the sums involved, for I think Will would find it shocking, but he is very intelligent and seems to appreciate my questions are not empty flattery. His opinions have been very helpful, for he understands more of the "everyday" world than I do and can explain it to me without making me feel an idiot. He has an excellent grasp of how business is done, for other clients speak as openly in front of him as they would in front of a chair, but he always listens to what is said. He is as well-informed as most businessmen in London, but blushed when I told him so. I do not think he believes he is as intelligent as he is, Susannah. It must be the schooling they get in Scotland.

The real piece of news is the visitor I had. Two days ago, as I was going through my correspondence, Constance came to the doorway of the drawing room, face pale and ashen. Taylor was standing as usual near the fireplace. Then Constance announced the caller at my door. It was Lady Shardley. Taylor blanched and made a rather strangled noise. I was flustered, and then Taylor's eyes begin to roll into the back of his head. Shades of Will in high summer. I ran to him, smacked his face and told Constance to lead him out to the veranda, then back through the kitchens to his room and alert Prudence to help tend him in case he began screaming, for it would not do for Taylor to collapse in front of Lady Shardley. She might crush him again trying to help. Once they were gone I went to the foyer myself and greeted her.

Susannah, it was the most pitiful sight. I have not seen her since the inquest, and she has deteriorated most alarmingly.

Lady Shardley has lost a great deal of weight, which normally I would find admirable, but she has also aged terribly. Hughe accompanied her, hovering behind and clearly concerned that her walking-stick would not be enough to maintain her paltry equilibrium. She gripped my hand and peered around the Hall. Her voice was papery and it was clear that even at that early hour she had been partaking. I have not seen such a rapid decline since the party we attended at Grovesnor Square back in our school days, when Millicent Braeburn discovered that her beloved had proposed to someone else. I welcomed Lady Shardley warmly regardless and ushered her into the drawing room, asking Foxx to find someone to bring tea and cakes.

Lady Shardley entered the room regally and then faltered, so I helped her sit in a chair near the fireplace. I sat down and waited for her to speak. After a moment it was clear she did not remember why she came, so I inquired after her health. It is the custom, but I was nervous as to how she might respond.

She was fine of course. Never better. Happy as a lark. She had come to see the Hall before deciding if she was going to attend the Opening Ball. It would not do for her to be seen at an inferior social event, she explained. Then she sighed.

Things were all right, actually. She was quite content. I offered my congratulations, and complimented her on her figure.

Well, not much appetite lately, came her reply in a more lackluster voice. Not hungry at all. Slept rather more than usual as well.

Constance came in with the tea and scones and put the tray on the table. I caught her eye and mouthed "Gwynneth" to her. She near dropped the teapot, recovered herself, poured out the tea and nodded slightly at me. Gwynneth and Gabrielle were just down the hall and Gwynneth sometimes left the nursery for lunch. If she and Lady Shardley met face-to-face the resulting scene might end in more renovations being required. After setting out our tea Constance quickly left to avert possible disaster.

After an uncomfortable silence during which the only sound was of tea being sipped Lady Shardley said she was feeling unwell of late, but believed it was a spring cold hanging on far too long. I inquired after her summer; had she travelled? Gone to London?

No, she rarely left the house of late. Too bright out. Perhaps she needed glasses, she had headaches so very often.

This was terrible. Lady Shardley may be overbearing, imperious, arrogant and high-handed, but she was also proud. Although I had no idea what possessed her to visit, I was concerned that this was not the first time she had decided make calls. If she had it could be ruinous. I knew the reason for her decline and could thus be more charitable, but were I not I am sure I would be as harshly judgmental as she is under normal circumstances.

I offered a tour of the main floor so she could decide on the acceptability of the Opening Ball invitation. It took a moment for her to regain her feet, and we slowly moved through the hallway as she peered at the work that had been done. She only glanced through doorways, and I kept her away from the nursery, as Gwynneth and Gabrielle were both there. Then we returned to the drawing room. Lady Shardley regained her breath and said Wetmoor was satisfactory, and could attend without fear of losing her status.

I asked if she went calling often.

No. The visit to the Hall was the first in months. She had only attended Baron Gurthwant's inquest, but her cold prevented her from accepting the many invitations and callers she always received. In fact callers were turned away for fear of the cold turning into something worse.

Well, that was a relief. Perhaps no one else had seen her in this state.

Then she announced that with her inspection done she would return home. I quickly left to find Hughe.

Hughe was in the kitchen in deep conversation with Prudence, who explained that Taylor would not come out of his room, even if I let him go for the impudence. That was the last thing with which I was concerned. Had I lived through what he did I would have felt the same, although I told Prudence to inform Taylor I would have to dock him a half-day's wages. There should be consequences for the abandonment of one's post regardless of the reason.

I then asked for a moment alone with Hughe.

Once Prudence and Cook had taken their leave I apologized to Hughe for having sent him away so abruptly, but he waved it away. Lady Shardley needed him. He haltingly confirmed that the visit to Wetmoor has been the only visit she since her difficulties began, that the other times staff had been able to put her off until she was distracted by something else. He said her heart was broken and her spirit tested by the embarrassment of her widely-known situation. Lord Shardley was no comfort to her even if he had been so inclined, but has added insult to injury and taken to staying for days on end in London, rumoured to now be gambling as well as profligate.

I thanked Hughe for his candor, assuring him discretion, and he said he should get Lady Shardley home, as she was exhausted from the carriage ride. I went ahead of him and we found Lady Shardley in the drawing room sleeping in her chair. She must have wanted more tea but had fallen asleep before it could reach her mouth. The entirety of it had spilled down the front of her gown. I asked Hughe to go to the foyer. She had suffered enough embarrassment.

I took the cup from her hand, cried "Oh, no!" and waited. As soon as she stirred awake I began to apologize. I had not meant to spill the tea on her, I was merely trying to put it back on the tray and was very sorry. She glanced down, saw the stain and started wiping it. I was terribly clumsy, she said. Did I know that? Yes, yes I did and was so sorry, I would pay for any damage.

After we had blotted up what we were able she announced that she had to go home and lie down, her "malady" having sapped her energy. She had just completed the labourious process of getting to her feet when Will entered.

He had clearly been out working with Mr. Seaverton, for his coat was off, his cravat loosened and his sleeves rolled up, with dirty hands and various bits of greenery stuck to his skin.

Everyone came to a dead stop. He had not expected to see a caller, I had not expected to see him until later, and Lady Shardley did not expect him at all. I must say, he looked splendidly sweaty.

He recovered swiftly and apologized for such a rude entry, but Mr. Seaverton had an urgent question. Lady Shardley suddenly looked quite focused, and was focused specifically on Will.

"What are you doing here?" she barked.

I intervened. Will was teaching me croquet and helping with the bridle path being laid out on the grounds. She nodded and said she heard he was. It was a bit unnerving, for she was unable to take her eyes off him.

Lady Shardley said, "Come to my home on the morrow. I wish to begin shooting again and require instruction. You have been before to help with our hunts. Be there at three o'clock." He bowed again and she tottered out of the drawing room. I motioned for Will to wait for a moment and went to the foyer to make my goodbyes to Lady Shardley. She kept peering back at the drawing room and as she left I heard her mutter that Mr. Ploughgoode would be very satisfactory. This alarmed me, as I have seen the havoc she has wreaked on others sent to serve her.

I returned to the drawing room where Will waited. There had been no question from Mr. Seaverton, Will had merely wished to say hello to me with the sun up, and told me I looked even lovelier in the day. I asked him to be careful with Lady Shardley as she was not well, and that he should not be alone with her; she had very nearly killed Taylor. He smiled and said he would be fine, she would not be the first nervous client he had and doubted he was in danger. I was worried that if he should suffer from another bout of heatstroke she might crush the life out of him, which would be horrible for me. He said he would not faint in her presence and would tell me all about it when next we met, for that night he would not be able to come to me.

His landlady has become accusatory of his character – he is so rarely home – and he does not want to find himself turned out. I did not know that this had been happening, but he said it was nothing to worry about, he only had to make sure he was there on occasion and had made up visits to friends and long trips to clients for most absences. Still, I did not like to think he might be unhomed, but he laughed and said it would be more than a fair trade in his eyes, so I should stop frowning and let him handle his affairs the way he saw fit, the same as he did for me.

Well, that ended that discussion, for he was right. With that he departed, kissing me on the cheek, and I returned to the business of the day.

I knew that you would want to be apprised of Lady Shardley's condition, as it all ties in with your house in a way. I do not see how there can be a happy ending for her, but will add her to my prayers that she find some peace with her situation.

I must away and back to overseeing the unpacking of drapes and furniture, or the Hall will appear very barren for the Ball.

I will write again soon, and know that until then, I remain

Your Dear Friend,

Annabella

9 September, 1821

Dearest Susannah,

You must be thrilled to be back in London, even if it is only for a few weeks. What a disappointment it must have been for you to return after a long absence to find your house in disarray! Your house has always been so beautifully maintained, more reason for your distress. To come home and find such a mess is unprecedented – Miss Ditworth has been so exemplary in the past. However, given your sterling reputation, I am sure you shall find no trouble finding a suitable replacement.

But the news I am happiest about is that I will see you when I come to London. An entire afternoon! I so look forward to seeing you, and will meet you at three o'clock sharp on Wednesday for tea. I have missed your face so much, Susannah. It will be the high point of my visit to London.

I read your comments about Will and I with a great deal of interest. I had been bothered that we sometimes sleep, to the point of discussing it with Will, but he was right: we have to sleep sometime. I did not realize it is not normal to sleep with your lover until I received your letter. Per your concern: Will does not seem to be bored or bothered by our clandestine arrangement. Truth to tell, things between us are lovely. And we do not always sleep, of course, but every few days we are too exhausted to do anything else.

One thing that might pique your interest and allay your fears is our discovery of a new pastime. We are in the middle of a particularly high-stakes chess game (I was thrilled to find he is an excellent player). We have modified the rules and the latter portion of the evening is decided by what pieces are taken and by whom. A pawn gains a kiss, etc., etc. It makes the game itself much more interesting than if we play for fun. Although come to think of it, we are playing for fun, simply a different kind than a chess master might envision.

As play continues we muse aloud on how the loss (or gain) of a piece shall be enjoyed, in specific and interesting detail. Last night he took both my rooks, which meant I could castle him twice, and he loved it. Although it will be difficult for me to recover the game without those pieces, it was well worth the loss. For both of us.

That hardly seems a loss of interest, does it not? Do you really think I need worry? I will wait for your thoughts before deciding if I need broach the subject with Will again.

Progress on the Hall is finally commencing at a pace of which I approve, even if Taylor's collapse upset the Hall schedule. Yes, he fell apart after the visit from Lady Shardley. He quivers, occasionally faints, and has woken most of the Hall almost every night with screaming, which began the night after Lady Shardley's visit. Of course Will and I did not hear it in our very quiet room, but apparently Prudence near expired from the sound, thinking the demons had returned.

Taylor stops screaming once he has awoken and always apologizes to everyone the next day, but that seems to be cold comfort. It should only continue for a week or so, if past experience is any indication, but disconcerting nonetheless.

The day after Taylor's rude interruption of sleep Will went to Sumwattle for the first time as an instructor, and the next night gave me the latest on what is occurring there.

Lady Shardley met him on time, seeming recovered from her less balanced state the day before, but inappropriately dressed for shooting. Truth to tell, she was wearing an evening gown that had been soaked to display her charms. I have done the same myself, for certain evenings in London with Quince, but it is inappropriate for a shooting lesson.

As Will had not planned on letting her anywhere near a loaded weapon until he evaluated her faculties and level of skill, he ignored the alarming display (it was rather chilly), and asked to see the rifles so he could determine the most appropriate one for her frame, ignoring the display.

Apparently Sumwattle Estate houses a veritable arsenal within that is impressive by any standard, for Lord Shardley and Lady Shardley have always enjoyed blood sports, and held hunts for anything that could be killed. This made it simple for Will, and he chose for Lady Shardley a suitable rifle. He then began to instruct her on the precautions to be taken, which is when she began to become vexed.

Lady Shardley explained that she does not stoop to menial tasks during hunts, including the cleaning and storing of the rifle afterward, something he well knew.

Will told her that what occurred before and after hunts was none of his concern unless hired to do so, but formal instruction was a different matter. She needed to understand how the rifle was to be checked for shot, the barrel in good working order and the like.

Lady Shardley decided that was charming, intimated that Will had a beautifully solicitous nature, and giggled. This met with my consternation, but Will sighed and told me it was a by-product of the work he did, and he had long ago learnt to ignore it. I had never thought about his work frequently putting him amongst the company of women, which gave me pause. He had not ignored it in my case, grounds for even further pause. He saw the look on my face, laughed and told me to not bother myself a whit about it, for his heart was taken and not to be given to another, and certainly not to Lady Shardley.

I must have still looked dismayed, for I had never thought of such things, and it made me feel queer. He became impatient and told me that I had asked for the tale, and should not now become upset with the teller for relating the truth of it, as it had no bearing on any other part of his life. I strove to compose my face, and bade him to tell it all without regard to whether or not he believed I would find it upsetting.

The lesson went well after that, although Will had to take pains to ensure he did not come too close to her, for her balance has been compromised by her indulgence, and she tended to stumble back into him. With giggles, I imagine. The rifle was in good working order, and Will procured another in less satisfactory condition, so she might see for herself the importance of understanding how such a dangerous weapon both functions and malfunctions. That led her to muse on the hunt of '16, when Baron Theosophus lost his little finger, so now we know how that happened.

When the lesson was completed, Will was taken aback by her invitation to supper, which he declined. (Thank God!)

Lady Shardley was vexed at Will's refusal, however, and he was relieved when Hughe came to the veranda and told Lady Shardley it was time for her nap. She greatly relies on Hughe now, and he is solicitous of one who has been so cruel to him in the past. She immediately acquiesced to Hughe, and Will left with no further incident, although he shall have to return two times each week to further her training.

I did not know how I felt about that. Will is an excellent instructor, and if Lady Shardley is going to be shooting in her current condition she can only benefit from lessons, but I did not like her behaviour at all. However, I maintained my composure, for I had seen how my jealousy was affecting Will, and bade myself to put it out of my mind as he had asked. I tried to think of the positive aspects of the lessons, not the least of which is to be better informed of the goings-on at Sumwattle from someone who speaks more or less proper English. And following the tale Will made it clear where his affections lie, which made me feel better about everything. I had taken one of his bishops in our chess game, which resulted in a toe-curling, spectacular evening for me. I think he lost it on purpose. We are both playing more outrageously than we might normally, for a checkmate will test the ability of the walls to muffle sound. I know it will for me.

On a much less romantic but more violent note, we have had yet another casualty of this county's bad luck, but this time it cannot be blamed on Walker and Molly. Baron Theosophus and Duke Twitwhistle have returned from Africa. They loved the hunt, of course, what there was of it, for it involved shooting things and setting an example of proper behaviour to the strange people they encountered.

They were having a marvelous time until the third day. They tracked those rhinoceros things and in the meantime satisfied themselves with shooting some little deer-like creatures and drinking a great deal around open fires every evening, playing at life in Africa.

That was a mistake, for a hand shaking from the after-effects of a long bout of drinking local spirits should not then tote a rifle, even if it is the best rifle money can buy.

To cut to the heart of the matter, Baron Theosophus shot off Duke Twitwhistle's big toe. He is far too cavalier with his weapons, as it was he who near shot me at Lady Shardley's hunt all those months ago.

It was quite awful, with a lot of screaming and fainting on the part of Baron Theosophus and an impressive amount of swearing on the part of the duke, who tried to kick the baron after the baron fainted, which proved a poor notion. The bleeding was staunched but the hunt had to end, for the duke could not track through the grasses tripping at each step. Fortified with vast quantities of medicinals they have come home.

The duke was lucky he did not expire from infection, but I suspect he made certain he had enough spirits in his system every minute that he could not have caught the ague, the pox or anything else. Once back in London he was presented with a beautiful cane by the Baron Theosophus, who is abjectly apologetic for what occurred, and now the duke stumps about, much as Driver does.

Although the duke's amputation is not nearly as impressive as Driver's, Driver apparently trips less than the duke. But a return to London was in order. The friendship between the duke and the baron has remained, for it was an accident, and may somehow even out the loss of the baron's little finger. Have you noticed how many in our set are missing bits of themselves, Susannah? These are dangerous times, I think.

I knew you would want to know and perhaps send him a note – I found out from Prudence. I think all our servants talk to each other which, although indiscreet when it comes to my life, is very helpful in being aware of the lives of others.

I am very pleased the Hall is going to be properly completed for the ball, as most of the furniture, hangings and draperies have finally arrived and been installed. The piano has also arrived, and with it another calamity, which seems to be a pattern I am not certain I find pleasing, although it does make me approach each day with a keen sense of curiosity.

The piano arrived on schedule but needed tuning. The shoppe from which it was purchased had no available tuner that could leave London, as everyone and their brother has need of one after all of the rain and damp there. A tuner from another company was arranged instead. That seemed straightforward enough, which is exactly how the strange event began.

On the appointed day the piano tuner arrived, and Prudence announced him as I was going over some fabric samples for one of the guest baths. His name, and I may have it incorrectly (you shall understand why in a moment) is Zlot Bagniewzsku. I think.

Zlot is Hungarian, if I understood correctly, and appeared hat in hand to tune the piano. I do not know any Hungarians, and hope his aspect is not representative of his people. He appears to be made entirely of squares. He has a square body, square hands (with thick and wiry tufts of hair sprouting from strangely feminine knuckles, which mirrored the tufts sprouting from his nostrils) and a square head. In fact, his head appears to be attached directly to his body, for I could determine no neck in evidence. His hair is wiry and dark, standing in independent patches all over his head. His form was so unusual that his suit was unable to disguise it. I wondered if such a person would be capable of tuning a piano, but realized if he could not I would have an excellent opportunity to remonstrate someone, which is something that has been sorely lacking in recent weeks. He was led to the piano and I told him to inform Taylor or Mr. Wicklestaff when he was done. He haltingly explained that my piano was very fine, but such fineness was sometimes delicate, so the tuning could take some time. This was not an issue, and he was given the usual instructions regarding how things in the Hall are done, so he would be as little in the way as possible.

He unabashedly complimented the music room, which seemed to awe him, before being left to his task.

A Herculean task it appeared to be. For Zlot (I cannot call him Mr. Bagniewzsku, it would take me many hours more to complete this letter if I had to write it out every time) tuned the piano for three days. Without stop.

At first everything seemed to be going fine, with the usual plinking and plonking noises, and a pause, followed by more plinking and the like.

Then the music began. Initially I enjoyed it, for Zlot is a gifted pianist. The Hall echoed with Haydn, Handel and Bach, a lovely change from the sounds of hammering, sawing and pounding, which are the normal accompaniment of my day. Each piece was then followed by plinking and plonking, and then more music. The first day was quite enjoyable, and I believed the work to be complete.

I was so very, very wrong, although I have since become aware that the fault was not with the piano, it was with the tuner. Zlot returned the next morning to continue his work.

It proceeded in much the same fashion, but the musical pieces he chose became more dirge-like. However, I was willing to withstand a great deal in order to have a functioning piano for the ball, and paid it no mind.

That is, I paid it no mind until he did not leave. The melancholic music echoed through the Hall until Zlot was told he had to stop for the day. He left after dark and I forgot about it, for Will had another lesson with Lady Shardley that day and I was bursting with curiosity.

Lady Shardley was again discomfitingly flirtatious with Will, who ignored her advances, simply continuing the instruction. A target had been arranged, and it was time to determine if her skills had atrophied as much as she thought.

Lady Shardley was correct that her skills had deteriorated, never hitting the target at all, but did take down a tree branch and a small gopher that had the misfortune of poking his head up from the grass at the exact wrong moment. Will must continue the lessons for some time. I held my tongue regarding her untoward behaviour, but Will was aware of my discomfort and strove mightily to allay my fears. However, it was still on my mind.

Until the next morning when Zlot returned. I told him the piano seemed perfectly tuned but he advanced the idea that his ear was more sensitive than mine, and more work was needed.

That day the Hall was filled with music that made me want to jump off the roof. I did not know such sad and awful music existed. It persisted throughout the day and well into the evening. I finally told Prudence that Zlot should be escorted out. I was quite surprised when she came into the library and told me that Zlot would not leave.

I myself went to the music room, for it was unthinkable for him to refuse the request. Imagine my shock to find Zlot at the piano, playing perhaps the saddest song ever written that I have never before heard, sobbing terribly as he did so.

Of course. My piano tuner is mad, I thought, for what else could it be?

I strode to the piano and demanded that he immediately stop playing and leave even faster, for the piano was tuned, although the music was dreadful, and his services were no longer required.

He did not stop playing, but somehow managed to turn his square, neckless head to me and sob out the words, "She does not love me," before collapsing onto the keyboard and wailing. Prudence's eyes were the size of saucers.

I told Zlot that I was sorry he had had such bad luck in love, but it was no one's affair but his own, I should like to maintain that tradition, and to please leave.

Then he said the thing that made it all clear. For he loved one whose voice was like a songbird, he had been intoxicated with its beauty, as well as the personage in which it was encased, for her spare, square frame reminded him of the women at home.

Lillienda Stonekup.

He had seen her some months before at the musicale I had also attended and been smitten. Then he had returned as often as his purse and schedule would allow.

Then, a month ago, he had begun to pitch woo. He wrote letters which were returned and, except for the first, unopened.

Flowers, trinkets, the usual offerings sent to declare affection followed the letters, all sent to her at the theatre, for no one could tell him where Miss Stonekup resided. Each gift was returned without explanation.

He began to write music, song after song about Lillienda's wondrous, sturdy loveliness, and tried to go backstage so he might hand-deliver them. He was rebuffed each time. Yet he purchased tickets at every opportunity, in order to experience the voice which had so captivated his heart and soul.

Obviously I am embellishing on Zlot's broken English, but believe this is a fair representation of events.

Zlot's hopes and love were dashed at every turn. Finally, just three nights before, he had been turned away from the theatre. He would be allowed to attend no more. This was caused by his previous attendance, when he had stood in the middle of a song and screamed his adoration of her, his desire for her and his overwhelming love which would continue unabated for all time.

He is a broken man, bereft of his love and unable to even bask in the sound of her voice. It has completely undone him.

Zlot is mad with love.

Of course I could not tell him why he had been rejected so out of hand, for I did not believe it would be in the least bit helpful. I cast about for something to say and resorted to the platitudes I had heard myself.

I told him he would recover from his pain. Time would pass, and one day he would look back on this time in disbelief that he could have been so hurt by one who had cared so little for him.

I should point out that when dealing with Hungarians these are not helpful things to say. Zlot merely wailed louder. Taylor actually came to the door, although he is the last person to look askance at those who scream in the night, and I told him to give Zlot a draught to calm him, and then see him home.

I did not see anything else that could be done, for Zlot is in an impossible situation. He has fallen in love with the wrong man.

And I must away, for there are duties pressing on me, and the day is fast slipping away. I hope I can write again before I see you, dearest friend.

Fondly,

Annabella

14 September, 1821

Dearest Susannah,

I write to you with the heaviest of hearts, and although I shall see you in only a few days' time, could not stop myself from writing now, as I am utterly bereft, and I cannot explain the cause of what shall surely be visible distress when I see you in London, for I do not know if I can bear to relate the tale face-to-face without embarrassing us both by weeping.

Will and I have broken with each other. That is my punishment for embarking on such a course, of course, but the knowledge is no balm for my spirit. I am writing this late at night, a time when I would have been engaged in far more pleasurable pursuits than letter-writing, but I that is my Fate, as Quince has left me educated, wealthy and constrained, and therefore unfit for a husband.

I am sure you are not shocked at this news, you advanced concern about how our affair was progressing even as I mistook the same events as evidence that we were happy.

It is ridiculous that I am shocked and heartbroken. Do they not all end this way, when begun with no hope of a future? I knew all of that and merrily ignored it. Now I am left sitting in my rooms alone, a cold and untouched supper reproaching me from a table and the sight of a small carved cat causing me to sob. It is unbearable, yet bear it I must, for there is nothing to be done about it.

It happened only two days after Zlot had been dispatched, and I thought everything was back to normal, or as normal as things at the Hall ever are. The workmen have by and large finished their work, and the sounds of their rough trades have been replaced by feet striding up and down hallways as drapers drape and the floors are polished and all of the other work of preparing for a ball goes on.

That day had been fruitful, for I finalized my tasks for London, and made out a schedule so I could insure everything was taken care of during the trip, as there are considerable arrangements underway and time is of the essence. I have not detailed them to you before now and find now that I do not care what tasks are done and left undone, for it does not matter in the end. Everything turns out badly.

But enough of that. You had asked to be apprised of how my romantic adventure fares, so I may as well just tell you.

Will and I had fallen into a comfortable routine in the evenings, telling each other of the day's events and seeking the other's counsel on various matters. That evening seemed no different, although Will was quiet while he ate his supper. To fill the silence I told him of the latest work done on the Hall and of guests who had thus far accepted their invitations to the ball. It was then that he set aside his napkin and said he needed to discuss something difficult with me. I suddenly felt fearful, as if I was not going to like what he was going to say. I was right.

Miss Paget has made it clear that she expects Will to ask her to the Opening Ball, as she wants to attend and has no invitation. Unfortunately he has no public reason to not escort her, for he cannot say there is a prior claim. He had not asked her, for he felt that it was not proper to raise hopes where none were warranted, but did not know what to do. He is marriageable, and apparently without constraint, so seemingly without reason to decline to invite her, for she is acknowledged to be desirable and his refusal would be commented on, and he thought perhaps I could help.

I was taken aback. First that Miss Paget should be so bold, and then that Will believed it a fit discussion to have with me of all people, and told him so.

He sighed and said he felt the same, but it changed nothing, were it not Miss Paget there would be some other woman, the issue would not simply dissolve into nothing by the ignoring of it. Imagine if we found ourselves at some dinner party, sitting across the table from each other, but with other partners at our elbows. He could not bear the idea, and hoped I could not either. He had been bothered quite enough when I went to the musicale with Mr. Castleton.

I of course had not thought of this, as in my state it would not be strange to simply be unescorted, no one would think anything of it. And I had perhaps fancifully deluded myself that the simple fact that he is a Scot would prevent any such situation from ever arising.

However young the conversation was, it made me see too clearly that our liaison was hopeless. We cannot publicly acknowledge our private hearts. There will be no courtship, no marriage, nothing except what we have right now, or had, and there is nothing to be done about it, which would be fine if there were no real feeling involved. But there are, or were, and suddenly those things loomed large. He is not titled, I am, and constrained on top of it. Were we to declare ourselves he would lose his clients and his livelihood, for who would engage a person who woos and wins the hearts of clients, and the estate would be lost to the vagaries of Quince's will. It would be the end of both of us.

With those thoughts crowding my mind, I asked why he wanted my opinion on the issue.

He said he valued my counsel in everything else, so wished for mine in this. Then it became clear to me what was really happening. He was bored by me, for what could he do but become bored, locked up in my stupid rooms, and wanted me to know he had ample opportunities elsewhere. I already knew about Lady Shardley's flirtation, the time he spent with the lissome girls of our County. He wanted leave to spend time with another, for I could not be seen with him, and others, apparently many others, could and would. It hurt that he would be so very callous with my feelings.

"What do you wish to do?" I tried to wrap my heart in stone. If he no longer cared for me, I would not give him the satisfaction of seeing how much it hurt.

"I coul' take her, but – "

There it was. He wanted to go with her to MY ball. It was such a blatant insult that I realized I was right, he did not want me, he wanted some cheap girl with a fat bosom and pocked face who could walk with him down what passes for the High Street in Wimbish. Well, two could play at that, I thought. "Then you should take her."

When Will stopped choking on his wine he asked me to repeat myself, so I did. "You said she is pleasing. You should escort her <u>somewhere</u> at least."

"You want me to spend time with another?"

I waved my hand at the room, hoping I would not vomit my dinner onto the table, as I let him know I knew what he was thinking. "This is all there is, is it not? We cannot be seen in public together. Miss Paget can, so you should consider it."

His voice was cold. "I have." Vomiting was suddenly no longer a concern; my dinner thudded into my feet with dismay. I was right. He wanted a wife, and I cannot be one to him.

"So I suppose there is nothing else to say." I sipped my wine and hoped it did not dribble down the front of my nightdress, my lips felt numb. I found myself wishing I was mistaken – perhaps he meant something else. My wish was not granted.

"I suppose not." His voice was light, which was hideous. "It's been an amusin' diversion, aye?"

I realized your assessment was correct.

The simple sleeping together, which I had taken for a good thing, as proof that Will wanted to be with me for more than trysts (ample and lovely as they were), was instead evidence that he was bored. I naively had not thought what we had as a diversion but he did, else he would not have asked it. I was not going to admit that I had adored him from the first if he had not adored me from the first. I actually stammered. "It . . . it was . . . "

He stood and began looking about for his things. As he pulled on his waistcoat and began fitting his cuffs his voice was distant. His true feelings were showing. "You need not say anythin' else, Bella. I've been toy to a lady's whim before." He began looking for his cravat, tossing pillows aside.

That is how I found out that he had done this before and had learnt through experience the best way to end it: with the lady thinking it her idea, so he would not feel guilt for such shameful abandonment. I began to feel angry, for I already felt very much the fool. "You should leave." He looked at me as if I had gone off my head.

"In case you'd not noticed it's what I'm preparin' to do. You'd not wish me to leave your house undressed. God knows you don' want your reputation to suffer."

"How chivalrous of you." Anger felt so much better than nausea. He pulled on his boots, taking care to sit on the divan instead of the bed, as he normally did.

"God, you're a cold one," he muttered.

"That is not what you said last night." I could be as unfeeling as he, at least in my outward aspect.

He stood but did not move to leave. "I thought you were different from the others," he said.

The words were a knife in my heart. There were others. Plural. More than one. Likely dozens. I was surprised my voice was so light. "What do you mean?"

His face was getting red, a sure sign he was angry, which was unfair. He was leaving me. "You're like the others of your class, which, in case you're unsure, is an insult."

I could not believe what I was hearing. Was I not already injured? Did he have to add insult to it as well? "You think the peerage is the lesser class?"

"In many ways, yes."

My disbelief turned to fury. The peerage is the only thing keeping civilization afloat, everyone knows that. "I suppose I should thank you for deigning to lower yourself to be with me. Or, should I say, lowered yourself onto me." I was viciously satisfied to see shock on his face, before it smoothed into a blank visage.

His voice was a hiss. "Oh, now you're insulted? At least the lower classes don't ask each other to play the whore, which is exactly what you've asked of me."

He was playing the poor, wounded victim, when I was the one being abandoned! I actually sputtered. "You are the one telling me about others that want you, you could have, that what we have is so little – "

"Wha' we have is so little tha' we may as well be with others." The burr in his voice had gotten thick but there it was, the admission. He wanted another. The idea hurt horribly. He was searching for his things and would not look at me as he said, "I won't burden you further wi' my presence."

I felt tears stinging and cursed my watering eyes, even as I turned my back on him. I was a task to be done, a chore completed and now I was not even worth simple courtesy. I could not bear for him to see me cry but inexplicably did not want to make it an easy thing for him. "You are cruel."

"I'm only followin' your example, Lady Upton-Church."

I was no longer his Bella, I was just a lady he had bedded, now he was bored and ready to find another. How could he not become bored, locked up in my rooms? I cannot even walk down the street with him. I do not know what I had thought would happen, well, I had thought about it. I did not think it would take such a short time and hurt so much. I glanced at his reflection in the looking-glass. He was trying to tie his cravat without success. He gave up on it and began looking for his coat, clearly desperate to be shut of me.

It was all I could do not to scream. "The situation is impossible – "

"I know that!" He had never, ever raised his voice to me before, and I flinched.

He yanked me around to face him and I could not look him in the face, I could not stand seeing it so closed to me. He took my chin and forced me to look at him. When he spoke again it was in a whisper. "I love you, Annabella."

I could not believe it. How could I? He had never said it before. He had said many lovely, romantic, passionate things, but I suddenly realized he had never, not once, said he loved me. Because he did not. I hated he would use the word only when it meant nothing, so I said nothing. It seemed fitting.

He looked down and when he looked up again his face was quite blank of any expression, as was his voice, and I realized I was seeing how he felt about me: nothing, in spite of his words, and his voice was low. "You can wall off this tunnel for all I care; it won't be travelled again by me. I'll not attend your lovely Opening Ball, for I have another engagement . . . I'll be wooing a more <u>suitable</u> girl. I'm sure you will be with someone <u>suitable</u> yourself." He was through the door in an instant, slamming it behind him, and I heard his footsteps fade as he left. Forever.

I know not what else to tell you, Susannah.

I love him and he is gone.

I continue to get up in the morning and go about my business, but it all seems meaningless. Staff is quietly solicitous, for it is clear that I have been crying and sometimes have to lock myself in my rooms to cry still more. I did not know a person could shed so many tears.

I miss him so dreadfully. I know I should not, he is not worth my tears, it took a total of ten minutes for him to break with me. I wonder if my name was entered on some list, comparing me to others, and how I fare.

Then I wonder if perhaps he had loved me but grew tired of me, but did not want to say it because he did not want to be cruel. Or more cruel.

I cannot even look at the tennis courtyard. Or the boathouse. Or the games room. My rooms rebuke me, cold in spite of the fire, and an unfinished chess game sitting on a small table makes my heart hurt. I feel very, very empty.

So please be kind when you see me in London, Susannah, for I am heartsick. I shall see you in a few days' time, and until then I am

Your Grieving Friend,

Annabella

☙ London ❧

20 September, 1821

Dear Susannah,

What a balm it was to see you! I know I made that abundantly clear when I saw you in London, but such is the force of my feeling that I must state it again. I so appreciate your generosity in allowing most of the afternoon to be taken up with my romantic misadventure.

The time was well spent, for at the end of it my spirits had been soothed. They are not as high as they were before my heartbreak, but I know I shall recover from this or, at the very least, be able to continue. As you said, how many can look back on their lives and know that even one time they were truly happy? The ruin to which it came does not nullify the joy of it, and I intend to keep that thought firmly in mind when I want to cry. I still rage at the fact that everyone else in England is doing unspeakable things with everyone and their brother (sometimes literally), but I cannot be seen with Will because of his station. He was worth more than any one hundred of them and, as you said, may never have broken with me if I could have at least acknowledged him in public.

Unfortunately I still cry every night, both in London and at home. However, the succor you provided gave me the strength to complete the tasks I had set for myself in London.

I met with Mr. Sinclair, who has been doing research for me and preparing some papers for the ball. He has a great deal of work to do, most of which has confused him, but I found I did not have the strength to explain. As it was clear I was distressed he did not press me on the issue, saying only that if it would help me he would be honoured to undertake the tasks, even when they have nothing to do with my companies. He has handled working with a woman so beautifully, Susannah, and I found that when he asked if there was anything else he could do to help I near began crying again. It was awful. I told him I was very sad and there was nothing to be done about it. Any kindness turns me to jelly. He promised to do everything I asked and said he was proud to be invited to the Opening Ball, even if it is to provide legal counsel, beaming when I said he would have been invited regardless. At least something I have done has made someone happy.

The morning after I saw you I went to the cemetery to visit Sarah and Quince, which proved a very bad idea. I wished they were both alive, for then I could have remained the light-hearted, shallow and ignorant woman I had been, a state to which I would give almost anything to return. Everything I have done in the last year was because the life I had was ruined, and it seemed to be going well until it went so terribly wrong. I thought the last grieving I would ever do was for Quince and Sarah, which shows how very ignorant I was. I stood in front of their graves for a long time, Prudence standing a ways away to give me privacy. But my wish did not come true.

I shall always be alone.

The last day in London I had one more task to complete, and that was go to the watch-maker. I did not tell you when I saw you – I was afraid you would try to dissuade me from it – but I had ordered a watch specially made for Will and had to fetch it. He had given me so many thoughtful gifts and I wanted to return the sentiment. I wrote my watch-maker to have a gold pocket-watch made for Will, back when we were happy.

Will's own watch kept poor time, and he needed to insure promptness in his work, so it seemed the perfect gift. It was custom-made to my specification: the fronts-piece is a tree in bas-relief, to remind him of the day of the storm, and on the inside is engraved a small twined "W" and "A."

As it was specially made I could not cancel it, so I went to the shoppe on the High Street and retrieved it. Prudence, who accompanied me everywhere in London, was tacitly curious about why I should purchase such a thing. I told her I had always meant to order just such a watch for my father before he died and had decided that his being dead was no reason not to have it. Thankfully I have such an eccentric reputation now that this reason was accepted without comment.

I was glad to be done with my errands, and as we left the shoppe I was thinking I could finally go home when I saw Mr. Castleton. He was walking to his club and stopped in amazement when he saw Prudence and I in London, for it was the weekend of the Filson's ball. I faltered; I was having difficulty maintaining my composure after such an upsetting day, and he immediately approached and inquired after my health, clearly surprised to see me.

As my voice was shaking and my eyes red from tears he assumed what I had told him at the musicale was correct: I was not ready to enter Society again. I told him I was in London to see my physician, quietly stepping on Prudence's foot to silence any query she might make. He called for my carriage to take me home, and told Prudence to take good care of me. I felt terrible. He is not an awful man, he is a thoughtful man, and deserved better than my insincere attention. I hope he meets someone that can return his kindness in full.

Prudence said nothing during this exchange, but once we were settled and on our way, said Mr. Castleton seemed a nice man. The rest of the ride home was silent, for Prudence is aware of my current state, although not the reason for it. I had supper sent up to my room, and left it untouched.

All the things which once loomed had been done, and it was with great relief that I left London for home. I never thought I would not think of London as home, but its bustle and pace now distress me. Noises from the street drifting up through windows that used to be such a comfort when I sat in mourning now jangle my nerves and prevents sleep. I required a sleeping draught every night that I was there. Wetmoor Hall, with all of its strangeness and obligation, is now my home. Quince was prescient in his own way. I shall maintain the London house, but suspect that the caretakers shall be the least-worked caretakers in all of England.

When I returned home I put Will's watch in a box which now also holds a small carved cat, a comb, a pin and other once-heartfelt tokens. It is locked tight and hidden in the secret tunnel room, although I am reluctant to admit that I have sometimes, deep in the night, crept there, taken the box out and cried over the contents. I miss him so! Then I take a deep breath, as you instructed, and a good hold of myself, and stop my tears by sheer determination. The box is then re-locked and left there. I know what you said is true, the hurt shall fade in the fullness of time, but for now it is still too near to bear reminders of the happiness that preceded it.

And it is of utmost importance that I recover myself. The now-dreaded Opening Ball will still be held. You will be the only ally I have in attendance. When I was in London I did not even call on old friends. It has been so long since I have seen my peers that I fear they might not recognize me, so much have I changed, had they been the slightest bit inclined to see me or extend an invitation to their balls and dinners and outings.

I had not noticed it, it has been in gradual degrees, but you have always been such an excellent barometer for me, and if you believe I have changed from the carefree wife I was not two years ago, it must be true.

I shall write again soon, and know that I remain

Your Recovering Friend,
Annabella

7 October, 1821

Dear Susannah,

I cannot believe it has been just two weeks since last I wrote you, for so much has happened that I want to get in my carriage and come to London, pound on your door unannounced and spill forth the tale.

When last I wrote you I was in a state of deep melancholy which, you will be grateful to know, is completely gone. The reason, however, is somewhat outlandish.

My melancholy is gone because of Lady Shardley.

Of course now you are confused, which is understandable. How could Lady Shardley have exiled my melancholy when she herself is in such terrible straits?

Will did not return to Wetmoor for my lessons, something for which I had both dreaded and hoped, torn between wishing to see his face and praying I would never see it again. I had fantasies that he would return and as we volleyed back and forth he would suddenly leap across the net and beg my forgiveness, foreswearing all others, etc., etc., etc., and when I was done clubbing him with my racquet I would throw myself into his newly broken arms and find happiness again.

But he did not return, killing my hope of reunion, and the courtyard again a simple piece of filigree on the grounds. The bridle path was being worked on by Mr. Seaverton, although he grumbled that his inquiries to Will regarding certain areas had been ignored.

By the way, Mr. Seaverton accepted my offer to become the land steward for the Hall, replacing that other man, although he must take some time to complete other commissions already accepted, but they are small and shall soon be finished. He will be a fine addition to the Hall, and shall take over the cottage (I am embarrassed that I did not know I have a cottage as well) that the soon former land steward occupied.

You do not care about Mr. Seaverton, I know. I am in a complete dither.

I was in the library doing what I have come to think of as my private studies, reading Mr. Shakespeare's exquisite sonnets, ignoring the happy ones and reading only those that spoke to heartache and loss, as those mirrored my frame of mind. There was a knock at the door and Prudence entered at my call.

"Might I have a word, Lady?"

"Of course, Prudence." It was so odd for my taciturn maid to ask for a word that I set down my book. Perhaps her heart had been broken and she wanted to resign so she could wander the world alone, filled with bitterness and grief. Were it so, I would make sure she had enough severance to do so for at least several months.

She surprised me. "Lady, why did you not tell us of Mr. Ploughgoode?"

I was aghast, for what could ever make her think I would tell staff about Will? How <u>did</u> they know about Will? Oh, no, he had done the unthinkable: he had told everyone about us and everyone knew. He not only did not love me but had painted me as a harlot and a fool. I would never be able to go out in public again, for I had been made sport of and spurned by my tennis instructor.

Those thoughts must have taken too long for Prudence's taste to whirl around in my head.

"We should have been told, Lady. We all are fond of him."

"I did not think it any of your business." I was having a great deal of trouble thinking clearly, I was so mortified.

"Well, it is not exactly our business, Lady, but still – "

"What do you all . . . think about it?" I wanted to know how badly I had been maligned.

"Any woman who would do such a thing is no lady in my mind, Lady, title or no."

"Prudence! That is very harsh!" Oh, he must be saying awful things about me. He had not seemed the type of man who would do such a thing, I had staked my reputation on that assessment and was so horribly wrong! My own staff thought I was terrible. I would have to move to the Americas and start over after all, and that place is positively barbaric!

Prudence did not notice my discomfiture, or if she did, chose to ignore it. "I don't understand how you can defend it, Lady. From what I heard, it's the most awful thing anyone has done here in a long time."

Prudence is so naïve, perhaps if I could explain that the wrong people fell in love constantly her assessment would be more forgiving. "I do not believe that what occurred is unheard of. In fact, I understand it is more common than generally discussed."

Prudence's tone was actually arch. "I certainly have never heard of such a thing. I hope she goes to gaol."

"You can go to gaol for that?" Why did no one tell me it was illegal? I just thought it was not done. I might go to gaol . . .

"Lady, people are hung for less, although her being a lady, it likely won't happen."

Suddenly a thought broke through my jumble of anger, embarrassment and humiliation. Prudence was saying "her," not "you," so I was not the lady to whom she referred. I thought my heart could not break any further, but I was terribly wrong. It shattered. Will had had an affair with another lady at the same time he was with me. He must have the constitution of a draft horse and be near-dead from exhaustion. Had he been seeing her during the day and come to me at night? Did he prefer her?

Another thought intervened: They might hang Will for that? It is a hanging offense? It should be, playing with the affections of two ladies, but it happens in London all the time and I have never heard of anyone hung for it.

"I do not know what to say, Prudence." I did not, truth to tell. My mind had stopped working.

"I just feel so badly for Mr. Ploughgoode, Lady."

Oh, he was the victim in all of this. He, who apparently had the scruples of a hyena and the stamina of a stallion. I hated him. "Yes," I murmured. "Poor Mr. Ploughgoode." Poor, rotten, perfidious, cheating, scoundrel Mr. Ploughgoode. I was seething.

"Do you think it hurt terribly?" She was concerned about his heart! How did he become the one to be pitied in all of this? I was the one crying myself to sleep every night!

"I would think not," I finally said. How could he have a broken heart when apparently he did not have one at all?

"Mr. Ploughgoode is very strong, Lady, but being shot had to hurt awfully."

I shook my head. "I beg your pardon?" It sounded as if she said Will had been shot. Clearly it was a case of wishful thinking on my part.

Prudence clarified herself. "It must hurt something terrible to be shot like he was."

"Mr. Ploughgoode . . . was shot?" I actually felt the blood drain from my face.

"Of course, Lady. Lady Shardley shot him ten days ago. That's what we were talking about. Weren't we?" She was now as confused as I, but all I could think was that Will had been shot.

"Is he . . . Is he dead?" I could not believe I was saying those words. Will might be dead. Dead and in the ground and I had not even known. I was the worst person ever born to have not known somehow that he had been killed.

Prudence interrupted my ruthless self-remonstration. "Gravely injured, to be sure, Lady, but not dead. The shooting was bad, but there was an infection, too. He's still at Sumwattle – he cannot yet be safely moved. The physician thinks he will live, but it was a near thing, they say."

He was not dead, I near fainted with relief, only to be followed by the thought that I was still the worst person ever born, for during the twelve seconds I hated him I would have cheerfully heard exactly that news. Until I heard it, that is.

"Lady Shardley shot Mr. Ploughgoode," I said. I must have sounded terribly stupid.

"She was angry with him, and she shot him." She was looking at me with curiosity, and I realized how strange the first portion of our conversation, before I knew that horrible, murderous Lady Shardley had shot Will, must have sounded to her.

I tried to gather my wits, which were in disarray. "I did not say anything to you, Prudence, for I did not know what to say. But I should have. I should have done right away. I am sorry."

She started twisting her hands. "Oh, Lady, please don't apologize, I just wondered because you and he seemed to be friends – well, not friends, really, I know he is only a workingman – but he was always so nice, and then he stopped coming and you never said why, it's because he was shot, I suppose – " My formerly nearly mute maid had suddenly sprouted the gift of oratory, but now was not the time.

"Prudence, have my carriage prepared immediately."

I was going to Sumwattle, for Lady Shardley had much to answer for. That woman! She is wantonly destroying all of the best men in this county! I was furious, frightened, and alarmed at the depth of my concern. Will clearly had no affection for me any more, that was obvious, for he had not written to tell me what happened. I was a mere former client.

Unfortunately I am not a Scot stoic and was in a state, for even if we broke badly I did not want him to die! I wanted him to grow old alone and lonely, with very few of his own teeth and only a mangy, smelly dog to keep him company, until he was found dead in front of a long-dead fire holding an empty bottle of poor-quality Scotch. Not shot by client! I wanted him to live a good, long, horrible, desolate life and, with any luck at all, suffer as I did.

Driver brought the carriage around in a trice and I embarked for Sumwattle Estate. Luckily it is a long drive, and I was able to calm myself somewhat and regain my senses. The bottle of chardonnay I found wedged between the seat cushions was helpful in that regard.

When I arrived at Sumwattle it was Hughe who greeted me, not with a little surprise. I told him I had come to speak to Lady Shardley, as I understood she had injured Mr. Ploughgoode, which was causing problems with my bridle path.

Hughe told me Lady Shardley was seeing no one and had taken to her rooms, for her remorse at the "accident" had stolen what little dignity she had left. I am afraid I stamped my foot and insisted on seeing her at once. He sighed and said he would try to arrange it, for the staff had been unable to affect any improvement in her condition and perhaps another lady could.

He returned in a moment, and near caught me peeking around to see if I could tell where Will was located, and said Lady Shardley would see me in her rooms. I followed him to her rooms and her maid showed me in.

The room itself was a reflection of Lady Shardley's condition: dark, shuttered and in disarray, and Lady Shardley herself lay abed at two o'clock in the afternoon, piled upon pillows and surrounded by the leavings of someone who has not left her bed for many days: boxes of chocolates and crumbled kerchiefs surrounded her. She looked at me with weeping eyes and said, "I have come to utter ruin. I shot Mr. Ploughgoode."

I asked her what had happened. It was complicated, she said, and proceeded to explain.

She had been having trouble with her nerves of late, she said, brought on by some kind of dropsy her physicians were unable to cure or improve. It caused her much pain and anguish, and although she had tried everything to assuage the pain, it continued. It began to affect her judgment, and she had been concerned that her reputation could be tainted if she did not somehow dispel the affliction which so sorely tried her.

The prettiest description of uncontrolled drinking I ever heard, though I kept that thought in my head.

She decided to take up pheasant hunting again, for it gave her great pleasure to take down such difficult birds. She knew it would require focus, patience and diligence, and would perhaps affect a cure where everything else had not.

In other words, I thought cruelly, she knew it was high time she pulled herself together and began behaving like a lady.

She had engaged Mr. Ploughgoode, as she always referred to him, and it was a good thing, for her skills and abilities in shooting had deteriorated from their former high standard. Due to her illness, of course.

Too drunk to shoot, I mused meanly.

But the other day she had awoken feeling more poorly than ever, and been required to partake of strong medicinals before her lesson. As the lesson progressed Will proffered that she was in no condition to shoot. Lady Shardley became angry, for it was infuriating that a hired hand speak to her so. She insisted they continue but he refused, telling her that shooting was not a sport to engage in when ill. He bowed preparatory to taking his leave.

Lady Shardley screamed she had never heard of such a thing, an inferior daring to dictate to a lady what was appropriate and what was not, and he was not only permanently discharged, she would see to it he found no more work amongst his betters. He said he understood but would not in good conscience continue the lesson, and begged her leave.

So vexed was she at his impudence (her word, not mine) that she threw the rifle down on a table on the veranda, preparatory to storming into the house and writing letters to her friends and telling them to refuse Will's services.

She was prevented from doing that because when she threw the rifle down on the table it went off, and thus Will found himself shot.

I was mortified. She had spoken so viciously to him, and he was trying to prevent such an occurrence!

Clearly Lady Shardley was aware of that as well, and she continued her tale.

The bleeding was awful, and while a footman rode for Mr. Gibberwilly, Hughe attended Will. He was in shock, and kept saying, "She shot me. I canno' believe she shot me." Hughe was able to stem the bleeding somewhat, the spilling of which, Lady Shardley noted, ruined much of the grout around the tiles of the veranda. It was only a half-hour before Gibberwilly arrived, but by then Will was pale and unconscious. The wound was in his left side, and Gibberwilly was relieved to announce that it passed clear through, apparently missing anything important. However, he was in grave danger from blood loss, and needed to be kept quiet and still.

Gibberwilly then closed the wounds (front and back, which makes me feel faint when I think of it), gave instructions for poultices to ward off infection, which was the greatest danger, and commended Hughe on his skills in stopping the bleeding. The fateful bullet and bits of clothing it took with it were retrieved. Thank God it was not bird shot! A single piece of shot is wicked, but had the rifle had been loaded with birdshot Will would have been, at best, horribly maimed by many small pellets instead of a single large ball, and the chances for the infection to be fatal would have been much higher.

Lady Shardley collapsed, and when she awoke in her rooms she was told that Will appeared to have recovered, and been taken home by Hughe, along with the poultices Gibberwilly had prescribed.

Well, that was altogether different than what I had been told and found I could breathe somewhat. Until Lady Shardley continued.

Hughe had gone to Will's rooming house two days later to discover what the constable had been told. Will had not told Constable Pukeston anything, for he did not answer Hughe's knock but could be heard muttering within. Hughe finally forced the door and found Will alone and fevered, an infection settled in the wound, the poultices having failed. I felt very much as if I were going to faint, for I could picture him lying there, sick unto dying, alone.

Hughe brought Will back to Sumwattle, realizing that if Will died, Lady Shardley would be in far more trouble than she already faced. An actual physician, not an apothecary, was brought in and had tended him every day since, but the infection was stubborn and Will's fever worsened.

When I managed to interrupt her, for I did not think I could bear to hear another word, my voice sounded remarkably normal. I asked if the physician had been successful.

Thankfully he was, Lady Shardley said. Gibberwilly was summoned, and after a gruesome treatment involving boiling water, wine, and scraping, Will's fever retreated and the infection appeared to have been bested. He would likely make a full recovery.

I actually almost heaved my breakfast up right then and there. He was boiled and <u>scraped</u>.

Lady Shardley could not stop fretting, but it was not concern for having nearly murdered Will, but because Constable Pukeston wanted to speak with her at her earliest convenience.

She had not left her rooms since for fear of arrest. She had, after all, shot Will when yelling at him, which made it appear perhaps less accidental than it may have been.

I asked if Mr. Ploughgoode, as I was careful to call him, was truly recovering, for if he did it would be difficult to arrest her. I informed her I am not very conversant in the law when it comes to shooting an instructor and the resultant consequences. She said she only knew he was alive, and Hughe was taking care of that, for she was too afraid of what would happen to her if she were arrested and (then she began to sob) put in gaol to worry about such things.

I found that the idea of Lady Shardley imprisoned did not concern me overmuch. We might all be safer were she not running around free, given what I know of the two people who have had the unfortunate luck to cross her riotous path, but did not say so.

Although I could have happily strangled her, I told her I was sorry for her plight and asked if her dropsy had abated, for that was surely at the root of this unhappiness. She snuffled that it seemed to be so, for she had not had any medicinals since that day, although she felt very weak and frail. In fact, she was rather tired and wanted to sleep, perhaps it was time I took my leave. I stood and thanked her for seeing me. When I reached the door her very small voice stopped me.

I would not tell anyone what she had said, would I? I sighed inwardly, and turned back to her.

I would not. It was not my business. Unless the constable was given cause to think I had any information bearing on the matter, which was unlikely. She thanked me and I left her to her self-inflicted sorrow. I did not add that if Will died I would make sure she hung for it.

I came down the stairway where Hughe waited for me. He asked after Lady Shardley and I told him the truth: she was in a poor state indeed. He nodded. I then asked after Will, pleased that my voice did not tremble, explaining that Lady Shardley was not able to elucidate his condition. Hughe said I could see him if I desired, for he was in the drawing room. As Lady Shardley had not left her rooms, since recovering his senses Will was allowed to sit there for a short time each day to enjoy the sunshine.

I hoped my thrill at those words did not show on my face, and managed to calmly say I would like to give him my regards.

Hughe seemed to be thinking about something carefully, and he did not open the door for me.

"Hughe? Was there something else?"

"Mr. Ploughgoode, Lady. When I went to him and he was sick, he thought I was his . . . how do you say it? Hughe not know word. His woman. He thought I someone called Belle and was so sorry to me for hurting."

"He did?" My heart fluttered in my bosom.

Hughe's face did not indicate his thoughts. "He was very sick, but she not come here. I not know a Belle. Maybe you find out and we send for her so she knows he good again."

"I shall speak to him about it, Hughe."

With that the drawing room door was opened, Hughe quickly announced me and withdrew. Thank God they do not attend ladies all of the time in Austria or wherever he is from!

Will was on a settee and covered with a light blanket as he read a book. He looked shocked for a moment and then smiled, but his voice was very quiet. He said he was glad to see me.

I found I did not know how to proceed. I wanted to rush across the room and fling myself into his arms, but his manner did not indicate if such an action would be welcome, whether from his injury or from how we had last parted.

Oh, Susannah, how very pale he was, with such dark circles under his eyes!

I remained near the door. "I came the moment I heard what happened. The very moment. Are you all right?"

He tried to smile. "No, actually, I'm shot an' somewhat putrid. But the surgeon and physician were very thorough, an' I'm told I'll make a full recovery." He yawned. "The medicines they give me are pleasant. I sleep most o' the time." His casual tone was at odds with the clear seriousness of what happened and I finally ran across the room, actually wringing my hands, and sat down next to him. The room had no windows, but I believe that had there been French doors leading to the High Street in London I would not have cared.

I laid my hand on his face and said that no matter how we had parted, I would not have had him shot. He said he was glad of that, for he felt the same, at which we both laughed a little. He was cool to the touch, which meant the infection truly had abated, but he was in a fair amount of pain, for although properly dressed he was sitting awkwardly, keeping his left side from touching anything.

"I'm sorry, Bella." My heart leapt – he called me Bella and felt badly about breaking with me! – "I shoul' have taken your warnin' about Lady Shardley to heart." My heart fell; he was not sorry about breaking with me, but for being shot.

"I am sorry as well, it is so awful." He thought I meant the shooting, but took my hand regardless.

"Don' fret. I don' remember much. I remember gettin' shot, bein' sewn up, and goin' home. . ." He shook his head slightly. "I started to feel poorly, and had strange dreams. That man Hughe came. Then nothin', until a few days ago. That was . . . rather unpleasant." He looked odd. "It was kind of you to come."

He closed his eyes for a moment, I had begun to think he had fallen asleep when he opened them and said he would be allowed to leave Sumwattle Estate in a few days' time and perhaps we could meet once more and talk, if I were amenable to the idea, for he had thought a great deal since we had parted, especially since he was shot, and would like the opportunity to perhaps put things aright. "I've been thinkin' of our last conversation, especially the endin'," is what he said.

I am afraid that tears came to my eyes at his words. When he saw them he asked that I please not cry or he would be forced to faint in response and that would not do in his current condition. I managed to blink the tears back and smiled instead. He said that on his release he would come to the Hall, and perhaps we could find a better ending than before. This wounded me, for I had begun to think *rapprochement* was possible instead of a new parting. I would not have refused him anything at the moment, so I agreed. Except for the tears that sprang anew to my eyes at his words I believe I appeared quite serene.

There was nothing left to do but to leave, which was wrenching. I wanted to stay and make sure he was comfortable and would soon be put to rights. But it was not my place, if indeed it ever had been, so I chastely kissed him on the cheek and went home.

It is a good thing the Hall's demands are constant, else I may have done a passable imitation of Lady Shardley, waiting in my rooms and drinking myself into a stupor. But there is always something that needs to be done, either instructions given or letters written or decisions made which kept me busy during the days. I slept poorly, for I wanted nothing more than to go to Sumwattle Estate, but there was no acceptable excuse I could make, so I strove to keep busy, retiring early in case Will returned.

Gwynneth is done with my ball gowns and they are beautiful. She has now become so filthy that she appears for all the world to be a huge toadstool, and whispered to me that my instructions were successful thus far. I had to think for a moment what she was talking about before remembering my admonishment to make sure that her husband stayed away from her. It seems so long ago now! As that all fit in with my plans I congratulated her.

She seemed sad that the gowns were complete, as well as the work on my other gowns, until I told her I would need her help the day of the ball and to please arrive no later than 10:00 a.m. in order to help me prepare. It was only two weeks away! She brightened and thanked me for letting her return. She likes the Hall much more than the pub, she said. With that arranged I bade her leave, feeling satisfied that everything just might be in place for the ball.

Which left only one thing left undone, and that was to have a final conversation with Will, one that would hopefully be less harsh than the one before. My heart lifted at the thought of seeing him, only to plunge down again when I thought of the reason.

On the fourth evening I retired to my rooms and waited. I had begun to think my waiting in vain and was preparing for sleep when I heard the catch on the door in the wall. Suddenly I was atremble and Will slowly came through the door. He was clearly in a great deal of pain and I saw the trip had been difficult for him. The same day, he explained, he had been transferred to his home, slept until dark, then saddled, mounted and rode his horse down the side of the road until he reached the Hall, tying the poor thing to a tree in my little forest, and then came through the tunnel to me. I had never before thought of how difficult it had been to come to me in the past.

I helped Will to the settee and poured a glass of wine for him, which he drank straight down. He then asked for something stronger. I took out a bottle of the Oban Scotch, which made him smile, and poured a healthy dram. That seemed to ease his discomfort somewhat and he looked around the room, saying he thought he would never see it again. I told him I had feared the same thing. He caught my words properly and asked if it had been something I had truly feared.

I nodded and was about to spill forth my heart when he asked that he be permitted to speak first, for he was quite exhausted, having undertaken to see me sooner than advisable, and the medicines he had taken made thinking rather difficult. I nodded again, and after a moment he surprised me.

"Would you accept my apology for the cruel things I said to you?"

"I cannot accept your apology unless you accept mine. I behaved badly as well." I tried to not fidget, as Miss Penelope taught us.

"I accept. With thanks," he said with no small amount of bafflement, and then there was an awkward silence, which had never happened between us before. I did not know what to say, for although we had apologized it did not seem to be resolved. After a moment Will looked up from the fire. "I'm sorry for my harsh words, but what you said hurt, Bella. Very much. That's no excuse for the things I said."

I sat carefully down next to him, trying very hard not to jostle or hope. "You were not a diversion, Will. I hated hearing that I was one to you, and it caused me to say things I wish I had not."

He seemed confused. "How could you think you were a diversion? I never said that. I don't want Miss Paget, nor Miss Bryce, nor any o' the other girls in this county, or country even. I didn't say it before, for which I'm sorry. I thought you knew . . . but you should have said somethin', asked me, before findin' someone else."

"What are you talking about?" Had he gone to others because he thought I had done the same? Is that how it happened?

Will sighed. "You tol' me to go to that stupid Paget girl because you found someone else. Just . . . please tell me it isna that Mr. Castleton. He's a dandy and a ponce, Bella. I couldn't stand for you to choose him over me."

"You are being ridiculous. Mr. Castleton?" I shuddered at the idea.

He looked grim. "You sent me away because you were done with me or you'd not have asked me to see Miss Paget. I'm not a complete fool."

I was becoming confused myself, without the assistance of medicines. "I never wanted you to leave. There is no one else. There never has been. Mr. Castleton? Ughh." I shuddered.

"But we fought . . ." His voiced trailed away and he closed his eyes. "I canno' remember wha' I was going to say."

It suddenly became clear what had happened. "Will, I think there has been a terrible, horrible mistake."

He sighed. "Bella, I understan'. I just wish you told me instead of startin' a fight."

"You were with others even when we –"

"I couldn't be with anyone else, how could you think that? I was finishing what you were saying. <u>You</u> found someone else."

Will had not been with anyone else! I was right, we were both wrong! I might be able to fix it! "Will, please stop talking." I sat down at his feet and looked into his face. "I was not trying to break with you. There is no one else, there never was." I said the next part slowly. "I thought you were done with me, why you had brought up that girl." I thought it best not to use her name, as names seemed to make us go in circles.

He sighed. "Bella, I was sussin' out your feelings. <u>Somethin</u>' was botherin' you, but you wouldna say what it was. Then, you said that what we had, well, it was no' enough for you. God, I wanted to die when you said that. Even with the constraints on us you'd always shown me respect."

"I do respect you –"

He held up his hand. "Let me finish. I knew about the constraints, about everything, before I ever kissed you. How could I not?" He looked down. "I know what I am. I'm a hired hand, a servant, a person who is helpful, but with no feelings, no thoughts worth knowin'. Until I met you."

I was stunned, this was much more than I had ever thought Will might say, but he was not done. Drink and medicine had loosed his tongue to an unprecedented degree. "I pursued you knowin' everything I'd never have and did it anyway. I believed you'd done the same until that night." He sighed. "I know it's hopeless. No one will ever know, and I'll never have the pleasure of walking down the street with you on my arm, none of the things one expects when one is bound to another."

"I know." My voice was as quiet as my heart.

"But I thought what we had was enough. I didna know it chafed you. I'm sorry, Bella, the only reason I've not asked you to go anywhere publicly wi' me is because your reputation'd be ruined, and I won't be the cause."

"I do not care about going out with you." His face fell. "You misunderstand. I would walk down the High Street in London on your arm if you wanted me to. How could you destroy a reputation already ruined? I know what it would do to your livelihood, and I won't have you starve because of me."

"But you're a Lady –"

"A rather odd one by all accounts, I know that. I don't care about the Ton, or going to balls or any of those other things. I never thought you might feel the same as I."

Will seemed confused. "I know what I had in this Hall, in these rooms, in your grand bed wi' you . . . I love you, Annabella. I have for a long time." He shook his head, seeming to need to clear it. I could not believe it; he had said it again, that he loved me and it was in the present tense. I burst into tears. He put his face in his hands. "Please don't cry." I could not stop. "Why are you cryin'?"

"I never thought you might love me," I managed to choke out, and he looked startled.

"How coul' you ever think that?"

I had spent long nights pondering my Life, such as it was, when Will had left. So I actually knew the answer to his question. The real question was if I would have the courage to tell him. But he had said he loved me, so I decided I should.

"Will, I married three days after my seventeenth birthday, and went from girl to a Lady in a day. It was strange, being a grown woman overnight, running a London house and taking care of a husband. Quince loved me, but like one loves a child or a pet. I could not even give him children. Such a simple thing is beyond me." He cocked his head to the side and looked sad, but I kept on. "I loved Quince because he was my husband and one should love their husband, and he was truly kind to me. He could have divorced me. Most men would have done. There were some offers from others, but they were from men who treat love as a game. They were easy to refuse. I was lucky, even if I was treated as a doll."

The next part was difficult, for it was true. "What I feel with you is different than anything I have ever known. I wait every night for the sound of the door opening. I yearn to hear your voice, know your thoughts, see your face, feel your touch." I blinked back the tears in my eyes. "And whatever my feelings are for you, one day you will want to get married, have children and live your life without pretense, not ride in darkness to a woman who reads books and talks of mining operations and plastering costs, who treats you like a servant in front of others." I wiped my eyes with the back of my hand, it would not do to fall apart before I was done. "Then you told me of Miss Paget, who can, <u>wants</u> to see you publicly, who is young and can almost sing and is charming. Who can be a wife and give you children. The only reason I could think why you would tell me of her was if this no longer suited you. And my heart broke. I could not even follow when you left." I worried that I had been too forthcoming, but there was nothing to be done, I had already said it all. I took his hand and held it so he would look at me and then held my head high and spoke clearly, for if one is going to be without pride, one can at least strive for dignity.

"I love you, William Ploughgoode. I do. I loved you even when I hated you for leaving me. I know all that I cannot offer, can never offer, and that I am not enough to keep you here." I could not keep looking at him, instead looking down at my hands, fighting to keep them still. There was a long silence. Then he took my face and gently tipped it toward his own. The burr in his lovely voice was pronounced.

"I came here before, I'm here now, because even wi' your tears – which, by the way, are considerable for such a merry woman – all th' constraint, everything, I'm happy wi' you. I know how rare tha' is . . ." He smiled a little crookedly. "We're very similar, for I couldn't believe you'd choose your tennis instructor when you could have any man in England, one who'd shower you wi' gifts an' furs an' jewels. Things I can't give you. I may not be titled, but I know wha' happens in your circles. You likely receive offers from wealthy an' accomplished men every day beggin' for your favour."

He sighed. "I can't compete with them, Bella, wi' little carved cats and jewelry made of glass. I thought you'd met someone who could give you the things I can't. I thought you'd never loved me, nor ever would, even though I love you so much tha' sometimes it makes my chest ache."

He had said it again, that he loved me, even if his words were lightly slurred, the Oban was taking its course.

I was in wonder. "Why did you never say it before?" None of this would have happened if he had, but I did not say that. I am not stupid.

"I knew you cared for me – you made that plain." His voice was tiring. "I confused a dalliance wi' love once long ago. The details don't matter, but it's why I never said it. I thought you might say you didn't feel the same. I didn't want to know, not for certain. I felt the luckiest man in the world when we were together, even if it couldna last. You're a Lady, Bella, your world is different. Do you know how many times since we argued tha' I began to come here? My horse starts this way whenever I leave my house. I probably helped cause my own shootin' – I conducted a lesson wi' a hangover tha' shoul' have killed me. I started drinkin' the night I left and didn't stop until I was shot. I've been miserable, but I couldn't beg. I couldn't beg and be refused." He stopped because my tears had begun again, rolling down my cheeks. What he was saying was not what I had imagined. I was afraid if my tears did not stop he would leave, for I was clearly insane, which made them continue. I was in such a state. He touched one as it trailed down my face.

"No one's ever cried for me."

"I have cried every night since that night. My eyes are swollen all the time and I have had to tell everyone I am ill. I have missed you so much, Will."

Will kissed a tear on my cheek and said, "You're still cryin'."

I sniffled and tried to smile. "I know, but it is so . . . I have loved you for the longest time, I should have said it, I should have said it over and over, and when you left all I could think was that I had never said it and you would never know, and I love you so much. I thought you were coming tonight to say good-bye nicely and leave me again, and then I would cry for weeks. Not <u>this</u>. Telling me you love me and are happy with me. And you are shot and came anyway, I cannot believe you went and got yourself <u>shot</u>. How could you do that? It was awful!" I vaguely waved my hand around, and he took and kissed it.

"I'm very tired, and if you don't mind, could we agree that we were both stupid and leave the rest alone? We've now said the things we shoul' have long ago. Those are the ones tha' matter. Can that be enough?" I nodded, but the tears kept on rolling down my face. "You must stop cryin'."

"I am trying, but –" I hiccupped, and he grinned.

"I'm too weak to kill anythin' for you, Bella, and I canno' think of a poem, which leaves only one thin'." He paused and my tears stopped, for I had the feeling it was very important that I pay full attention. "Would you marry me?"

"What?" I was sure I heard him right, but worried I misheard, because I so much wanted to have heard correctly. He still smiling, but there was also a nervous look in his eyes.

"You know how tears affect a Scot, therefore the remedy should be Scots. So . . . would you marry me? If you could?"

"Yes, in an instant." I was feeling queer, light-headed and faint. He seemed to be waiting for something.

I took his hand in mine. "I, Lady Annabella Christina Honorah Upton-Church, would marry you, William Bartholomew Ploughgoode. If I could." He smiled.

"Then you're my fiancée, an' I am yours. Do you understan' what I am sayin'?"

I did, and I was very, very grateful. "Yes."

Will grinned. "We'll marry in fifty years. You'll look like a shrivelled, adorable apple, I'll have a cane an' spectacles, an' we'll totter together out o' the church."

The aching hole in my chest was suddenly filled with a burst of happiness. I leaned forward to kiss him but he blanched and I realized he was in more pain than he had let on.

The reunion I had dreamed of was curtailed by reality, as his energy had been depleted by the mere act of coming to me. He was exhausted.

For him to try to make such a trip home alone at night would surely finish him off so I insisted he stay. I helped him to the bed, and as I tugged off his boots I asked if his bandage needed to be changed. He said it needed to be done but knowing how I feel about the sight of blood, if I turned away for a few moments he would do it.

I tried to sound as if changing the dressing of a wounded and, by his own account, putrid man were something I did every day. "I can change a simple bandage. I refuse to risk you to infection again." That silenced him and I helped him remove his coat, waistcoat and linen. I took an old sheet and ripped it into strips, knowing Walker and Molly could be blamed again. Since we are they it seemed appropriate.

I removed the old wrapping carefully in case it was sticking to him. I was glad it was not, I would likely have gotten sick on him. It looked awful. There was no sign of infection, but it looked lumpy and the stitchwork – I daresay Prudence would have done a better job. Come to think of it, I could have done a better job. I felt dizzy while staring at the stitches and Will grabbed my hand.

"You don' need to do this, Bella."

"It would not do for you to leak, would it?" I said lightly, trying to keep things normal, or as normal as they can be when one is changing the dressing on a man who has been shot and nearly killed by a deranged client. I am thinking of writing Miss Penelope and requesting that she augment her courses of study: there are many things that happen in the World which were never discussed in her classes.

I blotted the wounds in front and back with wine and soaked part of the new bandage in it as well. I then wrapped the linen around his torso a few times, tying the ends into a bow in the front so he could reach them if needed, which made him smile. It took a few moments as I clucked over him and when it was done he was limp with exhaustion against me, and I helped him lay down on his good side.

I gathered up the old bandage and tossed it into the fire, adding the ruined sheet to a large pocket in his jacket for later. Perhaps I should become a nurse, I did very well.

Finally I could sit next to him and smooth the hair back from his forehead to check that the fever had not returned.

"Thank you," he whispered.

"You are quite welcome." I kissed his forehead, the fever was gone.

"You do love me," he whispered.

I smiled. "Yes, I do."

"That's very nice." He closed his eyes.

It was odd, Susannah, for although it was awful I was glad I had changed the bandage for him. I was tucking the coverlet around him to keep him warm when Will opened his eyes again and took my hand in his, tucking it next to his heart.

He said he had never been so forthcoming in his life, and would not ever again, as it apparently did not agree with him to do so, and must have been brought on by all of the medicines the surgeon was making him take. He could barely move, and asked if I would mind very much if he laid down.

Before I could say a word he was asleep and I contented myself to curl up next to him and hold his hand, keeping the vigil I had wanted to keep since learning he had been shot.

Before dawn I woke him so he could be home before Hughe appeared to check on him. He was chagrined by his seeming weakness, both physical and emotional which, given his condition, proves how Scottish he is. I was not chagrined at all; it was the most peaceful night I spent in weeks. I helped him through the tunnel, onto his horse and bade him promise to not return until well enough to withstand the trip. I would be waiting when he did. With that his horse gently carried him away, weaving through the trees, and I returned to the Hall.

So now you know the reason for my complete recovery from heartbreak, as unexpected as it is welcome.

I knew you would want to know all that transpired, as you have been so patient in hearing of the heartache. I will attempt to write again before the Opening Ball, but until then, I am most sincerely,

Your Joyous Friend,
Annabella

☙ *Engagement Gifts* ❧

9 October, 1821

Dear Susannah,

Thank you for the lovely engagement gift, and even greater thanks for your happiness on my behalf. I was obliged to tell Will who had sent such a stunning chess set to us, it is the most beautiful either of us has ever seen. Wherever did you find it?

Once Will recovered from his shock that not only does someone know about he and I, but the person is a lady who greatly approves, he set about to very trounce me in our first game. He is still recovering so the things we normally would have done were postponed, so he wrote them on a piece of parchment so we would not forget any of the moves.

Will loves that the chess set is ours, not mine or his, and wanted me pass along his sincere thanks for your generosity of spirit and acceptance of our odd arrangement. You are the dearest friend in the world to have done such a thing. His letter is enclosed here.

(By the way, he does not know I have told you exactly how we play chess.)

Dear Lady Carollton,

Please accept my most sincere thanks for such a beautiful gift. I have never seen it's equal. I can guarantee it will be put to great good use, for we are both very fond of the game. She is the finest player I have ever had the pleasure of challenging, and the chess set itself is very beautiful.

More important, your approval of what at the least is a most unusual arrangement means a great deal to both of us.

Should you ever require anything that I might be able to provide, please do not hesitate to ask and I will provide whatever is needed. You mean a great deal to your friend, and therefore to me.

Yours Very Sincerely,

William Ploughgoode

He has a very fine hand, does he not?

I am so pleased that you engaged Miss Abblesham as your London housekeeper. The wheeled contraption she uses to move about will not bother you a whit. She was a delight in Quince's and my London house, and I am sure you shall find her an asset to yours. She shall put it to rights in a trice. I did not know she was not enjoying her retirement and am glad you wrote her.

I am sure she is thrilled to be in such a lovely house. I was sad when she left after the accident, but understood she was too heartbroken to stay. She loved Quince like a son.

At Wetmoor we are all working toward the Opening Ball, which is five days away as I write this. The deliveries seem to come on the hour: foodstuffs, wines, tapers and firewood (the dreaded tree now nearly used up) and the Hall is bustling with the tasks that must be completed: silver polished, linens aired and pressed, grates blackened, the guest rooms aired and prepared for unexpected guests, for I have had few refusals. It would seem that everyone is bursting to see the improvements that have been made. I even received a note from Sir Manfredson, thanking me for his invitation and telling me there was nothing he had looked forward to more in years. It was addressed to King George III, but I appreciated the sentiment nonetheless, and look forward to showing his former Hall restored to glory.

Wetmoor looks stunning, Susannah. Of course Constance's baby must be settled somewhere else that day and the nursery made to look as if it has never been occupied, but Constance and Prudence have sworn they will take care of it themselves, as my generosity should not be burdened with additional obligation.

I daresay staff is excited that the most glittering event of the year is one in which they have had a hand, for all have worked under strange conditions for the last year, what with renovations and ghosts and children and whatnot. I am proud of them for staying the course. In fact, they do not know it but they shall each be presented with a bonus for their efforts, save for Hortense and the new staff, for Hortense is too short and the rest are too new. I was also pleased to find that Cook has taken Hortense under her wing and begun teaching her to read. As Hortense and Prudence's family is poor – there are 12 children – it was not possible for Hortense to attend school, working instead since the age of five, but is getting on very well. With all of the girls sprouting under my roof I feel as if I am headmistress of a school.

Another happy event has occurred which underscored how little attention I have paid to staff but also warmed my heart.

I was in the library seeing to some last-minute issues when Taylor entered and begged a moment. I was concerned that perhaps Foxx had broken another bone, but he assured me it was not the case. He began to shift from foot to foot, which was interesting. It had been a long time since Taylor had reverted to his younger mannerisms.

"Lady, I have news for you that you may not find to your liking but it cannot wait until after the Opening Ball."

I was concerned. "Has Zlot the mad Hungarian returned?"

He smiled. "No, Lady."

"Is Lady Shardley at the door to maim another of our best?"

He frowned and gulped. "No."

I was running out of ideas. "Has Sir Manfredson shown up and declared us all to be thieves and immediately turned out?"

"No." He began to look nervous and blurted, "Prudence and I are engaged and soon to be wed."

I was astonished. "You and Prudence are <u>engaged</u>?"

He mistook my shock. "When I was recovering from the accident we became good friends. She has shown all of the qualities one could ever want in a wife: loyalty, kindness and devotion. She's very pretty, too," he added with a shy smile.

I was stunned. I had no idea this sort of thing was going on under my own roof and said so. He had the grace to blush, and said he understood if he or Prudence had to be discharged, which is why he had come to me earlier rather than later, so I could begin to find suitable replacement(s).

I asked him to wait for a moment while I thought. I had some questions.

"Does Prudence like her post?"

"She does now that the ghosts' torment has ceased. I know you hate to hear it, but she says you are kind."

"I am not kind, I merely believe it in one's best interest to keep a well-functioning staff, Taylor."

"Of course, Lady."

"Except for the unfortunate incident with Lady Shardley, which shall not be repeated, for you shall not be sent away again, are you satisfied in your post?"

"From what I hear of other houses, I am working in the best house in England."

I am clearly not strict enough. But I had not made up my mind about what to do about my favourite footman and personal maid falling in love. "Do you mind living away from London?"

"I thought I would, but find the Hall and the work I do to be very satisfactory."

I pondered the issue further. I did not wish to lose either of them, for they have both proven their mettle, and it has taken so long to train them. I at last came to a decision.

"You may both stay, conditioned on your performances remaining at the high standard required." He positively beamed his happiness, for it is not the normal response one receives, especially for a Lady's maid.

I added (for I was feeling lighthearted and very much approving of love) that the wedding party could take place at the Hall in the ballroom, if they so desired, and that would be my wedding present to them, as well as a wedding gown for Prudence, as long as it was made by Gwynneth.

He was astonished, but my spirits were much improved, for though I had not seen Will, he had written me every day to tell me of his steady improvement and desire to see me.

With a smile larger than the ballroom Taylor readily agreed, thanked me and, completely forgetting his station, grabbed my hand and shook it as if I were a man, which made me laugh. I then told him that his future wife was surely dying to know my answer and that he should go to her. As he was dashing out the door I thought of one more thing.

The boathouse. It is not used, but is a perfect little house for a newly-wed couple. As long as it did not inconvenience anyone for Prudence and Taylor to be out there, they could have that space once married. And only once married. With that Taylor actually let out a huge whoop, and said I was the cruellest and most parsimonious of ladies, since hearing that seemed to make me happy, but was also the best, most well-thought of in the county. With that he ran out of the door and I could hear his feet running toward his love.

I felt a thrill of excitement for both of them. How lovely that they are to be married! Is it not the greatest of ironies that they would be allowed what I never shall?

A moment later Prudence burst through the door, ran back out, closed it, knocked and re-entered. I tried not to smile. She bobbed a curtsy and handed me a letter that had just arrived. I thanked her and turned back to my desk to read it. She coughed behind me and begged a moment.

She began to thank me for my kindness, until she saw the look on my face at the word. She began again, and thanked me for my callousness in allowing she and Taylor to both marry and continue working in the Hall. I was the most awful lady in history, and would be spoken ill of at every turn by staff. The gift of a wedding dinner and wedding gown were the most vicious and thoughtless gifts anyone could have ever given her, and thanked me so very much.

That pleased me terrifically, and I thanked her. I wrote out a quick note summoning Gwynneth back to the Hall: she had another gown to design, and asked Prudence to have it sent immediately. Then I opened the letter in my hand. It is simple enough to copy out here:

> Tonight.
>
> *W*

The letter meant I had to re-arrange the rest of my day, for I suddenly felt the urge to terrifically pamper myself with a bath and washing my hair, wearing a nightdress just arrived from the shoppe you recommended in Paris.

I found myself in my rooms quite early, having dismissed everyone for the evening, altogether content and happy, brushing my hair and smiling at a small carved cat that was once more on my vanity table.

Although Will arrived late in the evening and moved rather slowly, I found there were special delights in being with him again after such a terrible row and unexpected reconciliation. He has always brought me a token when he comes and that night he pressed something into my hand as he kissed it, before kissing me properly. It was the lead ball that had pierced him, thankfully cleaned of bits of himself. He grinned at my shocked face. "Perhaps if we argue again we could write each other," he said.

Our reunion was worth the wait, for Quince and I never had such a row, so I had never been acquainted with the happy act of making it up to each other, and Will seemed to feel the same. I showed him our chess set and explained why we had received it, bracing myself for remonstration about my indiscretion. After reading your note he said he understood, for he knows women need to confide in each other in ways that men do not, but such a gift and sentiment showed that you are a true friend, and he did not mind. I think he was as unwilling as I to argue again so soon.

Much time was spent in quiet re-discovery, curled up on cushions in front of the fire, for our separation made us both keen to make sure nothing had changed. Oddly enough, it seems improved.

We did not discuss the fight or our talk afterward, for I think we are both clear on what happened and would both prefer to leave it alone, for it makes us both look stupid, really. Insecurity is not a terribly attractive trait. We have found our way back to each other courtesy of a drunk woman and a piece of shot and that is enough. However, the making up to each other – I am thinking that perhaps we should argue more often.

I shall write you again before the week is out, and I remain

Your Fondest Friend,
Annabella

☙ Susannah's Injury ❧

10 October, 1821

Dear Susannah,

It is the day before the Opening Ball and I just received your letter. It is unthinkable what has happened to you! I am devastated I will not see you! It was of utmost importance that you be here.

How could you have fallen in the bath? It is a bath, one simply lies there in comfort. And broken your leg? It is untenable! Thank goodness Randy was there and heard your cries for help, else you could have found yourself with pneumonia as well. I am crushed that you find yourself so cruelly injured and that the most looked-forward to and honoured guest will not be in attendance. It is so kind of you to send Lord Carollton along without you, and I am very glad Randy will be able to attend you closely during this difficult time.

That means I shall have to re-think the promenade to dinner, but those silly things do not matter right now. What matters is that you lie still and rest your bones so they knit properly, for you owe me a visit. I only wish it were to be on what I believe will be the most interesting night the Hall has ever seen. So many arrangements have been made and I so wanted you to be apprised of them before the ball, but it is not possible to detail them now – it shall take pages and pages to describe the plans as well as my hopes for each one. If any go awry it will all go terribly anyway. You are therefore going to have to wait until it is over, and I shall tell you both the plans as well as the outcomes, for the Opening Ball is the only opportunity I may ever have to gather all of the people needed in a manner that shall not raise any alarm.

So please know that my next letter will be gargantuan in proportion, for it is much more than a mere ball now. It is a chance to Put Things to Rights, Susannah. Please pray that I am successful, for if I am, this ball shall be legendary.

I shall write as soon as I am able, and please know that I am

Your Friend and Defender,
Annabella

ᏤᏕ Things Go Awry ᏤᏕ

15 October, 1821

Dearest Susannah,

I finally have the opportunity to pen to paper and detail to you the events of the Opening Ball, but the events following the ball shall have to arrive separately, as I believe it would not fit into the post without crippling the carrier. Regardless, it shall cost you a small fortune. I am pleased your leg is knitting properly, but the ball, unforgettable as I believe it was, was diminished by your absence.

I know you are aggrieved that you missed what in retrospect may have been the most exciting event of the Season, but it was the most exciting for only a very few of us. Although I was initially astonished that Lord Carollton's only comment to you was that it was "nice," on further reflection I realize he is endeavoring to spare you the embarrassing details of his youth, not knowing you are well aware of them. Fortunately I am in possession of the entire tale, and shall tell you all, but in the same way I would were we sitting to lunch and I was able to regale you in full about every detail. I hope you do not mind and assure you that you will be satisfied, with all of your questions answered.

The night before the ball everything was in readiness: the Hall was polished to a high sheen, Mr. Seaverton had been able to finish the grounds (only barely, and the workmen were given an extra measure of stout when they finished their work). The food that could be readied beforehand had been, and the rest was as prepared as possible for the next day.

The wines were chosen, ices and sorbets packed the ice house, the linens were aired, silver glittered, the chandeliers sparkled, and the infamous piano into which Zlot had poured his heartache was a glossy black, ready for hopefully more cheerful songs to be played. The dance cards had arrived and only two dances were out of order. I was not nervous about the ball at all, which was strange. Do you remember how agitated I used to be before a dinner party for Quince? How I dithered! How I trembled! I suppose I was not nervous because I had so many other plans that needed to come off perfectly during the ball that I had not the time to be concerned about the ball itself.

Will arrived soon after dark, coming through the tunnel, almost restored to himself, although the scar shall always remind him of the importance of rifle safety. Everyone had been dismissed early, for morning would come soon enough and it was important for us to be well-rested. Because of this Will and I enjoyed a wonderful evening together, the fire crackling in the grate and candles providing a nice glow. I felt altogether content and marvelled at how life has changed in the last year.

It was later in the evening, we had finished our supper and I was scratching Will's back, up between his shoulders where he cannot reach, as it fair makes him purr with pleasure, whilst he rubbed my feet. Then I remembered. I had never given him his gift, for I tend to forget many things when we are together.

I asked him to close his eyes, fetched the box from my vanity and laid it in his hands. I told him he had given me such lovely things, and I wanted to do the same for him. He opened his eyes and did not say anything, but opened the box with care. When he took the watch out of the velvet bag and held it up by the chain, he still said nothing, merely staring at the fronts-piece with the tree spread across it. Then he opened it to see the watch itself and saw the small engraved "W" and "A" twined on the inside of the fronts-piece. He rubbed his thumb gently over it. "I've never seen a watch like this."

"It is the only one of its kind." The watch did not seem to please him, for his face was grave.

"Where did you find it?"

"I had it made. It was ready when I was in London last."

"That was when . . . You had it made before . . ." His voice trailed off. When I had been in London I thought I would never see him again.

"Yes."

"You purchased it anyway?"

"I could not bear to think of anyone else having it. And then I kept forgetting to give it to you." He did not say anything. Oh, we were going to have another argument, it was too formal, too expensive, I had emphasized the difference in our stations. I could forget I bought a custom-made gold watch, how many people can do such a thing? I was also forgetful enough to forget to give him a gift, which he would think meant I did not think much of him. It was not personal enough. So many of my gifts to Quince were met with indifference, although in retrospect many of my gifts were quite silly. I was thinking that I should have waited until Christmas or his birthday and not be allowed to choose gifts again on my own as I was deficient in the skill when I found myself the recipient of a kiss which was not remotely indifferent. Indeed, it took my breath away.

"It's beautiful, Bella. Not as beautiful as she who gave it, but beautiful."

"You like it?"

Will cradled it in his hand. "I'll treasure it. No one has ever given me such a gift. Thank you." I was so pleased he liked it and my pleasure must have shown on my face, for he kissed me again and then again, each time lingering more, still holding the watch in his hand. Then he asked if I would mind if he ignored it for a time, as he believed he needed very much, right that moment, immediately, to pay specific attention elsewhere, to show me just how he felt about what I had done.

If words give weight to acts, then Will was completely true in his. In fact, he found the watch so pleasing that we did not gain the bed for urgency, instead claiming the floor in front of the fire. Susannah, Highland cures will remedy whatever might ail you. Trust me.

It was not a little while that we showed our appreciation, and the ways in which he showed his were both very inventive and absolutely splendid. Splendid.

So splendid were they, in fact, that we both fell asleep much later. I woke first, blinking at the light streaming through the windows and sensed Will's body curled warmly around mine. I luxuriated in the feel of it, snuggling back under the coverlet when I realized he was still there. After dawn. On the day of the ball!

I woke him quietly and he did the same as I: looked at the light streaming through the windows and crawled back under the sheets. Then his eyes opened again and we stared at each other.

"We did not wake up," he whispered.

"I know that. And Prudence shall be along to begin preparations for a very long day." I was whispering for no good reason, no one could have heard us talking in normal tones, but it seemed the thing to do. Will looks lovely first thing in the morning, although I could never tell him that. I might be able to tell him he looked manly, but that is not the same, so I smiled instead, tracing the outline of his lip with my finger before kissing him. He picked up his watch from the table and looked at the time. It was only seven o'clock, he noted.

I did not realize it was still that early, and informed him Prudence would not be along for a full hour.

He observed that an hour was a pretty portion of time. As I agreed I found myself being drawn back under the coverlet. After a moment Will asked that I be gentle with him, else he would not be able to dance with me at the ball, for had I not noticed he had been shot? Scot though he is, there are limits, after all.

At eight o'clock Prudence arrived with my breakfast. Will had just left and I barely had time to put myself into a semblance of decorum. I called her in and she was fair skipping with excitement and nerves, and said I must be so thrilled, for my face was glowing and I had the largest smile she had seen in a long time. I thanked her and set to my breakfast with zeal, for I was famished.

Then I got ready for the day.

The Hall was bustling when I came down the stairway, there was staff everywhere, including an army of temporary help come from London the night before to assist. They were being shown by Taylor both the Hall and where everything was before all the preparations were checked and re-checked. I felt certain all would go well. I was reviewing the promenade list one more time – was Duke Twitwhistle above or below

Baron Theosophus? I could not remember, and was just looking up what war service meant when determining placement when Prudence announced Gwynneth. That is when the real business of the ball began.

I bade Prudence stay and took a good look at Gwynneth. She had indeed taken my instructions regarding appearance to heart and for the first time mine faltered a bit. To say she was slovenly would be an insult to those who are. She had reached new heights (or lows). I asked Prudence if she had noticed that her duties had been somewhat circumscribed for the day. She had assumed it meant I required extra help for myself. She was incorrect, as help so often is. Then I explained what was in store for Gwynneth.

Prudence was to spend the next three – well, perhaps several – hours bringing Gwynneth's aspect to an acceptable standard, although I privately thought I was hoping for more than could be achieved on such a timetable. She was to be bathed, her hair combed out, trimmed and forced into a semblance of a glossy sheen, and to be done up in a style appropriate for a young lady (but not a young Lady, for we are not miracle workers, after all).

The gown Gwynneth had made, the one for me to wear the next day, was to be altered to fit her, for it was for her and always had been. Gwynneth, who had been gaping through the first, made a startled squeak and sat down in a chair. I continued.

Prudence would then spend at least one hour with Gwynneth doing everything she could to teach her to walk, talk and sit like a young lady. Finally, she was to help Gwynneth make herself up with rouge, face paint and colour for her lips.

Gwynneth was going to the ball.

At the end of my startling speech Prudence stared and Gwynneth gulped. I reassured them that Gwynneth would not be going to the entire ball, but would need to attend a part of it, and until summoned she was to stay hidden in the servants' quarters, where no one who mattered would go.

I then sat down next to Gwynneth.

"Gwynneth, I know none of this makes sense to you and I wish I could explain it, but more than three hundred people will be arriving soon and I do not have time. Please trust that what I am doing is in the hope of helping yourself and Gabrielle. My reasons are too complicated to detail now. I did not tell you earlier for fear you would run off. But as bewildering as this is, please look back on our acquaintance and ask if anything I have ever asked of you or done has brought you to any harm. If the answer is no, then please indulge me in this request."

She sat for a long moment. Then she asked if I was going to play a joke on her.

"You are accustomed to those who would use you for sport, Gwynneth. I assure you that is not the case of everyone. I am trying to correct something, but I need your help. Can I count on you to do so?"

Another long moment went by before she nodded. Prudence was still gaping. I asked that they be done by six o'clock, for I would then be preparing myself. I made them both swear silence regarding the arrangements, and was quite stern with Prudence. If anyone asked what they were doing, Lady had gone off her head and there was nothing to do but indulge me.

It was going to be a very busy day.

As I oversaw the flowers being arranged and made sure the quality of Mr. Calloway's desserts was up to scratch (his chocolate peacock was stunning) I occasionally heard Cook screaming things from the kitchen. Lunch was a hurried affair, and I saw Gwynneth once or twice, both times appearing less and less filthy. She seemed nervous, so I told her to have a glass of sherry to fortify herself. I sent Constance in the carriage to get Gabrielle from the pub and take she and Hope to Prudence's mother, with the admonishment not to inform Gwynneth of it. Constance is getting better and better: she did not even blink at the unusual request.

The master of ceremonies arrived at five, we went over pronunciations and titles, through the promenade list for dinner and he made only two corrections, which is the best I have ever managed. He did note that the guest list was the most diverse he had ever seen. I replied that it was a very large Hall and there were many who wished to see it.

The conservatory was set up as a place to rest between dances and it looked as if the weather would hold so the doors from the ballroom to the veranda could be opened. The tennis courtyard had a temporary floor laid on it to protect the grass and was filled with candles for light and little tables and chairs, to be used for dining and conversation later. It was going to be a marvelous night.

Near five o'clock I had a quick bath and bolted down a cold supper as Prudence did my hair in the newest style. I was assured that Gwynneth was settled in her room and, although still bewildered, was too exhausted to think of running away. It took twenty-five minutes to finish my face and get into my gown, at which point it was just fifteen minutes until the ball. My jewels were the diamonds Quince gave me on each birthday, including the little circlet of them worked into my hair. My fan was of made of copper filigree worked into the shape of leaves and I wore white gloves, of course. As a final touch I added the pin Will had given me to my décolletage. It matched beautifully, for it perfectly set off the fabric of my gown. Gwynneth swathed me in the colours of autumn, finding a silk that was cross-woven with different hues of scarlet, gold, bronze and soft copper, so it shimmers and changes in colour according to the light. She embroidered a motif of leaves over it with copper thread. It was a spectacular gown, if I do say so myself.

After checking in the looking glass one more time that I was ready I reminded Prudence to stay near me at all times, so she could get Gwynneth and bring her to the door of the library when I told her to, and I would bring her in myself. Then I went to my jewels box, finding what I thought would be perfect. I asked to see Gwynneth, to make sure she looked all right.

Staff in the servants' quarters near fainted at the sight of their mistress walking through their halls, but managed to stifle their amazement and go about their business. Prudence let me into her room, where Gwynneth was waiting.

Susannah, she looked lovely. Prudence had done a beautiful job in scrubbing the detritus away to reveal a girl that is pretty underneath, and I told her so. Then I asked Gwynneth how she was feeling. She replied that her stomach felt queer and her hands were tingling, but she had never been in such a fine dress, even if she made it, and was concentrating on that to quell her fear. She told me that she was pleased I had chosen her to design my dress for such a special night.

I thanked her and told her she did not look completely dressed. She needed jewels, and I showed her the opals Quince gave me after what happened in Tuscany with the villa and the fire. She gasped and said she could not. I replied lightly that she could and would, and proceeded to help her put them on. They were perfect. No one would have ever known that she was Fallen. Quite frankly, no one would know that it was Gwynneth.

I took her hands in mine and told her she would be coming to the library later to meet some friends of mine. She would be asked some questions, and would not understand the reason for them, but I made her promise she would answer all of them without protest and honestly, no matter how unseemly they might seem. I added that everything, including Gabrielle's future, depended on her truthfulness, and I knew I could trust her. She merely gulped, for she was overwhelmed. I told Prudence to have Hortense keep Gwynneth company until Prudence fetched her, and added that an occasional drink of something to calm her nerves would not be unwarranted. I left them with only five minutes to check that everything was ready when the guests began to arrive.

They arrived in droves. It was extraordinary. Curiosity about the Hall and its owner was more abundant than I knew, for everyone arrived on time and before I knew it I was welcoming guest after guest. Prudence stayed close, occasionally bringing me champagne or lemonade to slake my thirst as the guests were announced throughout the Hall by the master of ceremonies.

There were a number of guests with whom you are acquainted: the Carson-Coopers, the Stavelys, the Galworthys and the Thatchers came up from London. There were also the Plumwythers, the Cotterwoods, the Kingsley-Wyttons, the Driversalls, so many people I could not name them all. Baroness Gurthwant could not attend, she was in full mourning, but I had written her to say how sorry I was she could not come. She wrote back to say I would have to have another ball next year, when she can leave her house again.

Mr. Castleton arrived. I hoped he would find someone amongst the ladies in attendance and wrote a note to that effect on his invitation, for I did not wish him to think the ball invitation was prelude to a more personal one. After he was announced he bowed to me and told me he thought me very kind to have included him on the guest list. He was a little stiff as he said it, and I am sure I hurt his feelings by making it so clear he should abandon hope for me, but I give him credit for coming regardless. Also in attendance was Mr. Gibberwilly, who would have climbed down the front of my gown if he could have done, Duke Theosophus and Baron Twitwhistle in tandem, the Bargesniffles, and awful Vicar Carthinston, who seemed to be calculating what the loss of my tithe was. Finally your husband arrived, preceded by Constable Pukeston (who looked as if the sole purpose of the ball was to denounce him, but came anyway). Mr. Sinclair arrived breathless from London (he was crucial to the enterprise) and very thankfully, Lord and Lady Shardley. It would have been a disaster had Lord Shardley not been dragged away from the London gaming tables to attend. Lady Shardley appeared recovered and whispered to me that Mr. Ploughgoode had told the constable his shooting was an accident, and for his generosity of spirit she had decided not to destroy his livelihood. I murmured that she was a gracious woman.

Then Will arrived. He looked decidedly splendid, wearing the dress kilt of his clan, a gorgeous linen with froth spilling through the throat of his formal waistcoat, and the gleam of a gold watch-chain going from one of the buttons to a pocket in it. I near swooned at the sight, I do not mind admitting. He was announced by the master of ceremonies and approached me with a smile. He bowed formally, I curtsied in response and he kissed my hand, saying there was not a lovelier woman in the county that night, nay, in England, and was so pleased he could attend. He saw I was wearing the pin he had given me and grinned. Lady Shardley saw him and fair ran to the other side of the room, which made me laugh.

I was distracted immediately after, for Sir Manfredson arrived, and left Will so I could at last meet the architect of my folly. Manfredson was escorted by his son, who thanked me profusely for including his father. Sir Manfredson looked stunned and said the Hall looked like he always dreamt it might. I offered to take him on a tour later so he could see what I had done and he accepted with grace, although he did refer to me as Queen Elizabeth, at which point his son steered him away.

It soon became a whirl of conversations, and although I could not spend much time with any one person, it seemed to be going beautifully. All too soon we were sitting to supper. I noted with satisfaction that everyone seemed to be enjoying themselves, even Constable Pukeston, who had relaxed somewhat when he had not been announced as Lillienda Stonekup, County Degenerate. There was an awkward moment when Mr. Castleton brought up the musicale – thankfully leaving out who had attended with him. Will looked angry until I caught his eye and fingered the pin on my gown. At that his shoulders relaxed and he smiled. That evening now seems so long ago!

As it turned out, many other guests had seen Lillienda, and Constable Pukeston was blushing furiously at the extravagant praise paid to "Miss Stonekup," which turned to a stricken countenance when Miss Stonekup's gowns were discussed in less complimentary fashion. The gown she wore for the finale was particularly noted. I kept my head down to hide my smile.

When supper ended the master of ceremonies announced that the dancing would begin.

I stood alone in the middle of the floor and looked about. It was beautiful – jewels shimmering, gowns sweeping, everyone had worn their finest. It looked much as I imagined it would. Up until that moment I had not looked at the group of musicians from London who were providing the music. As Duke Twitwhistle tottered toward me with the odd hitching step he has whenever he does not use his cane, I saw that the piano player was none other than Zlot, the deranged piano tuner. I cast my eye about for Constable Pukeston. This was not foreseen, but there was nothing to be done about it; I was standing in the middle of a crowd I had invited.

Duke Twitwhistle was finally standing before me and bowed. As the most senior there he had to lead me in the first dance. I had chosen a waltz in deference to his toe. I curtsied, and wondered if this dance might be rather strange, for he cannot walk properly without his toe. He looked nervous, but managed to step forward well enough. The music began and the crowd fell silent, waiting for us to begin. My fears about his toe seemed silly as he took the first step with the lesser foot.

On the second step the duke tripped, lurched, gasped, let go of me (in more uncharitable moments the word "threw" comes to mind) and I flew through the air.

I shall never know how, but I did not land on the floor with my gown over my head. Will realized what could happen and moved swiftly to catch me. Even with what I was told later was a spectacular dive I found myself sitting on Will with my gown somewhat rucked up. Of course, that is far from the first time that has ever happened, but I had never dreamt it might happen in the ballroom. In front of an audience. Thank God the underskirt stayed in place! And Will's kilt, as well. I shudder to think what may have happened had our respective skirts wound up over our heads, although I have the feeling most of the women in attendance would not have minded.

The music faltered for a moment, the audience gasped as one, I tried to behave as if nothing had happened while I scrambled off Will, he helped me to my feet and the duke stood mortified. There was a dread silence from the crowd.

Will waited as I got my gown back in order, then took my arm and walked me back to the duke as if nothing had happened. He bowed and silently presented me to Twitwhistle, who appeared to wish someone would shoot him, and whispered to Will, "Thank you, sir. That was very agile." Will inclined his head in acknowledgement and began to step back, but the duke grabbed his arm and hissed, "You dance with her!"

"I'm sorry?" Will was startled, as was I. The musicians continued to play and I wished they would stop, it was silly to keep on when no one was dancing.

The duke shook Will's arm. "You do it! This damned toe of mine – if I pitch her again –"

I could not believe I was interrupting a duke, but this did seem to be a conversation that should have been had before the dancing, flinging and catching began, without a room filled with onlookers. "Duke Twitwhistle, Mr. Ploughgoode may agree to cut in the very moment the dancing begins by everyone else, but to give up now might be seen as less than gallant." He stared at me, then nodded in dismal agreement. Will withdrew and I realized the song was being played again – if it was not the dance cards would be useless.

The duke took me in his arms once again, preparatory to a second and, I hoped, more successful attempt. There was such a collective intake of breath from the crowd that I was surprised the candles in the chandeliers were not snuffed. I whispered that the duke could perhaps take very, very, very small steps.

"My deepest, most abject and sincere apologies, Lady," he whispered.

"It is not a ball until something untoward happens, duke. Now I need not be concerned what it shall be." I smiled at him in what I hoped was an encouraging fashion.

The music was continuing but we were not moving. "My feet will not move," he stammered, sounding panicked.

"All we have to do is begin, Duke Twitwhistle. After that no one will notice if you leave the floor."

"God, I hope so," he lisped, sweat beading on his upper lip. He took a large breath and a very small step. I remained upright and people began to applaud as we went in a tiny circle.

As I predicted, the moment we began to dance people streamed onto the floor. The drama was finished so no one was paying any attention to us at all, instead concentrating on the possible drama they might find with their own partner.

Suddenly Will was at the duke's shoulder. "Duke Twitwhistle, would you mind terribly. . ." he murmured.

"I would be quite grateful, sir." He stepped back from me and Will bowed.

Will was quite formal. "Lady Upton-Church? Would you do me the honour of accompanying me in a dance?"

Duke Twitwhistle bowed to us both. "I would beg your leave to end our dance now, Lady, to preserve your health."

"Of course, sir. But I do thank you for your courage." It was brave to have begun again after such a disastrous start.

Will smiled and took me in his arms. It was something I had not dreamt possible in public, let alone in my ballroom, crowded with titles and neighbours, none of whom were throwing rocks at us and screaming that I was a harlot and he some kind of kept man. I realized they thought the smile on my face had to do with the success of the ball thus far.

So for lack of a duke's toe, Will and I danced together in public for the first dance of my first ball, whirling amongst the other dancers, no one looking askance or twittering behind a fan. It was wonderful. Well, we danced part of the dance, perhaps an entire minute. He is a lovely dancer, and I felt entirely happy. When the music died away – all too soon – he stepped back and bowed low as I curtsied.

"Thank you, Mr. Ploughgoode. I do not know what I should have done had you not caught me."

He proffered his arm and continued in a whisper. "Had I known his injury would allow me to dance with you I would have shot off his toe myself, Lady." We kept our voices low so as not to be overheard.

"You look quite handsome tonight."

"You are stunning. Your hair –" His voice died away.

I patted at it with alarm. "Did it get ruined when –"

He smiled. "Reminds me of another night you looked to have diamonds in it."

I am sure I blushed. "That is the most romantic thing you have ever said to me," I whispered. He actually blushed back. "I must take your leave now, but please accept my most sincere thanks for . . . everything."

"Accepted," he said, and continued in a whisper as he escorted me from the floor, arm tucked through his. "I'd like to say that I'd not have done tha' for just anyone. I'm chivalrous, but no' overly so." He grinned. "Had it been Lady Shardley, she'd still be on the floor."

With that I needed to find Constable Pukeston and warn him about Zlot. When I found him he was not dancing, but paying close attention to the musicians, looking as if he may actually approach them.

"Constable Pukeston, may I have a word?"

"Of course, Lady." His voice was courteous, but I could see droplets of sweat beading on his brow.

"Please stop being so nervous every time you see me, Constable. It is rather insulting. And damp."

"Yes, Lady," but he did not stop perspiring.

We were walking toward the library when the younger Manfredson came down the hall at a near-run, stopping in front of us. "Lady Upton-Church, there is a difficulty."

"What is wrong?"

"My father, Lady. He's gone missing."

Constable Pukeston was immediately officious. "What do you mean?"

"He said he wanted to meet the musicians, sir. No one has seen him since. He's, well, he's addled, sir. Thought you were Queen Isabella." This was to Constable Pukeston, which I found amusing. Had Sir Manfredson been to a musicale in the recent past? My amusement turned to consternation. Did I not have enough to attend to without a mad architect roaming loose? Was I not already occupied with enough other tasks?

Pukeston turned to me. "Fear not, Lady Upton-Church. We shall form a search party to find him. He cannot have got far, and shall be back safely in no time." I believe he was grateful that the issue was a very old, very mad guest who had wandered off and needed rescue. He turned back to Manfredson. "We shall begin with the musicians."

"Constable Pukeston, thank you, but that is not why I wanted to see you." I saw Foxx standing at the door to the conservatory and waved him over to us. He was dispatched to form a discreet search party, so as not to upset the other guests, and to start the search near the musicians.

The younger Manfredson said he would join them, and apologized for the upset, but his father had been better the last few days. His family thought no harm could come by attending, as he had been so looking forward to it.

I said I understood and that we would do everything possible to find him without alarming the other guests.

As Foxx and the younger Manfredson began to make their way back to the ballroom I gestured for Constable Pukeston to precede me into the library. Once the door was closed and locked I told him to sit down.

"Constable Pukeston, I thought you should be aware of a disturbed person who is in attendance tonight."

"Of course, Sir Manfredson."

"Yes, well, you should be aware of <u>another</u> disturbed person in attendance."

"Please provide the details, Lady Upton-Church."

"He is the pianist. I did not know was one of the musicians, whom I was given to understand are from London. He has developed a mania for someone."

"Is it yourself?"

"Oh, no. He is passionately, desperately in love with . . . your sister. Lillienda."

Daniella paled. "Love?"

"He was banned from the theatre where she sings, sir. He had been sending notes, writing love songs, and finally – "

"Stood and declared his love in during a performance," Daniella murmured.

"You have heard of him."

"Yes." He began to perspire more heavily.

I tried to behave as if we were having a normal conversation. "I think it might be a very bad thing, Constable, to personally interview musicians, or talk to them at all about their craft, given your relationship to Lillienda." There was a long pause.

"You are a very surprising woman, Lady Upton-Church," he finally said.

"People keep saying that; I cannot imagine why," I said with a smile, hoping to keep the conversation light.

"I had my things packed, you know," he said, looking down at his hands. "And found it an unnecessary task."

"It is always good to inventory one's belongings, I think."

He looked at me with confusion. "Why did you keep silent?"

Oh, goodness, it appeared he might starting thanking me, which I tried to prevent. "In case one of my guests went missing and I needed a constable to help find him."

I was not successful, although my response did coax a smile from him. "Thank you, Lady."

"It was my pleasure." With that he left to join the search party and I went back to the ball, hoping Sir Manfredson would be found unharmed.

Guests not dancing were taking air on the veranda, or a rest in the conservatory, or in the games room taking to billiards or cards. It was all going very, very well. I danced with Constable Pukeston and was quite relieved to find that there was no confusion as to who would lead. I danced with

Mr. Sinclair, who beamed throughout as I pointed out various girls worth pursuit. I even managed to partner again with Will during a quadrille, seemingly quite by accident but entirely on purpose, ignoring the fact that he seemed quite popular with the eligible ladies there (and several ineligible ladies as well), as he did not seem to care. It would appear his gallantry during the first dance had enhanced what is a stellar reputation despite his station.

During our dance I managed to whisper to him that I would be gone for some time and not to worry, but I very much hoped he would not exhaust himself dancing, as I would like to engage his attentions in a more personal way after the ball ended. He smiled and said he would never dream of refusing the hostess of such a smashing ball.

And it was, Susannah. You would have loved it!

I danced with Baron Theosophus, a rather odious task, and then with your husband. I hope you do not mind. He sent your regards again and reminded me that I am expected to come to Paris soon to see you. You are a very lucky woman, Susannah.

After a time it was clear that everyone was occupied with each other, and would not notice if the hostess disappeared.

It was time.

I stepped to the side and my hands began shaking. Perhaps I had taken on too much in one evening, perhaps I was not as up to snuff as I believed when recklessly bashing about in other people's lives. I must have paled, for I saw Will looking at me across the room with concern, and Prudence appeared at my elbow.

There was nothing to be done; everyone needed was there and it was up to me to actually do what I had so carefully planned. I asked Prudence to fetch me some champagne, which she brought with an alacrity that made me glad I had decided to retain her even if she was to be married. I asked her to make sure that brandy was set out in the library, along with my best crystal snifters, and to make sure the room was cleared out. I nodded to Will to show I was fine and he continued talking with Mr. Castleton (how I would have loved to know what that conversation entailed!) and began the chore of gathering those concerned.

Those tapped? Lord Carollton, your darling husband. Then Mr. Sinclair, who was told to bring the papers I had requested, and Lord Shardley brought up the rear, which I found appropriate under the circumstances. When they had each been asked to go to the library for a special toast they disengaged themselves from their various conversations. Mr. Sinclair looked excited. When I was sure they were on their way I told Prudence to keep a close eye on the Bargesniffles and Vicar Carthinston, they would be needed when I gave the word. Foxx trotted past me, nodding a "no" to my raised eyebrow regarding Manfredson. Hopefully he would be found soon. I took a deep breath and went to the library.

The men had not waited for their hostess to pour themselves each a glass of my lovely brandy. When I entered they toasted me as the hostess of the best ball of the Season. I thanked them and bade them sit. I said that I wanted a moment to speak with them, for although they were not all acquainted, they would be in a moment. They each sat in chairs arranged so I was facing a little audience looking up at me. I felt a bit faint, and pressed my hands together. Then I began.

I told of Lord Carollton's indiscretion 18 years before. He looked pained, even as Lord Shardley slapped him on the back and said that those things happened, nothing to be embarrassed about. I ignored him, and detailed how Lord

Carollton had provided as best he was able for the issue that sprang from his indiscretion, even as he looked as if he would like to crawl under his chair. Lord Shardley looked up and barked at me.

Who did I think I was to bring up such a thing? I was only a woman, after all, and such things did not concern me.

I replied that it did concern me, and if he would have a measure of patience all would unfold. He threw back the rest of the brandy and held his glass out to Mr. Sinclair to pour another, as he was closest to the bottle.

That would have been the end of it, I continued (a bit shakily, but I had started, and now it would have to be finished), save for two things: the woman had never told her child of the arrangements made for her, before dying suddenly three years ago. At this your husband looked sad. I continued.

Without her mother, the poor child was forced to go to work as a maid.

At Sumwattle Estate.

In the kitchens.

At each further clarification Lord Shardley looked more and more nervous, which I uncharitably enjoyed.

I then told of Gwynneth's Fall, but couched it in terms that I thought might make it less scandalous, leaving out the part about her screaming for her lover to rescue her.

When I finished that part of the telling it was very quiet and your husband was looking at Lord Shardley in a decidedly less friendly way. Lord Shardley did not appeared fazed. He said he was not sure who I was talking about, and who would take the word of some stupid downstairs girl over that of a Lord?

I continued.

The poor girl was flung out into the street and the world with nothing save a dowry of what she was not aware. Then I begged a moment, poked my head out of the door and told Prudence to get the Bargesniffles and Vicar Carthinston. She ran off and I returned to the room.

However, I went on, aware of how warm the room suddenly seemed, there were others aware of both the indiscretion and Lord Carollton's generosity so many years ago, and knew those arrangements would have profited handsomely given the times.

At that point Rufus Bargesniffle, his father and Vicar Carthinston were brought in. I whispered to Prudence to next fetch Gwynneth and keep her in the hallway until summoned. Your husband looked amazed as he looked at the elder Mr. Bargesniffle and said, "You were at Sumwattle Estate."

Lord Shardley added, "He was let go for sloth and eavesdropping." The three new attendees looked confused. I cleared my throat so that all eyes were on me.

Mr. Bargesniffle had been employed next at White's in London, at the same time Lord Carollton was staying there. Bargesniffle started at my information. I added it seemed his habit of eavesdropping was put to profitable use there, and Bargesniffle had become aware of the arrangements made for the girl. With that in mind, when he heard at his pub what had happened, he made his son Rufus propose to the girl, as the laws regarding property would then give Rufus the holdings that were hers. Mr. Sinclair looked with contempt at Mr. Bargesniffle, which I thought boded well for the overall enterprise. I told them Vicar Carthinston had been bought to do the "honours," and wed them. At this everyone looked at Vicar with surprise and not a little disgust. He almost spoke and then thought better of it, instead sinking into a chair and pouring himself a brandy. I realized I might well need brandy myself before this was done.

Lord Carollton looked horrified and said, stumbling slightly to keep his own part in it quiet, that he could not believe the generosity of a peer could be so debased. Mr. Sinclair nodded agreement.

However, I interjected, the girl's insult was not yet complete, for Rufus Bargesniffle could not even be bothered to consummate the marriage, so taken was he with a girl from Kingston Woods, that he had met on the very day of his wedding.

Rufus suddenly piped up, for he was not going to be accused of not being able to be bothered with relations with his wife.

"She's disgustin'," he spat out. "Filthy an' altogether awful. I only married her because me dad said I 'ad to, so's we could have the income. 'E never said I 'ad to like her." That was exactly what I had hoped for, Susannah! It was perfect! Mr. Bargesniffle rounded on his son.

"You did not consummate?"

"You said not to until the baby came, so it wouldn't get all bounced about and maybe lose it, and after she had it she were awful. You said yourself she smelt like the stables!"

"You stupid boy!" Bargesniffle realized what was afoot due to his son's failure.

"Stupid! No man could 'ave gotten near her and been able to do it – I tried twice – it were – she was covered in dirt and bits of things!"

The elder Bargesniffle tried to recover the damning admission. "Of course you did, you told me you did. They signed the marriage contract and it states that consummation occurred."

"Then why did he just deny it?" I tried to sound dim.

Mr. Bargesniffle was clever. "This is not a fit conversation to have in front of a lady, Lady." He faltered. "He's embarrassed, of course. Have you seen her?"

"I am inclined to believe he speaks freely when he has had champagne, but not when signing a contract that will give him a handsome dowry."

"That is ridiculous," Mr. Bargesniffle spat out.

"It is an easily remedied question. I would like to introduce Rufus' wife, Gwynneth Bargesniffle." I opened the library door and Gwynneth entered, walking fairly well, looking beautiful. She came and stood next to me, and I could see her begin to tremble when her eye fell upon Lord Shardley. He did not look at her, instead glaring at me.

The perfect "O"s made by the rest of the men made me very glad of the time taken to clean up poor Gwynneth.

"Gwynneth? Was your marriage ever consummated?"

"What?" She stared at me, this was a horrible question to put to her in front of anyone, but especially in front of Men, most especially the one who had ruined her. Actually, several of them had ruined her, but in different ways.

"Please answer, Gwynneth."

"No, Lady." She looked down as if embarrassed.

"Why did you sign the marriage contract saying you had?"

Her voice was low. "They said it would keep my babe – Gabrielle – from bein' illegitimate. If I didn't marry Rufus, they'd tell everyone I was a whore withou' the sense to keep from getting' – the way I got." Her voice dropped. "They said we'd starve." I was shocked at the manipulation, but now was not the time to discuss it.

"Did you consummate?" I asked again.

"No. Rufus said he might have to marry me but he'd . . . " She looked pleadingly at me. "Do I have to say?"

Rufus Bargesniffle broke in. "This is insane –"

Surprisingly enough it was Mr. Sinclair who interrupted him. He was started to understand why I had asked him to do the things he had done before the Ball. "I should like to hear her answer, sir," he said in a quiet voice. Rufus looked at Mr. Sinclair's face and closed his mouth. Mr. Sinclair turned to Gwynneth and spoke gently. "It's all right. Tell us what he said."

Gwynneth stood for a moment, took a deep breath and stared at a point on the wall. "He said he might have had to marry me but he . . . he wouldn't . . . he wouldn't put his . . . his – oh, I'm so sorry, but you said I have to say – he wouldn't put his cock in such a filthy, cheap woman as me," she finished in a rush. I gasped and tried to not think about bashing Rufus over the head with the heaviest book in the library.

Mr. Sinclair looked with a great deal of disgust at Rufus. "That is how you speak to your wife?" I have never heard a tone like that from him. It was quite steely.

Rufus turned on Gwynneth. "What kind of whore uses words like that in public!?" He turned to us. "She proves she's no decent girl right now!"

"But it's what you said!" She cried back. "And that's not the worst you said, was it?" Oh, goodness, she seemed to have found her spine at exactly the wrong moment.

"That's no one's business but ours!" snarled Rufus and moved toward her. Mr. Sinclair stood and stepped between them, which brought Rufus up short.

Mr. Sinclair spoke quite clearly. "Stand back, Mr. Bargesniffle. You'll conduct yourself like a gentleman in this house, although you shall never be one." Rufus stood glaring at him, which did not faze Mr. Sinclair in the least. "Mr. Bargesniffle, sit down. Now." I was astonished. Had Mr. Sinclair been possessed? Mr. Sinclair's voice was so firm that Rufus sat down without a word. Mr. Sinclair then turned to Gwynneth. "Gwynneth, I am very sorry." She gaped at him as he bowed before returning to his seat.

I tried to remember what I had been about to say, for things were going far astray from what I had imagined. Everyone was suddenly developing a spine, which did not bode well for what I wanted to happen next. I cleared my throat to get everyone to stop looking at each other with murder in their eyes and at me instead. Unfortunately when they did some of them still had murder in their eyes.

Suddenly Vicar Carthinston leapt into the fray. "The debate is irrelevant. The marriage contract was signed, and the baptism records will show Rufus as the father. It is a true and proper marriage." I tried very hard not to smile.

"Damn it!" The elder Mr. Bargesniffle realized what had been done. He whirled on Gwynneth. "You . . . you planned this, you ungrateful little whore –"

Suddenly Mr. Sinclair was grabbing that Mr. Bargesniffle by his chitterling and shaking him. "You'll not speak that way in this house!"

Mr. Bargesniffle ignored him, yelling over Mr. Sinclair's shoulder at Gwynneth. "Wanted to postpone the baptism until later out of sentiment?! You lying, whoring, piece of –" He stopped speaking when Mr. Sinclair slammed him against the wall.

Mr. Sinclair's voice was as quiet as Mr. Bargesniffle's had been loud. "Another word, Mr. Bargesniffle, and I will make sure you live to regret it. I can ruin your life in ways you cannot imagine. Do you understand me?"

"But –"

"I am only looking for an excuse to do so. Sit down and shut up."

Mr. Bargesniffle sat down stiffly, glowering at Mr. Sinclair. I was astonished that my seemingly genteel solicitor had such mettle. However, he and I were the only ones who were aware of what was next.

I regained everyone's attention. "It is clear that the marriage is a sham." Vicar Carthinston was staring at Gwynneth's bosom. It was time to finish this. "A fraud has been perpetrated on the Church and our fair county, and I request an annulment, for the grounds have been met." I readied myself for the reaction to the *coup de grace*. "Gwynneth is seventeen, and no one gave consent, which she legally cannot give herself until she is eighteen."

That caused a fair flurry on everyone's part, I do not mind telling you, Susannah. Two of my crystal snifters were dropped while various cries of "Oh!" and "God save the Regent, the King, whoever!" bounced around the room. When everyone regained themselves I asked Mr. Sinclair if I was correct. He said it was, glaring at Rufus for good measure. Then the elder Bargesniffle spoke.

"The marriage was true and proper, you're only saying mad things because you're mad, everyone knows it, living in a haunted house and poking your head into the business of other people, why should you be believed?"

Lord Shardley's voice was as unexpected as it was tired. "Oh, for God's sake, man. Give it up."

I turned to Gwynneth. "Was Rufus a proper husband?"

Gwynneth looked at Rufus and said he was not. She was a serving girl for the family business and nothing more. Nothing.

Rufus began to protest but I shushed him, and asked Gwynneth what she knew of her father.

"I never met him, but mother said he was kind and tried to do the right things." She brightened. "Oh, and he had a birthmark shaped like Italy on the left side of his bum."

That was more information than was strictly necessary, but there was nothing to be done about it.

I asked if Rufus had been a true husband. Gwynneth said no, he was not, not by the standards she understood. I asked one final question: Did she wish to remain married? She looked at him for a long moment and gave the perfect answer:

"Not to man who don't treat me like a man should treat his wife, who spends himself with other women and calls me a whore."

I turned a callous eye upon the vicar, who looked as if he was going to be sick on my newly polished floors, and asked if what he had heard provided grounds for annulment. He was clearly about to say no when Mr. Sinclair spoke.

"It meets all legal and, as far as I can tell, moral grounds. I hope the Church agrees. To compound one sin with another does not erase either, or so I have learnt in my own Church." I was so proud of him!

Carthinston was trapped and he knew it. He muttered that it met the grounds. Mr. Sinclair drew papers from his bag.

They were annulment papers, prepared and ready for signature. The elder Bargesniffle began to protest and Vicar Carthinston rallied to save his tattered reputation.

He had tricked by the Bargesniffles and would be not be party to such a union now that he knew the real reason for it. He would sign the papers and the Bargesniffles should as well. Mr. Sinclair filled in the blanks while we watched.

Gwynneth signed with a trembling hand. I was the witness, along with Prudence, who was dragged in, signed with an air of bewilderment and then immediately dispatched. The annulment was complete. Mr. Bargesniffle looked annoyed but the gleam in his eye told me he thought me rather stupid.

Then Mr. Sinclair took out a second set of papers with a broad smile. The second set reinstated Gwynneth's dowry in full, with interest, and an additional payment of 100 pounds for defrauding her in the first place.

Mr. Bargesniffle began to protest until I reminded him that Constable Pukeston could be brought in and we could discuss the legality of it with him. Thoroughly. Gwynneth started to swoon then and had to sit down. Mr. Sinclair scrambled to his feet and helped her to his chair. He then filled in the blanks properly and quietly, so very quietly, everyone signed.

As Mr. Sinclair notarized the documents I dismissed the Bargesniffles and Vicar Carthinston from the room and from my house. They were not welcome now or ever in the future. I added that Gwynneth would not be returning to the pub, she would be staying at the Hall.

Gwynneth began to hiccup, so as the vicar and the Bargesniffles were escorted out, Mr. Sinclair rubbed her hands in his and inexplicably thumped her on the back once or twice while murmuring apologies for the poor treatment she had received from those men.

I asked both Lords if they had anything to say to Gwynneth. Lord Shardley "hrmmphed" and looked away, not even deigning to lay eyes on one whom he had so casually ruined. Lord Carollton stared at her for a moment. Finally he came to a decision.

"Gwynneth, I am very sorry for what happened to you, and hope that the actions of my peers does not make you look with a jaundiced eye on your betters, for there are many who would have never allowed such a thing to happen, and once they knew of the treatment you received, moved heaven and earth to rectify it," he said, looking at me.

I must confess I had hoped for a tender family reunion, with your husband confessing the bond between them, but it was not to be. He simply looked sad.

I told Gwynneth that Prudence would take her to a room that had been prepared for her, and I would talk to her on the morrow, for she had been through quite enough and should have some time alone to reflect on it all. I explained where Gabrielle was, and that she would be brought to Wetmoor in the morning. Gwynneth stared at me for a moment, and suddenly threw her arms around me, whispering, "Thank you, thank you, I don't know why you did what you done, but thank you." She then let go, stepped back and curtseyed. Her exit was unsteady, and I was glad I had a bottle of port left in her room.

When she had left Lord Shardley made as if to stand.

"There is one more set of papers to sign," I said, even as Mr. Sinclair reached into his bag one more time. "Lord Shardley, gentlemen take responsibility for their actions."

"What are you talking about?" he asked in a low voice.

"You should take responsibility for your child, sir."

"How dare you!" Lord Shardley's face was turning purple.

I was surprised when your husband spoke up, Susannah. "How dare you! Lady Upton-Church is trying to right a wrong, a wrong which you began. If the Bargesniffles had to pay for their transgressions you should as well! You've saved a fortune in mistresses because you won't pay – this time you will."

Lord Shardley looked very put out. "How much?"

Mr. Sinclair cleared his throat. "Two hundred pounds."

Lord Shardley laughed. "Two hundred! That is insane!"

Your husband countered, "That is fair! Most men spend far more than that on mistresses!"

"It's why I don't keep them! One hundred pounds! That's all! The girl was already paid for silence – she should have to forfeit that! She didn't keep silent!"

Mr. Sinclair stared at Lord Shardley in astonishment. "The huge and helpful sum of five pounds, given by your <u>wife</u>, who did not know the truth of the matter, was included in the Bargesniffle settlement. She was good enough to have but not good enough to honour? One hundred ninety pounds."

"One twenty-five."

Mr. Sinclair remained adamant. "The daughter of a Lord should be provided enough for a decent life, schooling and dowry despite her legitimacy. One hundred eighty-five."

Apparently the gaming tables have not been kind to Lord Shardley. He refused.

Your husband looked at him with disgust. "You didn't know her parentage, that's true. But you ruined her nonetheless, and refuse to make it right. It's not the behaviour of a gentleman, Hubert." He went to the desk and began to write. "I took responsibility when the same thing happened to me. That's what a gentleman does." I wondered why he was writing a letter as he spoke, but things had already gone so oddly.

Lord Shardley poured another brandy for himself. "If you want to throw good money after bad, Carollton, it's entirely your affair. Her child could be anyone's."

Your husband's head snapped up. "Are you saying my daughter is depraved?"

Lord Shardley's answer was horrible. "What did you expect from such a girl, with a whore for a mother? Of course she was easy; she followed the example of her own parentage."

Mr. Sinclair and I both gaped, and I began to have a sinking feeling. This was not an argument. These were fighting words. They would come to blows, I could feel it in my bones. Your husband stood.

"Lord Shardley, your actions are a blight upon this county, and not only where Gwynneth is concerned. You are perhaps the strongest reason it is so hard to find good help. You have behaved with dishonour to your wife, your house and your peers." Lord Shardley was "toshing" and "shushing" throughout the recitation of grievances, until Lord Carollton reached the end of his statement. "You have called my daughter wanton, when you yourself caused her ruin. You refused to take responsibility for your issue. Your behaviour is not that of a gentlemen, it is the behaviour of a cad, and I challenge you to a duel." He threw a piece of paper into Shardley's face.

I gasped, this was not foreseen! I was not the only one, Mr. Sinclair looked as if he were going to fall out of his chair. Lord Shardley read the paper quickly and peered at your husband as if he had just sprouted antlers.

"What the hell for? I'm sorry the silly girl is your daughter, had I known it I'd not have touched her, but to act like her downfall was my fault is stupid." He threw the letter back.

Lord Carollton replied with ice in his voice. "You are a dissolute lout with no honour and can only prove that statement wrong by a duel. I am her father, and I demand satisfaction."

Mr. Sinclair coughed, trying to remind them that a lady was present. He was ignored, and I was trying not to faint.

Lord Carollton stood. "If you do not meet me at dawn on the veranda, then the charges not only stand but are proved true. You should find yourself a second immediately, although it's doubtful someone with no scruples can be that quickly found. Perhaps Vicar Carthinston will volunteer."

He turned to me and apologized for speaking coarsely in front of me and for not having taken more care in making sure that Gwynneth was safe, which he would always regret. Lord Shardley strode to the desk and began writing his own letter. I have no idea why they were both writing letters in the midst of an argument. Your husband then asked if there was a room in the Hall where he could stay so he would be refreshed enough to duel come morning, even as Shardley handed his own letter to Lord Carollton.

"I accept," was all he said.

Your husband looked grim and said it would have to be in the morning, for he had to return to Paris the next afternoon.

Shardley sighed and drained his glass. He informed your husband that, as the accused, he had the right to choose time and place, but if the duel had to be at dawn, the weapons would be pistols, and the duel would take place on Wetmoor grounds, so there would be no question of Lord Carollton running away.

Mr. Sinclair actually gasped at the insult, and your husband was very quiet when he agreed. Both men looked at me and I nodded. What else could I do?

Lord Carollton asked if I had dueling pistols.

I told him Quince had a brace of pistols, I would make sure they were ready by dawn, and Taylor would see him to a room in the guest wing. He smiled and patted my hand. "Do not worry, Annabella. I have right on my side."

I know you will want to kill me for this, Susannah, but as I am sure you can see from my handwriting, my arm is about to fall off from the story thus far. I must ice and rest it, so I will post this now, and resume my tale when I can grip my pen, for the duel was not like any duel of which I have ever heard. And so very much happened before and after the duel as well!

I will close now, put my seal on this letter and have it sent by courier, and the next and then the next if that is what it takes for you to have the whole story of how your husband courageously defended the honour of his daughter, even if she may never know of it.

Your Very Sore-Handed Friend,
Annabella

☙ Things Go Terribly Awry ❧

16 October, 1821

Dearest Susannah,

I have had the opportunity to rest my wretchedly lacking in stamina writing hand and am continuing my tale where I left it last, and beg your forgiveness for any caesura you may have experienced in not knowing all that happened at my ball.

When I wrote you yesterday, your husband had challenged Lord Shardley to a duel and been accepted, and it was to occur at dawn at my own Hall.

Then things got complicated. Both men went to find seconds. Mr. Sinclair assured me that he would never divulge the truth of Gwynneth's parentage, for the information was obtained by accident, in the heat of the moment, but it did explain why she had an elegant air. He added that I was a very interesting person who was now going to be responsible for overseeing the duel itself, as it was I who had been the instigator of the proceeding.

Oh, my. I was going to have to supervise a duel. This was not how I planned on things turning out. There was supposed to be private censure of Lord Shardley as well as reconciliation between Gwynneth and her father, and a happy ending, not a duel to the possible death between two old friends.

I also had 350 guests dancing, drinking and dining in my Hall who needed attention.

I did not know what to do, for I have never attended a duel, and told Mr. Sinclair so. He explained that the men would bring seconds, and surgeons, but I needed to know the laws of duelling in order to insure it was proper, one that would bring satisfaction to everyone. He was abashed that he did not know what they were.

I am not a font of that knowledge, either, I snapped.

He said he knew only that the rules were strict, perhaps someone at the ball with discretion could help, and if there was a surgeon in attendance he should be retained.

I might have blood spilled on my Hall. You know how blood makes me feel faint. Mr. Sinclair added that as mistress of the Hall, and no husband, it was up to me. I could refuse and the men would find somewhere else to go and shoot one another.

That observation led to my cursed curiosity raising its large head. If I did not host (I have not a clue what the proper word is) the duel, I may not know the outcome for a very long time. That thought settled it, for I very much wanted to see how it All Turned Out In The End.

I thanked Mr. Sinclair and told him I would take care of everything, and would notify him of the outcome. He looked disappointed, and said he would be happy to stay, especially as he could provide legal counsel afterward, especially if someone died. I had not thought of that, and told him a guest room would be arranged for him. He beamed. I do not believe solicitors find themselves in the position he was in very often, Susannah, for he seemed to think it all thrilling.

He drained his brandy and said he knew he would long to tell the entire tale someday, although he knew he could not, but I had become a prized client. If I ever had any more balls he hoped he passed muster as a guest at this one so as to receive more invitations.

He then said I had done a good thing for Gwynneth and was pleased he could be of assistance, even if he had no idea when I had asked for his help that it would all be so very dramatic. Finally he took his leave, to make notes on what led to the challenge, leaving out the real truth of it. "Just in case," he said as he patted my hand. After his departure Prudence ran in, almost falling over herself in her panic to know what happened.

Of course she was disappointed, for time was of the essence. There were several things that needed to be accomplished simultaneously, I needed her help and discretion and told her so.

First, she was to make sure the guest rooms were properly made up. The sudden and not aware guests would be Mr. Sinclair, Lord Carollton, Mr. Ploughgoode and Mr. Gibberwilly, and I told her which rooms they should each be given in the east wing. I told her that if anyone presented themselves to her as a "second" a guest room was to be provided for them as well. I then asked for Mr. Gibberwilly, with Mr. Ploughgoode to follow. She came close to asking me to explain myself, but the look on my face must have shown it was a most inopportune time for the query. She repeated back my instructions and left.

I poured myself a generous brandy, for I was feeling shaken. The fireworks were supposed to begin, what if someone needed me, what if people began to notice and comment on my absence? I then realized that discretion or no, what was going to happen at dawn would become part of county lore, and everyone would later understand my disappearance. As I comforted myself with this logic Mr. Gibberwilly arrived.

He came across the room and clasped both my hands in his, whispering that he had hoped for a private moment with me, and was pleased I felt the same. He leaned in to kiss me, I saw with alarm, released his hands quickly and stepped back.

"Mr. Gibberwilly, there is going to be a . . . meeting . . . between two men here in the morning, and you should be in attendance. In case something happens." Mr. Sinclair had told me surgeons were never to be told they would be attending a duel, in case there was a trial.

I added that a guest room was being prepared so he could be on time and ready for whatever might happen. He smiled at me and said he understood, and was more than happy to offer his services in whatever way required. It would be his honour. I was actually pleased he had been invited. I knew he was good with people who had been shot, in case your husband was wounded.

He bowed, kissed my hand and said he would be delighted to attend the meeting, and what a very special ball I had held. In a spectacular Hall. Too bad his wife was now more dead than alive, she would have enjoyed it, but life did go on, did it not? My distaste for his discourse must have shown on my face, and he took his leave.

A moment later Will entered, and thought that I had managed to arrange a private moment for us. (He actually picked me up, thoroughly kissed me, tossed me on the settee and began to fiddle at his kilt with a grin.) That would have been thrilling and I wished I had thought of it myself. The look on my face and the fact that I bounced back to my feet instead of pulling him down to me made him realize something was very wrong. As he re-arranged his kilt he asked what had happened.

I explained that I could not tell him the details at the moment, I had been gone far too long from my guests as it was, but there was going to be duel at dawn and I was to host it, but did not know anything about duels and prayed he did.

He blinked a little and looked speculatively at me. He was dying to ask what was happening and I adored him all the more when he simply nodded. He explained that there was a code duels had to be fought by for legal reasons and purposes of satisfaction, he had trained several clients who had been challenged and acted as second for one, when the first second fainted, so was well versed in how to conduct them.

I told him Quince's duelling pistols were to be used and asked if he would check them for readiness and then teach me everything I needed to know about what to do. That did nonplus him. Did I know what time it was? It was nearly midnight.

I did not know that, and was suddenly overcome with everything. I sat gracelessly in a chair and dropped my head in my hands, for I very much wanted to cry.

Will crouched next to me and patted my hand. I need not worry. He would see to the pistols so the seconds could have no argument and would teach me about duels, but that meant I would be up all night, and did I know there were hundreds of guests still in my Hall who were mostly inebriated and likely to stay until the wee hours?

I said it was all too much, I could not do it, and everything was going so very badly.

Although Will had no idea what I was talking about, he said he would assist me without question if I promised, when it was all over, to explain everything to him.

I promised and sealed it with a kiss. He then asked where the pistols were and I told him to see Taylor. He took his leave to recover and check them. There are so many more advantages to having a Scot lover than the usual reasons, Susannah. They can help with duels.

I then had to see to my guests, and Will was right: they were very happy, mostly inebriated, some were inappropriate, and it appeared that my ball was going to be more successful than strictly desired. I found myself nodding and accepting compliments as if I had not another care in the world.

Unfortunately no one apprised me of something, for I had been so careful in keeping my plans and details secret that no one knew what they should be looking for.

Lady Shardley saw Gwynneth leave the library dressed like a lady, altogether scrumptious, dripping in jewels and recognized her. She then saw her husband leaving the library a few moments later looking furtive and guilty. She immediately put two and two together and got twenty-two instead of four. She assumed that Lord Shardley had continued his affair, and had the gall to bring his mistress to a ball when his wife was also in attendance. This was more than her nerves and dignity could tolerate and, as I later learnt, was seen gulping champagne as if it were tea. She then excused herself.

Who could have known she would return to Sumwattle in order to retrieve the rifle that had so recently blooded Will? Who could have guessed she would return to Wetmoor? Who might have foreseen that she would find herself lying in wait on the grounds, chilled, drunk, and find a bottle of Irish whiskey tucked into the roses growing over the outside wall of the tennis courtyard?

The answers to those questions is no one, Susannah. Not even I, armed with all of the facts in my possession, could have anticipated that, and things might have turned out differently if I had.

Instead I found myself shooing everyone outside for the fireworks, as they were to go off at midnight. Soon pretty explosions were going off over everyone's heads to applause and laughter and I realized things could go on until dawn, and no one was noticing me. Armageddon itself could rain down and no one would be the wiser. What a ridiculous turn of events! I should have been giddy at the success of my Ball (first dance notwithstanding), and I just wanted everyone to go home so I could think for a moment. This is what happens when one pokes their nose where it does not belong, and I remonstrated myself.

Then I started planning again, for there was nothing to be done about it. Dawn was coming in a few hours, and with it, a duel.

There was also the matter of Gwynneth. The girl was locked in a room with nowhere to go and no one to whom she could talk. I went to where she had been deposited without so much as a by your leave.

At my knock a small voice bade me enter, and I found Gwynneth sitting on the bed, still wearing the gown and opals, staring at her own meagre things, which had been put out for her, along with an old nightdress I had given Prudence last year. She looked surprised to see me. I said I knew her mind must be a whirl and she surely had a thousand questions, but asked that she abstain for at least a few hours more, for everything had become very complicated, not that she needed to concern herself at all, but I did not have any time.

She nodded, and tears filled her eyes. This made me stop. I was running around doing everything and this silly girl was locked in a room with no idea of what was happening. I sat next to her and asked her what was wrong, for suddenly I was all over cold at the thought that popped out of my mouth before I could stop it: Had I done the wrong thing? Did she want to have everything go on as before?

She laughed at me, Susannah! How could I think such a thing! Being free of the Bargesniffles was like being sent to Heaven, but to find out she had money and means and never had to go back there, but could stay in the Hall for now, it was all so much for her and she was reeling with it. She said she had no idea why I had done any of it, but I would be in her prayers forever, for I was an angel, how could I not know that?

Well, that was bit hyperbolic and more familiar than I would have liked, but I put it down to her overexcited state. I replied that I was glad, for I would have hated to have been made a fool. She said a "fool" was the last thing I should ever be called. I then told her I would speak to her on the morrow, in the afternoon, and would she please stay out of sight until I came for her? She nodded acceptance and I took my leave again.

I stopped on the stairway to think. What was next? Oh, I had to learn about duels, the perfect finale to the evening.

The music had ended with the fireworks and some of the guests began taking their leave, so I arranged for the master of ceremonies to make my goodbyes for me, as I could not spend hours standing at the door. Then I found Taylor to tell me where Will had gone. He was in the mud room off of the kitchens with the pistols.

I swept through the kitchens to the great surprise of the staff, told Cook she had outdone herself and had my greatest thanks. She actually smiled and said it had been a pleasure, though the girls sent from London to help could not hold a candle to our own. At that point there was a veritable bucket brigade of people washing the china and silver and crystal, and the kitchens were steaming from the hot water being used.

In the mud room I found Will working on the pistols. I had only seen them when presented, and was relieved when he told me that they were beautiful and very well-made, and needed only a good cleaning in order to be ready.

I asked if he thought they would find their mark, and he replied that it depended on the skill of the man wielding it, but the fact that they were detonating pistols would help, and there was a chance there would be no duel at all.

He asked if a cause would be publicly given, and when I said I thought not, he nodded and said there were other ways to avoid one, which relieved me. He thanked me for the room that had been arranged for him, it made him feel a proper guest, although it came at the expense of spending the night in a room he far favoured, and we both laughed. I left him to the cleaning, and told him Taylor would find him later.

I returned to the ball, helping to see people out and having those that were too unsteady from champagne to leave gracefully helped to their carriages. The servants were clearing up as people went, so that the work later and in the morning would be somewhat eased, and I sighed that except for the whist fanatics in the games room, everyone was clearing out relatively well. I then decided to walk outside and get some air, for it was a lovely night. I wish I had not, for I found Mr. Sinclair entangled in a romantic posture with Miss Paget near the boathouse. Actually, Miss Paget had pressed him up against the wall, which confirmed my belief that she is a tart. It was rather startling. However, it did mean it was likely that Mr. Sinclair would favour me even more regardless of the duration of his acquaintance with the girl and pesky Miss Paget would no longer occupy herself with Will. I told them to have a pleasant time and went back to the ballroom.

Foxx then came and told me Sir Manfredson had not yet been found, which began to concern me. He is very old, Susannah, and quite mad, rarely knowing the year and thinking everyone he is talking to is royalty. I was thankful the night was mild and said a prayer that he would be found safe by morning. My ball was already going to be scandalous with the duel, and I did not want anyone to trip over a dead guest.

At around three o'clock the last of the guests not staying for the duel were dispatched. The search for Sir Manfredson had expanded beyond my grounds and I asked Constable Pukeston and the younger Manfredson to notify me if he were found.

I paid the master of ceremonies for his good work, paid the London staff and musicians, sent them to the inn in town and looked around. The Hall looked more or less in order, and I went to the kitchens to see how things were going. Cook said that of course everything went well, she was the Cook, after all, and she wanted to make sure our staff was not overburdened the next day, so had worked the hired staff to bits for as long as they were there. She said there was enough food left over to make a lovely luncheon for everyone the next day, and asked to finally go to bed. I gave her heartfelt thanks and her leave, and she stumped out, limping heavily, for her bed and sleep.

Which I was not going to be able to claim for myself, for now I had to learn about duels.

Taylor's last task was to bring Will to the library to instruct me. Normally Taylor would never leave me unattended with a man at night, but the man was Will and Taylor was exhausted, so when I bid him goodnight he thanked me and closed the door behind him when he left.

Will told me the pistols were ready, showed them to me and then began duelling instructions. It was all very business-like, as he realized I was in a terrible quandary.

What an education that was! Men, Susannah. They have made up rules on how to properly shoot each other. It is even has a name: the Code Duello, and is followed by anyone with any standing, so had to be followed by me. It was invented in Scotland years ago, so Will was the best person at the ball to tutor me in its intricacies. He saw the look on my face when he explained its provenance, laughed and said he never imagined knowing the Code Duello might be helpful to me.

There are levels of offence and levels of what is considered to be an appropriate response, how many shots can be fired and what is defined as a shot being made. After about one and one-half hours I thought my head would split open with the various permutations that were possible within the rules, as I really did want to make sure the duel ended all between the two men, and Will was very patient. It finally seemed that I had it all clearly, and Will said I looked as if I would drop right then and there, and I thought I might. He said I should go to bed, for morning was coming quickly enough, and would be as full as the day had been.

I apologized for not being able to entertain him the way I had promised earlier, for it made me a very poor hostess, but perhaps he would consider meeting some other time, at which point I would endeavor to remedy the slight in whatever way was most agreeable to him. This made him happy, and he said being owed was a nice thing, as he was exhausted and had not planned on attending a duel in the morning, so would accept my demurral and ponder carefully the best way for me to make up the insult, warning that it would be exhausting, complicated and drawn-out, to which I told him I would be delighted to indulge any whim that might cross his devilish mind.

I left him in the library, for he wanted to check the pistols once more before retiring, and it would not be appropriate for us to go upstairs together.

It seemed to take a long time just to get to the foyer. My footsteps echoed as I made my way down the empty hallway leading to the grand stairway and I stopped in the middle of the foyer, looking up at the ceiling so far away. Climbing the stairway seemed a gargantuan task and I wished that Quince had been successful in his plan for a box that would take me up to my rooms without having to move my feet. It would be very popular, I think, were such a thing possible.

I was exhausted, for I had scarcely slept in two days, with another full day to be gotten through before I could be done. I admit I was thinking rather unkind thoughts about your Lordship, Susannah, for had he not issued the challenge I would have been able to rest, but there was nothing to be done about it.

My exhaustion is what caused me to not hear someone behind me. Suddenly an arm snaked around my waist, encircling it roughly, and I was rudely pulled back into a person I knew was not Will, for he knows how to touch a woman properly. I struggled to turn and see who would behave with such impudence, thinking it was Sir Manfredson, for then I could tell him I was Queen Elizabeth, and take the wind out of proverbial sails. Then a voice, borne on nasty breath, whispered in my ear.

"Annabella, how I have waited for this moment. I have thought of nothing but duelling since you bade me stay."

It was Mr. Gibberwilly! He had been lying in wait for me! I slapped at his hands and he was so surprised that he let go. He must have thought my squirming was a sensual response, the fool! I turned and smacked his face, giving him my most imperious glare as I did so. That idiot thought I had requested a tryst. With HIM!

He grabbed my hands. "I know you are high-spirited and need to be put to bed, as you are surely enervated from the strain of the ball – Mr. Castleton has intimated you are nervous – I would be happy to attend you as your personal physician." He pressed himself against me. "I have something that will make you feel good, Annabella. Very good indeed."

I was disgusted and pulled away, but he still had my arms held tight. The nerve of that man, in my own Hall, to behave so coarsely and without provocation!

I hissed at him. "You are drunk and confused. Release me or I will scream." I did not want to scream, I did not want any more chaos than had already happened, and there were at least six men in the Hall that would want to kill him for what he was doing, and ending the ball with a duel was bad enough, I did not want murder added to it. There was Will, your husband, Mr. Sinclair (he was a solicitor but had shown his mettle with the Bargesniffles), Taylor, Foxx and Driver. I did not know if Driver would do anything, but would have given much to have his leg as a club. I thought I could talk sense into Gibberwilly, Susannah. I truly did.

Gibberwilly leaned in to me and I reared back from the stench of my liquor, which he had clearly poured liberally down his throat. "Of course you won't scream. You won't cause a fuss in your own Hall, not on such a glorious night. If you do, I'll tell everyone you made an offer and then refused. Women are so fickle, after all." He began pulling me toward the stairway.

"Let go of me," I spat, pulling away as hard as I could, but to no avail.

"Come, Annabella. You are not the high and mighty lady everyone believes you to be. Your feigned outrage is charming, but we both know it is a ruse. I do not think the less of you for having needs." He began to drag me toward the stairway.

"It is no ruse!" I snapped, kicking at him and trying to make it very hard for him to keep hold of me. "There is a real duel at dawn and that is the only reason you were asked to stay, for blood will be shed and you are the only one who might be able to staunch it. It would be better to let someone die than for you to think I want you."

(I was not thinking at that moment that your husband might be the one to die without a surgeon in attendance, Susannah, I was that upset. Please accept my apologies.)

Gibberwilly thought I was dissembling and laughed. "I know what widows want, and that is to be under a man again as soon as possible. If you want to call it duelling it is fine with me." He leered. "As a surgeon I am uniquely qualified to make sure you enjoy yourself."

I was speechless. He was not letting me go. He crushed me closer to him and leaned in to kiss me, hideous tongue in evidence. Without thinking I spat in his face.

This was not the proper course, for he turned red with rage and pulled his hand back to strike me. I opened my mouth to scream and damn the consequences when a quiet and most beloved voice caused us both to freeze.

"Lady Annabella, the pistols are ready." Mr. Gibberwilly froze with his hand still in the air and I looked over my shoulder at Will, who was standing in the shadows of the hallway, a pistol aimed directly at Gibberwilly's head. The other was at his side. The look on Will's face nearly made me quail myself: it was so furied I thought he might shoot whether I was in front of Gibberwilly or not.

Will stepped into the foyer. "I'm most tempted to test righ' now tha' their aim is true. Step away from the lady." His Scots burr was thick and I realized I had never seen him truly angry, even when we had argued, for he had not looked as he did at that moment, as if he were perfectly content to kill someone.

Gibberwilly had the gall not to do as required. "Stay out of the business of your betters, Ploughgoode, this is only a little lovers' quarrel you've interrupted, nothing more – "

His voice died away in his throat when Will cocked the pistol, his aim never wavering from Mr. Gibberwilly's head, and his voice was low and tight.

"To be called inferior to you is an insult, Gibberwilly. No lovers' quarrel ever, EVER includes violence to the lady, which proves your words a lie. I'll only say it once more: Step away from the lady. Now." I was frightened, this was no bluff; Will was barely restraining himself from shooting. Gibberwilly realized it as well, let go of me and stepped away.

Will moved so quickly I barely saw any of it. He pulled me back from Gibberwilly, tucked me behind him, his other hand swung hard and I heard a horrid crunching sound. Then there was another. I looked from behind Will to see Gibberwilly on the ground, blood pouring down his face.

"You shouldna have touched her, Gibberwilly. Get up." Will stood over him. Gibberwilly did not move. "I said, GET UP." Gibberwilly still did not move. Will crouched down next to him, pistols still in each hand. "I know you're no' dead, you bastard. You're breathin'. However, if you don' get up you may no' be breathin' much longer."

Gibberwilly crawled to his feet. I have never seen anyone as angry as Will was at that moment. I tried to interject, but when Will looked at me I went mute.

"Lady Upton-Church, I'll take care of this. If it's unpleasant for you, you should go upstairs." I was torn between staying and leaving, and decided to stay. I may have to help Will move a body and hide it. Where does one hide bodies? They are so large and get so smelly – I was in a terrible state to have those thoughts – even as Will turned back to the terrified surgeon.

Gibberwilly's speech was hard to understand with all the blood, which made me feel faint even as he spoke. "Thee wanths me, thee athked me, you thtupid – "

Will aimed the pistol again and glanced at me. "Put your head down, Bella." He was going to do it, he was going to shoot. I put my head between my knees and tried not to faint. There was an awful thud, but it was not preceded by the banging sound I expected. I looked up and Gibberwilly was on the floor again. He was dead, I thought, and we were going to have to do something with him. Perhaps we could put him in the pond . . .

Will turned to me, looking confused and staring at the pistol. "I didna shoot, Bella."

"Then how did he – ?" my voice trailed away as Sir Manfredson stepped from the shadows of the hallway, holding a shovel from one of my fireplaces in his hand.

"Hello, Princess Maria."

"Oh. Hello, Sir Manfredson." I stood and curtsied, my voice sounding tiny, even to me.

"Who are you?" Will was completely nonplussed, and seemed disappointed that he had not been able to shoot Gibberwilly. Truth to tell, I was not sure how I felt about it, either.

"I am Sir Manfredson, my boy." I would have smiled were it not for all the attacking, smashing and possible murder going on; Will is thirty-five. Manfredson looked around. "I built this Hall."

"Oh." We all stood there, save Gibberwilly, who laid there.

Manfredson handed the fireplace shovel to Will and spoke in a conspiratorial tone. "These are better for this sort of thing, boy. Makes less noise, less fuss."

"Of course." Will was still confused, even as Manfredson came and took my hand.

"I was making my way to the bath for some relief, princess, overheard a quite upsetting conversation and realized rescue may well be in order. No one will allow me to carry a weapon anymore, I cannot think why, so I went to the drawing room. Fireplaces always have weapons."

"Thank you, Sir Manfredson."

"You are quite welcome, dear. Now, if you will excuse me, I need a private moment." He winked at me. "Don't worry, I know the way." He began to make his way up the stairway.

Will spoke quietly. "Thank you, Sir Manfredson."

Manfredson's hand waved airily back at him. "Quite all right. You'd have been well within your rights to shoot that man, but you are a Scot. We English are still nervous about your lot, what with the Rising and all. They may well have hung you for it, no matter the cause." He kept going and I stared at Will. He had risked hanging for my honour. Of course that made me begin to cry. Will sighed and sat me down on the stairs.

"It's all right, Bella." I kept on crying. He sounded exasperated. "Oh, go ahead and weep, it's warranted." He put the pistols next to me and went back to Gibberwilly, who was beginning to groan and move.

Will sat Gibberwilly up so he was leaned against a wall, smacking him more forcefully and frequently than necessary to bring him to consciousness. If I am being ruthlessly honest he punched him a few times. Had Gibberwilly not regained consciousness Will may have beaten him to death. However, Gibberwilly finally groaned and looked around blearily out of the eye that still opened. He could not speak properly. "Whad – whad habbened? I'b dot dead . . . "

Manfredson's voice floated down from the top of the stairway. "That was me, you sorry excuse for a Man. Were I not a gentleman, I would call you a scurrilous, wretched, deserving-of-gaol bugger, but as I am a gentleman, I will refrain from such pejorative language in front of the Lady. I bashed you in the head with a shovel and you deserve far worse. Don't give me cause to regret not watching you get shot instead."

Gibberwilly peered up at Manfredson. "Who are you?"

"King Olaf of Norway, of course," Manfredson replied, and wandered out of sight.

Will yanked Gibberwilly to his feet and took a deep breath, glancing longingly at the pistols left at my side. "One duel at dawn is enough or I'd call one myself. You'll stay in the stables tonight, that's where animals are kept. You'll attend the duel and then leave this property forever. If I hear that Lady Upton-Church is bothered by as much as a whisper from you again, I'll issue you a challenge, you'll have to accept, and I'll kill you. I'm an expert shot, Gibberwilly. It's what I do. I'll shoot you so that it takes days for you to die, and you'll be in agony the entire time. And I won't be charged. You touched a lady, Gibberwilly. Men have died for far less."

Gibberwilly muttered something through a bleeding mouth and I had to put my head between my knees again.

I heard Will walk Gibberwilly briskly to the front door. "You're lucky, Gibberwilly. If they weren't maybe needed for surgery tomorrow, I'd break your hands. You should leave before I change my mind, or give you to Manfredson . . . Oh, what the hell." I heard a horrible crunch. I looked up as Gibberwilly let out a thin shriek. Will flung him through the door, then closed and locked it behind him.

I was still crying, I thought I would stop but was unequal to the task. Will sat down next to me on the step and tried to mop my face with his kerchief.

"It's all right, Bella. He's gone, you're safe. He won't bother you again. I was very restrained, I only broke one finger." All traces of harshness were gone from his voice; it was very gentle.

I kept weeping, even as I tried to explain. "Everything has gone awry, I only wanted to have a ball and perhaps help someone. If you had not come when you had, he was going to strike me and . . . and . . . " I could not finish the sentence. He nodded and brushed some of my tears away.

"Shhh . . . " He helped me to my feet, gave me one pistol and kept the other and walked me up the stairway. At the top he must have heard a noise, for I was pushed behind him, his pistol was out and he was aiming into the darkness down the hall. He really did want to shoot someone, having been thwarted thus far.

Suddenly Manfredson's voice came from the dim hallway. "Hello again. It's me."

Will lowered the pistol while I used the back of his coat to wipe my tears. "Of course. Hello, Sir – King Olaf."

"King Olaf? You must have had a great deal to drink tonight, young man. I am Sir Manfredson. What is your name?"

"William Ploughgoode, Sir." Will bowed, and I began to feel odd.

"That is a good name. I like it." Manfredson was looking beatifically at both of us.

Will stepped back so he was standing next to me. As his hand rested on my waist everything began to go grey and I found to my great embarrassment that I was swooning. I felt Will pluck the other pistol from my hand, then his arms caught and lifted me as I heard myself murmuring, "Oops, I am sorry. So very sorry . . . "

When I regained my senses Will was laying me down on my bed.

"Well, hello, Bella," he smiled at me.

I was dreadfully confused. "What – what happened?"

"Oh, lots o' excitin' things, Bella, but I'm just going to put you to bed –"

Everything that had happened flooded into my mind all at once and I sat upright, smashing the top of my head into Will's forehead. He staggered back and I fell back on the bed.

"Oh!" I said it for my head and for what I had remembered, before remembering my manners. "Are you all right?"

Will came back to me slowly, rubbing his forehead. "Good God, Bella, that hurt!"

"I am sorry." I was rubbing my own forehead. Then I began to cry again, to which hiccupping was then added. I wished I cried more delicately, Susannah.

I began babbling about evil, attacking surgeons, Lords ruining girls, wicked vicars, duels and not making any sense. Will sighed and helped me stand, nodded at every inane utterance, peeled off my gown and underthings (oh, I had imagined that would happen differently, without the sobbing or the lumpy heads) and helped me into my nightdress. I was a blithering idiot even as he tucked me under the bedcovers and pulled them up to my chin. He finally put a finger over my lips and shushed me.

"I know . . . It's over, Bella. We'll talk about it later, but you're overtired an' overwhelmed. Manfredson is in my room – God, he's an odd one! – an' I'm goin' to stay here an' keep you safe. Dawn'll be here in a few hours." He turned away, preparatory to sleeping on the divan.

I could not stop fretting. "But you could have been hung, Will. I could not bear it if anything were to happen to you."

He turned back in surprise and then smiled, sitting down on the bed next to me. "That's why you're cryin'?"

"Of course. If you hung . . ." I could not finish the thought.

He looked into my eyes, which were still leaking tears. "You're the most wonderful woman I've ever known, which is mostly good, but sometimes quite annoyin'." His very soothing tone, so different than the one used on Gibberwilly, had calmed me and my tears finally stopped. "You should try to cry a bit less in the future, all right?" He smiled at me and I tried to smile back. "I'll be right here, in case Gibberwilly does somethin' stupid."

"What about Prudence?" I whispered. "Prudence will be coming."

He kissed both of my still teary eyes to close them. "I'll take care of tha'. Just sleep." He settled down on the divan with the pistols in his lap.

Knowing Will was there to protect me soothed me as much as what he had said and I drifted to sleep, for I was more tired than I have ever been in my life, more even than that first week after Quince died.

And I am exhausted now, Susannah, although I do not believe I will ever again be as tired as I was the night of the ball. However, I must stop here for now (please do not be angry), and pick up the threads of my tale on the morrow, for there is little daylight left, and I have ignored other duties that require my attention.

I shall write again tomorrow, and you will finally know what happened at the duel.

Your Exhausted Friend,
Annabella

☙ A Happy Ending for Almost Everyone ❧

17 October, 1821

Dear Susannah,

I have taken pen in hand, which has become an Olympian task of late, to finally tell you of the duel itself. I cannot believe that it is over a week since the events of that day. It seems like both years and only hours both since everything happened.

When I wrote you I had just fallen asleep, worn out by the ball, the impending duel, Mr. Gibberwilly's attack and being saved by Will and Sir Manfredson. Had I known when I awoke what would happen I would have refused to leave my bed for the rest of my life.

But I did not, and woke to find Prudence standing in my doorway with breakfast, staring goggle-eyed at my gown laying across a chair and at Will, who was sprawled near-indecently on the divan (kilts have become quite attractive to me), and just waking himself. Prudence exclaimed, "Lady!" At her cry Will bolted upright and with alarming speed had one of the pistols aimed at Prudence's head. She started and near dropped the tray.

"Will!" I called, hoping he was more awake than asleep and did not shoot Prudence. He looked at me, then back at Prudence, and put the pistol down.

"Mr. Ploughgoode, you – you –" I am not sure how Prudence was going to finish the sentence. I do not believe she did, either. I was ruined. Will went to her and took the tray out of her hands, put it on my vanity and closed the door.

I was woolly in my thinking and having trouble framing what to say, for I had an aching bump on the top of my head, when Will spoke for me.

He sounded officious, trying to offset the scandal of being in my room. "Lady Upton-Church was accosted last night by Mr. Gibberwilly and, although dispatched to the stables, I was concerned another attempt would be made. I insisted – over the strenuous objections of Lady Upton-Church – on staying 'til I knew Gibberwilly was off the grounds an' everyone instructed so as to insure he canno' return. Lady Upton-Church was beside herself." He shook his head a little, rubbing the bump on his forehead and wincing. "Sir Manfredson can confirm it. He's in my room." He looked abashed. "I'm sorry I nearly shot you."

Prudence's mouth was an "O" of surprise, but collected herself and turned to me. "Are you all right? Were you hurt?"

"I am fine." That was a bald-faced lie, I could feel my lip starting to quiver, so bit down on it. I did not have time to go into a dither. There was a duel coming on, after all. Instead I told Prudence the outcome may have been different were it not for the intervention of Will, and asked her to make sure he was given a perfect breakfast, for he had saved me from a horrible situation, and his gallantry needed to be rewarded. Sir Manfredson should also be collected and his family notified. She set my breakfast down and said she would take care of everything and return to help me dress.

Will looked at his watch and said the duel would begin in less than an hour and the rest of the principals would soon be gathering. That was a mistake. Prudence saw the watch with its unique fronts-piece.

She looked at him, then at me, and back at him again, but more carefully. I held my breath. Will had no idea he had given anything away, for he did not know Prudence was with me when I got it in London, but there was nothing to be done; it was too late.

After a moment she nodded and said she would oversee all, and Will should come with her for sustenance while I got ready for the day. They left and I tucked into my breakfast half-heartedly.

A short time later Prudence returned and I had to get dressed, which presented an unusual conundrum.

What does one wear to a duel? We chose a gown that was subdued, one that I would wear to Church but not a funeral, for I was hoping no funerals were in my immediate future.

When I was dressed Prudence stood for a moment, looking nervous. I wondered if I was going to be upbraided by my own maid. She is such a naïve girl, I am sure she was horrified.

Her voice was low. "Mr. Gibberwilly – he attacked you?"

"Yes. He thought I made an offer – which I most assuredly did <u>not</u> – it was terrifying."

I was surprised by the firmness in her voice. "Then I am glad Mr. Ploughgoode stayed. Mr. Gibberwilly – I don't like him." She looked at me with concern. "Are you truly all right?"

I did not know the answer to her question. "I do not think it matters, Prudence. I have to host a duel."

She turned to open the door for me and leaned against it instead, quite a startling thing for her to do. She seemed to be carefully choosing her words.

"I think it is lovely you gave Mr. Ploughgoode the watch. Such protection should be rewarded."

I sighed with relief; she had not sussed out the truth. We smiled at each other, she opened the door and I heard her murmur, "I do like that kilt," as I walked past her.

I went downstairs and was stopped by Taylor. The seconds were in the drawing room, trying to find a reconciliation. I began to have some hope, until Taylor finished his news: Sir Manfredson was not in Will's room. The bed appeared to have been slept in, but the man himself was gone. Again. I asked Taylor to have Foxx begin the search once more and sighed. I had believed that at least <u>that</u> issue had been solved, and also wanted to thank Manfredson for his fortuitous bashing of Gibberwilly. It would have to wait until we found him again.

I went to the morning room and found your sweet husband sitting to breakfast with Will and Mr. Sinclair, an unlikely trio. Your Lordship said Will had assured him the pistols were ready, he had tested them and they were of fine quality. As they ate they were discussing the duels and the Code Duello. Mr. Sinclair was taking notes, seeming thrilled to be in the thick of it. I was glad they were getting on.

In the kitchens Cook was preparing the post-ball lunch, grumbling that it was hard enough to do that and get breakfasts ready for guests, especially since one would surely go to waste. Then Taylor told me that Lord Shardley had arrived, the seconds had finished their discussion and the duel would begin as soon as surgeons arrived. I nodded as if duels were the thing one always does after a ball and went to greet the men.

On the way I met with Foxx, who told me Sir Manfredson was still missing, but the search had resumed, and he would hopefully be found soon.

Lord Shardley, Baron Theosophus and Lord Kingsley-Wytton were waiting on the veranda. Each one greeted me in turn, and it was explained that Baron Theosophus was seconding Lord Shardley, with Kingsley-Wytton as second to your husband. Baron Theosophus looked pale, watching the ducks paddling around the opposite end of the pond, and he appeared to fear they could attack *en masse*. I told Taylor to fetch Mr. Gibberwilly and have someone bring out tea and some food, although I did not know if it was correct or not.

After your husband, Mr. Sinclair and Will joined us on the veranda, Mr. Gibberwilly came around the side of the Hall (I was pleased to see he was not allowed re-entry to the Hall proper) with a dreadful black eye, a badly bent nose, cotton stuffing protruding from his nostrils, dried blood flaking from his face, a stick tied to a finger, bits of straw sticking to him and looking thoroughly put out. He was carrying his bag, however, which was all that mattered. When he glared at me Will walked to him and murmured for a moment. I know not what Will said to him, he will not tell me, but whatever it was caused Gibberwilly to pale and then settle down well away from the rest of us, never again looking at me.

Then Constance brought Lord Shardley's surgeon, Mr. Thimblequick. The kitchen maids brought tea and food behind him. I had not asked Will, but one always serves guests <u>something</u>, even if they are there to see someone shot to death. Everyone seemed to appreciate the gesture. As introductions were being made, I looked back at the Hall and saw the entire staff standing at the windows to watch. It was a horrible breach, but I could not upbraid them in front of everyone. When I turned back I saw heads poking up over the top of the wall separating the formal grounds from the rest of the property. The tenants. I hoped they realized they were poorly situated for a duel. For goodness' sake, one of my tenants might have their head blown off. I tried glaring, but they stayed. Hopefully they would work out the possible consequences for themselves before there could be any.

Everyone had a sip of tea and nibbled on something. It seemed like a garden party. I was hoping they might forget why they had come, but Will cocked his head at me to begin.

I thanked everyone for coming, which sounded remarkably stupid the moment I said it, and Will looked a little pained. Then I asked if the seconds had reached reconciliation. They had not, offering options throughout the night to both men without success.

I asked Your Lordship and Lord Shardley if they wished to publicly declare the cause of the duel.

They did not.

I asked what weapon had been chosen and they affirmed it would be pistols. At that point Quince's duelling pistols and Lord Shardley's were brought out for inspection. Will did the honours and the seconds confirmed: all was in readiness.

What was next? Oh, yes. I asked if any apologies or explanations were to be given or received by the principals.

No surprise there, there was no answer, but they did glare at one another.

I asked if the seconds had fixed the number of shots and they affirmed it would be two. That was alarming. I had hoped it would be one each and we would be done with it. Both men are very good shots.

None of us knew that Lady Shardley was under the roses, woken by all of the goings-on, so we continued unaware.

Then the seconds loaded the pistols. This took a moment, and I was suddenly too cognizant that all of the options had been explored and found wanting. There was going to be a duel. With pistols. And shot. And blood.

I said that since Lord Shardley had chosen the ground, Lord Carollton chose the distance. He declared seventeen paces, which everyone thought odd. Then I remembered that Gwynneth is seventeen years old. Lord Shardley snorted. I looked up at the Hall and saw Gwynneth's face at her window. I had hoped she would sleep through it, for I did not know if I could explain it without giving away anything.

I looked back at both men and asked if they were ready.

They were.

I asked if firing had been regulated, and the seconds' answer was what I expected: firing at pleasure.

I asked if the seconds were satisfied.

They were.

I asked if the men were ready.

They were.

Oh, my. They were going to go through with it. I thought about swooning to distract them but knew it would only delay the duel, not end it before it began.

Lady Shardley must have been watching her perfidious husband with loathing at that point.

I looked at Will, who nodded that I had fulfilled all of the requirements. I told the men to take to the grounds. As they began to move to the center of the near grounds in front of the pond I remembered something and called out. If Sir Manfredson tottered into the fray the duel would stop until he could be removed to safety. They each nodded, continued to their places and faced each other, the seconds mirroring them, albeit further away.

At that moment Lord Shardley and your husband hissed something at the other, but I do not know what it was. I asked them to please turn. Suddenly a familiar burred voice whispered in my ear that I had done it well, he was proud and it was good that I had thought of Manfredson's safety. Lord Shardley and Lord Carollton had turned away from each other, one pistol held in front of them, the other held at the ready. The seconds echoed their stances. I was grateful to note that my tenants were not complete fools, heads that might be in the way began to sink down behind the thick stones.

I could not think, for this was too real, Susannah, and the outcome too frightening to contemplate. Your husband might die right in front of me! I would be the cause! You would hate me forever! I am afraid I froze, until that familiar burred voice murmured that I must begin it, for it must come to its end.

With a shaking voice and a heartfelt silent prayer I began to call off the paces.

One.

Two.

Three.

At each call the men took another step away from each other. There was no other sound than that of my voice. Even the birds seemed to have stopped their song in recognition of the seriousness of events.

Ten.

Eleven.

Twelve.

I faltered for a moment in my cadence, which left the men standing with a foot in the air. I continued to the final number.

Seventeen.

At that dreaded number both men whipped around, pistols at the ready and a shot rang out.

Who had fired so quickly? There was a momentary tableau. Suddenly Lord Shardley crumpled to the ground and your dear husband was looking at his pistol in disbelief. Gibberwilly ran onto the grounds and as Lord Shardley began screaming, your husband called out that he had not shot, who had shot? The seconds raised their pistols to show it was not them.

Had Manfredson found a pistol and shot Lord Shardley? He knew the Hall better than I, perhaps there was a secret arsenal somewhere I had not found. He would hang, even if he thought he was the King and Lord Shardley a traitor. I looked about and did not see him.

Then we were running to Lord Shardley, who was keening and clutching what appeared to be his stomach. As we reached him Lady Shardley stood up from under the rose bushes. I will never forget the sight of her, covered in dirt and thorny scratches, holding a rifle and a nearly empty bottle of whisky. We froze.

"He deserved it!" She screamed. "That rotten, cheating husband of mine deserved it! I have always been a good, loving wife and he brought a whore to the ball! It cannot not be tolerated, it <u>will</u> not be tolerated, I SHALL NOT TOLERATE IT. . ." She trailed off and suddenly crumpled to the ground. No one moved, for no one knew what to do – attend Lord Shardley or the wife who shot him? Suddenly a hideous scream issued from Lord Shardley, the sound of which caused everyone to sort themselves.

I ran to Lady Shardley alone and the other men continued to Lord Shardley's side. Lady Shardley was in a dead faint. I turned her over and took the rifle from her before turning back to the others.

The men had stepped back from Lord Shardley, who was whimpering dreadfully. Even Gibberwilly stood back, the coward. Each of them looked sick and poor Mr. Sinclair suddenly was. I ran to them but Will caught me. "It's no sight for a lady," he said, and turned me away. He gulped, looking ill. "It's no sight for a man, either." It was also not a sight for the tenants brave enough to have watched the duel itself. They lost their nerve with all of the pistols being waved about and Lord Shardley's screaming, and had disappeared.

I thought Lord Shardley was dying, for the sounds he was making were terrible and I fought to be let through. Will kept me back, whispering in my ear. "The wound is likely not mortal, though Shardley will wish it to be." Mr. Sinclair stopped wiping his mouth with his kerchief long enough to agree with Will.

Lady Shardley may have hoped to kill her straying husband, but her aim proved true in a more just way.

Lord Shardley was wounded in his lower region. Much lower. With birdshot. Pellets and pellets burying themselves in the region of which men are both the most proud and protective.

Thimblequick and Gibberwilly called for the seconds to carry Lord Shardley to the boathouse, where he would be attended to the best of their ability. Gibberwilly added in a lower tone, "I do dot dow ib the best surgeon id the world can helb hib." The seconds picked up Lord Shardley, which agitated his injury, and he screamed again as he was carried to the boathouse. Everyone looked stunned and Mr. Sinclair was sick again. He apologized to the other men for his weakness, and Lord Carollton said he was only doing what everyone else felt like doing.

I then asked if the duel was over, ignoring the fact that everyone goggled at me for asking.

Will said that although no shots were fired by the participants, a duel was considered over when one man or the other could not shoot, although he had never heard of a case of someone getting shot when neither principal had done the shooting, but the duel was probably over regardless, with Lord Carollton the winner. He thought.

Mr. Sinclair piped up his agreement, for even if a rematch could be demanded, it was unlikely that Lord Shardley would want such a thing.

Lord Carollton said it gave him no satisfaction, but he would accept it. Then we stared at Lady Shardley, and Will murmured that the woman was a menace and was grateful she had only shot him in the side. All of them then looked back at the boathouse, where screaming could still be heard.

I looked back at the Hall and saw everyone still standing there staring. I made a shooing motion with my hand and they all scurried, including Gwynneth.

I asked what would happen to Lady Shardley. They thought for a moment, and Mr. Sinclair was the one who finally spoke.

Lady Shardley was clearly out of her head both from drink and humiliation. She needed help, not a trial, and thought that Lord Shardley would not take kindly to his injury being disclosed to all and sundry. The other men murmured agreement.

Mr. Sinclair said it was also a private matter; Lord Shardley had come knowing full well he could be shot, so what had happened to him was partly his own fault, in more ways than one. He finished by saying that he thought we should all keep our counsel on the matter, as much as possible, and the injury perhaps was more appropriate than anyone would like to admit, given what he had heard about Lord Shardley's behavior. Since it was not mortal it would likely be ruled an accident in the end, so making the affair public would not serve any cause. He had collected all of the challenge letters and attempts at reconciliation – everything in writing, and added his own notes, and could discuss it with Constable Pukeston if the need arose.

Will said that all of the weapons should be removed from Sumwattle Estate until Lady Shardley had recovered herself, for she would not escape punishment were anyone else to find themselves shot.

He did not know he was holding his side when he said it.

That seemed to settle the issue and we were suddenly all looking about for something to do. I invited the men in for tea while we awaited Gibberwilly's report and I could have Lady Shardley taken home. They felt it a capital idea and we went inside. The seconds returned from the boathouse and begged to leave, for their work was done and both were feeling queasy. I had them carry Lady Shardley into the Hall so she could be put in the east wing until we determined how to get her home. They heaved her into their arms and disappeared.

Mr. Sinclair pulled me aside and apologized again for having sullied my lawn, and said he hoped his momentary illness and his dalliance with Miss Paget had not spoilt his reputation in my eyes. He would never have insulted my house in such a way. I smiled and said it had not, for the rains would take of the former and the latter was none of my business. He said it was the best ball he had ever attended.

When we entered the Hall, door opened by Taylor, whose eyes were huge in his head after what he had seen, and he whispered that someone was in the drawing room waiting to see me. I sent Mr. Sinclair to meet with the other men and went with Taylor to the drawing room. Perhaps Sir Manfredson had been found.

Taylor opened the door but did not follow me in. He closed the door as I stared at Hughe. He turned to me and I saw he was distressed.

"Lady Shardley gone," he whispered. "She not come back from ball last night."

"Oh, Hughe," I murmured, wondering how I would ever manage to explain what had happened in a way he would understand.

"She came home and left again," he said. "She was crying hard but not let anyone help her. Hughe not know what to do."

"Hughe, Lady Shardley is here."

His face brightened. "I see her?"

"Not right now, but you should wait. She will be brought to you soon and you may take her home."

"You took care of her?"

"She is alive, but she needs help, Hughe. A great deal of help. When you take her home you must send for a physician immediately – not Mr. Gibberwilly – a proper London physician. Do you understand?"

Hughe frowned. "Gibberwilly is bad man. Good surgeon, bad man."

I wished I had had this conversation with Hughe before the ball. "Yes, Hughe, Gibberwilly is a bad man. You are a good man to care so for your mistress."

He shrugged. "She lets me stay, Lady. No where to go. She not so bad as everyone say. Just sad."

"Yes, she is very sad."

"Hughe will try make happy."

"I am sure she will appreciate it." I realized there was one thing he could do to help. "Hughe, when you return to

Sumwattle, have all of the weapons brought here. Until things return to normal." I did not add that if that is the condition required I may have them for years.

"If Shardleys allow, Lady." He was their man first.

"I do not believe that will be an issue, Hughe." Lord Shardley likely would not protest, I thought, and Lady Shardley should not have a say in the matter at all.

There was nothing left to say. He bowed and I turned to leave. Just as I reached the door his voice stopped me.

"Is Annabella happy now?" I turned back to him and smiled.

"I am very happy, Hughe. Thank you for asking. And you?"

"Hughe good. I not see you in long time, Lady." He seemed somewhat sad, and I worried that perhaps somewhere in that foreign mind there might lurk feelings for me.

I spoke carefully. "I know. It is for the best, Hughe."

"But – "

"It is for the best." I spoke gently but firmly, for no matter where he came from he must know that we were ultimately unsuited to each other in every way.

He stood for a moment and then nodded. "For best." I sighed with relief. "Lady nice to me, glad Lady happy now."

"And you? Are you happy?" I did not mean to ask it, but his English was so improved, and I found I did wish to know.

He said, "I miss home," and my heart went out to him.

"You will find your way back there someday."

"Someday," he said softly, and looked out the window.

I did not know what to say, for homesickness is not something kind words from a near-stranger can cure. Maybe one day he will find his way home. I hope he does.

I took his leave knowing Hughe would indeed make sure Lady Shardley was well cared for. She would be aware of what she had done soon enough and perhaps would see that she needed to pull herself together. I hope. I do not think one can keep shooting people without it coming to the notice of the authorities.

I then joined the men for tea and it was amusing to see your husband, Mr. Sinclair and Will trying so hard to be solicitous and graceful in front of me. All offered their congratulations and I made sure your husband and Mr. Sinclair understood the very important role Will had played in my performance, which pleased him very much.

I left them to discuss more manly subjects and went to see Gwynneth. I have a strong suspicion that the nature of Lord Shardley's injury was resolutely unmentioned by the men. No matter what Lord Shardley's transgressions may have been, I think no man would find the outcome just. I, a mere woman, thought it rather appropriate.

Gwynneth was in her room, Gabrielle with her, and I remembered that Driver had been dispatched in the morning to collect the child who had caused such a fuss, all unknowing, from Prudence's mother. They both looked quite happy.

Gwynneth asked if the duel had anything to do with her, and I said that it had, but no one had died and she need not think on it ever again.

She was amazed that she had been the cause of so much by so many, and I said that not all of my class were awful, just some, and was glad my friends had risen to the occasion to help me put everything right, for now she was as she should have been: with means and aware of it. She had a fresh start, and a beautiful child as well, for Gabrielle was the only thing that mattered in all of this. The fact that her father was horrible did not matter, for he would have no hand in her upbringing.

Then Gwynneth asked what would happen to her. I had spent some time thinking on it and had an answer.

I asked her to stay on at the Hall, which was is so huge she would scarce be noticed. She had to design and make Prudence's wedding gown, but it was also important that she learn to read and write elegantly, and do sums well, for with her own money she would need to know such things. Cook would be happy to help, I believed. Then she could decide what she wanted to do with her life. Mr. Sinclair could help her with advice regarding her funds, and she would never again find herself in danger of being out in the cold.

She nodded that she would like to stay at the Hall very much, and had spent most of the night thinking about what she might do. Most important was to make a good life for her daughter, for she dearly loved her child. She was thinking perhaps she might someday become a dressmaker, for she seemed to have some small skill in that area, and my gowns had turned out so very well, she had the means to start a small shoppe and did I think that very, very stupid?

I said I did not. In fact, I thought it an excellent idea. If she moved to London she could say she was widowed; no one would be the wiser there, especially with the lovely transformation she had made less than 24 hours ago.

She smiled but I saw that large tears had gathered in her eyes, and she whispered that she had a favour to ask, but I had already done so much that she did not know if she could. I said a favour asked and refused left her in no worse a position than before, but the granting of it might be an improvement, so she should ask.

Gwynneth wants to baptize Gabrielle instead as Gabriella, as a private nod of thanks to me and also have me stand as godmother, but knew that with Gabrielle being illegitimate I might find it all an insult.

I was absurdly touched by the request, Susannah, and found I had tears in my eyes as well. I said I would be proud to stand as Gabriella's godmother. Of course I would need a new gown for the christening, so Gwynneth now had two gowns to make. She told me they would both be beautiful.

With that settled I found myself very pleased indeed.

I went back to the drawing room to find that Gibberwilly had come to the back door and was prevented entry by Foxx, to whom he gave his report.

Lord Shardley would live, we were told, although most unhappily. The injuries individually were not horrible, but the sum total of them were. The pieces of shot had been removed and although the scars would never show, they would also never truly heal. He would never function properly again. It seemed a just outcome, for he could never again inflict himself on poor, stupid girls who believed his lies. He had been taken home, Gibberwilly in attendance, to recuperate and face the wrath of a very angry wife.

I saw your husband out, my respect for him greatly increased, for be assured he conducted himself very much as a gentleman, Susannah, even all those years ago when his lapse began everything. As we talked, he cocked an eyebrow at Mr. Sinclair, who brought a set of papers out of his bag and gave them to your husband. He rifled through them and smiled at me. "I knew I had right on my side," he said. "But if that wasn't enough, I made some arrangements. Mr. Sinclair would have delivered them for me."

The reality of everything that happened suddenly struck home, Susannah. Your husband could have been killed. Lord Shardley could have been killed. The seconds – a baron and a lord! – could have been killed. The rest of us could have been put on trial and hung, or locked away in for years for our part in it. I had to sit down.

Mr. Sinclair took his leave at the same time and said he would not forget my Opening Ball for the rest of his life, and looked forward to seeing me again. He even kissed my hand!

After both men departed I saw Prudence waiting for me. She stepped forward and asked if she could have a word.

I knew I would not get out of this without some penalty, Susannah, and braced myself for unmasking. Prudence is naïve but not a complete dolt, she had ground out the truth of my affair with Will for herself and was now going to resign and destroy what little reputation I have left.

After a long pause, Prudence told me Will had been sat down with the rest of the staff for their luncheon, for though he was not an official member of the household, he was greatly liked by all and believed he would be welcome any time, if I would forgive her impertinence.

I did immediately.

She was not done. "'Course please. I'll not say anything about Mr. Ploughgoode being in your rooms. He was acting as a guard. It would not do for his protection to be seen as anything but chivalry and people can be very small in their thinking. He should have slept on the floor in front of your door, but he is a Scot. You should not suffer for his coarse ways. I think they do things differently up there." She waved her hand upward.

"Yes, I believe they do." That much was true, but in very different ways than Prudence meant. I was relieved; she was not going to unmask Will and I.

We looked at each other for a moment, and then she smiled, curtsied, and asked to be let go for the luncheon. I gave her leave with a happy heart. My maid does not think me a harlot.

I did not want to interrupt the servants' party, for even if I had intentions of adding to their gaiety I would surely dampen it by my very station, so I wandered through the Hall, finally finding myself in the games room, one of my very favourite rooms.

What a morning! What a strange year! What a very strange Hall! I was musing on the events that had taken place over the last year when I solved the last puzzle of all. I went to the hidden wall panel and gained entrance to the tunnel. With the panel closed behind me I travelled down the narrow space and all too soon found myself standing in front of a closed and locked door.

Holding my breath, I knocked. After a moment, just when I had begun to think I was wrong, it was opened by Sir Manfredson. He beamed and asked me in, bowing ever so slightly. I was finally in the room that had so confounded me! I looked around in delight. It was decorated in the same dreary bachelor style that had so affected the rest of the Hall when I took possession. There was a small writing desk and chair, a little pair of stuffed chairs with a table between them, a large and battered table around which sat five chairs, one of which was tipped forward so the back rested against the table. Along one wall was a row of filing cabinets. The old man smiled at me and asked me if I were well. I replied that I was very well, with no small thanks to him, for he had saved me.

Sir Manfredson's eyes sparkled as he told me it was lark for him, and he had not had the opportunity to do anything like that in years. He then grew serious, and said he hoped I did not mind his having come to the secret room during the ball, and he had done it without anyone the wiser. He looked around and his voice was wistful. "I missed it very much. More than I thought I would." He did not seem to be mad at all, and when he saw my astonishment he laughed. "I am only a somewhat mad, Annabella, but I was very lonely. Although the latter state did not bother my son, the former caused him to bring me to live with the family. I can spend time with my grandchildren."

I laughed myself, for this was a most delightful discovery. He asked if I had learned all of the secrets of the Hall. I said I believed I had, all save the very one we were in, and that they had both saved my life and given me great pleasure to discover. I asked him the purpose of the tunnel to the boathouse. He smiled more to himself than me and asked that he be allowed to keep at least one secret for himself. I nodded my agreement. He looked at me for a long moment.

"Quince was right to purchase Wetmoor for you."

I was surprised until I realized that was what Quince must have told him, to spare an old friend's pride, and decided to do the same. "I did not know he had done such a thing."

"Annabella – I hope I have earned the right to call you by your Christian name – Quince purchased Wetmoor because he knew he would likely die before you and wanted you away from London if, or when, it happened. He said redecorating a Hall might be the only way to accomplish such a feat."

This was unsettling information. "Why would he want me away from London?"

"He thought London was not a happy place for you, in spite of your gaiety. He knew he was not the most attentive husband, his work took most of his energies. And after Sarah. . ." He sighed. "I am very sorry about Sarah, Annabella."

"Thank you." Was I was wrong about why Quince bought Wetmoor? Whilst I pondered the issue Sir Manfredson seemed to be weighing something himself, and after a moment he took my hand.

"After Sarah he said you were different – do not think he was angry or upset by that – but he said you were sad in a way no mere diversion could cure. He knew when he died you would be all alone and very aware of that fact, and worried you might fall into despair. He thought managing the estate yourself and restoring Wetmoor would help you realize you have far more to offer the world than a light laugh and sparkling eyes."

My eyes were sparkling with tears by his words. "I did not know he thought of such things, Sir Manfredson."

"He loved you very much, dear. He knew your worth, even if you did not. He wanted you safe when he was gone. I hope you're not upset," he added hastily, as a small tear leaked out of my eye.

I tried to smile. "No, no, of course not. I never knew he thought so carefully about it."

Sir Manfredson smiled gently. "He thought about everything carefully, including choosing you for his wife. He never regretted a single choice he ever made, but he was proudest of that. You made him happy, Annabella."

"Did I?" I had been wondering about that. We were so different, Quince and I, perhaps it had been pity that made him stay with me.

"Yes. You were kind and thoughtful and never harped at him about his work. A bluestocking would have driven him mad, he once said. You made and gave him a home."

We sat in silence for a moment. I was thinking about Quince and how he spent more time worrying about me living without him than he ever did about my life with him. I suppose he was correct. I was a good wife to him and in the end he did everything he could to ensure I might be all right without him. Sir Manfredson watched me as I thought it all through.

I smiled at him. "You are very kind, Sir Manfredson. Thank you for telling me."

"I have my moments," he smiled at me. "Also, did you know that you can hear everything going on in the library from this room?"

"No," I said. "Oh!" He had heard everything!

He patted my hand. "Do not fret. I will likely forget it in a week or two and even if I do not, I am very discreet. I want you to know that I liked what you did. I liked it very much." His voice drifted away and I thought perhaps his mind had with it when he nodded briskly, seeming pleased. He took a key out of his pocket and laid it on the table between us.

"This," he explained, "is the key to this very room. I determined long ago that it would only be held by the true owner of Wetmoor Hall." He picked it up. "Last night you proved your worth." He placed it in my hand and closed my fingers over it. "The cabinets hold information you may find . . . upsetting. Some are quite funny. Some are scandalous." He sighed. "And some are dangerous. If you choose to read them and find you have questions I must ask that you come to see me. Put nothing in writing. There is a fair amount of information regarding the residents of Wimbish and London as well. I trust the information will be safeguarded and treated with appropriate respect."

Although unnerved and itching to get into the cabinets immediately, I instead took the key, slipped it into my pocket and kissed him on the cheek. "I give you my oath to do exactly that."

Sir Manfredson then said he was tired and very much in need of a water closet. He had come back at dawn to enjoy his hideaway one last time and the sounds of shooting had caused him to assume that other, more urgent, duties had claimed my attention. I asked if he would accompany me back to the Hall proper, as his family was beside themselves with worry. He accepted my offer and we left, locking the door behind us. After the unnervingly long time he spent relieving himself, we went to the dining room.

The party seemed to be a great success: there was Will, Driver, Cook, Prudence and Taylor, Gwynneth and Gabriella, Constance and Hope (the little ones in their mothers' arms), with Foxx, Hortense and all the others enjoying a wonderful lunch. They had laid out the table beautifully and I liked the sight of it. Foxx jumped to his feet when he saw Sir Manfredson. I told everyone that Sir Manfredson had been found in the conservatory sleeping behind a potted palm. Sir Manfredson looked appropriately addled and I asked that after the luncheon he be taken home.

Sir Manfredson sat down, addressed Constance as Queen Mary, and asked that she not behead him. Constance pretended to consider it and said she would spare him, as it was rude to behead those with whom one has dined. I did not know she had the wit, Susannah! Then Sir Manfredson spied Will. They nodded to each other and Manfredson said I must be famous indeed to have Robert Burns grace my table.

I was turning to leave when Taylor stood, cleared his throat and requested that I stay for a moment. He instructed everyone to charge their glasses and I found myself facing a room of people standing to face me.

Taylor said he wanted to toast the mistress of Wetmoor Hall, for she was the worst mistress ever to grace its halls.

Prudence said I was a most cruel and thoughtless mistress.

Constance said I was horrible and frightening.

On it went around the table, each toast more outrageous than the last: I was also drunk, clumsy, illiterate, the list of deficiencies was seeming endless. Sir Manfredson said I was a terrible singer and could not paint to save my own life. Will said I was scandalous, which I quite liked. When each one had gone in turn Taylor raised his glass and said they would not have it any other way. There was a general cheer and everyone drank to my awfulness. I really do not think I am strict enough, Susannah. I must work to remedy that.

When the luncheon was over Will came and found me dozing in the library, for I had thought I could not sleep and decided to spend my time reading. He woke me gently and begged to finally be told what he had been part of that morning.

It took a long time, but I related the entire tale (save that your Lordship is Gwynneth's father, that is not for me to tell, describing that part instead as an old and quite dead friend in whose memory he was acting), leaving him by turns astonished and amused. When I was done he shook his head in disbelief.

"You did all this – while renovating a Hall, runnin' an estate, an' carrying on a love affair – you somehow ferretted out the tale, generally bein' a nuisance an' fixin' it?"

"Yes, although it all started before I met you and began the affair part."

He looked thoughtful. "Bella, it must have taken a fair amount o' effort. You never said anythin' to me about it."

I had hoped he would not notice that. "I wanted to. I was afraid it would go wrong and did not want you disappointed in me. It may well have had you not been there. I hope it does not diminish my standing in your eyes; it was fear of losing it that made me keep my tongue." This made him quiet and I thought I must have said the wrong thing, even if it was true.

His voice was quiet. "No one has ever wanted my good opinion of them, Bella. Your wish for it is a better gift than the watch," and he kissed me. "Next time you tell me what you're doin' beforehand, all right? I'll make sure I'm armed." He sat back. "But why did you do it?"

"What happened to Gwynneth could have happened to any woman, even to me, and seemed a harsher punishment than the sin which caused it, so I tried to put it to rights, although it was more of an endeavor than I initially imagined."

He smiled. "You did a good thin' an' my opinion o' you is higher than ever." He yawned. "But I've broken every instruction from the physician at least six times over in th' last three days an' have had less sleep than you. Please give me leave to go home, for your bed is not available to me now."

"Only if you promise to return as soon you are properly rested. It would not do to exhaust you to death; I would be as bad as Lady Shardley."

I went to bed early that evening, skipping supper and immediately fell asleep. I woke several hours later by the now-familiar sound of a secret panel in the wall opening and tried to wake for my visitor.

Will entered and as he lit candles and lamps, asked if I minded the intrusion. I was quite happy for it and said so.

He stood at the end of my bed and as he pulled off his boots, coat, linen and everything else, skin gleaming alabaster in the low light, told me he had to return, for although I had done admirably well during the duel, I had not resolved everything.

I was distracted from what he was saying as each article of his clothing dropped to the floor but managed to ask what I had overlooked, for I really could not think of anything undone.

He sighed and said I had been a poor hostess, for I had slighted my own fiancé, promised to make it up and then appeared to have completely forgotten about it. Also, I had nearly caved in his skull with mine own, when he was merely being gallant.

I agreed instantly: I was truly a poor fiancée, very poor indeed, and most abjectly sorry for my clumsiness. He crawled onto the bed and up next to me to play with the ties of my gown, acting quite innocent even as they came undone under his fingers. As I slid down to his side I added that I would be happy to remedy it twice if I could perhaps be forgiven.

Perhaps, he echoed me, brushing my skin with his lips. He would consider it, he continued, beginning to taste my shoulder, nibbling along it even as my gown slid from my shoulder. I rolled atop him carefully, pinned his hands with mine and kissed the bump on his forehead. He smiled and said I had clearly suffered a hideous head injury, for I missed his mouth, so I tasted his lips for a moment to show I had not gone dotty. Growing increasingly thorough in my ministrations, I promised to endeavor with all my skill to provide a suitable balm for his very great insult, as it was very great indeed. When he caught his breath he replied he would not mind such an attempt at all, but if it appeared that I repaid him too fully he would be obliged to respond in kind. After all, fair was fair.

I was very glad for the thickness of the walls in my rooms, Susannah, else everyone might have thought ghosts walked again that night. Although they are very happy ghosts.

I then slept for two days.

And that is the end of it, Susannah. I hope my solution meets with your approval, for it was you I hoped to please. Your house's reputation is intact, your husband's reputation will surely increase, for his gallantry in defending a poor defenceless girl will become legendary, with no one the wiser regarding the true cause, and a young girl has a fairer chance than she had before this all began.

I look forward to seeing you soon and feel confident that the next time I shall be in much better spirits, for the twists, turns and surprises of the last year have left me in a very happy place indeed.

And you still owe me a visit.

I will close now in the hopes that I have satisfied you with the tale. I am so very glad I could tell someone the whole of it, both the good and the bad.

Who would have thought back at Miss Penelope's what life had in store? Without your friendship I know my life would be the lesser, and will always have you in my prayers for that very reason.

I will write again soon, but in the meantime, I remain

Your Very Happy Friend,

Annabella

Acknowledgments

First let me say that any mistakes or omissions are mine alone.

There is a real Wimbish in Essex County. I picked it because I loved the name and it was situated in the right place. After reading the history of the town it seemed I could neatly fit Wetmoor Hall in the area without causing any difficulty to anyone. I hope its residents don't mind.

Biggest thanks must go to Jenny Deason Copeland of Crazy Red Head Publishing. This book would not be in your hands (paper or otherwise) without her. She believed in this book and held my hand every step of the way, always guiding and supporting while letting me feel I was finding the way. A finer publisher and friend would be a difficult thing indeed to find. Her husband Charles Copeland also supported this book, encouraging Jenny and I to work together on it. He also wrote my little bio, something I found myself unable to do.

There was a group of readers and supporters from all walks of life that need to be named:

Peggi Tabor, my first international reader (she was on a mountain in Lesotho at the time and I rightly assumed there was little competition for her entertainment dollar). She was my first reader of any kind and read the very first draft which was, unbelievably, longer than this version.

Deb Crudele and Miranda Richardson have been staunch friends and allies for years. They'd help me hide a body.

Andrew Zimmerman Jones is a writer in his own right and been a huge supporter of this endeavor from the start. He gave me a crucial bit of advice during a critique that improved the book and made me a better writer.

The best roommate ever, Rachel Diegel, sets an example of humor, grace and strength in everything she does, including being my friend, which I'm sure is sometimes taxing. Also, she does all this while looking like a super model.

Special thanks to the men who read this and encouraged me: Kurt Buker, Peter Brown, Mike Crudele, Tim Grennan and Bob Stofflett. A finer group of hooligans, hellraisers, ne'er-do-wells and men I will never find.

Jaclyn Duysters is the closest thing to a sister I've ever had, as well as the best friend anyone could hope or ask for. She knows all my weaknesses, foibles and failures and is still my best friend. She never stopped thinking I could write a novel and be published, even when I did. Now that it's happened she'll lord it over me forever, and I'm very happy she can.

Everyone has guardian angels, and some of them are people you meet at the worst moments in your life. I am blessed enough to have many angels. They'd not like to be named here, but they know who they are, and I thank God every day for each and every one of them.

My family put up with my muttering about this book for far longer than could be reasonably expected, and always believed I could do this. Mom Marilyn Grennan, brother Tim Grennan, brother John Grennan and his wife Deb, and my nephews John and Chris – I'm so lucky you're in my life, in so many ways.

Finally, thanks to Dad, who is no longer with us but never forgotten, and who gave Annabella her name.

To any of you that expected to be included but weren't, I owe you an apology and a drink, not necessarily in that order.

☙ Bibliography (partial) ❧

If you're compelled to read non-fiction about this period, here's a not even remotely complete list of the reference books consulted during the writing of Shagging, Shooting & Death, but they're the ones referred to the most. I'm not even going to try to list the articles, essays and general trivia I found in other books and periodicals. I'm sorry I can't list the book I found on the history of undergarments, because that would be titillating, but I can't find it.

Isabella Beeton, *Mrs. Beeton's Book of Household Management*

Carolly Erickson, *Our Tempestuous Day: A History of Regency England*

Kristine Hughes, *The Writer's Guide to Everyday Life I Regency and Victorian England*

Ian Kelly, *Beau Brummell: The Ultimate Man of Style*

James Lansdale, *The Last Duel*

Marc McCutchen, *The Writer's Guide to Everyday Life in the 1800's*

Venetia Murray, *An Elegant Madness: High Society in Regency England*

Josephine Ross, *Jane Austen's Guide to Good Manners, Compliment, Charades & Horrible Blunders*

Diana Sperling, *Mrs. Hurst Dancing & Other Scenes from Regency Life*

☙ About the Author ❧

Andrea Grennan was born in Grosse Pointe Woods, Michigan longer ago than she cares to admit, even in the internet age. She attended Grosse Pointe North High School, then Wayne State University. She finished her Bachelor of Fine Arts degree at the University of Detroit.

She has had jobs that included stock girl, usherette, the receptionist for a yacht sales company, actress, pizza delivery girl, executive assistant, magician's assistant, office manager, and an account analyst in the automotive industry. So a straightforward career trajectory which resulted in her decision to write a novel.

Writing a novel is a funny thing. In her case it was a good thing she didn't realize what she was doing until about a third of the way in. Backing into writing a novel made it less daunting, but she will never forget the feeling she had when she typed "The End". She sat for a long moment, stunned, drained, exhausted and exhilarated.

Then she went to bed. It was 1:00 a.m., after all, and she had to be at work in the morning. Such is the life of a writer.

Shagging, Shooting & Death is her first novel.

CPSIA information can be obtained
at www.ICGtesting.com
Printed in the USA
FFOW03n1247071017
40728FF